Dolores Stewart Riccio

The Divine Circle of
LADIES
BURNING
THEIR
BRIDGES

The 10th Cass Shipton Adventure

ISBN: 150096493X
ISBN 13: 9781500964931

Also by Dolores Stewart Riccio

Spirit, a novel of past and present lives
The Ghost Who Came Home from the Auction

The Cass Shipton Adventures:
Circle of Five
Charmed Circle
The Divine Circle of Ladies Courting Trouble
The Divine Circle of Ladies Making Mischief
The Divine Circle of Ladies Playing with Fire
The Divine Circle of Ladies Rocking the Boat
The Divine Circle of Ladies Tipping the Scales
The Divine Circle of Ladies Painting the Town
The Divine Circle of Ladies Digging the Dirt

For my daughter Lucy-Marie,
with thanks for the trip to Stonehenge

A Grateful Acknowledgement

Special appreciation is due to my intrepid and meticulous proofreaders, Joan Bingham and Leslie Godfrey.

A Note to the Reader

This novel is a work of fiction. All the characters, places, and events are either products of my imagination or used fictionally. Although I've researched the traditional meanings and uses of herbs mentioned in the Circle books, their efficacy remains in the realm of folklore. I have also studied Wiccan ways extensively, but magic spells, chants, and love potions from the Ladies' grimoires have been totally concocted by me. (In other words, *do not try this at home*.)

Plymouth, Massachusetts, is an actual town, but many of the streets, locales, businesses, and shops herein are my creations. The same is true of the Circle's adventures in Britain, where well-known landmarks such as Westminster Abbey, the Tower of London, and Stonehenge are real monuments to history, but many other places mentioned in this story have been made up by the author.

Greenpeace is a true crusading organization which has been involved in some of the issues described, but the ship *Gaia* and its misadventures, and various Greenpeace educational and fund-raising activities alluded to in this story are fictional.

Recipes for dishes enjoyed by the Circle may have been taken from actual kitchens, probably my own. You'll find a few in the back of this book.

DSR

The Circle of Five

Cassandra Shipton, an herbalist and reluctant clairvoyant, the bane of evil-doers who cross her path. Her online business is *Earthlore Herbal Preparations and Cruelty-Free Cosmetics.*

Phillipa Stern (nee Gold), a cookbook author and poet. Reads the tarot with unnerving accuracy.

Heather Devlin (nee Morgan), an heiress and animal rescuer. Creates magical candles with occasionally weird results. Benefactor of Animal Lovers Pet Sanctuary in Plymouth.

Deidre Ryan, a young widow, prolific doll and amulet maker, energetic young mother of four. She's the owner of *Deidre's Faeryland* at Massasoit Mall.

Fiona MacDonald Ritchie, a librarian and wise woman who can find almost anything by dowsing with her crystal pendulum. Envied mistress of The Glamour

The Circle's Family, Extended Family and Animal Companions

Cass's husband **Joe Ulysses**, a Greenpeace engineer and Greek hunk.

Phillipa's husband **Stone Stern**, Plymouth County detective, handy to have in the family.

Heather's husband **Dick Devlin**, a holistic veterinarian and a real teddy bear.

Deidre's new love, **Conor O'Donnell**, a world-class photographer and Irish charmer.

Cass's grown children

Rebecca "Becky" Lowell, the sensible older child, a family lawyer, divorced.

Adam Hauser, a computer genius, vice president of Iconomics, Inc.,

married to **Winifred "Freddie" McGarrity,** an irrepressible gal with light-fingered psychokinetic abilities. They are the parents of twins, **Jack and Joan Hauser**.

Catherine "Cathy" Hauser, who lives with her partner **Irene Adler**, both actresses, mostly unemployed.

Thunder Pony "Tip" Thomas, Cass's American Indian teenage friend, almost family, whose tracking skills are often in demand.

Fiona's family
Fiona is the guardian of her grandniece **Laura Belle MacDonald**.

Deidre's family
Jenny, Willy Jr., Bobby, and **Annie**.
Mary Margaret Ryan, a.k.a. **M & Ms**, mother-in-law and devoted gamer.
Betti Kinsey, a diminutive au pair, a.k.a. **Bettikins**.

The Circle's Animal Companions
Cass's family includes two irrepressible canines who often make their opinions known, **Scruffy**, part French Briard and part mutt, and **Raffles,** his offspring from an unsanctioned union.
Fiona's supercilious cat is **Omar Khayyám**, a Persian aristocrat. Phillipa's **Zelda**, a plump black cat, was once a waif rescued from a dumpster by Fiona. Recently, Phil has added a rescued boxer, **Boadicea** to her family.
Heather's family of rescued canines is constantly changing, and far too numerous to mention, except for **Honeycomb**, a golden retriever and so-called Therapy Dog who is Raffles' mother. Deidre's two miniature poodles are **Salty** and **Peppy**.

The atoms that make up your body were once forged inside stars, and the causes of even the smallest event are virtually infinite and connected with the whole in incomprehensible ways. If you wanted to trace back the cause of any event, you would have to go back all the way to the beginning of creation.
    Eckhart Tolle

Everything is energy and that's all there is to it.
Match the frequency of the reality you want and you cannot help but get that reality.
It can be no other way. This is not philosophy. This is physics.
    Albert Einstein

Magic: The movement of natural (but little understood) energies from the human body and from natural objects to manifest change.
    Scott Cunningham

London Bridge is falling down,
Falling down, falling down...
London Bridge is falling down,
My fair lady.
        Traditional nursery rhyme

CHAPTER ONE

*The untold want by life and land ne'er granted,
Now voyager, sail thou forth, to seek and find.*
Walt Whitman

A Samhain séance on Burial Hill, Plymouth's historic cemetery: who could resist such a deliciously spooky prospect?

Heather could, that's who.

The ceremony, after all, was to take place at the Morgan family vault, Heather's family, where we were proposing to contact her great-great grandfather Nathaniel (actually, two or three additional "greats" would be more accurate, but Heather simplified) who'd made his fortune in the early19[th] century China Trade, with a sideline in opium. So Heather was more than a little apprehensive about what skeletons might emerge from the Morgan family's checkered past. The rest of our circle of five were all for it and persuasive enough to talk Heather into the plan.

We depended on Phillipa's word magic to compose a rhyme offsetting any possible ghostly harm. Fiona, our librarian and wise woman, had researched the Morgan family history and discovered no curses or hexes to confound us. Deidre, however, was almost as apprehensive as Heather, because of a recently developed talent for actually seeing the dead. But Deidre is always up for an adventure, and her streak of daring won out over fear every time.

"It's four to one," she declared to Heather.

"But it's *my* damned family," Heather countered, hazel eyes flashing. "So to speak."

Our circle had come together a few years ago, in a women's study group sponsored by the Plymouth Library. The history of women's issues had led us inevitably to goddess myths and legends. As we'd delved into ancient matriarchal societies, we'd discovered this modern equivalent to the old earth religions—Wicca, "the wise ones." We'd liked the way Wiccans revered nature and recognized female spirituality. And Wiccans believed life energies could be used to control events—*the power of magic*. There's something very attractive to women about magic, after centuries of struggling to take control their own destinies. But as we've discovered, the purest intentions don't always turn out as planned.

Samhain (Halloween) is one of the high holidays, or Sabbats, of the Wiccan year. On Samhain, the veil is thinnest between this world and the next, and sensitive souls are more likely to communicate with the dead at this sacred time. Like the Spanish *Día de los Muertos,* Samhain has its roots in pre-Christian times; it honors and celebrates dead family members with candles, incense, food, music, and stories.

"The dead come back to finish what is unfinished," Deidre had explained to us and to herself. "I just wish they wouldn't bring their troubled past lives to me. Good grief! I don't fancy myself as some kind of Dr. Phil of the Spirits."

The cemetery séance was to take place at midnight, so we held our Samhain Sabbat earlier at the stone circle Heather had created for us on a wooded hill that was part of the Morgan mansion's extensive grounds.

෨෭

It was a crisp starry October eve of the quarter moon. To avoid cumbersome parkas, we wore heavy sweatshirts with hoods, which in silhouette made us look like robed witches or an urban gang, depending on one's frame of reference.

Tall, lithe Heather pushed her hood back, long hair glinting bronze in the light of the altar fire. She called the quarters, invoking blessings from the four directions, casting our circle, a sacred space "between the worlds" with her silver-handled athame.

We lit candles to welcome the spirits of our beloved dead. I sought the warm aura of my grandma and breathed in her scent of lavender and vanilla. Deidre was just as surely reaching out to her dead husband Will. Fiona, too, was a widow; Rob Angus Ritchie had drowned at sea. Phillipa's brother Josh had recently died of pancreatitis. Heather had lost her family housekeeper and old friend Ashbery, and then there were all the dear dogs she'd cherished through their briefer lives. *At our ages, it'll be more candles every year*, I thought, then immediately banished that image with a hand gesture learned from the *stregheria* in Italy.

Then we wrote our not-quite-so-secret life intentions with gold paint on broad autumn leaves and consigned them to the ceremonial fire where they would whirl up as smoke to the Goddess of a Thousand Names.

"I hardly dared to appeal for a new housekeeper, but I did," Heather said. Since her perfect couple, Max and Elsa, had resolved their legal problems and returned to their former lives as actors, she and her husband Dick had been casting about unsuccessfully for a replacement. Heather's relationship with housekeepers has always been somewhat doomed, ever since the first, Ashbery, was blown up in an explosion meant for her employer. But Heather, who was cooking-impaired and kept a lively, messy pack of rescue dogs at the Morgan mansion, really needed assistance. Silently, we had all echoed her plea, and we waited with uneasy anticipation for the solution that would surely come winging back from the Divine Cosmos.

Afterwards, we had the traditional merry supper, called "cakes and ale," packed by Phillipa in one of her elegant picnic baskets: a thermos of rum-laced hot toddies and hand-pies: mince, apple, and plum. Thus fortified, we put out our altar fire, then climbed into Heather's Mercedes with the dog-drooled-on windows and Phillipa's spotless BMW. We arrived at the cemetery and the Morgan vault a few minutes before midnight, "the witching hour."

∽

The aura of our Sabbat ceremony continued to hover around us, like the deep, disturbing incense of autumn.

I strewed dried dandelion flowers around the burial chamber to raise the spirits of the dead, with a handful of dried hawthorn and fennel leaves to protect us from whatever troublesome vibes might pop up with them. Heather, dubious but intrigued anyway, fixed a few of her handmade candles (violet and indigo for the sixth and seventh chakras) on the top of the vault, and lit them. The fragrance of cardamom and coriander rose into the cool night air, vying with the overwhelming scent of pine that permeates the hills of Plymouth.

No doubt disturbed by these goings-on, an owl hooted nearby and spooked us all, except for Fiona who claims the bird of night as her familiar. "A fortunate omen," she said, and raised her athame, an ancient Scottish dirk, to inscribe a sacred space around us, while Phillipa recited.

> *"Rise, O Captain Morgan, from your rest,*
> *Be our honored Samhain guest…*
> *As your spectral presence grows,*
> *Tell us secrets no one knows,*
> *Keep us through this midnight charm*
> *Safe from any ghostly harm.*

"Let's dance around and chant Phil's rhyme," Deidre suggested, rubbing her arms enclosed in a navy blue "hoodie" sweat shirt. With her pink cheeks and dimples, she looked more like a school girl than the mother of four. "It's cold as Hades out here, and my feet are frozen stiff." So we did that; shuffled around the burial vault and began to recite the chant the customary thirteen times. When we got to the ninth, however, we had to stop abruptly, because Deidre screamed and pointed. "Look there! Look over there."

Phillipa said afterward that she saw nothing but a reflection of the quarter moon bouncing off a granite monument. Fiona had glimpsed a column of silvery fog. The momentary vision of a man with a knife scar from his eye to his mouth flickered across my inner eye, but that was nothing new to me. Being a clairvoyant, I see things that may or may not be there on a regular basis. Deidre, with her fairly recent talent for encountering restless ghosts, was able to describe Captain Nathaniel Morgan more or less as he appeared in the portrait hanging in Morgan mansion's parlor, except that the specter had a scar not shown in the painting. She added that there was a second ghost standing right behind the captain, a brigand with a noose around his neck, dangling a length of rope. He was holding something in his hands, gesturing as if he wanted her to take it from him. Deidre shut her eyes, wanting to close out even the memory of that specter. "I couldn't see what it was, but gauzy things were hanging off it."

"Ectoplasm," Fiona said. "It's rare to see real ectoplasm, Dee."

"Ugh. Why me, O Holy Mother?" In moments of stress, Deidre reverts to the Catholic roots of her youth.

Throughout these awed exchanges, Heather said nothing. Nothing at all.

"Hey, Heather," I said. "Didn't you see something? You must have. If that was Nathaniel Morgan, he would have wanted to contact his great great granddaughter. That's why we thought up this whole expedition in the first place. After you found your great, great grandmother Alyce's prayer book and all.

"As I recall, I warned you at the time that I'd already learned as much about the Morgans as I ever needed to know," Heather reminded us. "For instance, the family legend that Benedict Morgan had been hanged in Boston for piracy. His son, Horatio, brought his father's body back to bury in this family vault. A year later, Horatio made a voyage to an unnamed island off the coast of Britain and somehow came into a fortune in French gold coins, Napoleons, which he used to finance his Cousin Nathaniel's expeditions to the Far East.

"Thus laundering the loot," Phillipa said.

"We all thought there was more to the story," Fiona said. "That's why I suggested this séance."

"There is more," Heather said. "Deidre saw the ghosts, not me. *But I heard a voice.* Like in my head but not in my head, if you know what I mean."

"One too many rum toddies?" Phillipa suggested.

"Clairaudience," I said. "Shut up and listen, Phil."

"A man's voice, very low and raspy, as if there was something wrong with his throat," Heather said.

"Because he was *hanged,* Heather," Deidre said. *"Duh!"*

"The Hanged Man!" Phillipa dark eyes shone with belated enthusiasm. "I could read the tarot with The Hanged Man as the significator. A symbol of sacrifice and suspense. A state of timelessness. Odin hung from the World Tree for nine days to receive the wisdom of the runes."

Ignoring the rest of us, Heather fixed her eyes on Fiona. "I heard this gravelly voice, saying, *I have waited a long time for you, and I am tired to death,"* Heather intoned with a shudder. *"Gather ye sisters in Salisbury at the Winter Solstice. Find the Crossed Keys Inn. Something that belongs to the Morgans is laid in the chimney, a gift of great power. You will know what to do."*

"Oh, sure," I whined. "Is this just your revenge for our setting up a séance *for your own good?* Are you cooking up a plan for getting us all to Salisbury, which also happens to be the location of Stonehenge, for the solstice?"

"Don't be daft, Cass," Heather said. "Have I ever doubted your visions? Well, hardly ever. Won't you at least credit my ... what did you call it?"

"Clairaudience," I said reluctantly.

"But you have a great idea there," Heather said. "Stonehenge! Why didn't I think of that?"

"You did think of it," I pointed out.

"An expedition into the extraordinary," Fiona declared. "This ancestor of Heather's has promised us *something,* something waiting for us at the Crossed Keys Inn."

"But it's impossible for us to simply pick up and go to England!" Phillipa cried. I imagined she was already rummaging through the closet of her mind's eye, looking for just the right outfit to wear for luncheon at the Savoy.

"If we're meant to go, everything will miraculously fall into place. Just you wait and see," Fiona promised. Her round face shone with enthusiasm under the crown of carroty-gray braids. "Maybe we should have another go at Benedict about what's stuck up the chimney"

"Probably the bones of some little chimney sweep," Phillipa said. "Those poor boys."

Their incipient wrangle was cut short by the wail of a police cruiser's siren that had just spotted us and our candles at the Morgan burial vault. It pulled up beside us, cut off the siren, and one of the officers stepped out of the vehicle.

"I could have told you that the cops always expect vandals in the cemeteries on Halloween," Phillipa muttered.

"Then why didn't you?" Deidre whispered back tartly.

Heather stepped forward with an unexpected chuckle. "Is that you, Cliff? It's only me, Heather. Paying my respects to the Morgan ancestors, you know."

"Oh, Heather," the officer said. "I might have known. Are these gals the rest of the Crazy Five?"

"These are my friends," Heather said in a reproving tone. "Hey, ladies. meet my cousin Clifton Morgan. Isn't it nice that he's out here protecting our gravesites from juvenile delinquents?"

"I can't believe there's *another* cousin," Phillipa said.

"Heather's cousins are legion. Literally," I said.

"Cliff is my second cousin, or maybe third? His Morgan lineage goes back to Horatio. Cliff and his family moved here recently from Vermont, which is why I may not have mentioned him before," Heather said. "New on the Plymouth force, actually."

"That's why I'm out here cruising for weirdoes on Halloween," Officer Morgan said. But he seemed cheerful enough about it, a small man with the muscular, wiry frame and hardened face of a lightweight boxer, but when he turned his head, the patrician Morgan profile came into evidence. "What's with the candles?"

"Respect," Heather s said. "It's All Souls Day, after all. Or it will be, tomorrow."

"Right," Officer Morgan drawled. "Better wrap it up now, though, before you give ideas to the druggies and vandals." He gave half a wave and half a salute to his cousin, got back in the cruiser, and said something to the driver, who threw his cigarette out the window before driving off.

Deidre stamped on the butt ostentatiously. "No thought to the piles of dry leaves," she complained.

Fiona took out of her reticule a small brass bell, shaped like a lady in a long skirt, and rang it three times. Heather was quenching the candles. Then she opened the magical space she had drawn with her athame. *Merry meet, merry part, and merry meet again.* We got back into the two cars and headed home. Possibly each of us was quietly thinking over the events of the séance, and whether we would be impelled to visit some haunted inn near Stonehenge in December.

It just didn't seem possible.

CHAPTER TWO

The Moving Finger writes; and, having writ,
Moves on; nor all your Piety nor Wit
Shall lure it back to cancel half a Line,
Nor all your Tears wash out a Word of it.
    The Rubaiyat of Omar Khayyám

There's no sneaking into a house where there are dogs on the premises who consider it their primal duty to announce all arrivals. And then, of course, they will want to take a run outdoors to relieve themselves.

Hey, Toots…where've you been all night? That furry-faced guy forgot our bedtime Milkbones again. Scruffy cocked his head and gazed straight into my eyes with his best alpha dog stare.

"Again! Again!" Raffles always provides an echo and back-up for his sire.

Scruffy and Raffles probably weren't speaking aloud (so I'm told) but somehow I always hear what they're saying quite clearly.

Joe came into the kitchen, yawning and stretching. He wore an open terrycloth robe with blue sleep shorts, showing off a muscular body and a permanent sea tan that gave his graying hair a silvery luster. He looked so good, I walked straight into his arms. He felt good, too, so we kissed a while. Meantime, Scruffy and Raffles paced around us restlessly.

"Where have you been all this time, Cass? I was beginning to get worried," Joe whispered in my ear. His neat beard tickled, but his breath was sweet and warming.

"You were asleep, honey. Worrying about me in your dreams? After the Sabbat, we went up to Burial Hill for a while.

Very atmospheric." I moved away only to open the kitchen door and let the dogs, who were now dancing around in an agitated fashion, onto the porch where they could avail themselves of the pet flap. "Did you by any chance forget their bedtime treats?"

"As a matter of fact, I was dreaming of you, and it was quite pleasant," Joe said. "If those two ruffians say I forgot them, they lie through their teeth. I split a slice of leftover *pastitsio* between them."

"Let's say they subverted the truth," I said.

When the dogs came in from their jaunt around the pines, I said, "You did, too, get bedtime treats. Liar, liar, tail on fire."

But no Milkbones, Toots. We canines need that biscuit crunch to keep our teeth clean and sharp.

"Clean and sharp. Clean and sharp."

"A treat is a treat, and you've had yours. Okay, I'm knackered, and I'm going to bed now," I said.

"I could tell you about my dream," Joe offered.

"Sure. Maybe I can make it come true." And maybe I wasn't all that tired.

Before we shut the bedroom door on the two inquisitive noses, I did pass out a couple of Milkbones. Dog discipline is not my forte.

The next morning, over coffee and a potato frittata, Joe said, "Greenpeace closed up a bunch of Shell stations in Britain last week. It's their Save the Arctic campaign against drilling for oil, you remember. Blocked the entrances and shut off the petrol flowing to the pumps. Mounted a bunch of wild life banners and posed in polar bear suits.'

I giggled at the mental image of strapping young activists in polar bear suits.

"Some guys I know were arrested for malicious mischief." Joe's tone was almost wistful.

"Missing all the fun, are you, honey?" I teased, but at the same time, I noted with a quickened beat of my heart that the action was in Britain, as if underscoring last night's séance. Still, Joe was a ship's engineer not a land activist, so no connection, really. Just synchronicity at work in its usual uncanny way.

"No, not at all. I've seen the inside of enough jails to last me a lifetime," Joe said. "A judge in Amsterdam has ruled that it's a legal protest in the Netherlands, but Britain got tough. Still, the guys are probably free already. More coffee?"

Despite disclaimers, his Aegean blue eyes took on that inscrutable expression I knew so well. I didn't have to be a clairvoyant to perceive that there was something in the wind, but I let the subject go. For the time being. The secret of ferreting out a husband's secrets is to spar, duck, weave away, and dance back later with a surprise attack.

My cell phone rang as Joe was filling our cups. It was Patty Peacedale. "Cass, dear, I wonder if you'd help out a young mother who's come to us with a problem that's a bit beyond Wyn and me." Selwyn Peacedale, Patty's husband, is the pastor of the Garden of Gethsemane Presbyterian church, just around the corner from our house.

Now what, I thought. Patty was a lodestone for gals with unusual psychic dilemmas that her husband avoided like the plague. "Oh, dear. I have such a stack of orders to fill today. What's the nature of the problem, Patty?"

"Do you remember my mentioning Fanny Fearley? Her husband went out to Suffolk Downs one day and never came home? She reported him as a missing person, but no trace of him was ever found. Two years later when the poor girl became pregnant, it was all the Ladies League could talk about, wondering just how it happened. The ladies do not exactly move with the times," Patty admitted.

"Immaculate conception? Shower of gold? The choir master?"

I could hear Patty struggle to submerge a chuckle. "So you've heard the gossip, then? But that's not why I called you. It's not Fanny herself that's the problem. It's her nephew, who's come to live with her while his mother, Fanny's sister Emma, is in rehab. Her son is twelve, used to be the glory of the choir before his voice broke, a lovely boy really. Except for that one disconcerting thing. Rather too much for Fanny, with her new baby and all."

Instantly I thought of Tip, Thunder Pony Thomas, whom I had first met when he was about the same age. "Tell me about it," I said.

"His name is Edward Cook Christie. He's taken a paper route, you know, to help out. So it's a reading thing, really. He reads headlines aloud," Patty said.

"And that's troubling, how?" I began to clear the table with the phone cradled between shoulder and ear.

"He reads them the day before. That particular headline hasn't actually been printed yet. Do you remember the accident last week? Three teen-agers drove off the road after a dance at Plymouth North, one of them hospitalized? That was Mavis Pynchon, the driver."

I put down the plates I was carrying and sat again at the weathered oak table. "Yes?"

"Fanny's nephew had read that headline to her the day before it happened. Poor boy knew Mavis from TNT, our Thursday Night Teens, and he'd had a sort of crush on her, though she's four years older. So he cautioned Mavis about the accident that hadn't happened yet. Mrs. Pynchon heard about Eddie's warning later. Mavis is her husband's cousin's girl, that's a second cousin I guess. So now Mrs. P. wants to know if Eddie did something to Mavis's car, or, if not, how could he say such a thing? Even if he didn't tamper with the Mustang, he was guilty as sin of *wishing evil on the girl. The devil's work*." Patty sighed deeply. "Wyn is beside himself. Fanny and her family are a thorn in his crown, he says."

"How does Eddie explain all this?" I asked.

"Eddie says he can't help it. When he picks up his bundle of papers, the headline just pops out at him in black and white. A few minutes later it fades away, and the real header for that day reappears. Fanny's fit to be tied. She told Eddie he'd better quit the paper route and get some other job after school. But he hasn't been able to find anything else at this time of year. Maybe not until after Thanksgiving, when the stores gets busy again. Oh, the poor child! Fanny says Emma warned her about the boy's vivid imagination, but Fanny thinks Eddie's not quite right in the head. Wyn calls him a juvenile delinquent, and Mrs. P. believes he's one of Satan's imps."

"What do *you* think, Patty?"

"I think Eddie's just got one of God's quirky gifts, similar to you and your friends' special ways. So that's why I'm calling you. The boy needs guidance. I pray for him, but the Lord expects us to do more than pray for those who are beset with difficulties."

"Amen. I tell you what, Patty. Tell Eddie to stop over to see me. I might have a few chores for him to do in place of the paper route. Joe keeps everything shipshape when he's at home, but I expect he'll be going back to sea soon."

Joe, who'd taken over clearing up the dishes when the conversation with Patty took a serious turn, looked around at me from the kitchen sink where he was cleaning the old cast iron fry pan, his eyebrows raised. "What the hell...?" he mouthed. I held up a finger to indicate that I'd explain in one minute. He shook his head in disbelief. Patty said she'd speak to Fanny. Maybe the boy could stop over after school to discuss employment. "God bless you, dear. That's a load off my heart."

Joe sat down at the kitchen table. "What does Patty want now? Who's this kid you've invited to work for you? And how the devil do you know when I'll be getting my next assignment?"

I answered his questions in reverse order. "I just feel in my bones that something's coming up for you, a new assignment. You'll see. I'll give Eddie the sort of jobs that Tip used to do for me. Stacking wood. Putting the herbs to bed. Wrapping orders. Schlepping them to the post office. If he's been delivering papers, he must have a bike. Patty wanted me to talk to the boy. Some worrisome incidents."

"Your bones always have a lot to say," Joe remarked. "What troublesome incidents?"

I told him the story of Eddie's strange ability. Marriage to me for a few years had taken the edge off Joe's incredulity.

"Taking this weird boy under your wing could get you into a mess of controversy," Joe said. "Not that I've ever known you to steer away from controversy."

"I wouldn't call him *weird*, honey. He's just a little different from his friends. I know what that's like. The first thing he has to learn is to be more guarded in his revelations."

"Going to get hanged for a witch, is he?" Joe sailed into the wind with that one.

"It's no joking matter, Joe! The witch hunts didn't end in Salem. If Eddie's lucky, the only penalty for being himself is that he'll be sitting at a table all alone in the school cafeteria. If he's not lucky, he'll end up accused of whatever he prophesizes. I wonder..."

"You wonder ... what?" Joe asked.

"I wonder if Mavis had paid attention to Eddie's warning, would she still have crashed her car and been hospitalized. Or would she have driven slower and got home safely?"

"That's a weighty wonder," Joe said. "Can the foreseen future be changed?"

"Or at least, swerved a little away from danger."

"What do you think?" Joe asked.

"I think we're going to find out," I said.

"Uh oh," Joe said. "Hoist the red flag."

CHAPTER THREE

Just then, with a wink and a sly normal lurch,
The owl very gravely got down from his perch,
Walked round, and regarded his fault-finding critic
(Who thought he was stuffed) with a glance analytic.
    James Thomas Fields

I needed Fiona!

Ignoring all the herbal orders piled in my cellar workshop, I drove over the next morning to consult with my pixilated Pisces pal in her fishnet-draped cottage in Plymouth Center. We conferred over a pot of lapsang souchong tea poured steaming into her thistle mugs. Bright sunlight spilled through casement windows illuminating the scarred cherry coffee table and a number of book shelves crowded with arcane volumes and instructional pamphlets. I couldn't help but notice the absence of dust and cobwebs, as would have met my eyes in the old days, before Fiona became the foster-mother of her grand-niece Laura Belle.

Fiona was wearing a rather subdued outfit: moss green, cable-knit sweater over an ankle-length blue and green skirt, the MacDonald hunting tartan. Only one pencil was stuck in her crown of carroty-gray braids, the sign of a fairly stress-free day.

She said, "I'm thinking of adopting an owl as my familiar."

"Really! And what is Omar going to say about that?"

"There will be an adjustment period, of course."

Omar Khayyám, her Persian cat, who at that moment was sunning himself on the arm of the sofa where Fiona sat, looked up with a scornful mien, blinked his green eyes, and stretched out his claws. *Not on your life.*

"Owls eat live whole animals, Fiona. They wake up at night and want to fly around the house," I said. "What about a lovely stuffed owl, instead?"

"Blessed Brigit, how revolting! Who would do such a thing to a magical bird? What a blot on one's karma!" Fiona exclaimed. "But don't be concerned, my dear. I'll not bring a wild bird into the house. Too cruel. I'm going to *call* my owl to take up residence in that lovely rowan tree right outside this window, where I will seek its advice on pressing psychic matters and send it on magical errands. Owls are great spiritual teachers. Surely you recall that an owl once lived in that great oak near the library? I named her Blodeuwedd after the Celtic flower goddess who was turned into an owl."

Omar settled back into napping mode, but his ears remained alert.

"That should be okay, then. Meanwhile, let me tell you what I'm working on." I related the story of my conversation with Patty.

"Dearie me, the poor child, and so young," Fiona said. "Christie is a Scottish name, you know. There's many a seer under a kilt."

"I bet." I shook my head to dispel the bawdy image. Sometimes it was difficult to keep on topic with Fiona. But I plowed on. "Do you believe that knowing about the future gives us a chance to change it?"

"All time is one, in a sense. So, just like Dee says, there's little point to wearing a wristwatch," Fiona said.

"You're wearing a watch," I pointed out. It was a silver nurse's pin watch fixed to her sweater. The face was upside-down so that it could be easily read by the wearer.

"Sentimental value. It belonged to my Granny. And I wouldn't want to miss Laura Belle's bus, dear. Bus schedules notwithstanding, past, present, and future exist at the same time. That's how you, Cass, can sometimes see what's going to happen, and that's how this little Christie boy can read tomorrow's news. Modern physics teaches us that the things of this world may look quite solid, including ourselves, but actually they are made up of energy and information taking physical forms. Atoms with a great deal of space between them. We are immortal spirits, too, of course, but physicists haven't got to that, yet. The point is that reality, not being all that real, can always be bumped a little. That's what magic is all about."

"So that's a *yes?*" Trying to follow Fiona's logic can be a tricky business.

"That's an *it depends*," she said. "Of course if a disaster is foretold, the seer will naturally try to avert it, just as Eddie did with his friend. You've done the same yourself, as I recall."

I remembered once frantically trying to get in touch with Deidre who was driving Jenny and Willy to school, when I "saw" that the car's brakes had been damaged. Deidre had averted a crash by driving up onto a grassy hillock off the road. "Not a definitive success," I said. "She still ended up on the Town Hall lawn."

"Perhaps we're going to get another chance to test the theory," Fiona said.

"That's what I told Joe, but I'm a little uneasy."

"Clairvoyance like yours is one of the Thirteen Powers. So is Prophecy, but that's somewhat different," Fiona said. "Clairvoyance may miss the mark, timewise. Drives you crazy, Cass, doesn't it? Knowing *what* but not *when?* And what you 'see' may be pieces of a puzzle, from which you cannot make a whole picture. Eddie Christie, on the other hand, has the gift of prophecy, which predicts a future event in precise detail. It is indeed as if he read a report of it in the news. And there's no escape for the prophet. Psychic gifts, once given, must be honored. So then, there's an overwhelming impulse to warn those who may be harmed."

"Honor aside, this particular gift is only going to get Eddie into plenty of hot water."

"But if he can save someone from injury?" Fiona gazed hopefully at the tree outside her window as if expecting her owl to appear at any moment. "That's the dilemma gifted folk have faced since time immemorial."

"What should I do to help him?" I asked.

"Teach him to be discrete and to use his gift only for good. Not to just blurt out everything he knows, but if there's a real danger, find a way to ward it off that doesn't implicate himself."

"For Goddess' sake, Fiona. The boy is only twelve years old!"

"That's why he's been sent to you. You'll just have to run interference."

I sighed. How many times, when we ask a particular friend for advice, it's because we already know exactly what she will say. Something we needed to hear, a confirmation of one's own inner voice. "Well, maybe when Eddie gives up his paper route, the prophecy thing won't keep happening."

Fiona laughed until the many silver bangles on her arms jingled like tiny bells, that deep infectious chuckle I couldn't resist joining. She was right. It was entirely ridiculous to think either Eddie or any of us would escape our psychic karma.

"So, what kind of owl are you expecting?" I asked, wiping away the laugh-tears.

"Silver Owl. Also known as Ghost Owl or Barn Owl. There are several quite suitable nest hollows out there, although I would prefer that she choose the rowan," Fiona said with perfect authority that her desire would be manifested in reality. "*Cailleach-oidhche*, in Granny's Gaelic. The natural companion to an older woman, an owl carries the wisdom of the Goddess. She who is wise and inquiring, and from whom nothing can be concealed."

"Sounds like you, Fiona," I said.

But Fiona was already humming to herself, a tune with a Scottish lilt. "Is that an old Scot ballad?" I asked.

"Indeed it is, dearie. It's called *Ye Cannae Shove Yer Granny Aff a Bus*. Very popular with kiddies. It was at Granny's place that I first made friends with Silver Owls. Granny had cut out a pentagram portal into the barn's loft, and a pair of the creatures went through and nested there. Oh, it's also called a Demon Owl, but that's nonsense. Heart-shaped, white face. Doesn't hoot. More of a *shree* scream that will put the fear of Hecate into any intruder."

"The neighbors will be thrilled. Literally," I said. As I looked out at the bare tree branch, I could almost see Fiona's familiar owl perched there.

༄

At home, I found Joe packing his duffle bag in the bedroom and the dogs pacing around him nervously. He looked up and smiled sheepishly. "You were right. The call came through right after you left for Fiona's."

Hey, Toots. What's the furry-faced guy up to this time? You're not going to abandon us again, are you? This bag on the bed business is a bad sign.

Bad sign! Bad sign!

"Pipe down! I'm not going anywhere," I said.

"I assume you're reassuring the canine contingent?" Joe folded his good Italian suit very deftly in tissue so that it wouldn't wrinkle ... much. He was an amazing packer, married to a woman who couldn't even fold a fitted queen-size sheet.

"Why in Hades are you packing dress clothes, Joe?"

"The *Gaia* is docked in Boston. We're sailing to Canada, a protest against exploratory Arctic drilling, but after that, we're heading to this fundraising thing in Philadelphia. We'll be giving public tours of the *Gaia* at Penn's Landing, and later there's a meeting with some of the Kirkup Foundation people. Might be a dinner."

"Public tours? I wouldn't mind looking around the *Gaia* myself."

"Someday, sweetheart, for sure," Joe said. "At the evening meeting, we'll be showing videos of the African over-fishing campaign, and someone *up there* has got the idea that schmoozing with the actual crew will provide extra motivation to shell out a hefty donation. In truth, though, Greenpeace is mostly financed in small amounts from committed supporters and face-to-face fundraisers." He stopped packing to pull me into his arms and gaze at me earnestly. "I'm not looking forward to this show biz jaunt, sweetheart. I'm like the Old Man of the Sea among all those eager, hip young activists. Even the directors are younger than I am."

"Not as old as all that," I said, feeling his solid, muscular body against mine. "Oh well, I'm not surprised that Greenpeace wants to show off someone who really looks as if he's sailed the seven seas.;" As soon as I'd said that, I felt a buzz, a quiver of an idea, a shudder of premonition, that there would be more to this fundraising thing, and not just in Philadelphia. It made me dizzy even to think about it. I pulled away and sat down on the bed abruptly.

Joe recognized the cloud passing over me. "What's the matter, Cass? What are you seeing now?" He sat down beside me and put his comforting arm around my waist.

"If you get too popular," I warned Joe, resting my head on his shoulder, "they'll be sending you to Europe next."

"In that case, you'll come with me. We'll steal a vacation for ourselves, what do you say to that?"

I don't like the look of all this cuddling, Toots. Are you sure you're not planning to dump us with that pack of mongrel refugees?

Refugees! Refugees! Raffles was so alarmed by his sire, he jumped up on the bed and crashed on the duffle bag. In the general consternation to follow, the subject of Joe's fundraising future got lost for the time being.

It didn't come up later that night, either. We had more engrossing matters to occupy our hearts and minds. But after we finally went to sleep, I dreamed of an Elizabethan inn on a narrow dark street. The rasping screech of an owl keened in the distance, and the wind shrieked down the streets of the town. A lamp caught an image on the inn's sign as it banged against the building.

Crossed Keys!

CHAPTER FOUR

Just at the age 'twixt boy and youth,
When thought is speech, and speech is truth.
    Sir Walter Scott

I was unprepared for the boy's beauty, which brought on an immediate attack of acute worry. The curly blond hair, the clear sky-blue eyes, the sheer vulnerability of his open, honest expression, the brave set of his fragile shoulders. Who in the world would ever suggest that Eddie was "Satan's imp"? Mrs. Pynchon should choke on those words.

Oops! One ought to be so careful about those casual curses! *Take that out of the law! No harm to Mrs. P.* The Divine Cosmos has its own way of dealing with the mean and mouthy without any help from me.

"My name is Eddie. Eddie Christie," he introduced himself after we'd said hello at the door. "Mrs. Peacedale said you might have some chores for me, Mrs. Shipton." An old but decent black bike leaned against the porch.

"Call me Cass," I suggested immediately, so I wouldn't have to confuse the boy right off. As a married woman, I am legally Mrs. Ulysses, but I have retained my maiden name for business purposes. Or so I claim. In my deepest heart, however, I know it's because I'd given up my family name once for Gary Hauser and that had not gone well. Joe didn't mind. He never felt diminished by my eccentricities.

Scruffy and Raffles, after some *pro forma* barking, checked the boy out by sniffing his hands, sneakers and pant legs thoroughly. He patted heads and smiled sadly. "I wish I had a big dog like these guys," he said. "I bet they're real good company." Instantly, in my mind's eye, I saw the figure of a lonely boy biking down a long road by himself.

Hey, Toots, does this guy play ball? If he doesn't play ball, you'd better send him away.

Away! Away! Raffles checked out Eddie's pockets and made him giggle. Scruffy brought over his green sponge ball and thrust it into Eddie's hand. It was somewhat gooey, but Eddie took it anyway.

"Stand down, you two," I said sternly. "Sure, Eddie, I do have some chores that need sorting," I said, motioning him toward the kitchen table. "Sit down, and we'll have a talk. But you'd better drop that old ball and wash your hands at the kitchen sink. You can play with the guys later."

I poured him a glass of milk and myself a cup of tea. I put out a plate of Joe Froggers between us. When he took a cookie, I noticed that his hands were very clean, white, and unmarked. I thought about meeting Tip for the first time, his work-worn hands and questionable fingernails, his dark eyes that had seen too much for his years. Eddie ate with good appetite, and we agreed on an hourly rate which I was certain was better than whatever he'd made on the paper route.

I gave Eddie a pair of Joe's work gloves and started him on an easy enough job, moving the truckload of wood that had been dumped at the edge of our property, neatly stacking split logs between two pines nearer the house. Scruffy and Raffles ran back and forth with Eddie, and occasionally he threw the green ball a distance away where one or the other dog could chase it down, making two devoted friends.

Samhain was past now, and Samhain is the earth cycle's last warning to get our homes winter-ready. Perceiving Eddie's frailty and resolve, I determined I'd send the boy home early, well-paid. Working for me, he should be able to drop the troublesome newspaper route, as his Aunt Fanny had decided he must.

So I was keeping an eye on Eddie's progress when Heather called me, caroling with joy that she had found a housekeeping couple to replace the departed Max and Elsa, who had headed straight for New York once they'd been cleared of the assault charges which had forced them into hiding. "The Divine Cosmos has come through for me once again," she cried. "You're going to love these dear children, Cass. "Fleur and

Roland de Vere. Talk about the answer to a Wiccan prayer! By the most extraordinary synchronicity, they simply wandered into our grounds carrying their dear little Italian greyhound, Fra Angelico, who had a thorn or something in his paw, and of course someone at the firehouse suggested that they bring the limping pup here. We got to chatting while Dick was treating Angelo, and it turns out that they've wanted to settle down in one place for a good rest-up."

"Rest-up from what?" I asked.

"They're ... well, the only word for it is, *troubadours*," Heather said. "They've been working their way from Robin Hood's Faire to Medieval Manor's theater-restaurant, and so forth, but they've been wanting something more secure. And I must say they look worn out. He plays the lute, and she sings medieval ballads. *Charming* couple."

"Really. What about cooking, cleaning, and dog-minding?" When Heather waxed rhapsodic, I had to worry.

"Along with performing at the Medieval Manor, Fleur sometimes worked as a kitchen helper while Roland was employed as a busboy. The Manor's official menu is rather limited, but the chef had made a study of medieval food, and he taught her a lot, she says. Pottage, sallets, spitted birds, and skewered fish. It's going to be a whole new experience."

"Larks' tongues?"

"Don't be obscene, Cass. Like me, the De Veres are practically vegetarians. Free-range and wild-caught all the way. They're very attached to their darling greyhound, and all our dogs seem to respond affectionately to them, especially when Roland played the lute and Fleur sang. Isn't it extraordinary how animals love music!" Heather was still ebullient. I decided not to throw any more buckets of cold water on her delight.

"It does sound as if you lucked out, Heather. What about Dick? He must be pleased, too."

"Yes, it's getting a tad chilly to be grilling outdoors, poor guy. I admit I'm not much of a cook. We're both looking forward to having good helpers again."

"Have you told the glad news to Phil? What does she say?"

"Oh, you know how Phil is. A bit of a food snob. Calls the Medieval cuisine 'pease porridge slop'. Also, she seemed to think that checking references is a really big deal, whereas I trust entirely to my psychic instincts. Never look a goddess gift in the mouth, I always say."

"You sound like Fiona," I said. "Has Fiona told you yet about calling an owl to be her familiar?"

"I wonder if she wouldn't be better off with a nice little Scottish terrier," Heather said reflectively. "There's a homeless little Scottie over at the shelter. I'll speak to her about that. Oh, and Fleur has another talent as well. So Roland tells me. She's got a natural green thumb. It's something about singing to the plants. She's promised to sing to the potted plants in the conservatory. Anyway, you and Joe must come over to meet dear Fleur and Roland. We'll have dinner."

"Joe's gone to a new assignment in Canada," I said. "But I wouldn't miss this for the world."

"Super! I suppose I'd better give the De Veres a day or so to settle in. How's Saturday night, about seven?"

"I'm looking forward to it. Is there anything I can bring?"

"Just a suspension of your usual skepticism, my dear. Hey, maybe I'll invite Fiona as well. I'd ask Phil and Stone, too, but you know Phil. She'd scare my new little cook to death. And Conor's taking Deidre to be presented to his folks, at last. Well, his grandparents anyway. His parents are in Africa, running some kind of medical set-up. Conor's been more or less keeping the family under wraps, hasn't he? Embarrassed to admit his grandfather, Dermot O'Donnell, is a big wheel in the Irish Technology Group?"

"Yeah, Deidre only learned how rich they are because of that ransom deal in Rome," I said. "I wonder if Conor's told the O'Donnells that his sweetheart is a poppet-maker who comes with a built-in family of four little ones?"

"*Love triumphs over all!*" Heather declared. At the moment, her beatific mood was obviously triumphing over every cloud on the horizon. I hoped fervently that the De Veres would be the perfect answer to Heather's Samhain wishes, but if they were not, sooner or later I would sense it.

∽

In his after-school visits, Eddie had finished the wood pile, and I had moved him on to mulching a few perennial herb beds that Joe hadn't got to before he left. That's when the prophecy problem hit again. There was a stack of newspapers in the shed beside the garage where we keep the bales of salt hay we use for mulching. The fact that they were old news indeed didn't seem to make a difference. Eddie came out of the shed white-faced, holding a yellowed sheet.

"Missus, Missus ..." (Apparently he was too polite to call me Cass, as I had suggested.) "Did you know there was a hold-up at the Mayflower Bank? Aunt Fanny's a teller there. So how come she never even told me about the hold-up? Should I call her and see if she's all right, do you think?" If a youngster could be said to wring his hands, Eddie was wringing his in much distress, crumpling up the newspaper he was holding in the process.

"Let me see that paper, dear." I eased the page out of his grip and straightened out the wrinkles. It was a copy of the *Pilgrim Times* dated several months ago, and the headline was "Power Struggle: Relicensing the Pilgrim Nuclear Power Station." I read the first paragraph. "With the end of its 40-year license approaching, the owners of Pilgrim Nuclear Power Station in Plymouth have applied for a 20-year extension. But opponents of the plant, including some local and state politicians, question the reactor's safety after three sister reactors in Japan experienced explosions and likely meltdowns this past year." Then I scanned the rest of the front page. Nothing whatsoever about a bank robbery.

"I think you're mistaken, Eddie." I smoothed the page again and handed it back to him. "No bank robbery. Just a fuss over Pilgrim."

Eddie looked at the newspaper incredulously. "But it was there just a minute ago, Missus. I'd better call Aunt Fanny" He took a cell phone out of his pocket. "Or maybe I should just text her in case she can't answer right now."

"*NO!*" I said emphatically. "What you've read hasn't happened, honey. But maybe it's *going* to happen, you know, like the accident with the Pynchon girl? You remember what trouble you got into over that one?"

Eddie looked down and scuffed the toe of his sneaker on the gravel path. He'd taken off his gloves earlier, and now he rubbed his eyes with the back of his hands. I sure hoped he didn't have any allergies. "I don't know why I keep seeing stuff that isn't there," he said, with a sob buried somewhere underneath the words.

I put my arm around his thin shoulders and led him into the kitchen. "Wash the hay off your hands, honey, and I'll fix us some hot chocolate while I think what to do." I took out the small heavy pot I like to use for hot chocolate. Then it hit me, if the robbery hadn't happened yet *but it was going to,* perhaps it could be prevented.

I grabbed my cell and punched in Phillipa's number on my speed dial. "Listen, Phil. Someone's going to try to rob the Mayflower Bank, or already has. Call Stone right away!"

"Oh, come on, Cass. Are you sure this isn't one of those figments of your imagination?" Phillipa complained.

"Are you going to wait until it happens, *or are you going to call this minute?*"

My tone must have conveyed enough sharp urgency to penetrate Phillipa's doubts.

She sighed heavily and ended the call with a click.

I waited, busying myself with mixing cocoa and sugar in the saucepan, gradually adding milk and a dash of cinnamon. My cell finally rang its tinny tune.

Phil said, "Too late, Lady Soothsayer. Stone was already at the scene of the crime. First time in its history that the Mayflower has ever been involved in a stick-up. Can you imagine?"

Eddie was at my elbow, trying to hear what was being said. "It's all right, honey," I said to him, and then to Phil, "No one's hurt, then?"

"A new teller got a bump on her head, but that's all. Fanny Fearley was reaching for the alarm button when the robber tapped her with his cane," Phil said.

"Cane?"

"Apparently, judging by the cane and his voice, the robber was a senior citizen. But how did you know? Was this one of your visions?"

"Hang on a minute, Phil" I poured the hot drink into a cup for Eddie, added a fat marshmallow, and reassured him. "Your aunt is going to be fine, honey. Just a little bump on the noggin." Leaving the boy at the kitchen table, I carried the cell phone into my office, the old borning room, and eased the door closed.

I debated for a moment, but then I realized that, sooner or later, Phillipa would have to know all about Eddie. "The boy, Eddie Christie, the kid that Patty Peacedale talked me into hiring. He's here today, finishing the mulching. Apparently, he has the gift of prophecy."

"Sweet Isis! Does this mean that my poor husband is going to be saddled with two soothsayers? How does the kid do it? Crystal ball? Chicken entrails?"

"Eddie's gift is somewhat different than mine," I knew that Phillipa likes to sound more cynical than she actually is, so I didn't mind patiently explaining. "My visions are scenes I see and occasionally hear, but Eddie reads the future as if it were a newspaper headline. Apparently, any old newspaper will do. He read about the bank robbery in a discarded copy of the *Pilgrim Times* that actually featured a story about the nuclear power plant."

"*Oy!* Thanks a lot, Patty! Where does she find these weirdoes?"

"I think they find her, Phil. Something about Patty's compassionate aura draws young people in need of guidance, including psychic guidance, like bees to nectar. She's simply a sweet, helpful soul."

"Unlike the dear Reverend," Phillipa said.

"I think the Peacedales find a balance between them. Wyn keeps Patty from wasting all her energy on the needy, and she shames him into sharing her empathic impulses. But here's the thing, Phil. I'm almost sorry that Eddie didn't come up with his prophecy a little earlier, aren't you?

Phil was wise to me. "You wanted to find out if the bank robbery could have been prevented. *Can the future be changed?*"

"That's the big question, all right. On the one hand, I want to encourage Eddie to get control of his gift so it won't overwhelm him. On the other hand, if we knew in advance about some terrible event, could it be averted?"

"You've consulted Fiona, I imagine," Phillipa said.

"Of course. She doesn't know either." I gazed out the window. Eddie had gone back to work, ferrying salt hay to the last rosemary bed with two happy dogs at his heels. Following a wheelbarrow was always a good time. The sun glinted off the bright red metal right into my eyes.

Phillipa sighed. "I'm going to have to meet this little boy."

An image danced across my inner eye. Phillipa and Eddie. "He's a dear, and you're going to love him," I said. *And want him for your own,* was the thought that followed. *Oh, I hope this doesn't end in tears.*

CHAPTER FIVE

We have fallen into the place
where everything is music.
   Rumi

Fiona and I arrived at the Devlins' circular driveway at almost the same time, so we made our entrance together. The November night was overcast and bone-chilling, but we were both well wrapped up, Fiona in her tartan cape, leaning on her silver coyote cane, and me in my L.L. Bean parka, but suitably dressy underneath with sleek wool slacks and my green Armani jacket; my hair (freshly retouched at Sophia's Serene Salon, with a color called "Sahara Spring") was not in its usual wilding state but smoothly shoulder-length. Joe would not approve. Like most men, he believed that he preferred "the natural look," having no idea of how much artifice was required to maintain that illusion while keeping the years at bay.

The big dogs, although tucked up in their kennels, announced our arrival, and immediately a tune was struck up indoors to welcome us. I think it was "Greensleeves." After a while, the dogs quieted and there was only the medieval music.

"I wonder if the De Veres will serve eel pie." Fiona smiled at me impishly, arranging the folds of her shawl (red-and-green dress MacDonald). A silver pen and an ivory crochet hook were stuck in her coronet of braids.

"Eels! Oh, good Goddess," I exclaimed before the front door opened and Dick Devlin welcomed us into the Victorian red parlor, where a slim young man with fair hair was playing a lute by the fireplace. On second glance, he was more than slim. That boy was unhealthily thin. I was suddenly glad that he'd landed with the generous Devlins where food and (Goddess knows!) wine were always plentiful.

Pewter goblets had been unearthed from somewhere, and Heather waved a jug at us merrily. "Come in, come in, my dears, and have a dram to start things off. Fleur is in the kitchen, finishing up the feast. Doesn't it smell divine! And this is Roland, our marvelous musician."

Roland bowed, smiled, sang out "Greetings, good ladies," and nearly toppled over before he went back to his lute playing. Fiona reached into her green reticule for her medicine bag of corn pollen, no doubt to bless the boy.

The contents of the jug proved to be honey mead, which was pretty sweet stuff for an aperitif, but with Heather and her frequent changes of housekeeping themes, one tended to simply go with the program. Fleur came in from the kitchen, still drying her hands. She, too, looked a tad undernourished but lovely in a pre-Raphaelite way, with wavy chestnut hair and expressive dark eyes. After introductions all 'round, the young couple joined in a duet, something about a wandering lover: "My life is faren in londe, Allas why is she so? She hath my herte in holde, Wherever she ride or go."

We applauded warmly. Fiona beamed at the musicians and kissed each of them on the cheek, her silver bangles tinkling. They didn't seem to mind at all. Right after the singing and the mead, we were ushered into dinner. A refectory table, draped with brocade, was set with pewter plates. We were dining in the conservatory as we had often before at the Morgan mansion. Even at this time of year, the many-windowed room was warm and very pleasant after the reality of November outdoors. Subliminally, I noticed that the potted palms and ficus trees that surrounded us were vividly glossy and the forlorn hibiscus had come out with two crimson blossoms.

"Of course I wanted Fleur and Roland to dine with us," Heather whispered while the couple retired to the kitchen to bring out the feast, "but they would have none of it. Fleur said they'd eaten earlier and preferred to attend to the food and perhaps sing a few songs later." Heather, in her egalitarian way, always wanted her hired help to be treated as guests not servants. As it worked out, the help often preferred to be autonomous and private.

"Don't fuss, dear," Fiona advised, tucking her linen napkin into her collar. "Let the wee darlings find their own way for a while."

Right now, "the wee darlings" were bringing in platters and bowls of steaming food. I tried my best to memorize every dish, knowing that Phillipa would want a full report. "A dauce agre," white fish in a sweet and sour onion sauce, was followed by the main course, chickens braised in a clay pot with sage, rosemary, and thyme, then finished with a saffron sauce, and rice flavored with almond milk and white pepper. This was accompanied by a bowl of artichoke hearts with cinnamon, butter, and vinegar, and "boiled sallet," cooked greens with currants, garnished with hard-cooked eggs. Several bottles of wine from Cypress and a coarse round loaf of bread accompanied the meal. Dessert was wine-flavored peach tart in rich pastry.

It was all quite delicious, and we complimented Fleur extravagantly. It was evident that she had paid close attention to those lessons from the Medieval Manor chef.

After dinner, we gathered by the fire in the parlor again. The De Veres sang: "O West Wind, when will thou blow? that the small rain down can rain. Christ, if my love were in my arms, And I in my bed again." I thought of Joe at sea somewhere this night, perhaps feeling lonely. As if in sympathy with the song, the cloudy November night turned to rain pelting the velvet-draped windows. Roland dashed outdoors to check on the comfort of the larger dogs in their heated garage-kennel. The smaller ones, including the De Veres' own Italian greyhound, were tucked up in wicker basket beds in a room adjacent to the kitchen.

Roland disappeared to help Fleur clean up, and the four of us remaining in the parlor drew closer to the cheery fire.

"They seem like a lovely couple," Fiona said, musing on the hypnotic flames.

"Devoted to their little dog, Angel," Dick remarked, stretching out his long legs toward the fire and sipping a mug of mulled wine, poured from a pitcher on the hearth.

"And Fleur certainly knows her way around a kitchen," Heather noted with satisfaction.

I had no impression myself to share, which made me realize that I should have shaken hands with Fleur and Roland when we were first introduced. That's the way I "read" people usually.

But with Roland clutching his lute, and Fleur constantly holding some dish of food in her hands, the occasion had never presented itself.

Well, later will be good enough, I thought.

At that moment, a burning chunk of wood shot out of the fireplace and over the half-screen; it landed on the hearth rug. Heather and Dick jumped up and stamped it into ashes, which had the appearance of a merry little jig.

"The magic science of fire-watching," Fiona said, "is called pyromancy. I was trained as a pyromancer by a Hawaiian shaman, a kahuna, which means 'keeper of balance'. Pele, goddess of fire, lightning, and volcanoes, is an important deity in the islands."

"Of course," I said, wishing that Phillipa were here to exchange glances, as we often did when Fiona came up with these gems.

"Now that exploding brand may be significant," she continued. "I'm sure nothing is amiss with that sweet little couple who've just come to live with you, and yet I wonder ..."

"Cut it out, Fiona," Heather said sharply. "We are pleased as Punch that Roland and Fleur have joined our little family."

"I've always found canines to be excellent judges of character," Dick said, sweeping ashes off the rug and back into the fireplace. "And our dogs have really taken to Fleur."

"Oh well, then," I said. "Nothing to worry about at all."

Fiona took the silver pen out of her coronet and made a short note in a tartan-covered notebook she retrieved from her reticule. "Yes, of course, dear." She put the pen and notebook away.

Time for a change of subject. I related the story of Eddie and the newspaper headline that wasn't really there. Everyone else had, of course, heard about the Mayflower bank incident.

"Better if no one learns of the boy's prediction," I said. "He's got himself into trouble that way before."

"I heard the robber got away with several thousand dollars, and there was no dye deterrent," Dick said. "Mayflower had not expected to be a target, I guess."

Heather sighed. "Probably some poor old guy who can't make his Social Security stretch far enough. Or maybe a homeless Vietnam vet."

"Perhaps the next time the boy reads the future, we can get in there ahead of time and prevent a crime," I said.

"You're just itching to test that time theory, Cass," Fiona said. "But keep in mind the butterfly effect in chaos theory. One minor change in a nonlinear system may result in a chain of unexpected results, even a major event."

"You may call that the "butterfly effect," Heather said, "but I call it magic."

CHAPTER SIX

... Tomorrow's fate, though thou be wise,
Thou canst not tell nor yet surmise;
Pass, therefore, not today in vain,
For it will never come again.
      The Rubaiyat of Omar Khayyám

Deidre stopped by the next morning, eager to share her story, (saving me the trouble of prying the details out of her). I noticed that, after months of keeping it on a gold chain around her neck, she was finally wearing on her left hand the ring that Conor had given her. It wasn't a diamond, though, but a jade ring with a tiny carved parrot. Deidre had told us the ring was an amulet of peace and love because famous paintings by van Eyck and others depict the Madonna holding a green parrot.

"Holy Mother, what a third-degree I got from Conor's grandmum!" she exclaimed. "Do you happen to have a drop of the Irish to sweeten this coffee?"

I raided the parson's cabinet for whiskey and poured a liberal swig into Deidre's cup. She was looking a trifle subdued today. Even her golden curls were less bouncy, and the mischievous spark in her eyes had definitely been quenched.

"Never mind staring at this ring, Cass. It's a friendship thing. Conor and I are not even engaged, but I guess his bringing me to meet his folks is almost the same thing, because Mrs. O'Donnell's main concern seems to be whether I'd be keeping a good Catholic home for Conor, not to mention a Catholic future family," Deidre continued. "She asked me to call her Eileen, but she's so imposing, lacy bosom and all, I just couldn't bring myself to do anything but clutch my cross, which thank the Goddess I had sense enough to wear, and bob my head in agreement to whatever the old dame said."

"She doesn't know you've gone over to the dark side, then?"

"Blessed Lady, no! But she asked me about my 'little one' quite sweetly. So I had the distinct impression that Conor's not told her how prolific I am."

"It's very Catholic," I suggested.

"It's ready-made-by-another-man's-genes, truth be told! So I said to Eileen that my 'little one,' and that would be Annie, was in nursery school, and I never really did get around to mentioning her three siblings," Deidre confessed. "Anyway, there's this trip the grandparents want us to make at Yuletide. To the British Isles, to see the palatial manor house the old man's bought in *ye merrie olde England*, although why any Irish would show such anglophile leanings beats me. The thing is, Conor despises all that rigmarole and will only go if there's an assignment in the offing to keep him creatively occupied."

A familiar ghostly chill walked over my future grave. "Conor will get an assignment that takes him to Britain in December, of that I'm sure," I said. "Maybe even something to do with photographing old pubs and inns."

"Oh! You mean the fates are aligning its witches all in a row to get us to Stonehenge for the Solstice? Like Heather's spooky pronouncement at Samhain?" Some of her characteristic sparkle was returning to Deidre's eyes, and that dimple was in evidence "As long as I'm home by Christmas Day for the kiddos, I'm game for a Solstice adventure. And so will Fiona be."

"What about Phil?" I wondered.

"Something will turn up," Deidre said. "And for you, too."

"I already know what my twist of fate will be," I said. "I've already 'seen' Joe and I on Westminster Bridge. It's a Greenpeace thing, I'm pretty sure."

"The Goddess moves in marvelous ways." Deidre reached for the bottle of Bushmills to warm up her cold coffee.

❧

I couldn't decide whether I should remove all newspapers from my property to protect Eddie's sensibilities, or leave them around deliberately to see what might turn up. I was mighty tempted toward the latter strategy. Fortunately, I was saved from making that decision by Eddie's arrival the next day with a newspaper already in hand. He had picked it up, he said, from the street. His expression was worried and wondering.

I didn't bother to take the paper from him and read the headline myself. I was sure it would be unremarkable, as Plymouth news generally is. "Read it to me, dear," I said, rather ingenuously.

"*Faulty Safety Relief Valve Shuts Down Nuclear Power Plant,*" Eddie appeared to be reading from the page. "See, it's right here."

Eddie handed me the soggy newspaper. I read, '*Town Meeting: $550,000 to restore Burial Hill unprecedented.*"

What to do? This was not the kind of thing that Stone Stern could help me with. *Curses! I would be forced to call my ex-husband, the berserker.* As ironic twists of fate would have it, after majoring in Chemical Engineering, a stint at a Boston firm managing hazardous waste, and a graduate degree from MIT in Nuclear Engineering, Gary Hauser happened to be currently employed at the Plymouth Nuclear Power Station (practically over my dead body, but what could I do?) My children were pleased to have him living in the same general area as their mother, especially Cathy, his favorite, who spent most of her time with him on her rare visits.

"It will be all right, Eddie," I said soothingly. "You're probably reading the news in advance, as you have often done before, and I believe I'll be able to divert this event before it becomes a hazard. I know someone at the plant I can contact."

Eddie looked at me trustingly. I almost wished he were less credulous and more suspicious of his elders, purely as a survival instinct. Meanwhile, I put him to work sweeping up my cellar workroom while I retired to my office to call Gary.

"Gary, it's me, Cass," I said without preamble once I had reached his extension, "I have reason to believe there's a defective safety relief valve at the plant which will shut down Pilgrim if not repaired."

"Ah, Crazy Cass and her Curious Cautions," Gary said in a delighted tone of voice that seemed at odds with the gravity of my news.

"I think you should take me seriously, Gary. I have a pretty fair track record in the predictions department."

"Don't I know, darling. Don't I know! But in this case I think you've screwed up some important details. Such as your geography."

"What do you mean?"

"It's an official secret at the moment, but you'll be hearing about the incident soon enough. Will you swear on whatever you're using for a Bible these days not to spill the news before it's public knowledge?"

"Okay," I said cautiously.

"There's a leak happening in Pickering, Ontario, dear Cass. Not Plymouth, Massachusetts. A finicky pump. They may have to release radioactive water into Lake Ontario. The reason I know this is because Pilgrim and some other older plants have been ordered to check our pumps as a precaution."

Silently, I reviewed the exact wording of Eddie's "headline." I couldn't remember his actually having said "Plymouth."

"When did it start?" I asked. The Ontario leak was not following Eddie's usual pattern. It should not have happened yet.

"Days ago," Gary said with that air of superiority that at one time would have undermined my faith in my own intuition. *But not anymore.*

"Will you tell me if you find anything irregular at Pilgrim?" I asked.

Gary laughed at my foolishness, as he had so many times in the past. "Not on your life, civilian. But I'd stake my life that everything here is in good working order."

"Lives are always at stake at a nuclear plant," I said. "Not just the pumps, check the safety valves as well." But no way was Gary going to tell me if there was a problem at Pilgrim. I'd never really know, and the unalterable nature of the future would remain intact. Still, if I were a betting woman, I'd put money on Gary finding that faulty valve.

"I suppose you're one of those paranoid environmentalists who have tried to block the renewal of our license." Gary added. "Solidly aligned against the cheap clean energy of the future."

"The Pilgrim plant is old and prone to mechanical failures, such as the recent compressor problem. But I haven't been taking around a petition, if that's what you mean," I said. How this man could irritate me!

"Well, as long as I have you on the phone, I wonder if you've heard from Cathy this week?"

"Heard what?"

"I guess that answers the question. Our youngest and her pal Irene are on their way East. Got themselves some minor parts in a mobster movie being filmed in Providence. They're talking about spending Thanksgiving with us."

"There is no 'us,' Gary," I said, annoyed by the way he'd blown off my warning.

"There's no reason we can't spend a civil holiday together, Cass. Maybe with Becky and Adam as well. I'm sure that sailor you married would agree."

I'm not much in favor of forcing children to endure two holiday dinners in order to please two sets of parents, but a blended Hauser-Shipton-Ulysses family Thanksgiving was never going to happen. I would think of something. I might even resort to a little spell-working, if it became absolutely necessary.

"How nice it will be to see Cathy and Irene again," I said evenly. *Sailor I married, indeed! Let's see, what herbs do I need?* "Well, thanks so much for your help, Gary. And good luck with the valve thing." That ended the call on a good note, I thought. I went off humming *I'm gonna wash that man right out of my hair.*

Thanksgiving! It *was* time to plan for the holiday. How much we had to be grateful for! Always remembering the first shared Thanksgiving we five had spent together at Deidre's, when her husband Will was still alive. An air of melancholy had pervaded the feast that year, Heather, Phillipa, and I especially wanting something (someone!) that hadn't yet happened. We wouldn't have guessed then that Deidre's cozy family would soon be fatherless as well. Nor could we have imagined all the adventures we would encounter and dangers we would pass through in the years ahead and what surprising events would bring love into each of our lives.

There's something to be said for the unknowable future. *Let go and let Goddess.*

∽

"Don't make dinner," Phillipa ordered. As it happened, I was looking in the refrigerator when she called. "I've been testing meat pies, and I'm bringing over a sample."

Actually, I'd been getting lazy about cooking when Joe was away, preferring to forage in the freezer for leftovers despite their hard-to-identify anonymous shapes, since I often forgot to mark them. But I didn't want Phillipa to scold me for being a kitchen wimp and, worse, begin a regime of care packages. "What kind of meat?" I asked cautiously, and ungratefully.

There was a small pause. "Moose," she said. "But moose is not exactly against your quasi-vegetarian principles. This isn't some factory-farmed and tortured animal. This fellow ran proud and free in the wild woodland before a Penobscot hunter took him down. No doubt with appropriate prayers. Each hunter is allowed one moose per season, and that's over a thousand pounds of meat. My guy sold me a goodly chunk for the new cookbook, *More Native Foods of New England.*"

"Okay, I'll be your guinea pig, *again*," I said. "What's it taste like?"

"Beef. It has a beefy taste. And I've flavored the gravy with wild mushrooms and a decent Bordeaux. You'll love it."

"*Wild* mushrooms?"

"Yes, wild, *oh ye of little faith.* You're not the only one who knows her fungi, herb lady. Is the boy still there?"

"Eddie Christie. Yes, he is."

"Not to worry. It's a big pie, enough to feed him, too." Phillipa ended the call before I could cross-examine her on the subject of her mushroom expertise. Fifteen minutes later she was at my kitchen door (she lives only a mile away) with a basket of goodies. She was well swathed in a black wool poncho against the bitter November evening.

"Ah, little black riding hood," I greeted her, taking the basket from her hands. The pie was still hot. I took a cautious sniff. "I have to admit it smells divine."

Scruffy and Raffles were quick to agree. *Hey, Toots, save us some of that meat stuff! Real beef for real canines.*

Real canines. Real canines.

"It's not beef, it's moose, smarty."

Phillipa looked at me sharply, but I indicated that I was talking to the dogs. "I hope you're not planning to feed any of my puff-pastry-topped masterpiece to those mutts," she said.

"Of course not." *Not the pastry part anyway.*

I had suggested that Eddie call his aunt to see if he could stay for supper. "She won't care," he'd said, and that now proved to be the case. Eddie returned from the office phone with a big smile. "Aunt Fanny says I can even stay over if supper runs late. She says she doesn't want to be woken up because she's hoping for an early night for once."

Eddie's angelic face and delicate build would go straight to anyone's heart. Phillipa's sharp features went all soft as soon as she saw him. When I introduced them, she smiled brilliantly at the boy, and said, "I brought cupcakes, too. Pumpkin and apple." Then she began asking Eddie all about himself, and soon he was telling her how his ma was away at "a hospital" and his Aunt Fanny, who was awfully busy with her new baby, had been obliged to look out for him, and how some of the boys at his new school called him names and teased him about Aunt Fanny (a problem he had not shared with me).

"Hmmm, I might be able to help you with those bullies," Phillipa said, putting a comforting arm around his thin shoulders and ignoring me violently shaking my head out of the boy's sight.

No magic, I mouthed silently.

"Tomorrow's Saturday, no school," Phillipa said. "Why don't you bring Eddie over and I'll find some jobs for him to do. He'll be well paid. Would you like that, Eddie?"

He smiled and nodded shyly. Phillipa hugged him before she left. After dinner, we watched a Harry Potter movie, and I sent him to bed in the blue bedroom upstairs. Scruffy followed Eddie upstairs, carrying the favorite green sponge ball, and Raffles trotted after them. Eddie said he didn't mind at all.

After breakfast the next morning, I paid Eddie and drove him to Phillipa's house. With suitable compliments to Phillipa for the moose pie, I left the boy to her care. It was obvious that she already doted on him. I rather wondered why Eddie's Aunt Fanny was so indifferent to his absence from home. He seemed to charm everyone else.

The dogs were waiting anxiously at the kitchen door when I got home.

Where's the boy? You forgot the boy!

The boy! The boy!

Apparently he'd made a hit with Scruffy and Raffles, as well.

CHAPTER SEVEN

Every day is a journey,
and the journey itself is home.
    Matsuo Basho

Late Sunday afternoon, Phillipa drove Eddie back to his Aunt Fanny; on the way back home, she dropped in to see me. She had a kind of "look" on her face that I read as a psychic surprise of some kind. "What's going on now?" I asked while putting on some strong coffee I knew we'd need.

Instead of answering immediately, Phillipa rummaged in her Gucchi handbag and took out the silk drawstring bag which protects her tarot; she shuffled the deck. "Stone's been invited to Britain in December to visit the Sussex Constabulary, including a side tour of Scotland Yard. Isn't that *incredible!*"

"*Welcome to my world*," I said. "I've known since Samhain that this solstice thing was all going to fall into place. But how did this come about?"

"I'm just going to lay out a few cards on some of these issues" she said. "It's an exchange program that some public relations genius dreamed up. There's a chief constable from Brighton who's going to be given the grand tour of our South Shore law enforcement at the same time." While she was talking, using the Four of Wands as a significator (possibly to represent the Circle in merry days), Phillipa placed the cards into the Celtic Cross arrangement, and studied them quietly. Then she began to move them around and to add a few extras, so that the resulting shape represented more of a free-form pentagram.

In the intervening silence, I said, "So we may as well tell Heather and Fiona that it looks as if we will be able to celebrate the winter solstice at Stonehenge, as we imagined. Conor and Dee will be there, you and Stone, and I feel in my bones that Joe's next assignment will be in Britain."

"Those marvelous bones again? There are a few things of interest here." Phillipa leaned over the lay-out, the glossy raven wings of her hair falling forward; she began tapping various cards with her cook's square-cut unpolished fingernail. "Here's the Two of Wands indicating travel across water. That's our trip to Britain. And here's a battle, Five of Wands, connected to that enterprise. No surprises there. But first, what's before us *immediately* is some kind of dangerous situation. The Tower plus this Seven of Swords. I read this as a warning, Cass, specifically to you."

This was the moment in her reading when Phillipa leaped to conclusions that, if not in the cards, were inspired by her reading them. "And here," she continued, "this Page of Cups, must be Eddie with his sudden inspirations. Three of Swords, a heartbreak or sorrow connected to him. That poor little guy!"

I thought I would change the subject back to our trip before Phillipa got any more maudlin about Eddie. "Laura Belle will likely be whisked away to her grandparents for the Christmas holidays, as usual. I believe the mother, Belle, will be on leave from her State Department gig in The Hague as well. So Fiona will be free, very much at loose ends. Isn't it wonderful how the MacDonald family is quite content to foster Laura Belle with her great-auntie all the rest of the year!"

"Laura Belle is adorable, of course," Phillipa said, "but always a problem for the MacDonalds with her slow speech and her inconvenient penchant for telling the truth when she does talk. Fiona need not fear losing that child. As for Heather, she never needs an excuse to travel ... expensively. Let's see if we can prevail upon her not to book us in at the Savoy."

"Right. But I do have a feeling that we may all end up at the Crossed Keys Inn, wherever that is," I said. "And by the way, Phil, what's the final outcome in the cards? Do we all *live happily ever after?*"

"Three of Pentacles. That's some kind of material gain or mastery of one's craft. As for the Crossed Keys Inn, I'm betting it's in Amesbury," Phillipa said. "Largest town on Salisbury Plain."

෧෨

Joe came home from Philadelphia in not such a great humor with his new role as one of the poster boys for Greenpeace. He had duly circulated at various events to showcase their important current activities and to meet with representatives of charitable foundations. Greenpeace was fussy about their donors: no corporations or political parties, please. "But I think we're better off subsisting on small donations," he said.

"I don't know. Greenpeace must be an expensive proposition, running all those impressive ships and spectacular protests. Oh, well, that's probably the end of your part, anyway." I turned away to continue making roast lamb sandwiches for lunch. *Best to hide my knowing smile.*

Joe put his hands on my arms and whirled me around to face him. "It's hell living with a clairvoyant, unless she's as beautiful and sexy as you," he said. It was getting nearly as difficult for me to fool him as it was for him to deceive me. "You know damn well there's another trip in the works, and ..."

"And it's going to be Britain in December, right?"

"*Jesu Christos!* That's damned accurate, even for you, sweetheart. Yes, it's something to do with the Hinkley nuclear reactors at Somerset. Although why they want an old salt like me along on this project is a mystery. It's mostly legal wrangling. Delay tactics." This was accompanied by a warm hug and his lips nuzzling my neck, an implicit promise that I felt in parts of my body I shouldn't be thinking about when making lunch. "But—and this is the important part—now we'll have that vacation I've been promising you."

"Perhaps your role is being expanded, honey. How marvelous! I should mention just one little diversion while we're in Britain."

Joe drew back and fixed me with those Aegean blue eyes that are almost impossible to look away from. "*Jesu*, no. You can't mean you've got a hidden agenda here! I should have known."

I looked away anyhow, my gaze moving to the hollow of his throat, such a vulnerable place, so kissable. I wrenched my thoughts away and launched into my prepared explanation. "The ladies and I are planning to take in the winter solstice at Stonehenge. Other than that, I'm all yours. Oh, but *first*, Heather wants to make a little side trip to an inn called Crossed Keys where she believes her great-great-great somebody, uncle maybe or cousin, *the pirate,* may have left her a gift of some sort. You can come along, of course. Might be fun. Might be scary. Might need you to guard me from evil forces unknown. And help carry a pirate's treasure of gold coins, if necessary."

Joe groaned and slapped his forehead dramatically. So I knew he wasn't really angry at all. Because when he gets truly upset, he face turns whitish gray, his generous mouth tightens into a forbidding line, and his tender blue eyes get steely. The dogs take one look and run upstairs. Then Joe stalks away and goes for a long walk someplace until he masters his feelings.

Right now he was more amused and resigned than indignant and irate. Nothing I couldn't sweet-talk him out of before morning.

"As long as we're discussing upcoming events, we may as well think about Thanksgiving," I said, turning back to the sandwich making; slicing sour dough bread, layering on a little hot pickle relish and lettuce leaves.

The sliced lamb had the devoted attention of Scruffy and Raffles, who were lying politely and hopefully under the kitchen table. I put aside a few scraps on a sheet of wax paper.

Hey, Toots! Hold the pickle stuff on mine.

Mine! Mine!

"I've heard that Cathy and Irene are coming east to work on a movie in Providence. So I want to plan something nice."

"Did Cathy call? That's great," Joe said. Such calls were rare and welcome occurrences, he knew, and he was always on the side of my happiness.

"She called her father," I sighed ruefully. "To make a long story short, I had to get in touch with Gary about something, entirely unrelated, and he gave me the joyous news. He was harboring some fantasy that we could all get together as a family on Thanksgiving." I put the sandwiches on the table, and Joe poured some red wine to go with them.

"Is that something you'd like?" Joe asked cautiously.

"I'd rather have gum surgery. I'm wondering how I can get out of it and still enjoy having all my children home at once."

"Let me think," Joe said.

We ate. He thought. For that matter, I thought, too, but nothing brilliant came to mind. We went on to coffee and fruit. I peeled a tangerine, separated it into segments, and put half of them on Joe's plate.

"At the risk of sounding like a Zen master," Joe said, handing me a small bunch of grapes, "why not surrender to the situation? Encourage them all to get together on Thanksgiving but *without you*? It's not as though you'll miss out on the cozy family visit. Cathy and Irene will probably stay here, anyway. Didn't you tell me that Gary's place is a studio apartment at Governor Bradford Village? So then, the next day, we'll host a marvelous lobster and pasta party for everyone."

I thought about it. I thought *No!*

Then I thought *Maybe.*

And finally, *Why not?*

"Do you think we could cajole Johnny Marino into helping with the pasta?" Becky, my oldest, was again keeping company with the good-looking young lawyer whom I suspected of having some involvement with the FBI. I admit that I think Johnny's quite handsome because he looks remarkably like Joe in build and features, except much darker in all respects. Including some interior ones I haven't been able to fathom … yet.

"I'm sure. He's still hoping to impress Becky's family, especially you."

"And what excuse will we give for not attending the fatal family feast?"

Joe smiled, a playful, knowing smile. He loved saving the day, which he was doing right now so admirably. "You and I have been recruited to help Patty Peacedale and the good Reverend with their annual Thanksgiving Dinner for the Lonely and Elderly at the church."

"Oh, good Goddess. We will really have to do that, then," I said, but I could feel a smile of relief and hope beaming across my face.

"Small price to pay, I say." Joe was smiling, too. *Another crisis averted.*

Only that's not quite how it turned out.

CHAPTER EIGHT

Some hae meat and canna eat, -
And some wad eat that want it;
But we hae meat, and we can eat,
Sae let the Lord be thankit.
    Robert Burns

I always worry about Cathy, and my worry was all the keener when I saw her at last in the flesh and put my arms around her ethereal form. But her smile was luminous, and she was as lovely as ever. Irene, svelte and *soignée*, stood by her side watchfully. *Snow White and Rose Red.*

"Oh, *Muth-er*! You *can't* mean you're not going to celebrate Thanksgiving with Dad and the rest of the *family*? I thought you always prided yourself on being *très civilisée* about divorce. Never ranting and raving, I'll give you that. But poor Dad will be so *crushed*!" Her eyes closed dramatically, her mouth turned down in a sweet, sad moue. Clearly, Cathy was working herself up into full dramatic mode.

Irene put a calming hand on her shoulder. "It will be all right, *chérie*. I think we should give your mother the chance to explain, don't you?"

I did explain about our having volunteered to help with this tremendously worthy activity at the church around the corner, long before we knew that she and Irene would be coming East, and how devastated we were, but a promise is a promise, and how we planned to get together with Adam and Becky and her and Irene the very next day, for a really fun, relaxed time, although of course her father would be needed back at work on Friday. (I'd make it clear to Gary that he'd better agree.)

"Dad knows that Irene and I are vegan, doesn't he?" Cathy was suddenly cheerful again, her thoughts going straight ahead to the next production.

I smiled. "Oh, you know Dad. He takes everything in stride. I'm sure the Chez Reynard will have some lovely vegan entrees on offer." *Like Chez Reynard is a tofurky kind of place. Well, let Gary work that one out.* I was fairly certain he had forgotten about the vegan phase Cathy was going through.

Joe, being no stranger to my wily side, winked and inquired about the movie being filmed in Providence, and more importantly, Cathy and Irene's roles in it. The sun came out indeed, as the girls launched into a synopsis of the script, which sounded very much like *The Sopranos* meet *The Zombie Apocalypse.* The girls had scored similar ghoulish roles in small independent films on the West Coast and felt fortunate to be cast in speaking parts for this one, although not budgeted for travel expenses. It turned out that Irene had paid for that herself, and to save money, they would be bunking with some friends with a spacious loft in Providence during the filming.

"The important thing is to get good notices," Cathy said.

"I have a friend at Seven Angels Repertory," Irene added. "Maybe we can read for something while we're here."

I thought I would do a little spell-work on that account, after the whole Thanksgiving pageant had played itself out.

The Garden of Gethsemane Presbyterian Church was indeed "just around the corner" from our house, and close enough to the shore to have an ocean view from the bell tower. The Parish Hall was a separate building in the utilitarian style of an early Grange hall, and even may have been one in the early 1900's. The parsonage, to Patty's immense relief, was situated at some little distance on Metacomet Street. "Just a pleasant walk," Patty had said. "But not cheek-by-jowl with the church."

By the time we arrived at the Parish Hall, the aroma of roasting turkey was wafting into the dining room from a serviceable kitchen at the back of the large, plain room, dispelling the odor of dust and mildew that usually clung to it. Selwyn Peacedale, the pastor, was in full charge of the turkeys, a duty he discharged each year with skill, reverence, and a great deal of pride. Patty and I set the tables with festive paper tablecloths, ceramic turkey salt-and-peppers, and baskets of dinner rolls (donated by Heather and delivered by the De Veres). Joe went back into the kitchen to help lift the birds out of the oven to rest before carving.

Patty took the opportunity to share her newest concerns. "Dear little Eddie keeps getting himself into trouble with Fanny. She's asked Wyn about exorcism again. Definitely not his notion of pastoral duties! And he's mortally afraid that Mrs. P. will get wind of this matter and raise the devil, so to speak. I wonder if there's anything you can do to divert the child from making these alarming pronouncements, before Fanny takes matters into her own hands."

"I don't know what else we can do, Patty. My friend Phil and I have kept Eddie busy with weekend work to replace the paper route. And Phil has taken a special interest in the boy."

"Fanny's talking about consulting DCF," Patty whispered urgently.

"Oh, good Goddess!" I had a sudden vision of my friend's response to dumping Eddie on the tender mercies of the Department of Children and Families. Phillipa would swoop into battle like a valkyrie.

"Exactly, Cass. I'm counting on you to pull some celestial strings. I know you girls are always on the side of the angels, and I'll be praying for you to pull a miracle out of your hats." Patty's heart-shaped face shone with enthusiasm and confidence. A lock of hair fell limply across her broad fair forehead. Her hazel eyes were filled with innocent hope. I wondered if she'd ever seen Phillipa in the pointed black hat she liked to wear for *trick-or-treat*.

Our *sotto voce* conference was cut short as guests began to arrive in vans driven by volunteers; the guests were mostly elderly but also included a few young families of slender means. Fanny Fearley appeared with her little daughter in a stroller and Eddie in tow. He smiled and waved at me shyly before his aunt spoke to him sharply. Immediately he took charge of the inevitable overflow of baby equipment and sat down quietly in the corner. I thought I would have a word with them after I had helped with the vegetables.

Dinner was served family style, and once all the platters and serving bowls were out on tables, Joe and I joined the Fearleys. The pastor took the head chair at the longest table, and Patty sat at a different one. Others from the Gethsemane Ladies League who had been helping in the kitchen parceled themselves out likewise. The idea was to make everyone feel like a cherished guest. Underneath all the holy bluster, Wyn really had a good heart.

The stuffing was predictably bland and the potatoes watery, but the turkey was moist and tender, a credit to the Reverend, and it tasted even better when I reflected on not having to share it with my ex.

I admired Fanny's little girl, a brown-eyed sweetheart with a charming grin. After we had pretty much cleaned our plates, Eddie's aunt began to talk to me, and even confide. "You're that friend of Mrs. Peacedale's she says can help us. Here's the deal. I promised my sister Emma, you know, that I'd take care of things, but her stay in rehab is court-ordered, and I just can't keep on like this until she's kicked, you know." She glanced at Eddie. He didn't seem to be listening, but he was. "Eddie, you push Baby around the hall in that stroller for a while. Keeps her from getting fussy." Eddie did as he was told.

The ladies of the League began dishing out pumpkin and apple pies and frozen slices of ice cream. Fanny continued. "Lost my place at the bank, you know. Manager said I didn't fit in, the old fart. But now I have this really good job with Finch's French Maids, you know, and he don't mind if I bring Baby. But this kid of Emma's is so weird, God knows what he gets into after school. Except working for you. That's a good thing, for sure. But I'm thinking maybe, another home would be better, you know. Solve a lot of problems. Until Emma gets clean, you know."

I glanced at Joe for help, but he was deep into conversation with an older gentleman who had been a commercial fisherman and, like the Ancient Mariner, had stories he was eager to tell. I so didn't want to get in the middle of Fanny's family woes, but Phillipa would be a sword of wrath if I didn't keep Eddie off the DCF rolls. Just as I was pondering my reply to Fanny's situation, I became quite uneasy, and not about Eddie.

"The kid came up with another freaking scare yesterday, you know," Fanny said in an even lower voice. "Said he read in the *Pilgrim Times* that there'd been a fire at this church, doesn't that beat all?"

I jumped as if shot from my chair, and Joe looked up with alarm. "What's wrong, Cass?"

At that very moment, the whole room was jolted by the scream of a distraught pot washer, Harold the Sexton, as a cloud of black smoke rolled out of the kitchen. Several of the diners cried out in fear and began to stumble toward the front door.

With a muffled oath, Wyn immediately rang the fire alarm and ran for the fire extinguisher, aiming it into the kitchen like a sword of the Jedi. "Be careful, Wyn. Don't breathe," Patty cried anxiously as she and the other ladies began shepherding the parishioners out of danger. Joe and I helped some who were in walkers and wheelchairs to leave the hall safely.

"So ... you didn't sense this one coming, Cass?" Joe muttered in passing.

"I wish. But, no, I'm afraid not until it was too late." I was coaxing along an old dear with a cane and a satchel into which *I knew* she had tossed a turkey leg wrapped in her napkin, typical useless information, something I had *not* particularly cared to see. Visioning is not *on call,* and there's seems little rhyme or reason to one's flashes of insight.

Fanny Fearley, with a face like thunder, had grabbed her little girl and rushed outdoors, followed by Eddie pushing the stroller with all their gear. I was seriously worried about the boy but too busy to do anything about it right then. Fortunately, the fire trucks arrived only a few minutes later. Although the kitchen was destroyed, the fire was brought under control before it took the entire hall, and no one had been injured.

Because of its close proximity, the church was thoroughly soaked with water for good measure. Volunteers from the inevitable crowd of onlookers also helped with the old people who were milling about in a distracted fashion. I overheard Harold the Sexton explaining to Mick Finn, the Fire Chief, that a leaky aluminum roasting pan must have been set on a lit burner by mistake, and there was more about grease catching fire, dish towels, and some cardboard boxes. I didn't hear it all. After that, Joe and I were busy getting the more decrepit guests onto the vans that were to transport them home. Once, I caught sight of Patty's stricken look, and the wrathful expression on her husband's sooty face.

I felt sorry for the firemen who'd had to rush away from their own homes on this quintessential family holiday and football extravaganza, but in truth, they were cheerful enough now that the fire was reduced to a steaming carbon skeleton of the Parish Hall kitchen. I wondered if Mick Finn, available bachelor of a "certain age," might have been a guest at Fiona's, as he sometimes was. I couldn't tell if that notion was nosy speculation or intuition, the two always being difficult to separate.

Finally Joe and I went home ourselves to get ready for tomorrow's family party.

Hey, Toots, you smell funny. Aren't we going to get any turkey?
Turkey! Turkey!

"You two have some good smellers. That's smoke. There was a fire at the Parish Hall, so I couldn't bring you the turkey I promised," I explained. "You'll just have to settle for Milkbones."

"Oh, yeah? I was thinking about a pepper and cheese *frittata* myself," Joe said. He had his head in the refrigerator checking on the liveliness of the lobsters scrabbling around in their heavy bags. "What a weird thing to have happen. I hope the Parish Hall was well insured."

"Ugh. I don't want to be around when you boil those fellas alive," I said. "Yes, even weirder when you consider that Eddie read about it in yesterday's paper, which seriously freaked out his aunt. Did you hear any of our conversation? What do you think about Fanny?"

"That she's going to dump that boy as soon as she can," Joe said. "Don't worry. I'll spare your cruelty-to-crustacean sensibilities. All you have to do is make a big salad and clear the decks. A Greek salad would be my choice, nicely spicy. Along with the pasta course, Johnny's also bringing a tray of Italian pastries for dessert, so there you have it. While you're entertaining our guests in the living room. Johnny and I will manage the dinner."

Goddess bless a man who knows his way around a kitchen! And in this case, *two* men. To keep the range top clear for boiling lobsters, Johnny was bringing ziti casseroles that only needed to be baked in the oven.

"Shall we mark this down as one of our more eventful Thanksgivings?" Joe said. "Poor Patty and Wyn."

"Yes, *good intentions leadeth straight to hell* and all that. Honey, why don't you make us some coffee while I call Phil. Even though it's a holiday, I think I ought to tell her about Fanny and Eddie."

"Better you than me" Joe said.

∽

Phillipa and Stone were on their way home from Vermont where they had spent the holiday with his mother, who didn't cook. Just as well, considering Phillipa's outspoken food snobbery. It was only a matter of finding an acceptable restaurant; Phillipa had always claimed that a turkey dinner was a safe bet at almost any eatery, but then she'd never enjoyed a Thanksgiving catered by the Gethsemane Ladies League at a Parish Hall that caught fire as the concluding entertainment.

Luckily Stone was driving when Phillipa answered her cell; she got pretty excited. I related my conversation with Fanny Fearley to increasing exclamations of shock and horror, but finally a dangerous calmness prevailed. "That sweet boy is not going to be flung into the maelstrom of foster care while I have a breath in my body," she declared quietly, and that's all I could get out of her. "I'm going to hang up now, Cass. I have to consult with Stone. Enjoy your family tomorrow," she said and clicked off before I could add a word of caution.

∽

There was almost too much joy in having all my three children together in one place at one time, and it didn't happen often. The last time had been that strange Christmas when the twins were born, and we'd all converged at Brigham and Women's Hospital. Just thinking about that happy event might have made me all weepy if I hadn't been so busy watching out for the grandchildren right then and there, marveling at how relaxed Adam and Freddie were about a whole range of dangers that were perfectly obvious to me. But my daughter-in-law

Freddie, as always, brought her own brand of *joie de vivre* that kept me laughing instead of fussing.

I kept an eye on Becky and Johnny Marino as well. There was certainly something electric in the air between them. I'd given Johnny an affectionate hug when he arrived. Becky had said, "Don't let Mom fool you, honey. That's not just her gratitude for your ziti. She's having a go at reading your mind." He'd just laughed, poor innocent. Holding Johnny, even briefly, had already informed me of his true passionate interest in Becky, but there was still an area of his life that he was keeping hidden from her. The love I sensed was deep and strong, though, and that counted for a lot.

Becky had lost weight, although still softly rounded, and there was a radiant glow about her. Her shining, chestnut-brown hair was less stylish, longer and more casual. She looked relaxed and fulfilled. Naturally, my motherly mind leaped immediately from pleasure in their obvious joy in one another to the prospects of sealing their relationship with marriage. I would devote some thought and good energy to this later.

"We all missed you yesterday, Mother," Cathy was saying reprovingly, "Dad especially." Joe, who was weaving through the living room, filling flutes with Prosecco, winked at me, meaning to warn me off a tart rejoinder. But he needn't have worried. I was still beaming.

"*Alla famiglia*," Johnny lifted his glass for a toast, and we all drank.

"How was the Chez Reynard?" I asked.

Irene lifted her eyebrows expressively. "The butternut ravioli were rather dry and unappealing. I don't think Gary realized that we're vegan when he chose the Chez Reynard. Force-fed goose liver and crate-raised veal. *Gross!*"

Cathy said, "All complaints aside, the important thing at holidays is for *everybody to be together*."

"Oh come off it, Cathy," said her sister smartly. Becky was leaning against Johnny looking quite rosy and comfortable. "Mom and Joe were busy with good works yesterday."

Adam, sitting on the sofa arm, preferring single malt Scotch to Prosecco, said, "Isn't it strange how often Ma's good works end disastrously."

Freddie, who has her own paranormal problems, came immediately to my defense. "And how often Cass saves the day.

Especially, as we are speaking of the Reynard family." A spoon on the sea chest that serves as my coffee table moved slightly toward her hand, the way things do when she becomes agitated.

"What's this about Mother and the Reynards?" Cathy asked. "Another *crime sordide* perchance?"

"Let's not go into that now," I said hastily, pulling Jackie farther away from the fireplace where he was attempting to add some pine cones from the basket. "No, no, sweetie. Grandpa Joe will keep the fire going." Not all the details of our Circle's adventures had reached Cathy and Irene on the West coast, which was the best thing about the distance between us.

"After that scandalous home invasion at the Reynard estate," Adam said, "a guy broke in here and threatened Freddie and our kids. But something weird happened, and he had a heart attack."

Freddie and I exchanged glances. *Omertà*.

Joe came out of the kitchen in the nick of time and announced that dinner was served and invited all of us to take our places in the dining room, which was now filled to its utmost capacity, not to mention the two high chairs. An overflow of blessings for me, and nothing to do but enjoy them.

CHAPTER NINE

Come away, O human child!
To the waters and the wild
With a faery, hand in hand,
For the world's more full of weeping than you can understand.
        W. B. Yeats

On Sunday, Cathy and Irene went off to bunk with their friends in Providence and touch base with the independent production company that had promised the girls small parts in the movie *Goodfellas vs. Ghouls*. Rhode Island was especially hospitable to the film industry, offering a variety of cinematic possibilities, from mansions to seaports to a miniature Little Italy, all in a small area. The producer planned a climactic scene, Irene had confided, in which the gangster-hero would cling for dear life to the 4,000–pound termite (also known as the Big Blue Bug) that loomed over I-95. Not exactly Cary Grant on Mount Rushmore, but *they don't make 'em like that anymore*, I thought. As we hugged good-bye, I dutifully wished they each would break a leg *(take that out of the law!)* Secretly, I was harboring the hope that something better would work out for Cathy and Irene at the Seven Angels Repertory Theater to keep them on the East Coast.

That afternoon, the Circle met at Fiona's to talk over arrangements for our visit to Britain.

Fiona said, "The owl I called has been perching in my rowan tree. I fixed a barn nest box in my attic window, and she's found it suitable. I've named her Blodeuwedd after the library owl. I believe she may be the same bird following me home, rather like a guardian angel, wings and all. Blod comes to her branch at night, and I whisper my messages to her."

"How's that working out for you so far?" Phillipa asked.

"Time will tell, my dear. I have sent Blod with a message to my Salem friend Circe La Femme, and I'm awaiting an answer. Now, who's for lapsang souchong and who's for Phillipa's French Press coffee?"

We filled our cups while Omar Khayyám stalked along the top of the sofa glaring menacingly out the big window at the rowan tree, which appeared starkly picturesque at this time of year, a thick old scarred trunk and gnarled branches, absent green leaves and red berry clusters. Blod may have gone about her messaging business, but Omar remained on guard against her return.

"I thought if we all met in Britain about the 12th of December, we would have a few days in London to do the touristy thing before we journeyed out to investigate the Crossed Keys Inn and then to Stonehenge for the Winter solstice," Heather began. "To tell the truth, I was rather amazed that there really *is* such a place as the Crossed Keys Inn in Amesbury. But sure enough, it's there, it's real, it's online. You can all Google the place and have a look. Rather a charming 18th century Tudor style, judging by the images. I wonder what my piratical ancestor wants me to retrieve there, and if it's still intact after all those years in a chimney. Perhaps someone has already made off with the thing, or it's been smoked to a fare-thee-well."

"You must have faith in your great-great-great whatzit's mission," Fiona said. "Materializing is a deal of hard work, you know. A spirit doesn't attempt it just to play a merry prank."

"Yes, but it's easier at Samhain. So I can understand how Captain Nathaniel Morgan might appear at his vault in Plymouth on that one night," Heather said, "but how in Hades did that other fellow get there? I suppose I should just be glad that he still had a head on his shoulders and could speak up."

"His head was in the right place when I saw him," Deidre said. "With a rope dangling from the noose around his neck. *Ugh*. And, as we know, Heather, distance simply doesn't exist for spirits. Nor time."

"Speaking of time and distance," Heather said briskly, "I will be pleased to handle all the reservations in London and

Amesbury, except for Dee, of course, who will be staying with the O'Donnells?" Heather voiced that last as a question.

"Oh no, you don't!" Deidre exclaimed indignantly. "I'm not missing out on all the fun of finding the Morgan treasure, whatever it is. Conor's got the idea that he wants to do a Salisbury Cathedral feature anyway."

"Isn't that convenient, Dee. I wonder how that happened. Some cathedral gargoyle amulet under his pillow, perhaps?" Phillipa asked, sniffing one of Fiona's miniature cream scones before taking a bite. Still searching for the elusive spice that was Fiona's secret. Mace, yes, she'd included that in her written recipe, but there was *something else* less detectable. "But aren't you the least bit nervous, Dee, about seeing Heather's dead pirate again?"

"You have no idea. But let's face it, the spirits of the dead are everywhere we go, and also nowhere," Deidre said. "Usually, I only see a specter when he or she has some unfinished business in mind, like avenging murder. Heather's ghost seems more intent on revealing the location of his treasure."

"Those dates would work with Joe's assignment," I said, getting back to the matter at hand. "But I'm not so sure about your making the reservations, Heather."

"It's really the most sensible course," Heather said. "So we can all be together for the tour of London. And the *shopping!* Let's not forget the shopping."

"And just what hotel did you have in mind?" I asked.

"Oh, something central and reasonable," Heather said airily.

"Not the Savoy, then?" Phillipa said.

"No, no. Leave it to me. There's a place on Park Lane that might do, situated near the best shops."

"Fine, that's settled then," Deidre said. "The less time I spend at the O'Donnells' being grilled by Eileen O'Donnell on Catholic family values, the better. Phil, what's this I hear about the Boy Wonder you've taken under your wing?"

I think that was the first time I'd ever seen Phillipa blush. She looked at me as if expecting some objection when she said, "I've come to a mutually agreeable arrangement with Ms. Fearley, and I've been out to see her sister Emma Christie, Eddie's mother, at Cove Center. She's okay with the boy staying with me until she gets clean and clear of rehab and establishes a home for him."

I wondered if a gift of money hadn't changed hands to facilitate this meeting of the minds. "What about you and Stone going on this jaunt in Britain?" I asked.

"Yes, that's my dilemma. It's too late to get a passport for Eddie, and beside there's the problem of school. I guess he'll have to stay with his aunt those ten days, but I'll keep in close touch with him, see that no one gives him any grief. Like Dee, I plan to be home by Christmas Day. The solstice is the 21st, so no problem."

"What if Eddie comes out with another dire prophecy while you're away?" Dee asked. "Maybe he should stay at my house instead. He's only a couple of years older than Jenny. Mother Ryan and Betti Kinsey will be in charge."

"Isn't that rather an imposition, Dee," Phillipa said doubtfully.

Deidre chuckled merrily." I can almost guarantee that Mother Ryan will be as charmed by Eddie as everyone else seems to have been."

Phillipa said she'd consult with Eddie and his aunt.

଼ଆ

As it turned out, Eddie would be glad to stay anywhere else than with his aunt, although he didn't dare say so openly. He knew Jenny from Middle School, and had met the whole Ryan family at the Thanksgiving Pageant. Conor had remarked on the boy's beauty and had taken photos of him playing the part of John Alden.

But there was one more prophecy incident before we left for Britain, which was the most serious, and almost endangered our trip. Eddie was already living with Phillipa when it happened, and she had a glow about her that quite softened her usual acerbic nature, as love is liable to do. Eddie was a brilliant boy, she claimed, who far exceeded his grade level. They read together every night before he went to sleep, poetry as well as stories. Eddie had even shown a natural aptitude for cooking, and she enjoyed letting him help to prepare the evening meal in the late afternoons.

Eddie couldn't be more perfect if he were a robot child especially designed to enrapture Phillipa. *Too good to be true* sprang to mind, but I considered that to be an uncharitable thought and squashed it promptly. I reasoned that the change to a more stable, affectionate home had had a normalizing effect on Eddie; he appeared much less troubled and nervous, and there were no alarming incidents.

Then one day, shortly before we were to leave for Britain, Phillipa asked Eddie to wrap some mussel shells for the dump, and he found an old newspaper in the back hall for the job. When he didn't come right back to the kitchen, Phillipa went to see what had happened and found that Eddie had fainted and was lying on the floor of the back hall.

Fortunately, she took a breath before calling 911, because Eddie opened his eyes and sat up as soon as she took hold of his hands. "Oh, it's so awful, isn't it?" he cried.

"What is, dear? Tell me what you saw."

"It was at the theater. I read it all in the paper, an explosion at the theater," he sobbed. "There was a bomb under the stage."

Phillipa's heart had quailed in fear, but she reminded herself that Eddie's headlines always told of tragic events *that had not yet happened*. She was already calling me while she asked him, "Did the headline say *which* theater, sweetie?"

So the moment I answered, she whispered urgently into my ear, "Eddie says there was an explosion at some theater! Are you getting a vision or anything?"

Visioning was the last thing on my mind. I was in my cellar workroom packing up herbal orders. Pre-Christmas business had been brisk, and my mind was a clutter of Sweet Dreams Pillows, Quiet Child Herbal Tea, aromatherapy wish candles, aphrodisiac massage oils, Love Potion XXX, and, not to forget the family pet, Peppermint-arnica Muscle Rub (a favorite of Scruffy's) and Pennyroyal Fleabane. But the instant I heard Phil's frantic tone, the jumble of everyday business fell away, and I was fully alert to a horrible possibility.

"What theater? What theater?" I asked anxiously.

"A bomb under the stage. Sounds more like legitimate theater than a movie house, don't you think?"

At once the same saving grace occurred to me. This was Sunday. Whatever was going to happen, would happen tomorrow, Monday. "Didn't he say one other damned thing when he read you this headline?" I demanded.

"Speak to the boy yourself, but don't you dare scare him. Here, Eddie. Aunt Cass wants a word."

"I didn't mean to worry you." Eddie's voice was faint and trembling. I felt sorry for the boy, but with some nameless disaster looming, I needed to press on.

"Eddie, dear. We absolutely have to know what theater and where. Surely there's some word or two you can remember?"

"I don't know. I don't know," Eddie wailed. "I wish I never read that paper."

Another idea occurred to me. "What paper was it, Eddie? Did you see the masthead?"

"Masthead?"

"Put Aunt Phil back on the phone, dear."

Phillipa said, "You're frightening the boy to death. You'll never get anything that way."

"I just want to know what paper he was reading!" I demanded. My voice was getting urgent and quarrelsome, but I didn't seem to be able to control myself.

"Why, the *Plymouth Times*, of course. I have the paper right in my hands this minute. An old copy. Headline about putting the Mayflower in dry dock for repairs. Goddess knows I've tried to rid the house of every damned newspaper, but this one was out in the hall with the brown paper bags."

Eddie said something I couldn't hear.

"No, sweetie. It's the *Times*, see here?" I heard Phillipa talking to Eddie.

"Why? What paper does Eddie say it was?" I shouted.

"He's claiming that he read that headline in the *Providence Journal.* Maybe it was a church, he says. He remembers something about Angels."

I screamed. Unfortunately, I seem to have screamed directly into Phillipa's ear.

"*Jumping Juno, Cass.* I think you've broken my eardrum. You're worried about some church in Providence now?" she asked.

"*Seven Angels,* Phil! A bomb under the stage at Seven Angels Repertory Theater!"

CHAPTER TEN

All the world's a stage,
And all the men and women merely players;
They have their exits and their entrances...
William Shakespeare

"I suppose that's a possibility." Phillipa's tone was dubious. "But what can we do?"

"We absolutely have to stop this from happening! *What if it goes off when Cathy and Irene are reading there tomorrow?*" I screeched.

"Cathy and Irene are in Providence? At Seven Angels? I thought you said they were waiting to play parts in that wretched *Goodfellas vs. Ghouls* movie."

"They are. That's what brought them to the East Coast. But Irene has friends at Seven Angels. The girls are going to read for some part or other. I've got to go down there immediately and warn them. Or maybe I should call? Yes, that will be faster and surer, of course."

"Cass, dear, will they believe you? Or will they chalk it up to your general craziness? Being Cathy's mother and a clairvoyant makes you doubly suspect."

"Should I phone in an anonymous bomb threat to the theater, then? The police will have to evacuate everyone and search the place."

"I'll ignore the illegality of that notion, Cass, and just remind you that the bomb may not yet be planted. Maybe some psychopath is going to walk it into the theater *tomorrow.*"

"Then I'm going to have to drive down there today, right now. I'll get Fiona to go with me. Heather's candles and Dee's amulets are all very well, but Fiona is a finder, and we need to *find* the damn thing."

"You're too upset to drive, and Fiona...well, talk about your *extreme road hazard*!" Phillipa paused for a moment of reflection. She sighed. "I'm afraid I'll have to go with you. Stone can look after Eddie until he leaves for school tomorrow. Maybe they can do some male bonding or something."

"Oh all right, if you insist, Phil. But what will you tell Stone?" Actually, I felt relieved. I could always depend on Phillipa to keep a level head while I was running amok.

"What does one always tell a husband? I'll say *I'm going shopping with the girls*," Phillipa said. "Listen, you call Fiona and see if she's up to foiling a mad bomber this afternoon. That should do it. Fiona loves a psychic challenge. I'll pick up both of you in a few minutes."

Fiona said I sounded quite alarmed and of course she would come along and help to find the bomb and disarm it. What are friends for? Laura Belle could stay with her obliging neighbor, who had just adopted a darling kitten.

Then I called Joe on his cell. He was at Home Warehouse buying a strip of exterior wood to replace one that the woodpeckers had destroyed. "Providence? You're going to Providence *shopping with Phil and Fiona?* Listen, Cass. Can't you come up with anything more plausible than *shopping?* You hate clothes shopping, as we both know."

"It's for our London trip, honey. I'm going to need a few special outfits, and Phil knows this designer shop that's having a sale ..."

"Yeah, yeah. Okay. Just give me a call if you need bail money or male muscle or anything," Joe said tiredly.

"Love you, honey! Take good care of the boys. If I have to stay overnight, I'll text you," I said rather rapidly. I had only recently become texting proficient, and I'd found it a useful way to communicate without getting any direct backtalk.

"*Overnight?* Hey, what ..."

I ended the call abruptly. Probably Joe would think we got cut off. Immediately afterward, I called Irene's cell and asked how things were going with the film and the reading at Seven Angels. Irene said the movie crew had just got started, and the girls were still waiting for their scenes to be filmed. They were going to be hookers hanging around the bar in the mobster's nightclub, and they would each get to say a few lines of dialogue before they were torn to pieces when ghouls invaded the place. The special effects—blood, gore, and what have you—would be awesome, Irene declared. Meanwhile, she'd contacted her friend at Seven Angels, and she and Cathy would get to read for one of the directors that afternoon, or tomorrow. The theater was between productions at the moment. *The Dog It Was That Died* had just closed and Edward Albee's *Seascape* had not yet opened. I said we were on our way to Providence to do some shopping, could I take them to lunch, maybe someplace on Federal Hill? Irene asked, "Why? What's wrong? Your voice sounds funny."

What could I say? The clairvoyant's eternal dilemma.

"Where's Cathy?" I asked.

"It's okay. She's in the bath," Irene said.

"Don't upset her, but here's the thing. We have information that someone may be bringing a bomb into the theater," I said. "It will be set to go off tomorrow. Under the stage."

"*Information?* You mean, like, some of that psychic business?" Irene demanded.

"I know it sounds crazy."

"*Merde! Quelle catastrophe!* There's no way I can divert Cathy from this reading, Cass. Or me, either, for that matter. Isn't there something we can do? Call in the *gendarmes?*"

"The police won't credit the psychic thing, but if there *is* a bomb, we'll be suspected of having had a hand in the plot," I said. "So we're going to find the bomber ourselves. And the bomb. We should still have time to avert the danger, possibly another day."

"No shit! Well, as long as you're sure …"

One thing about young women whose lives are totally immersed in drama, their relationship with real life is tenuous, and danger seems more a plot contrivance than a real threat. *All shall be resolved at the end of the third act.*

I keep a little make-up and spell-working kit in the downstairs lav, with a travel-size, fold-up hazel wood wand. Just the basics in case I need to rush away without warning, as I did today. I'd grabbed that and added a few other necessities by the time Phil squealed into the driveway.

"Got your toothbrush?" was her greeting. I noted the Hermes overnight bag in the back seat, and her chic black leather jacket.

"Everything needed is right here." I patted the hand-woven Hopi bag, a gift from Tip.

We picked up Fiona, who came perfectly equipped, of course, with the miraculous reticule from which she is never parted. She was wearing her muted MacDonald hunting plaids and carried her coyote-topped walking stick. *Ready for action.*

Oh well, it's only theater folk after all, I thought. My jeans and Indian jacket would do very nicely, and I had tucked a clean black turtle neck and some underwear into my bag.

Fiona rode in back, as usual, and busied herself with a trade paperback she'd taken out of her reticule. I craned my neck to read the title. *Disarming Explosive Devices for Dummies.* One could only wonder what else she was carrying, but for once I didn't care. I have to confess that I was more than a little nervous, not only worried about Cathy and Irene, but also of winding up in some Providence police station trying to explain how I knew what I knew.

"Don't worry, dear," Fiona reached over the seat and patted my cheek, silver bangles jingling. "If we have to, we'll wrap the whole frigging theater in a protective white light."

As we drove into Providence, I texted Irene: "Where r u?"

"*Pane e Vino*, Atwell's Av. Waiting 4 u, hurry! Appt SA at 3."

"Cathy and Irene are having lunch on Federal Hill," I told the others. "We're invited to join them. Their appointment to read at Seven Angels is at three this afternoon. The theater's on Michael Street."

"You're invited to pay for lunch, you mean," Phillipa said. "*Pane e Vino* has been recently voted the best restaurant in Providence. I hear they make their own black squid ink pasta."

"Dear, dear," Fiona said. "Just a little meatball sandwich for me."

"Meatballs in a trendy Italian restaurant? Don't embarrass me," Phillipa said. "I'll order for you, Fiona."

"Prosecco?" I suggested.

"Oh, good idea, Cass," Fiona said.

We arrived just as a long black car with shaded windows drove away from an ideal spot in front of the *Pane e Vino*. Phillipa has a knack for always finding an ideal parking place, and she slid into this one right in front of another hopeful who honked crossly. The restaurant was expensively upscale in décor (no flashy statues or fake grapes) and redolent of delicious possibilities. Cathy flew into my arms with a dramatic and French-accented cry of *Mama* as if it had been years and not just a few days since our last embrace, which was rather sweet. Irene stood up respectfully as we joined the table for five where they had already been served their entrees. Both girls were wearing jeans, too, I observed. Cathy, of course, looked none the less ethereal in a delicate ruffled tunic that emphasized her fragility. Her perfectly oval face was framed in a cloud of pale gold. Irene's short dark hair had been judiciously gelled in pixie fashion, and she was brilliant in a flaming silk shirt.

After hugs had been exchanged all around, Phillipa immediately began to study the menu. While she was deeply absorbed, Fiona waved at the waitperson, urgently mouthing "Prosecco!" with a motion that included Phil and me.

It was a thoroughly satisfying lunch, even if we were teetering on the edge of doom. Phillipa was not disappointed in the black stuff and made several notes. Fiona and I were refreshed by a few glasses of Prosecco and comforted by the *Penne Ai Quattro Formaggi* we had insisted on ordering. The girls enjoyed such delectable vegan entrees that Cathy forgot to toy with her food. As Phillipa had warned me, I got to pick up the tab, not that I minded. Such a treat to have a civilized conversation with my youngest when she was not in a neurotic state.

Irene checked her watch. "Okay. You ladies may come with us if you will promise to sit quietly in the back of the theater," she said.

"*Sacre bleu, non, non!*" Cathy cried.

Irene said, "Cathy, *chérie*, the ladies have come all this way because they're worried about us.

"Worried about what? Irene, no one brings *la mère* to a reading! *Trop maladroit*. They'll ruin everything," Cathy wailed.

Irene told Cathy, as tactfully as possible, about the vision of a bomber. Not knowing about Eddie, Irene believed it to be my vision, of course. "It will be all right, dear. Remember that the director's assistant is a friend of mine. If we have to, we'll introduce the ladies as our agents and PAs. Nothing wrong with that," Irene assured her. "It isn't as if they look like ordinary mothers."

Cathy looked mildly interested in the possibility of a bomber, as if it were a sudden interesting plot twist rather than actual peril. "Oh, all right," she said ungraciously. "But don't any of you say *one word* or you'll ruin my concentration."

The theater looked strangely shabby, as empty theaters do, and smelled of dust and mold, lingering grease paint, a whiff of fresh paint, and memories of recent pizza. Not only did we sit in the far back rows, we staked out shadowy seats where we could see without being seen.

At the front of the theater, there were several young men lounging about in attitudes of boredom and despair and one older woman making notes at a table. A succession of actors read for parts in a play I recognized as *Les Liaisons Dangereuses* which was scheduled to go up after *Seascape.* Cathy's audition was a revelation. Although it was only a small part, *une amie de Cecile,* I'd hardly recognize her as my daughter. She even seemed to glow, more delicate than waif-like, with a shimmering innocence. I thought, without question, she gave by far the most convincing performance of any actor who read that afternoon, quite magical, and I believe I'm being totally objective here.

"Not bad," Phillipa leaned over and muttered quietly.

"It's the glamour," Fiona whispered. "Cathy's an adept, I see, as some of the best actors are. Now what do you make of that pinpoint of light over center stage?"

CHAPTER ELEVEN

There's no business like show business …
    Irving Berlin

"What light?" Phillipa and I cried out in unison.

"A cosmic nudge, I believe. I really need to dowse the stage," Fiona said. Reaching into her reticule, she took out a small forked hazel twig, the kind usually employed to find a hidden source of water.

"Good Goddess, no!" I exclaimed. "Cathy will disown me."

"At least wait until the auditions are over," Phillipa said. "I think they've wrapped it up now, don't you? That woman and her clipboard have disappeared in back somewhere."

Irene came back at that moment to tell us that she and Cathy were going on now for drinks with some friends from the casting call, and that Cathy had said good-bye and thanks for lunch.

"Aren't you auditioning, too, Irene?" Phillipa asked.

"Yes, but not today. I'll read for Puck later on. *Midsummer* will be the last production of the season. We can't decide if we'd want to stay in Providence, but if we both get parts in upcoming productions … well, the fates, *Les Sorts,* will decide. Any joy on the bomb?"

"Not yet. You won't be coming back today then?" I felt relieved. If we couldn't prevent someone from blowing up the theater (and I still hadn't totally ruled out calling in a bomb threat), at least Cathy and Irene would be safe.

"Only if we're called back, but that will probably be tomorrow. Cathy may have got herself a part, fingers crossed," Irene said with a delighted smile. With a carefree wave, she was gone.

We'd have to leave, too, before we could scope out the danger. I was devastated. This should not be. I would have to go to Plan B, the anonymous phone call, if I could get away with it with Phillipa nearby.

But Fiona said, "You two hang around the door as if you're about to leave. If anyone questions you while you're still here, just continue on out to the street. Here, Cass, you hold these for me, dear. I'm going to dowse the stage." She handed me her reticule and coyote walking stick.

Phil pulled me to the side entrance where we had come in (it was still unlocked) and we turned back to keep an eye on Fiona, expecting her to be kicked off the stage as soon as someone in charge spotted the intruder. As we watched, however, Fiona's plump, sturdy body underwent a subtle change, became stooped, frail, and slow. I could have sworn I was looking at a cleaning woman who had come in to tidy up after the audition.

"Holy Hecate, do you see what I see?" Phillipa said. "Has that dowsing wand suddenly become a feather duster, or do I need to have my eyes checked."

"I know," I said. "Phenomenal, isn't she?" I rubbed my eyes and looked closer. "She's dowsing all right."

Fiona continued shuffling around the stage in slow motion. She appeared to be wearing house slippers.

"You ladies had better leave now." We whirled around at the sound of a deep, rich bass voice. A grey-haired black man in a ragged green coat sweater had come up behind us. His shrewd dark eyes sized us up and found no harm, just inconvenience. "The open reading is over for today."

"Okay, we're just going," Phillipa said, pulling me out the door. "I don't think he even sees her," she muttered. We walked around to the front and stood under the marquee, shivering. No matter what the poet says, November, not April, is truly the cruelest month, at least in New England.

About fifteen minutes later, Fiona appeared at the side door where we had exited. She was saying good-bye to the man in the green sweater as if they were old friends. He leaned over and kissed her cheek as they parted company.

"I'm not even going to ask," Phillipa said. So we listened speechlessly when Fiona joined us and took our arms, bangles jingling.

"Small world," Fiona said cheerfully as we hustled toward the parking lot. "Claude and I were at Berkeley together. As soon as I came out of the glamour, he recognized me. We were colleagues in a few break-ins for peace and whatnot. He says he never forgot me. Isn't that sweet? You've still got my things, Cass? Good."

"Well, what did you find out?" Phil demanded as we got into her BMW. I handed Fiona her reticule and walking stick in the back seat.

"Something's under that trapdoor all right. My guess is that there's a remote control timer. No idea when it might blow. We've sorted out the danger, but now it's up to others to defuse it," Fiona said. "Either we call the police or I'm going back to warn Claude right now. Don't know how I'll explain our prior knowledge, though, when they find the thing."

"Not to worry, Fiona. Sorry, Phil, but what we are going to do is to call the police," I said, taking out my cell.

"No you don't!" Phillipa slapped my hand away. "Not if you want this to be anonymous."

She was right, of course. We got out of the car again and found a working public phone outside a gas station on Michael Street. Surprisingly, Fiona insisted on placing the call herself, and we realized why when she spoke in a voice we had never heard before; in fact, she sounded more like a young man than the mature woman she was. Meanwhile, Phillipa and I created a human barrier around the phone so that no one could listen in and perhaps remember the three ladies who'd called in a bomb threat.

"We need to keep an eye on the theater, see how this plays out," Phillipa said. "Just hanging around outside could lead to embarrassing questions, and besides, I'm freezing. But there's a Starbucks across the street from the theater. Maybe we can get a window seat."

"Of course we can," Fiona said.

Sure enough, soon after we entered the coffee shop, Fiona stood near the three guys sitting at the table we wanted and began to hum. Suddenly they became fidgety and hurried out, looking back nervously. We perched on the high stools provided for the front tables, which normally I dislike, and climbing up there wasn't easy for Fiona either. But we could see the theater entrance quite clearly when several cruisers, including a canine unit, screeched up to the door.

Phillipa went up to the counter and ordered three lattes, so we would appear to be paying customers not just busybodies taking in the local mayhem. While she waited, she craned her neck backward to watch the scene outside. Hearing the racket, other people got up and went to the window, surrounding our table.

But my attention was irresistibly drawn to a corner table where a young man sat alone. Somehow he looked familiar, although it was hard to tell *what* he looked like with that Paw Sox cap pulled down to his dark glasses and the kind of beard that boys grow to look older but in reality makes them appear to be wearing a grown-up disguise. Although I don't really see auras, I could have sworn that he was surrounded by agitated red vibrations even as he sat calmly stirring his espresso. And kept stirring. Something about that young man was definitely not kosher.

He reached for the leather laptop bag at his feet.

No matter how she may be compromising herself, a clairvoyant learns to go with her gut instinct rather than to berate herself later. So I screamed a warning and jumped down awkwardly from my high chair. "No, no, no! Don't let him open that."

Phillipa might have been startled, but she was quick on the uptake and more agile than I. In a flash she had set down the tray she was carrying and knocked the young man aside to grab his bag.

"Gently, gently," I cried, meaning the bag not the guy.

Other customers were incensed at this unprovoked attack on a quiet, nondescript guy, and some of them tried to interfere. That's when Fiona slid down and made her way toward us, swinging her cane from side to side, stepping between the Paw Sox cap and the bag Phillipa was holding.

"This man is wanted by the police," she announced in a commanding tone. Phillipa and I looked at her in some amazement. She appeared taller, younger, stronger, and somehow very *official.*

"Let go, you crazy broad. Do you see what she's doing?" he yelled to the other customers, who were standing up in attitudes of alarm and staring in fascination. "She's trying to steal my laptop."

A girl at the counter called "Hey, Rock, you'd better get out here. Someone's trying to lift a guy's laptop."

With the problem turned over to Rock, whoever he was, some customers returned to looking out the window to find the source of the sirens. "Hey, there's something going on at the theater." "Is it a fire?" "Might be a bomb scare." "Look at that drum thing they're bringing up to the front. They'll put the bomb in there."

"Yes, and this man is trying to set off that bomb," I shouted to the assembled melee. "He's got a long-range remote control in his bag." Sometimes my own pronouncements surprise me; this was one of those times.

Phillipa, who had been waving Paw Sox cap's bag out of his reach, seeing the man called Rock approach, thrust the bag into his arms with the warning, "Don't jiggle this, fella. But don't let him have it back, either. He may be trying to set off whatever he left in the theater." True to his name, Rock was a big bruiser, perhaps not too swift but staunchly faithful to an assigned task. His muscled arms closed around the laptop carrier.

Meanwhile, I'd forced my way back to the window. I looked down Michael Street. I cried out, "Oh, Good Goddess … it's Cathy and Irene coming back to the theater." I dove for the door, pushing the other patrons aside with my elbows.

Fiona grabbed my arm. "Easy, Cass. I'll go with you."

Several of the customers spilled out the door with us. Running to intercept Cathy, I was wildly impatient with Fiona's lumbering along with me, reticule and walking stick in tow. She would not let go of my arm, however, and she kept saying something. Slowly the words registered. She was telling me that the young man in the Paw Sox cap had run out the back and jumped on a motorcycle. He was headed away in the opposite direction, leaving Rock, literally, holding the bag.

"Oh, too bad I didn't get a good shot at that guy," Fiona said with real regret. "I might have at least winged him before he comes up with some other explosive idea."

"We're in enough potential trouble without you waving your Glock around," I said. "But you're right. He'll be back." I don't know how I knew that, but I did.

When we caught up with Cathy, I did a kind of body block to keep her from going any closer. Irene took one look at my face, and pulled Cathy away from the mess of cruisers and cops. "Come on, honey. There's something going on here. We've got to get out."

"But the director called me back," Cathy cried, stamping her little foot in high pique. "Let me go, René. I have to see him, *I have to*. This may be *my chance*!"

But Irene held on and wouldn't let go. "Later*, chérie*. Can't you see they're evacuating the theater now?"

Phillipa strolled casually out of the Starbucks in our direction, then picked up speed as she came closer. "Now is the time we have to fade to black," she whispered urgently. "When Rock saw how that guy took off, he said he'd bring the laptop carrier to the police, in case the crazy lady had it right after all. He asked me about you. Naturally I said I'd never seen you before in my life. We were just sharing an available table until you took a fit about that guy and his bag, but I wasn't taking any chances and neither should Rock."

Fiona said, "*It's never or now*, Cass. We can't get mixed up in this."

I hesitated. Irene said, "It's all right, Cass. Cathy and I will go back to the loft now. See you all on the Six O'clock News, ladies."

Tears were running down Cathy's face. "How could this happen to me? What if he never calls again?"

Fiona stepped up and hugged Cathy firmly, whispering in her ear. Instantly she calmed down. "You're sure?"

"It's written in the stars," Fiona assured her. Then she whirled around, took my right arm while Phillipa took the left, and they frog marched me back to Phillipa's car.

Cathy had the unexpected strength of many fragile-seeming young women whom you don't want to encounter at a sales table, but Irene was a match for her, and they hobbled away like three-legged racers who had decided to run in opposite directions.

We piled into the BMW in graceless haste. "What about the surveillance cameras?" I said as Phillipa raced us out of the theater district.

"Not to worry," Fiona said. "They'll have the guy sitting in the corner with his laptop bag, but the minute you sprung up to attack him, I put a bane on the cameras. As a precaution. You had a crazed look in your eye, Cass."

"You bet I did. Will the bane work?"

"Probably. I never tried it before, so we'll see."

"What I want to know," Phillipa said, "is whether there really was a remote control in that bag. If not, poor Rock is going to have a problem."

"On the other hand, suppose those cops rushed into the theater and then the bomb went off. How many lives!"

"Maybe there is no bomb at all," Phillipa said.

Fiona gave her an incredulous look.

"I'm just saying…" Phillipa said.

"That bomber guy in the cap. Did he look familiar to you?" I turned around in my seat to face Fiona.

"Now that you mention it …"

"Phil, let's book ourselves into a hotel somewhere nearby in case there's something tomorrow. I don't know what, but I just have a feeling," I said.

Phillipa obligingly pulled over and took out her iPhone. "What fun! There are other cool new restaurants I'd love to try."

"Yes, of course," Fiona said. "Under that sad little disguise, there was something about him that triggers a memory. It's as if he is a walking mug shot. Very curious indeed. Let me ponder."

Fiona pondered her way into a little snooze. Meanwhile Phillipa and I tried to think of where we'd seen that kid before.

"Oh, who can remember every mass murderer one has met before!" Phillipa cried impatiently. "Let's see what's on the news at six. Maybe that surveillance camera …"

"Ceres save us from seeing our own faces on it!" I said.

"Yeah. We took a chance, fleeing the scene like that," she said. "Stone will be beside himself. Well, maybe he'll cool down by the time we get home, if we're not held in jail."

"You're the one who was hot to get away," I reminded her. "Let's hope Fiona's bane fogged up the camera or whatever. Where are we staying?"

"The Providence Biltmore, of course. We can dine at the *Red Fez*. So *au courant* that it doesn't even have a sign outside."

Fiona jolted awake as we parked under the hotel. "What's up, girls?"

"We're booking into the Biltmore, watching the news to check out your bane, and dining at a trendy restaurant noted for its authentic Middle Eastern cuisine and hipster atmosphere," Phillipa said.

"Okay. I'm game," Fiona said. "I'd like to see for myself if the bane works."

CHAPTER TWELVE

The past is not a package one can lay away.
Emily Dickinson

"You're getting as delusional as Heather." I looked around at the swank suite Phillipa had booked for us. Muted tones, sweeping mauve drapes, soft lights, a king-size bed in one room, and a queen pull-out sofa in the sitting room. This was going to cost a fortune. Admittedly, though, it was convenient to be all together and not have to run down the hall to find one another in some worst case scenario.

"Fear not," she said. "I just got a rather decent advance on *More Native Foods of New England* and a follow-up, *Superfoods of the Algonquins.*

We were on the seventh floor facing west. Extravagant view; the setting sun was beaming into our window, so beautiful. I gazed at it for a moment too long, although I should know better.

As I drifted away from reality, the suite's sitting room began to fade around the edges, and I could see the street in front of the theater. In this vision, Cathy and Irene were again approaching the side door. A motorcycle was cruising down the street. It appeared to be the same young man I'd spotted in Starbucks, only this time he seemed to be holding a large green plant. I could feel the fearful beating of my heart, the cold sweat springing out on my forehead. *Weird*, even for me.

I sat down on the sofa, feeling distinctly ill. "Sweet Isis, Cathy's going to go back for a second interview tomorrow, and I don't know if that madman will make another try. But what was he doing with a plant?"

Fiona waved smelling salts in front of my nose, bangles tinkling. "Clairvoyants often deal in symbols," she said. "It will come to you, dear. Phil is ordering some strong coffee to clear our heads."

The coffee came, and it helped. Phillipa turned on our flat-screen TV; a local station was running a Breaking News special on the bomb scare at the Seven Angels Repertory Theater. A split screen showed the crush of police vehicles outside the theater on one side and a grainy photograph of the bomber on the other. The newsman said, "Law enforcement officials are asking the public if anyone can identify the man seen here wearing a Paw Sox cap and dark glasses. He is wanted for questioning about the incident at Seven Angels. Police would not describe him as a suspect, but he is a person of interest."

"You bet your sweet little besom he is, sonny!" Fiona exclaimed.

The newsman continued undeterred. "This photo was taken by a surveillance camera at the nearby Starbucks. Sources tell us that the equipment malfunctioned due to excessive steam from the coffee machines, and no subsequent images were retrieved. Other cameras on the street are being reviewed."

"Well, Fiona," Phillipa said. "That's another handy talent we can credit to you."

"Sometimes we don't know our own magic," Fiona said. "Women are the natural spell-workers, being outlaws in any patriarchal society. We've got used to keeping our power secret, since it's so frightening to men."

"Not all men, Goddess be thanked," I said. Suddenly I was longing for Joe's sturdy acceptance and protection.

While Phillipa was busy tracking down reservations at *The Red Fez*, I called Irene. The girls were back at the loft, and Cathy was taking a little rest after all the excitement. "Has Cathy been called back for an appointment tomorrow?" I wanted to know. Irene said that Cathy was in a fair way to be given the part of *une amie de Cecile*, but the cops were cluttering up the theater with that yellow crime scene tape. Her friend, the assistant director, Idylla Schimmer (she with the clipboard), had asked Claude, the maintenance man, who was still permitted to access the premises, to sneak Cathy into her office at eleven. Irene would, of course, go along and keep an eye on Cathy's well-being.

"Me, too," I said. "But I'll stay out of sight."

Just as I was about to end the call, inspiration struck, which to me is like a punch in the stomach—painful and not to be ignored. "When you see Idylla, ask her if there's been any trouble with a disgruntled actor recently. Just a crazy notion."

"I'll take any one of your crazy notions to the bank anytime," Irene said. Just the vote of confidence I sorely needed.

Phillipa, who had been listening to the end of my conversation with Irene, said, "Actor? That rings a bell, doesn't it?"

"A large green plant," Fiona whispered thoughtfully. She put her cup down on the tray and sat up at attention. "Would that be hemlock, do you suppose?"

"Yes!" I said. "Whatever happened to that nasty little poisoner Leo Deluca when he got out of Juvie, that's what I want to know? Deluca's idea of following his bliss was to murder his way into acting school. If only he'd been tried as an adult, he would still be in jail."

"The poison evidence was ruled inadmissible, thanks to that mellifluous attorney, Owen Llewellyn, defender of murderers, gangsters, and criminals of all descriptions, who was paid big bucks to take over the case," Phillipa said. "But we know that young fiend would let nothing stand in the way of the career he'd fantasized for himself. Could it possibly be Leo Deluca? Let me ask Stone if he can trace the boy." She was already punching her husband's number on speed dial.

"The only charge that the overmatched, panicky prosecutor could make stick was attempted murder in the Eel River incident," I reflected. "Deluca was due to be released when he was eighteen. Perhaps he picked up a few tips on bomb making from some of the other teen-age felons."

Fiona, who was rarely flummoxed, was twisting the *Welcome to the Biltmore* booklet into a baton. "Leo Deluca!" she exclaimed, smashing the baton against the desk. "If I had only known this yesterday, I'd have taken him down for the wee wicked demon he is. Deluca locked my darling Laura Belle into his Volks and drove it into the river. Dee's two youngsters, too. He's just lucky he was arrested that day, or it would have been his last." Her breathing was becoming fast and shallow.

"Now, now, Fiona," Phillipa said mildly. "If you'd got yourself in trouble with the law, who would have taken care of Laura Belle with her very special need for psychic understanding? Do you need a paper bag to breathe into, dear?"

"In my reticule," Fiona gasped. A minute later, her head inside a Whole Foods bag, she slowly relaxed, then emerged into her usual calm and in-command demeanor.

"By the way," Phillipa said. "*The Red Fez* doesn't take reservations, so we'd better get going."

"Oh, stuff the Red Fez!" Fiona was not amused.

"The cocktails are said to be fantastic," Phillipa said.

"Well, all right, then." Fiona picked up her coyote walking stick and swung it around in a lethal circle which fortunately did not include us. "Maybe the sneaky bastard will turn up tomorrow. After all, tomorrow is another day."

"That worked for Scarlett O'Hara," I said.

"And another shot at that evil creep," she added.

"Keep cool, ladies," Phillipa said. "Ask questions first and shoot later. We are only assuming the guy is Deluca because of Cass's vision in which he was toting a green thing. None of us has actually identified him in the flesh. Kind of a handsome young man, as I recall, when not hiding behind a cap and dark glasses. Liked to be called 'Lee'. Built small, but then many leading men are—Al Pacino, Tom Cruise. Lee had those attractive black curls, too. And he was always smooth, plausible, and convincing, so often the case with psychopaths."

"He'll have some grudge against the Seven Angels, I'm guessing. Let's see what Irene's friend Idylla has to tell us," I suggested.

∽

We were at the Red Fez, immersed in stuffed grape leaves and babaghanouj, when Stone called back. A year after his release from juvenile detention, Leonardo Deluca had been discharged from probation on the recommendation of his mentors at the MacLean drama therapy program for gifted juvenile offenders. Although he had been expected to continue working with counselors at the hospital, Deluca disappeared off the radar only one week later. Even his parents, Arthur and Jean Deluca, who had moved to the Jersey coast after the unfavorable publicity surrounding their son's arrest, claimed not to know his whereabouts.

After delivering his report, Phillipa's husband naturally wanted to know what was up with our interest in a former case. I could see Phillipa hesitate. Finally she put off his curiosity with an offhand remark about our talking over old times, and old crimes.

"I don't know why I didn't tell Stone about your suspicions," Phillipa said ruefully. "I guess I was afraid of getting him in trouble with the authorities again because of some crazy crusade of yours. Remember what a time he had explaining how he happened to find Molly Larsson and her kidnappers."

"Don't beat yourself up, Phil. We can always come clean later, when we know more," I said.

"As a general rule," Fiona said, "it's best not to burden a husband with too many pesky details when he's focusing on the big picture. Global warming, world poverty, and what-have-you." She tucked the swizzle stick with which she'd been stirring her Scotch Tom Collins into her coronet of braids, where she already had lodged a Biltmore pen, a pearl hatpin, and an ivory crochet hook. Obviously, we'd have to keep an eye on our friend's mental state, which was signaling A for Addled.

I had a hard time settling myself that night, no matter how seductive the hotel's pillow-top mattress. About three in the morning, hoping to change my brain's unceasing worry broadcast, I eased out of the king-size bed so as not to wake Phillipa. I found Fiona in the sitting room, dozing in a chair overlooking the street, her pull-out queen undisturbed. Every atom of her being must have been waiting for the reappearance of Leo Deluca.

Not only did I have to protect Cathy and Irene, but also Fiona from her own worst impulses. I thought I would start by quietly removing the Glock she was probably carrying in her reticule, which was propped against her chair as always.

Gently….gently…gently

"Not on your life, Cass!" Fiona sprang out of apparent sleep in an instant, clutching the top of the bag closed. "This bag is protected by a powerful mojo given to me by a Navajo shaman."

"Oh, sorry, Fiona. I was just looking for butterscotch." Personally, I wondered if she was overworking this Navajo mystique just a tad.

She gave me *The Baleful Look*. When delivered by a proper witch, that icy stare withers the will and freezes a person's lower chakras. The *streghe* we'd met in Italy called it *malocchio*.

Thoroughly chastened, I crept back to bed. *Que sera, sera.*

∽

"Jumping Juno! Fiona's flown the coop." Phillipa stalked into the bedroom and shook me by the shoulder for emphasis.

I had just got to sleep again around four, never really falling deeper than a doze. My mind was not as sharp as I could wish. "What do you mean, flown? Is she on the roof?"

"No, Cass, dear. Here drink this right down." She handed me a double espresso in a small round cup. "I mean that Fiona has gone, vamoosed, disappeared. And we'd better go after her."

"What time is it? Oh, my good Goddess, past eight already! The girls will be at the theater at eleven." Fortunately, the espresso was like an intravenous shot of caffeine.

Phillipa sat on the edge of the bed, sipping from her own small cup. "What's to prevent Deluca from coming to the theater, say at dawn, with some clever device to demolish the place later?"

"Would he dare? The police have an idea what he looks like, and it's only a matter of time before someone recognizes him through his current disguise and identifies him." Even as I said the words, I thought that Deluca would dare anything, always believing himself to be more clever than any pursuer.

"You're talking about a young man who probably knows everything there is to know about stage make-up, honey," Phillipa added to my alarm.

"Right. Let me throw on some clothes, then. We've got to catch up with him ... and Fiona."

∽

I can move fast when I have to. A splash of cold water on my face replaced make-up, and I pulled my hair back into a scarf in lieu of brushing. A few minutes later, we were embarked on our mission. Fiona was nowhere to be seen in the Biltmore common rooms, on the street, or anywhere near the theater. Phillipa had equipped herself with a camera, a pair of binoculars so small they resembled opera glasses, and, of course, her iPhone. Along with searching for Fiona, we strained to identify every passerby who might be Deluca in a fresh disguise.

It was a chill, gray morning, although not as bitterly windy as it had been. I probably should have brought something heavier than an Indian jacket, but at least it was fleece lined. Also the symbols painted on it would protect me from enemies, so Tip had assured me. I thrust my ungloved hands into my pockets and looked across Michael Street at the Theater marquee. *Seascape* by Edward Albee, the next production, was up in translucent blue letters. Starring Will Sharp, Larry Chandler, and Vanessa Barnard. Was it this production or some other that Deluca had set his sights on? Thinking of Deluca's cold-blooded program of advancement and penchant for revenge, I shuddered. *Better pull it together,* I thought, realizing that I was feeling mighty shaky on too few hours sleep and no breakfast except that overload of caffeine.

A quick fix presented itself across the street in the form of a little wheeled cart sporting a green and white striped umbrella. "Phil, you stay here and keep your eyes peeled. I'll just go over there and get us a couple of hot dogs."

"From a street vendor? At this hour of the morning? *Are you crazy?*"

"Does that mean you don't want one?"

"Two dogs, mustard, no relish, and be sure they've really been steamed," she said.

I jaywalked across the street, dodging the brisk morning traffic, to the hot dog vendor's cart parked at a kind of recessed half-moon area where people could sit on the concrete wall, a few doors down from the theater.

"Four hot dogs, two with mustard, no relish, and two with everything except onions." I fished in my bag for bills to pay the vendor, a bent old man with a gray pony tail. Then I looked up directly into his eyes.

"*You!*" I exclaimed.

"*You!*" Leo Deluca muttered. "The witch bitch from Plymouth!"

CHAPTER THIRTEEN

Like one that on a lonesome road
Doth walk in fear and dread,
And having once turned round walks on,
And turns no more his head ...
　　　Samuel Taylor Coleridge

We were both immobilized with shock for a few seconds. I have to confess, Deluca recovered before I did.

"*O day and night, but this is wondrous strange!* My nemesis delivered to my hands." The actor delivered his line with a nasty smirk. "If you move or make a sound, I'll blow us up right here on the street." Deluca's eyes slanted downward meaningfully toward his vendor cart; the steamer was issuing little puffs of hot dog steam. How could he manage that? A zany mental picture of hot dogs exploding into the air flashed through my fevered brain. Then I noted the ominous black backpack hooked onto the handle of the cart. My mind raced through every possibility of catastrophe or rescue at breakneck speed, which also describes my heart rate at that moment. But I knew this kid and his enormous ego. There was little chance that he would allow his precious self to be destroyed. On the other hand, did I want to bet my life on my ability to psychoanalyze a psychopath?

I hazarded a quick glance across Michael Street, hoping that Phillipa would catch sight of my confrontation with a threatening hot dog vendor and call the cops. But the morning traffic had increased, and there was little viewing space between cars. I thought I caught a glimpse of her peering at the theater marquee through her binoculars. How long would it take her to miss me?

Too late! As I'd turned to look across the street, I'd felt a cold metal cylinder pressed under my jacket against my shirt. The icy sensation moved down my spine, and Deluca pointed the gun into my jeans. "Start walking, if you ever want to walk again," Deluca ordered. "There's an alley just before you get to the theater. Turn in there."

"Crime scene tapes are up everywhere, and I'm pretty sure officers are guarding the premises." I can't imagine what possessed me to blurt out all this speculation, as if there were a chance of deterring Deluca when he was this deep into his evil plan, whatever that was.

I began to walk as slowly as possible in the direction Deluca had indicated. Although I couldn't at that moment feel the gun muzzle in my back, I could sense him following me closely. No sound of the trundling cart, which he must have left behind him. No doubt Deluca was carrying the ominous black bag, though. When I tried slowing down even more (anything to delay!), he prodded me with his weapon. How long, I wondered, before Phillipa would notice that I had not returned with the food? *O unconscious friend!*

The alley was narrow, dark, cluttered with trash, and evil smelling. Something scurried between old barrels. *Ugh!* We turned the corner and were in back of the theater, where it was a little brighter and cleaner. Not a cop in sight. *Probably all inside scarfing up coffee and doughnuts!* Deluca grabbed my jacket. "Stop right here, bitch," he said. "And don't make a move."

He shoved aside some wooden boxes and exposed a cellar window. It opened so easily when he pushed it with his foot, I had the idea that he had scoped out this area previously and unlocked the window. I glanced back to see him drop the bag inside and pull the window closed.

"*Though this be madness, yet there is method in 't,*" he muttered. "All right then. Let's get out of here."

"Out of here *where?*"

"Just move. No don't go back the way we came. Keep walking in the same direction."

That brought us around to the other side of the theater, more of a street than an alley. A bent, beat-up sign identified it as Gabriel Street. We walked past two cars half pulled up onto the sidewalk. One of them had a Seven Angels bumper sticker and the other a Seven Angels decal on the side window. A motorcycle was parked on the curb near the corner, where it could easily zoom out onto Michael Street.

Deluca pulled the motorcycle away from the curb into the street. There may have been a moment when his gun wasn't aimed exactly at me, but in truth I was too scared to test that theory. I just stood there like a dummy, awaiting orders.

He got on the bike. *Oh, goodie, is he going to leave me here? Possibly alive?*

"Get on the bike in back of me," Deluca said.

At last the Goddess energy flowed through my veins, and I felt the return of power and resolve, however foolhardy.

"No way," I said, holding the index and little fingers on each hand pressed against my body but pointed in his direction. In that brief instant, I did what I should have begun earlier, summoned the white light of protection to surround me. Short notice, but you never can tell.

Deluca smiled. *That one may smile, and smile, and be a villain ...* came to mind. Then he lifted his gun and pointed it, not at me, but across Michael Street, where I saw with horror, between cars zooming past, Phillipa looking up and down with an attitude of dismay.

"I could pick her off from here and still get away," he said. When he'd raised the gun, I'd noticed that he had a boxy thing in his breast pocket, which I took to be the remote control detonator. He started the motor and revved it in place, waiting for me to follow orders so that he wouldn't shoot my friend. "I can't leave you here to give away our secret package," he explained in an utterly rational tone.

What he meant was that he couldn't leave *my body* here, thus raising an alarm, but would have to dispose of me elsewhere.

"What about your hot dog wagon?" I whined irrationally.

"Not mine. Borrowed from a drunk purveyor of foul food. Now hop up here, witch, or die."

"Oh, all right," I said. *Where there's life, there's a chance to turn the tables on this terrorist.* I'd ridden on a motorcycle before, once, with Tip in Salem. There was a little backrest, but if I really wanted to be safe I'd have to grab hold of the driver. I got on awkwardly in back of Deluca, who was still holding his gun down by his thigh. I supposed he could twist around and shoot me if I got frisky. "Got another helmet?"

"You won't need a helmet," he said. I could see his point. Preventing damage to me was not high on his list of priorities. I grabbed his jacket, but I couldn't stand the sweetish smell of him and leaned back as far as possible, holding onto the seat more than the driver.

Then something unexpected happened. Well, even more unexpected than being kidnapped by a deranged actor.

A gunshot shattered through the little street. It seemed to zing between Deluca and me, where there wasn't all that much space. Or maybe past us. All I knew was, it whizzed mighty close. Either someone was a magnificent shot, if intending to *harm none,* or a rotten one, if meaning to hit one of us. Instead, the bullet had exploded into the Falstaff's Tavern dumpster across the way. Deluca froze, perhaps shocked into momentary paralysis, but not me. Filled with Goddess energy and adrenaline, I scrambled off the bike and raced toward the theater. I had the dim memory of a little step-down side door that I might be able to dive into, if it happened to be unlocked.

But someone had just emerged from the sunken entry. It was Fiona, aiming her Glock straight at Deluca. Sparing the boy was not on my agenda, but saving Fiona was. There was nothing for it but to tackle her before Deluca shot her or she got herself in a world of legal trouble by shooting him first.

When I threw my arms around her, a second bullet went wilder than the first one and took out a window at the tavern. Not an ideal result, but at least it should evoke a rapid police response.

Gunfire and breaking glass finally did it … awakened Phillipa to what was going on across the street. Once out of her coma, she wasted no time, zigzagging across Michael Street amid the honking of indignant drivers. She managed to race onto Gabriel Street two ticks before the police. Taking in the situation at a glance, she grabbed the Glock out of Fiona's hand, and dropped it into her Gucci handbag. At the same time, Deluca raised his gun to shoot one of us, who could tell which, but apparently decided against it when the cops burst into the scene from both sides of the theater.

Drop the gun! Drop the gun! Off that bike! Down on the ground!

But Deluca, still a daredevil, did none of those things. Before the orders were out of the officers' mouths, he had taken off and joined the heavy traffic on Michael Street, weaving like a serpent, leaving pursuing police cars trying to bull through the crush of cars. I could hear multiple sirens. Other cruisers coming in the opposite direction would try to intercept Deluca.

I still had my arms around Fiona. Phillipa stood in front of us like an angry Queen of the Night, explaining to the officers that the shots had come from Deluca's gun. I thought about the shell casings that might be found in the dumpster and the tavern across the street. There would be no way to tie them to Fiona's Glock, which they hadn't even seen. She was home clear.

The information I gave the officers on the scene was a perfect follow-up distraction from the questions that would naturally arise about Deluca's shooting in the wrong direction. "The guy's name is Leonardo Deluca, but he's probably using another name. I saw him drop a backpack into the theater window. I think it's a bomb, and he probably has a remote control to detonate it. He's an angry and vengeful actor."

I had to explain how I knew this, of course. "I saw that he had this oblong thing the size of a phone in his breast pocket. I assumed it was the remote control. He was trying to abduct me so I wouldn't report the bomb before he got a chance to detonate it. We'd met before, you see." I quickly related details of Deluca's earlier conviction as a juvenile attempted murderer who had spent two years in juvenile detention. All the while I was spilling this story, officers were moving us away from the theater, while others were evacuating the nearby businesses. Some theater people were hurried out of Seven Angels. I thought I spotted Fiona's friend Claude among them. The patrons of Falstaff's Tavern had pretty much run for it, anyway, when Fiona shot out their window. Mob shootings were not unknown in Providence.

Meanwhile, Phillipa had done about everything except throw Fiona's tartan scarf over her face to keep her "under wraps" literally. I could hear Fiona muttering about *just deserts* while Phillipa hurried her behind the barrier being set up by the police at each end of Michael Street, which also blocked off the alley, the theater, and Gabriel Street. But the officer who was taking my statement, Officer Trout, who had not yet dismissed me, was taking me to the opposite end of the barrier from the direction in which Phillipa had hustled off Fiona.

I was pushed into the back of a cruiser, where I repeated my story to another officer of obviously higher rank who seemed to be in charge. Meanwhile, the path was cleared for the bomb response vehicle to pull ahead just in front of the barrier. A bomb technician emerged in an outfit not unlike space travel survival gear and unfolded what looked remarkably like the robot in the movie *Short Circuit.*

"A robot! Oh, thank the Goddess," I murmured. "I was so afraid Deluca would set the thing off while officers were responding."

"Why do you say that this Deluca is using a remote control detonator?" demanded the new interrogator, whose name was Captain Kowalski. "And why was he shooting across the street at Falstaff's?"

"I saw it in his pocket. Today he has a gray pony tail, but he's an actor who knows how to change his appearance. He's probably using a false name as well. That guy in the Paw Sox cap who left a laptop bag at Starbucks yesterday must have been Deluca. Didn't you find a remote control detonator in that? Wasn't there a bomb under the stage in the theater? Maybe Deluca spotted a witness over at Falstaff's. How should I know?"

"What I want to hear from you is how you got your information, Ms. Shipton."

I saw it in a psychic vision was perhaps not the most sensible response under the circumstances. This wasn't Detective Stone Stern, after all. Despite the end-of-November bone-chilling day, I was having a definite hot flash, or *fear flash* might be the better term, so I shrugged out of my jacket and took a few deep calming breaths.

"Oh, here and there. I know some people at the theater. You ought to ask Idylla Schimmer if she's aware of a young actor with cause to feel revengeful toward Seven Angels. Look, can I leave now? I only came down here to meet my daughter, who is supposed to have a second interview and be signed for a part at the theater this morning. But I guess no one's going to get into Seven Angels today. I have friends who are waiting for me at the Biltmore, and when they see this disaster scene around the theater playing on TV, they'll be frantic."

The captain wasn't buying it, but eventually he allowed me to scurry out of the cruiser, first eyeing my license, verifying my hotel information, and taking down my home address and phone. I was inspired to give Detective Stone Stern as a reference. It sounded good, and Stone had lots of experience fielding such requests.

Before I went back to the Biltmore, I thought I would have a good look through the crowd of onlookers for Cathy and Irene. Cathy was going to be mighty cross, losing yet another interview, and she'd be looking for someone to blame. Mothers are always handy for that.

Sure enough, when I came across Irene trying to pull Cathy away from the barrier that blocked off Michael Street and the theater's main entrance, she cried out *"Oh, Muth-er, what did you do now?"*

She might have continued in this vein, except the attention of all of us was riveted to the removal of the bomb to a portable bomb containment chamber so it could be transported to a safe place for detonation. I wondered why Deluca hadn't set it off, after all. Perhaps he had raced too far out of range for the remote to function. At least the girls and my friends were safe, that's all I cared about. Well, I also cared about putting away Deluca before he could do any more harm, but I didn't feel terribly hopeful on that score. It would be like trying to trap Wile E. Coyote.

Irene was calling her friend Idylla on her cell. She looked up and shook her head at Cathy, who wailed softly, but Irene was still listening to whatever her friend the assistant director was saying. When they ended the call, Irene said that the theater was still being searched with canine assistance for other bombs or incendiary devices. Cathy's appointment was postponed until the theater was cleared. "And Idylla said there was a young actor who'd been with the company for several months, playing small parts, who seemed to be terribly distressed when he failed to get a leading role in Seascape, a role he felt would have been perfect for his talents, but let's face it, Idylla said, the kid didn't have it and Chandler did, including good reviews in several Broadway productions. Chandler's name would have drawing power."

'What was the angry actor's name," I asked.

"I think Idylla said it was Geoffrey Craig."

"Nice stage name. Also, Craig is Lee Deluca's mother's maiden name. Did she describe him."

"Puckish. Small with black curly hair and a devilish smile. Good thing he's gone, then," Irene said, "since I'm going to read for Puck myself if the theater ever gets clean again."

CHAPTER FOURTEEN

There comes a time in every woman's life
when the only thing that helps is a glass of champagne.
Bette Davis in *Old Acquaintance*

Heather had always told us to depend on champagne to clear the head in times of high stress and chaos, and this seemed to be just the moment for it, although Phillipa and I had had nothing to eat or drink except that earlier espresso. Nor had Fiona, who was sitting at the window, brooding on Goddess-knows-what.

"We're going to have several calls to field, so let's get breakfast from room service, omelets, melon, and champagne," I suggested.

"Sounds as if you've been possessed by the Morgan spirit," Phillipa said, but for once she agreed, taking the precaution to add a pot of strong coffee to the order.

I already had several "Missed" calls on my cell, all of them from Joe. And Phillipa would have to deal with Stone. *Breaking News* had done a fine job of shining a spotlight on our mission in Providence, which was not, as Joe had suspected, a shopping trip, but more of a stop-the-bomber caper.

"Why did I have to marry the most devious woman on earth?" Joe complained.

"Because you love me? Because I put you under a magic spell? Because I love you, too, terribly?"

He groaned. "All of the above. Do I have to come into Providence to protect you, or are you coming home today?"

"Rest easy, honey. The crisis is over." I didn't say that the peril had been personal, that I'd been kidnapped by the ghost of crimes past. "I'll be home this afternoon," I promised.

"That would be great news, if true. Especially as our trip to Britain has been confirmed, and I know you will need time to fuss about what to wear and what witchy paraphernalia will be needed at Crossed Keys Inn. So now I'm beginning to wonder what this Curse of the Morgans thing will turn out to be."

"The Samhain ghost promised an agent of change, a gift of great force. I wonder if we want that."

"As we Greeks say, *if you join the dance circle, you have to dance.*"

"You're making that up," I said, "but it may very well be true."

Joe repeated the proverb in Greek.

"That sounds sexier," I said.

"Everything is sexier in Greek," he said. "I can demonstrate this, if you like."

I bet he could. Time to go home.

After that, it was Deidre who got hold of me. "Was that *Leo Deluca* you went after, and you never even told me? Those were *our kids* he tried to drown, Cass. I should have been in on this."

I explained how we didn't really know it was Deluca until we got here. "And I'm sorry to report that he's still at large, Dee," I said.

"We've got to take him down before we can fly off to Britain," she said. "Who knows what form his revenge will take this time? I'm calling Heather. We're having a meeting as soon as you get back here."

Next it was Heather I had to placate. "Do you realize that all of us have plane tickets and our hotel reservations are *already made?*" she demanded. "Now Dee is saying we can't go until we deal with Deluca. Why exactly is this *our* responsibility? Can't the police deal with this kid without our magical help *for once?*"

"Decide where we should meet, and I'll see you this afternoon." I ended the call and turned to Phillipa. "Right after breakfast and we finish the champagne, we'd better get back to Plymouth. Dee wants us to have a meeting this afternoon about taking down Deluca before we go to Britain."

Room service knocked, and Phillipa opened the door. A waiter wheeled in our tray. Fiona screamed, a piercing Navajo scream. The scrawny young man jumped back into the hall with a cry of alarm.

"Oh, look, ladies!" Fiona cried. "It's a message from Circe La Femme on the ledge!" An owl was sitting on our windowsill, an odd enough sight in downtown Providence.

Phillipa gave the young man a huge tip and said, "It's not your fault, kid. My friend forgot her meds this morning. But don't worry. We're checking out right after breakfast."

"It's Circe returning my message!" Fiona exclaimed, leaping off her chair by the window. "The owl thing works, isn't that a hoot?"

"Have you ever thought of just getting a pager, Fiona?" Phillipa suggested.

But Fiona was wrapped in her own wacky world. "That's a very good bird, Blod! He means me to call Circe, and I do so in a tick. Oh, too bad I don't have a few beetles or something to give the dear owl for a reward."

"I would order beetles for you from room service, dear, but then the window won't open, and Blod will be so disappointed," Phillipa said. "Also, we'll be taken for a nest of vampires, so there would be the whole thing with the garlic and the silver cross. Such a bore." She refilled our flutes all around and we had a very merry toast. "I wonder what the group name is for vampires? Bats are a colony."

"Kindred," Fiona said promptly, pressing the speed dial number for Circe. "Some people say a Kiss of Vampires, but a Kindred of Vampires is preferred by the blood."

"*I'm not going to ask*," Phillipa whispered to me. We were silent, then, sipping and eavesdropping on Fiona's end of the conversation."

"Circe! So good to hear from you. What's in the wind?"

Apparently there was quite a lot "in the wind," because Fiona just listened for a few minutes.

"We can always count on Pauwau," she said finally. "You can't find a better guide than a deceased Indian princess, I always say. Perhaps the only people entitled to haunt this continent are its natives, don't you think? Do give her my best, and thanks from the heart of my heart."

As the call ended in a flurry of mutual compliments, Phillipa leaned over and poured the last few drops into our flutes. "Brace yourself," she muttered.

Fiona beamed. "At last, some sensible advice. Pauwau says, *a mother always knows where her child is.* Phil, dear, you must tell Stone to arrange to have Jean Deluca watched, and all will be made clear, the culprit will be found. Also, Pauwau insists that we must not let anything delay our trip to Britain. She says that the Morgan gift waiting for us will confer great spiritual mojo. And I say, *we cannot let our laurels rest on us without doing something.*"

"Right," Phillipa said. "Don't you hate when laurels do that?"

CHAPTER FIFTEEN

If you can look into the seeds of time,
And say which grain will grow and which will not,
Speak then to me.
William Shakespeare

It's about time you got home, Toots. I suppose you think we canines can't tell time, but our keen senses and ancestral instincts tell us when it's dinnertime on the exact tick of that kitchen thing.

"Dinner won't be until six o'clock, you phony. So you can stop trying to move it up by a quarter of an hour every night.

Yeah, yeah. We can tell moon time, too. Hollow Bone Moon is waning, and next will be White Bone Moon and then, Lost Bone Moon.

"All your moons are Bone Moons?"

The moon is a bone, Toots. Any fool rabbit could see that.

"Okay, then, I'll be back by dinnertime, I promise."

"Are you finished talking with those mutts?" Joe said, pulling me into his arms, the place where I always felt loved and safe no matter what mayhem was going on around us. I inhaled the lingering scent of him; he must have been infused with the herbs of Greece from his first breath. "And now what schemes are you rushing off to hatch?"

"It's a mercy mission, honey. Dee is very upset about our leaving for Britain with that dangerous Deluca kid still on the loose. A little group meditation to restore her spiritual harmony, and I'll be right back home, count on it."

He kissed me with all the summer sweetness that made me regret leaving him every time. Oh well, *I could not love thee, dear, so much ...*

✑

The mystique of Plymouth is distinct among South Shore towns. Its native lore and tribal ghosts predate by many centuries those weary pilgrims who first put a brave foot on the fabled 1620 rock. Devotion to its unique history as the first Massachusetts colony is apparent in monuments, museums, and faithfully restored settlements. Its main streets are charmingly lined with small-scale shops and eating places, nothing garish or terribly touristy. But it's a practical town, as well, with a working class population that keeps everything running for the people who summer in sea-side mansions along Route 3A. Its fatalistic townspeople live confidently with the looming icon of a nuclear power plant in Manomet. Above and below everything, the constant presence of the sea and its unpredictable moods makes the rocky shoreline a place of psychic energy. You might say this of any sea town, but somehow, Plymouth (like Salem) is home to an elusive "X-factor" that infuses the workings of magic with concentrated power.

Miserably cold though it was at the grim end of November, as I drove to Deidre's, I opened the window of my Rav4 a crack, the better to drink in the particular air that was Plymouth— essence of pine resin, salt waves, water-logged wharfs, fishing boats and their catch, and food grilling in various restaurants along the waterfront.

Deidre's home, a garrison house overflowing with her energetic handiwork and a certain Colonial kitsch, is usually a busy, noisy place, what with four youngsters, two poodles, a doting mother-in-law, and a hovering lover with a camera craze. But somehow she had managed to clear the decks for an hour and was serving a pot of excellent Irish tea with a plate of lace cookies and currant scones. Conor's influence had upgraded the Ryan hospitality from its previous reliance on store brands. Even Phillipa was impressed.

"Not to worry, Dee," she said, breaking a scone in half, the better to evaluate its texture. "Fiona's witchy pal in Salem came up with a notion that Jean Deluca is the key to finding Lee, which makes perfect sense now that we remember how obsessively protective Jean was of her darling son. And then there was that *strega* grandma with the stiletto in her purse.

Bianca. Misnomer, if ever I heard one! A black-garbed, black-hearted old gal. She may be involved in hiding him, as she has done in the past. The only problem (*same old, same old*) is that Stone has no way to follow up, which is making him very cross with me, with us, with the wyrding ways of Wicca in general. He keeps slamming out of the house, taking poor Boadicea for long walks in the sodden November woods. And you know how the poor dear hates rain."

"It won't hurt her, though," Heather said. "She's a tough old boxer and should thrive on meeting the challenges of the seasons."

I must remember to quote this to Scruffy, I thought, when he complains that canines ought to have indoor accommodations for inclement weather.

"What are you smirking about, Cass," Dee asked crisply. "This is a serious matter. I can't possibly go to Britain with Connor if that Deluca maniac is still on the loose."

Fiona put her plump arm around Dee's small shoulders, silver bangles tinkling softly. "There, there, dear. I have brought just the spell from that old grimoire of ours. It's simple and should be eminently effective. All we need is a picture of Deluca, which I have right here in my reticule, from an old newspaper clipping, and a very dark blue candle. Aren't we fortunate that this just happens to be the waning phase of the Beaver Moon, perfect for a banishing."

A.k.a. Frost Moon. And Scruffy's Hollow Bone Moon.

"Ah ha!" Heather cried enthusiastically. "I have come prepared with the very thing." Reaching into her Susan Nichole vegan handbag, she drew out a black candle.

"That's black." Phillipa pointed out the obvious.

"Nonsense," Heather avowed. "Just a very, very dark blue. Look here." She scraped a little wax off with her beautifully manicured fingernail and smeared it onto her saucer thinly.

"Nice color," Phillipa said. "What's it called?"

"Midnight Blue," Heather said.

"No, I mean the nail polish."

"*I'm Not Really a Waitress* by Opi. Sophia's Serene Salon has it,"

"Holy Mother of God!" Deidre exclaimed. "Can't we please get back to this hex?"

"Never, never call it a hex, dear Dee," Fiona said. "Just an Implacable Psychic Deterrent and Restraint. Heather's candle will have to do. The wax does look *almost* blue spread on that white saucer."

"Need a rhyme?" asked Phillipa.

"Of course. No spell is complete without the magical element of words," Fiona said.

Phillipa closed her eyes for a few moments, leaning back on a silk throw pillow embroidered with silver fairies.

"May he who would our children harm
Be hoist by his own evil charm."

Deidre clapped her hands together, a delighted smile and that irrepressible dimple in evidence. "Oh, that's super, Phil. I'd rather 'hexed' but 'hoist' is very apt."

"Recite the rhyme thirteen times, and away we go," Phillipa said, pleased with the praise.

So we did that. Burned the photo of Deluca while chanting Phillipa's rhyme and danced around Deidre's round oak coffee table as best we could in the crowded living room. Some antique poppets with malevolent eyes that she keeps on a high shelf seemed to leer at us, and one toppled down onto the hearth and had to be rescued from its proximity to the fireplace where a merry little fire was alight. The two poodles, Salty and Peppy, who had been sleeping in their crate near the kitchen door, commenced to howl and scratch the wire door, and they would not be easy until Deidre let them out into the backyard.

The meeting broke up shortly afterwards, and we all went home to await whatever the Divine Cosmos would send in answer to the banishing spell. Or whatever would happen next in the search for Deluca that might or might not be the result of our magical skill.

☙

It turned out later that Stone, despite his misgivings, had decided to contact a Providence detective friend with a hint about Jean Deluca's close attachment to her son during the Plymouth investigation of his earlier crimes. "You might want to keep tabs on the grandmother, as well," Stone had said. "There isn't much those two wouldn't do to keep their kid out of jail, and he knows it."

"At least Princess Pauwau can rest now that her message has been passed on," Phillipa said. We'd taken advantage of the sparse sunshine of early December to go for a walk in Jenkins Park with Boadicea, Scruffy, and Raffles. Never landscaped as a park, this disheveled stretch of woods only seemed like a chaos of broken and downed trees among the upright; the hidden harmony of new growth forever springing out from the old made it a sacred place to us. Our footsteps were almost silent on the carpet of fallen pine needles. The profound quiet was broken only by conversations of birds somewhere unseen, some cautious scampering of little animals, and the sharp barks of our companions. The woods smelled of wet decaying leaves, pine mold, and fungi, but the park was sheltered from the sharpest winds off the Atlantic, and a brisk pace kept us from being totally chilled. As usual, I carried my forager's basket over my arm, finding the occasional useful hazel wood branch or medicinal root. Joyfully off-leash, the boys had noticed that Boadicea was a girl, but alas, fixed. Still they were frisking about, showing off for the boxer queen's benefit, although she was clearly not amused.

"And now we can concentrate on our trip," Phillipa declared. "Stone is really starting to look forward to his tour of the Sussex Constabulary, however mysteriously arranged by the accommodating Universe of Infinite Solutions. So ... what are you packing?" Her black eyebrows rose inquiringly. "I will need a Sherlock Holmes stalking cap for our visit to Scotland Yard, *of course*, and *you* will need some chic activist togs for the Greenpeace gatherings, in case you get invited. Then we will both need an elegant afternoon outfit or two for the hotel. Plus we will require winter survival gear for tramping around Stonehenge on the solstice."

"Don't worry about me. Heather has taken my wardrobe entirely in hand. See you at the ... what in Hades *is* the name of that place on Park Lane where she's booked our rooms?"

"It's the London Hilton, Cass. Five stars. Spectacular views of London landmarks and Hyde Park. I had to talk her out of suites and connecting rooms. You'll find you only have an ordinary but exquisite double room on the same floor as the rest of us, which in itself was a neat trick. Possibly she has a cousin on the staff. See you later."

We parted at our usual midpoint. I had to be rather strict with Scruffy and Raffles to drag them away from Boadicea.

Feeling quite excited to think about packing, always a favorite part of any trip, I purposely avoided thinking about flying over the entire Atlantic Ocean "in the arms of fate." Seasoned traveler that he was, Joe would be my fearless comforter and safe anchor. As usual, he would take only his venerable duffle bag to check, and a modest carry-on leather bag, unlike me and my Heather-approved wardrobe for all eventualities.

Scruffy took a dim view of the appearance of luggage in the bedroom, presaging as it did a stay with Heather's dog pack.

Hey, Toots, my canny reasoning power tells me you're dumping us again at that prison camp for delinquent strays. How many dinnertimes will we be abandoned there? I hope you remember that the kid and I will be trying to choke down that dry kibble and sawdust stuff while you're off somewhere chowing down cheeseburgers. When you get home, all you're gonna find is our bleached bones in some dark snowy corner of that gulag.

Gulag! Gulag!

"Gulag? That's a new one."

A fling with a Russian wolfhound in my younger days, Toots. Taught me a lot, that saucy bitch. Descended from the Romanov wolfhounds, she claimed. But you and furry-face just go ahead and have fun. Don't worry about us.

Worry about us! Worry about us!

No one can heap on the guilt like one's canine companions.

∽

When our wishes work out exceptionally well, it sometimes makes me a tad nervous, wondering what amusing surprises the Goddess of a Thousand Names may have up her sleeve. Just before it was time to haul off to the airport, however, while Deidre was still stamping her size three shoe and stubbornly declaring that she simply could not leave her dear ones in danger, the news came through that the Providence police had taken into custody the young actor who was suspected of attempting to bomb the Seven Angels Repertory Theater.

It appeared that the magic *had* worked this time. The Divine Cosmos had arranged for the five of us to meet in Britain. Someone "up there" wanted us to find the treasure of the Crossed Keys Inn, and to dance at Stonehenge at the Winter Solstice. (Well...*lumber about* in our padded coats and heavy boots.)

Deidre's misgivings about leaving the children were set to rest. Deluca had been found hiding in his grandmother's cellar, although his family claimed to have no knowledge of his whereabouts. As I remembered Grandma Bianca, I could only imagine the dark-hearted Italian maledictions that had been called down on the arresting officers. *Buona Fortuna* to those guys.

How good it was to know that the lurking menace of Deluca would trouble us no more!

CHAPTER SIXTEEN

And marbled clouds go skudding by
The many-steepled London sky.
Thomas Moore

We straggled into the London Hilton on the 12th of December, having taken the flights that our various sponsors had booked for us, except for Heather and Fiona, who had travelled together first class on the 11th. Heather had wanted to get there ahead to check out our accommodations and arrange for our first get-together. She left messages at the desk for each of us. We were to meet in the Windows Bar (28th floor) between 10:00 and 11:00 PM when we arrived on the 12th, which would be dinnertime to us, but we could order a snack or a sandwich in the bar.

The spectacular lobby, all shining blue, gray, taupe, sparkling glass, and polished wood, was so dazzling to me I wondered if I could enjoy the wonder of it all sufficiently in the short time we would be here to justify what it was going to cost us. After all, I was just a simple herbal housewife from a small town on the Atlantic coast—*unsophisticated* didn't even begin to describe my utter naiveté and awe, but Joe appeared not the least nonplussed, even when the carefully expressionless bellhop hoisted his battered duffle bag onto the burnished brass luggage cart.

Our room on the 12th floor, was graded Deluxe (booked by Heather, what else?) and, as Phillipa had promised, was exquisite, with fresh, fragrant flowers and large windows with a view of the giant Ferris wheel on the Thames that I hoped never to be forced to ride. When we had finally sorted out our luggage

at Heathrow and checked into our hotel, it was already nine
in the evening. Taking in the luxurious room in one glance, I
nearly swooned (a nice Victorian word for ladies overcome with
emotion. I do prefer it to many contemporary exclamations of
awe involving bodily functions). The drapes were drawn back,
and London lit up was pure enchantment.

We were a little early for our rendezvous at the Windows
Bar, a respite in time we accepted as a welcome gift. Our
wondrous vacation had begun, and we celebrated by grinning
like two loving fools and falling together on one of the twin
beds (thoughtfully pushed together). Joe would not be put off
until later, and I was glad of it. Later could take care of itself.
The aroma of white roses was heady, the bed coverlet (that
we didn't stop to fold back) was silky and seductive. Joe was
already aroused, and it didn't take long for me to join him,
with the muscular heaviness of him close against my breasts.
Married love can be very sweet and certain. A way of conjuring
that "space between the worlds" that is the essence of magic.

Now we really were late, because of needing a quick shower
and a change from our wrinkled traveling casuals. Opening my
suitcases, I smiled with approval at the satin and lace lingerie,
actually matching, that I'd bought especially for this trip. And
bewitching nightgowns, too, that were really my size, or should
I say *age*. I'd not relied on Heather for that particular shopping
foray. I'd just bought what I thought Joe would like, although,
truth to tell, he liked me even in my plain white cotton stuff,
or without it.

Heather was responsible, though, for the crisp Nordstrom
navy pants suit and white silk blouse with which I had been
ordered to wear navy and white high heels. It all looked rather
plain to me, so I added gold earrings and the gold eagle pendant
that Joe had given me to commemorate our first encounter,
occasioned as it was by the rescue of endangered eagles. When
the Circle finally got together in the Windows Bar, after the
screams and cries of gladness had diminished, Heather gazed
at the eagle with a judiciously raised eyebrow. "I would have
thought, *pearls*," she whispered.

Although Heather and Fiona had checked in the day
before, the rest of us, arriving today, had taken different flights
with differing tales of traveler's angst. Joe and I had flown by
American Airlines (on Greenpeace), Phillipa and Stone on

British Airways (Law Enforcement International, UK), and Conor (courtesy of his Granddad) had booked some Irish flight that had stopped first in Dublin and taken nearly two days to arrive at Heathrow.

"*Hail, hail, the coven's all here!*" Heather caroled with delight, oblivious to curious glances from the bar. "And I'm happy to report that Dick's flying over to join us on the 15th. It's not easy leaving the Wee Angels Hospital, his holistic treatments are so popular. And not easy, either, talking his friend Dr. Wolf to come out of retirement and cover for him at the holiday season. It's just too much for his assistant Dr. Wu to handle all by herself, the poor little thing. Some of those patients are big bruisers. I once saw her flattened while trying to administer an arthritis treatment to a Great Dane. The big fellow was spooked by the sight of acupuncture needles, I guess."

Fiona, who was in full Scottish regalia, which is not entirely unusual in Britain, was beaming and leaning on her silver coyote walking stick. "*She rode all unarmed, she rode all alone,*" she paraphrased Lochinvar reassuringly at Stone. "*And save her good broadsword, she weapons had none.*"

"Thank God or Goddess for that," Stone said with feeling. "I'm off first thing tomorrow to meet with my Sussex guide and our confrere at Scotland Yard, and it will be good to do so without looking back nervously at whatever you gals are up to. Phillipa did confess about that contretemps on Gabriel Street, you know."

Fiona drew herself up regally (as only she can do.) "I don't know what you mean, Stone dear."

"*Shopping, darling*, that's all we'll be up to tomorrow." Phillipa interrupted, smiling brilliantly at her husband, enclosing him in her own captivating aura. Her silk suit was black, of course, but she did have a royal purple scarf wrapped in careless perfection around her neck, and wore amethyst earrings.

"Holy Mother, how I hate to miss Harrods!" Deidre exclaimed. "But Conor and I have promised to tour and admire the magnificent O'Donnell manor tomorrow. Grandpa booked our flight on Aer Lingus specifically for that purpose, so there's no escape. But we did get a reprieve about accommodations. Conor insisted that he wanted to stay in London. He has an assignment to do a spread on Portobello Road at Notting Hill.

The street market, the pastel houses, photos teaming up with essays by some famous British authors for a special issue of *London Life*."

"Living or dead authors?" Phillipa asked.

"Both," Deidre said. "But some of the living ones are teetering."

"Glorious idea!" Heather said. "We must do Portobello ourselves. Sometime after Harrods, of course. And the Tower of London. Tea at Brown's Hotel, in honor of Agatha Christie. Westminster Abbey."

"So many pounds to spend, so little time," Phillipa moaned.

"Let's not forget why we came here," I warned, feeling like a high school teacher chaperoning an unruly class through the grand tour. "At the behest of your dead forebear, I might add, Heather."

Amazingly, Stone got off on his exchange visit, Joe to his Greenpeace conferencing, and we ladies (except Deidre, who was in the clutches of the O'Donnells) rode sedately in a boxy black London taxi to Harrods. *Shop till you drop* was the order of the day, then an elegant light luncheon at the department store's restaurant, The Georgian, surrounded by our shopping bags. Mine contained a "map of London" silk scarf and a miniature gold-leafed statue of Isis that had cost me ninety pounds. I marveled at how easy it is to spend foreign currency as if it had no relation to American dollars. Still, the shining little Isis would add a perfect note of grace to my altar at home.

We were very tired, we were very merry, as the Millay poem goes, returning to our hotel at four, envisioning a restorative and serene tea time. Our buoyant mood was somewhat dampened, however, when Phillipa noticed several members of the City of London's Special Constabulary hanging around the lobby, looking officious.

After a little close questioning of a desk clerk just going off duty, Heather learned that, barely two weeks ago, a chamber maid had been found dead, brutally murdered, tossed in a rubbish bin at the rear of our hotel. Although no longer an official murder scene, parts of the rear service entrances were still cordoned off. An obvious effort was being made not to spook the guests, but a rising tide of horrified speculation was inevitable.

Details of the victim's particular injuries had not been released by the police, but rumors of sickening mutilations were circulating. Since we'd hardly had time to open a British newspaper since our arrival, we were startled to learn from a copy of *The Sun* Heather snagged off the rack that the Hilton maid's tragedy was the fourth in a string of shocking murders that had occurred in the last few months in or near London's five-star hotels. The tabloid referred to the murderer as *Five-Star Jack the Ripper*. This was not a tidbit that Heather's travel agent had shared with her when our rooms were being booked.

"We will just ignore the whole matter," I decided. "It's simply a string of tragic incidents that have nothing to do with us, as we are on vacation from all things sordid and criminal."

"How has that ignoring strategy worked out for you in the past?" Phillipa inquired.

"The poor souls." Fiona brow was furrowed with concern, at odds with the jaunty Harrods pens stuck upright in her coronet of braids. "Such a terrible event must have left a web of negative vibes right in this hotel. We ought to do some kind of a cleansing ritual before Dee gets back from touring the O'Donnell manor."

"I *knew* we should have stayed at the Savoy," Heather declared. "No one gets hacked about at the Savoy."

"Not since 1923," Fiona said, absently drawing on her vast collection of fascinating trivia, "when Marguerite Fahmy shot her husband the international playboy Prince Ali multiple times. Shocked the whole world when she was found not guilty. An amazing attorney, you know, known as The Great Defender, got her off because of her husband's depraved sexual appetites, so it was claimed, had given her a bad case of piles. Reminiscent of Owen Llewellyn saving Deluca from being found guilty of the hemlock murders we knew he'd committed. Just a few years in Juvie for aggravated assault, the little bastard. And now look!"

"Well, no murders at the Savoy *recently*," Heather said, nervously. Fiona's unresolved hatred for Deluca was a concern to all of us.

"Just shake your hands and feet to get rid of the nasty images," I suggested, demonstrating with a little hokey-pokey.

"For Goddess' sake, Cass," Phillipa muttered. "You're attracting the attention of that cute copper." But she smiled (her devastating smile) at the PC who was young and good-looking; he blushed and looked away.

"Tea is all very bracing and good," Heather said, taking Fiona's arm and heading toward sustenance, "but I believe we all need something stronger right now."

We repaired to the Podium Restaurant and Bar where tea was served every afternoon. While we were having tea and an excellent sherry selected by Heather, Stone called Phillipa to say that "something interesting had come up" at the Yard, and he would have to miss dinner with us, so we weren't able to pump him for details about the Ripper yet. But Phillipa did tell him, naturally, how distressed everyone was to learn of a murder in our very hotel. He assured her that we were all quite safe with members of the Constabulary keeping an eye on the premises.

Joe was tied up with Greenpeace people for dinner; it would be chiefly devoted to discussing strategy and therefore, he said, unutterably boring. But these events had bought us a trip to Britain, and so could be endured, he'd affirmed manfully. Deidre, who had begged off dinner at the manor house, claiming jet lag had caught up with her, called Heather to say she was going straight to bed.

"I'm a little fagged myself," Heather admitted, not mentioning the dead maid to our little friend who was plagued with ghost-sightings. Retiring to our respective rooms, we rested, watched the BBC news, and surveyed our many purchases with satisfaction until dinner, which would be necessarily late after a full tea in the late afternoon. *How do the British do it?*

So there were only four of us to meet much later at the Galvin, which was on the same floor as the Windows Bar: Phillipa, Heather, Fiona, and me. Our first dinner party in Britain was somewhat subdued, but we continued to make plans for Westminster Abbey and Brown's Hotel tomorrow, like the carefree tourists we should be.

It was none of our business, after all. We were on holiday. This British killing spree should not have affected us, and *would* not have if Deidre hadn't been visited by the ghost of Ameerah Sindi, the most recent victim. And Deidre was, understandably, quite upset about it.

"*Some fucking vacation!*" she'd screamed at us, summoned to hear her horror story later that evening, just as we'd collapsed in our rooms in the last throes of exhaustion. "I just looked up at this window, thinking I was seeing a reflection of myself, when the apparition came toward me with her arms outstretched, and *Mother of God*, no hands, just gruesome stumps, and her head wrapped in a bloody hijab. I've a good mind to go home on the next available flight, the O'Donnells be damned."

"I wonder if any of the other victims wore hijabs?" Phillipa mused.

"Possibly Stone will know," I commented lightly, but already I was seeing the dead girls in my mind's eye, and guessing they were all Muslims. "I hope the Yard is pursuing an ethnic connection."

"Where's Conor, dear?" Fiona asked gently, softly patting Deidre on the hand, silver bangles tinkling, while I fetched a cold wet facecloth from the bathroom.

"Placating his family at the spiffy formal dinner his grandparents had arranged for tonight. They even went so far as to hire footmen. There were family members and colleagues to be impressed and a prospective daughter-in-law to look over," Dee said. "Conor wasn't too pleased when I left early, but then, why do I have to be appraised by the O'Donnell clan when we're not even engaged?"

"Not engaged yet?" Heather inquired with that old matchmaker's gleam in her eye. "Why ever not, Dee? I mean, you're practically living together."

"The O'Donnells still don't know that I already have four children. Somehow it's never come up in my conversations with Grandma Eileen, and Conor keeps forgetting, so he claims."

"In the first place," Phillipa said, while making a cup of hot sweet tea for Deidre, "whatever kind of nubile, fertile virgin the O'Donnells are seeking to hang on their family tree should *not* make a damned bit of difference to whatever you two decide to do with your own lives, and in the second place, can we leave off the bachelorette drama for a few minutes and focus on this ghost?"

"Here, dearie, you drink this nice and hot. It will steady your nerves," Fiona said, taking the cup and saucer from Phillipa and holding it somewhere near Deidre's chin. "Isn't there some kind of biscuit, Phil? The more sugar, the merrier."

"Because when Dee sees a ghost, we know we're all in trouble," Phillipa said, handing over a box of chocolate digestive biscuits she found next to the electric kettle.

"We cannot get involved, my dears," Heather said. "We're due at the Crossed Keys Inn in a few days. Hardly time to solve a crime that's been confounding Scotland Yard for months."

I sighed heavily. Maybe if I didn't stare absently at bright lights I could avoid any troubling visions.

∽

"What the hell is going on around here?" Joe exclaimed. He pushed me into our room, whipping the Do Not Disturb sign into place, and chained the door firmly.

When he'd returned to the hotel around 11:30, he'd run into a couple of detectives cluttering up the lobby and plenty of gossip about the butchered maid before he even got upstairs.

I'd met him in the hall, returning from Deidre and Conor's room, looking like I'd seen death close up, which I rather had through Deidre's eyes. One look at my face, and Joe had insisted on an explanation. I'd told him it was only one of Dee's gory girl ghosts.

"You gals seem to invite crime like nectar attracts bees."

"That's not fair, Joe." I averted my eyes from his accusing blue gaze and busied myself moving gold-wrapped chocolates from pillows to night tables. The coverlets we'd left somewhat disarranged were now neatly turned down. "We didn't do anything at all, except to let Heather book our rooms. I'd really like to stay clear of this one, if it's possible after Dee saw that specter. I'm so looking forward to Westminster Abbey tomorrow!" I could hear my own voice hitting that unpleasant whining tone.

"Okay, okay, sweetheart," he said, enclosing me reassuringly in his arms, where I breathed in the solace of a familiar nautical after-shave that didn't overpower his own scent. It was the blessing of our marriage that Joe could never be cross with me for long and would immediately amend any criticism with a caress. I was always forgiven, even though I might not be quite so forgiving myself.

"You don't suppose we could move to a different hotel, do you?" he asked. I must have looked at him incredulously. "No,

I guess not. Well, here's the thing. Try not to 'see' anything, the way you do."

"That's my plan," I said.

"Because, as you know, I have to head out to Somerset tomorrow for that Hinkley business. I gather I'm to be the muscle, if any sort of protest against the lack of waste storage is arranged. Unless the energy committee decides to stick with legal jousting. At any rate, I'll only be gone a day or two. Is it too much to hope that you and your pals will stay out of the tabloids until my return?"

"That's our hope, too. We have far too much tourist stuff on our agenda to worry about Dee's ghost."

By some perverse law of clairvoyance, the harder one attempts to evade having a vision, the more likely it is to find you. On the other hand, if a spontaneous clairvoyant like me actually *tries* to have a vision, the third eye remains intractably blank.

It's a lose-lose deal.

I thought it a stroke of good luck that I had not brought my visions pillow. Of course, I did have a baggie of dried mugwort in my Wiccan kit. In a pinch, a good sniff of that stuff would send me reeling into la-la land.

CHAPTER SEVENTEEN

Rule, Britannia!
Britannia, rule the waves.
Britons never, never, never shall be slaves.
James Thompson

Convinced as I was that the "full English breakfast" Joe ordered would kill me, I opted simply for coffee and fruit from room service. Joe's tray included such a pile of toast and scones; I could certainly share that as well. And those darling little pots of honey and marmalade. Before I knew it, I had nearly polished off the basket of breads. Joe seemed happy enough, though, with his overload of eggs, bacon, sausage, tomatoes, and mushrooms, and the one scone I left for him.

After breakfast, we said good-bye, as we had so many times before, with the usual warnings to take care and stay safe and warm. He lingered in the doorway, looking like some World War II movie hero in his navy pea jacket and Greek cap set at a jaunty angle, the old leather bag handing from his shoulder. He was studying my face with a hint of skepticism.

"What can happen? I'm only going sightseeing," I scoffed, leaning forward to kiss him one more time on the threshold, *the liminal*, a place of magical transition. His lips were full and sensual, promising that he would always return.

"And I'm only going to be bored out of my skull at some strategy conference," he replied, then added with the familiar seductive smile that generally weakens my knees, "but once that's done, we'll have a few days to enjoy ourselves. Whenever I've been somewhere special, I've always wished I could share it with you. Maybe even before I knew you. And here we are in London, one of the world's great cities."

"Sounds like heaven, honey. But then we'll have to move on to the Crossed Keys Inn, Goddess knows why and what's there. And the solstice at Stonehenge, of course."

"Wouldn't miss the chance to freeze my ass off with you, sweetheart," Joe said, moving away toward the elevator with a cheerful wave of his hand.

~

It was good to have Deidre back again, completing our circle, even though it was sightseeing not spell-working we were up to today. Westminster Abbey! What a feeling of unbelief actually being in a historic site I'd only seen in pictures. Overwhelming to imagine the remains of so many important personages in one place. There seemed to be no way to avoid stepping on dead geniuses, then jumping back in horror. *Oh, my good Goddess. That's Sir Laurence Olivier!*

Seventeen British monarchs dating back to Edward the Confessor were laid to rest in the Abbey, plus the entire pageant of English history: statesmen and soldiers, heroes and villains, poets and priests, actors and artists. It's no wonder we had to practically hold Deidre upright in this magnificent mausoleum, sensitive as she was to dead souls.

According to Fiona, on our voyage to Bermuda Deidre had been favored by a sudden onset of the Seventh Sense, the perception of bodiless spirits. ("And now's she's stuck with it," Phillipa had said with a notable lack of sympathy. "There's no going back to five senses once the leap has been made. Just ask Cass, who's beleaguered by the Sixth.") Fortunately, the constant stream of visitors at the Abbey diluted ghostly vibrations or we might have had to carry Deidre out of there.

So many evocative sights and speculations, it was too much to take into the consciousness on one day. The Poets Corner with its revered names read like an index to English Poetry Volumes 1 and 2 of *The Harvard Classics*, Chaucer to Tennyson. It brought Phillipa as near to prayer there as I was ever liable to observe in my acerbic friend.

Personally, since I am somewhat timeless myself, I wandered about completely bemused in the cloud of history. I was especially entranced by the monument to Mary, Queen of Scots, erected by her son James I, which gives her every honor and crown denied her in life by Elizabeth I. Ironic, considering that the dour Scots regents who raised James Stuart to be a God-fearing Protestant would not permit him the comfort of his Catholic mother. Fiona filled us in on the whole Stuart saga from the encyclopedia of her memory. James I, although credited with sponsoring the King James Bible and its enduring poetry, was also quite swept up in the Scottish witch hunts. He even chose to witness in person the torture of those pitiable women accused of raising storms at sea. Every time a British ship sank, an order went out to "round up the usual witches." Poor old lady herbalists were an endangered species in Scotland.

Descendent of the sea-faring Morgans, Heather was much taken with the memorials to naval heroes, of which the British Navy has no end. Deidre was merely shivering and watching where she stepped. I slipped an arm around her, and we wandered over the chapel where a boys' choir was practicing for Evensong. The clear, sweet voices revived us both.

Before we left, Fiona proposed that we ought to say a blessing for the honored dead, as we once had for the ancient gods at the Pantheon in Rome. "Okay, but no dancing," I muttered. Phillipa and I managed to move our circle to an out-of-tourist-traffic wall, where we held hands while she improvised an appropriate rhyme.

Hail, Britannia, mighty goddess,
Bless the spirits of this place,
May they live eternally
In our hearts and in your grace.

Possibly it appeared to alerted guards that we were merely an observant religious sect saying an impromptu prayer—which was, in fact, the case. I thought it was heartening that the patriarchal British had resorted to a goddess to represent their spiritual might. Britannia in her plumed Roman helmet, holding a trident and resting on the lion's back, was quite a formidable image of motherly protection.

⟨∿⟩

We had skipped lunch purposely, the better to enjoy the fabulous tea room at Brown's Hotel. The lavishness of it all was justly famous, with seventeen kinds of tea from which to choose. (Phillipa chose for us, of course, Brown's own blend.) Three-tiered tea trays laden with finger sandwiches, scones, and pastries, followed by a trolley of freshly baked cakes. Pots of clotted cream and strawberry preserves. It was almost too much, but we soldiered through bravely.

Highly polished silver is always a problem for me, however. Just as we got ready to waddle out of there, stuffed with rich pastries and fueled by a sugar high, a tray suddenly held upright by a waitress reflected the overhead gleam of a chandelier directly into my eyes. In a moment, I felt that familiar drifting-through-time feeling. *A girl working in the kitchen at night. A girl wearing a hijab leaving by the back entrance. A raised arm with a short curved sword.*

I suppose I cried out and wobbled dangerously. The next thing I knew, Fiona was wafting smelling salts under my nose, and Phillipa was fending off solicitous waitresses, assuring them that her friend was not choking, just feeling a bit faint. "Jet lag, you know," she said. "And possibly too much clotted cream."

What nerve! Phillipa had eaten almost all of that herself. "Be all right in a minute," I assured everyone in a quavering voice. Ladies at nearby tables were looking startled and concerned. "I'll just stop by the loo for a splash of cold water. Phil, you'd better come with me." Phillipa took one arm and Fiona the other.

"I'll settle the bill," Heather said. "Dee and I will meet you in the lobby. And we want to know *everything*, don't we?"

My two guardians shepherded me along into the Ladies'. Fiona checked the stalls and found them all empty for the moment. Phil said, "Okay, Sibyl, what's up?"

"I just don't know what to do," I wailed. "Here we are in a strange city, no one will listen to us, and I just know there's going to be another hacking murder right here, right out back, maybe tonight, or tomorrow night, some poor girl wearing a hijab. I saw it, I tell you. *Ugh. Ugh.* I hate, hate, *hate* this."

Becoming aware that I was actually babbling, I deliberately slowed myself down and took a couple of deep calming breaths. I felt a cooling spray on my wrists; Fiona and her sage spritz.

"Sweet Isis, didn't we recently have a murder at *our* hotel!" Phillipa exclaimed crossly. "I thought these homicidal creeps took a longer rest between atrocities. Stone is a stranger here, just like us, and a guest of Law Enforcement International. I truly hesitate to dump this figment of your fevered brain on him right now, Cass."

"Fevered brain" was spot on. I rested my head on the cool porcelain of the sink. "You're right, of course. Let's just walk away and pretend I never saw the girl being attacked by some madman in the alley."

Fiona took out her cell phone and called Heather. "Where are you right now, dear?"

"Hanging around the lobby near the hotel desk, delaying. Hurry up," Heather said.

"Excellent. We'll be with you in a minute or two. Meanwhile, I want you to find out two things, what time the kitchen closes and whether there's a Muslim girl working there. Ask the desk clerk."

Two women came into the Ladies Room and gave us curious looks as they headed for stalls. Something about us always draws attention (except when Fiona puts on her invisibility glamour). Just because I was still cooling my brow on the porcelain sink, Phillipa was signing a pentagram over me, her long black sleeves reminiscent of Morticia, and Fiona was using her magical voice on the phone to Heather.

"May the peace of the Goddess envelop you with calm. Now let's get out of here," Phillipa said.

"Holy Hecate! Now what?" I could hear Heather's protesting voice faintly rising from Fiona's cell.

"Just do it," Fiona replied in that imperious tone that's so impossible to resist.

"Oh, shit," Phillipa said. "It's up to us, then."

"That would be totally crazy," I admitted. "Steven Seagal, maybe. Or Chuck Norris. Or even Charlie's Angels. But not us. We are hardly in shape to confront a sword-wielding maniac with a thing for Muslim girls."

This sentiment was heartily approved when we met up with Heather and Deidre, except by Fiona, who ignored our protestations and went trolling through her reticule. With a gleam of triumph in her eye, she brought out a handful of official looking bobby whistles, each on a silver chain.

"I want each of you girls to hang one of these around your neck. It's been said that the sound can be heard a mile away," Fiona said, "but that's probably an exaggeration. Still, my dears, if we all five blow these babies at one time, I doubt Abdul the Ripper will hang around to find out what happens next."

"You think the killer is a Muslim, too?" I hadn't seen that in my vision.

"There's intuition, and there's reason. Use them both, I say. In this case, now, my best guess is *honor killings,*" Fiona said. "Girls under Sharia law are not supposed to leave home and have lives elsewhere. Perhaps it began with a member of the Ripper's own family. I wonder if the investigating officers have looked into male relatives of the first victim. That would be where I'd start."

"*If only,*" Phillipa said. "But it's important to remember that we are not consulting detectives for the Met, that we're not even British."

"I'd have a word with Stone, if I were you," Deidre said. "You know how it is with men. They are often in need of a little tactful help."

"The Met doesn't give a flying fig for what Stone thinks!" Phillipa was obviously becoming a tad irate. "The Met just wants to get this international relations brainstorm handled, and return Stone to his home turf across the pond."

"What did you find out about the girl?" Fiona put her hand on Heather's arm. The thought came to me then that Fiona's tuneful gestures, that inevitable jingle of bangles, might have an extra element of magic that we'd never fully realized.

"The girl's name is Fatimah Khatoon," Heather said. "She gets off work at ten, but the kitchen itself never really closes. There's late room service for guests, and the bakers come in at three or four. Don't you want to know how I got all that information out of the desk clerk?"

"*Wait, wait, don't tell me.* The desk clerk is your English cousin?" Phillipa said.

"All right. I won't tell you, then, Ms. Smart Witch," Heather said. "This is worse, isn't it, when the girl has a name? It's as if we're *responsible* now for her safe-keeping. So I'm thinking we should do a little spell *thing* for extras. Back at the hotel. Meantime, we'd better move along out of this lobby. I think the Brown's Hotel staff is beginning to look at us askance. I'll hail a taxi."

Taxis are always throwing themselves into Heather's path. The Brown doorman didn't even have to raise his arm before a traditional British taxi screeched to attention in front of us. We piled in, managing not to discuss *murder* and *spell-craft* until we were back in the privacy of Heather's room. Not surprisingly, her room had what none of our other rooms had, a pleasant sitting area for guests and bottles of Drambuie, Chartreuse, and Strega, with liqueur glasses at the ready. Phillipa and I abstained, but the rest fortified themselves with wee drams of Drambuie.

"A pity our grimoires are not available on eBook readers," Heather said. "It might be worthwhile to have them scanned."

"Hazel's book, maybe, but the grimoire that turned up at the library book sale is far too decrepit and fragile," I said. "Let's just try to remember some suitable spell we may have worked in the past."

"Do you recall the spell we conjured early on, when we were just getting our magical feet under us that worked rather like a boomerang?" Deidre said dreamily. "That Q person drove himself right into a wall."

"But then he escaped and almost killed me," I shuddered.

"The fault of law officers who failed to guard him, not our spell," Deidre said. "How did that one go, do you recall?"

"I do," Phillipa said. "It was my idea, really, a way of protecting ourselves from Q, who had already found a way to threaten each of us. It was a dark-of-the-moon night, and we worked by candlelight. The incense was frankincense and sandalwood. Heather took the role of priestess and cast our circle. We blessed ourselves with salt water. Then we visualized the wall against which Q's evil intentions would rebound against him. And we used banishing sticks to describe our visions. Each wall was a bit different. Oh, and Cass burned herbs in the fireplace."

"St. John's Wort and dried periwinkle, 'the sorcerer's violet.'" It was all coming back to me now. "I have those two in my Wiccan first aid kit."

"Holy Mother! It's a wonder you weren't waylaid by airport security," Deidre said.

Fiona and I smiled at each other. "I packed all the dried herbs in a see-thru baggies and gave them to *Fiona with the Innocent Air* to get through the airport. Apparently, her claim that they were herbal teas for her rheumatism was not questioned. Don't you love it?"

"I not only love it, I want it," Phillipa said. "Every damn thing I bring on an airplane gets the fishy eye. Did you pack candles, Heather?"

Heather laughed. "*Never leave home without them.*" She opened a boxy Prada satchel upholstered in Louis Vuitton fabric (no leather for Heather!) and revealed a neat little set of candles, several colors and a bouquet of scents. She removed two of them and snapped the bag shut. "This burnt sienna candle is infused with frankincense, and the ochre has a touch of sandalwood."

"I didn't bring my banishing stick," Deidre said wistfully.

"Don't fret, Dee," I said. "Who brings a banishing stick on vacation?"

Fiona reached into her reticule and pulled out a bunch of chopsticks tied up with a silk ribbon decorated in Chinese characters. "These will do, suitably purified and blessed, of course. Oh, dearie me, I don't have any salt."

"What! No salt?" Phillipa exclaimed with a smirk. "Well, I never thought I'd catch *you* wanting any necessary magical paraphernalia."

"Not to worry. I have salt in my kit," I said. "I'll just pop back to my room."

A little later, we'd scraped together the rudiments for our impromptu spell and were ready to begin without waiting for darkness to fall. We'd have to be out on our mission later this night.

"Everything we're using here helps us to focus our intention," Fiona said, "but the intention itself is the only vital element. Everything else, in the end, is optional."

"Personally, I like the structure of a good spell," Phillipa said. "And we *do* have everything we need."

As she had before, Heather cast our circle and lit the scented candles; Phillipa called the quarters. We sprinkled ourselves and our improvised banishing sticks with salt water. I burned tiny sprigs of St. John's Wort and periwinkle in a little metal bowl from my kit.

Blessed be work for the good of all,
Blessed be tools to raise up the wall,

Now we proceeded with the visualization, each describing a wall against which the murderer's evil intent would rebound against him. At the least, the spell might give us an edge when we went back to Brown's that night. Our plan was to escort Fatimah to her home. She'd think we were crazy, but that would hardly be a first.

CHAPTER EIGHTEEN

It is not strength, but art, obtains the prize,
And to be swift is less that to be wise.
Alexander Pope

"We cannot keep depending on taxis," Heather had declared when she showed up in front of the London Hilton that evening in a rental from Auto Europe, quite a classy one. The only problem: Heather was driving it *on the wrong side of the road*. It was my bad luck to sit in the front next to the driver, while Phillipa, Fiona, and Deidre played it safer in back. No problem all squeezing in there, even in bulky winter coats, because the car was a roomy and comfortable Mercedes Benz. Metallic silver; not the most clandestine of vehicles, but perhaps that wouldn't matter at night.

"I figured the red Porsche might be too conspicuous," Heather said. She glided away from the hotel's portico, easily moving with the flow of traffic. Then, a few blocks later we came to a roundabout, which she entered hesitantly from the left. My alarm bells went off. To my American brain, she was heading straight into oncoming traffic! At any moment, as I pictured it, we would be mashed into a tangle of twisted metal. I drew in my breath with a sharp whistling intake and checked my seat belt.

"Cut that out, Cass. You're making me nervous," Heather said. "I think I almost have the hang of this. Soon it will be second nature."

"Actually," Phillipa interjected from the back seat, "it takes 21 days to adjust to driving on the left, the same as for any habit."

The Mercedes edged dangerously close to the curb as we made it out of the roundabout. I could hear tires scraping against concrete. It would be a wonder if we didn't have a blow-out.

Since I was on the "driver's side" of the front seat, it felt as if I should have had a steering wheel. Instead, my hands braced themselves against the dashboard with a panicked grip. I squealed and hit my non-existent brake.

"If you don't stop sniveling, I'm going to drop you off at the next bus stop," Heather said crossly. "Let me see now. There's a GPS here someplace." Her hand groped the dashboard. Obviously she herself was afraid to take her eyes off the road for a moment.

"I'll do it," I insisted immediately. The GPS screen was easily visible and centrally located on the dashboard. I selected the destination. Taking over the navigation got my mind off my imminent demise.

Soon a lovely female voice was guiding us to Brown's Hotel in the heart of Mayfair. The main entrance was bright and busy, with laughing, chattering people coming in and out, wrapped in lavish coats and handsome scarves against the bitter cold. I shut off the route finder, and Heather drove along the street past the hotel. She found an alley two blocks away and crept stealthily around to the back where there was a service door to Brown's kitchen.

She parked behind an old Peugeot in the shadows. We waited.

And waited.

Fiona hummed. Phillipa tapped her foot. At last the back door opened on a burst of merry talk, like a bunch of children just let out of school.

Fatimah was easily identified among the small cluster of workers, three men and two women, who left the hotel at ten past ten. A car came by and picked up the blonde woman. Two of the young men began jogging in the direction of a bus stop. Glancing at our Mercedes curiously, the older man stopped and said something to Fatimah, pointing to the Peugeot parked in the shadows. She shook her head and proceeded to follow the younger men, but at a slower pace. The Peugeot drove away. Soon Fatimah was alone on the street, except for us. With her black hijab, long black coat, and diffident walk, she looked like a nun.

"You speak to her, Fiona," Heather said. "Any of the rest of us might spook her. Offer her a ride home."

Fiona opened the car door, and the smell of frying fat floated into the air, sweetened by a trace of spices. Enveloped in tartan plaid and leaning heavily on her walking stick, she struggled out of the back seat to catch up with Fatimah. After walking continually all morning at the Abbey, her arthritis must have been flaring up. The silver coyote's pointed snout caught the light over the service door, winking as she moved toward the girl who was walking briskly now, a lone dark figure.

"Shouldn't someone else be with Fiona?" Deidre said. "I'm going, too." She jumped lightly out of the still open door of the back seat, looking like a pixie in her hooded blue coat.

Everything else happened in a blur, like a fast-forwarded film.

A short, hefty man leapt out from behind the rubbish bin. It was too dark to see his face, but his head appeared to be swathed in cloth. I heard him muttering threats and curses. He was swinging a murderous-looking curved blade that also caught the light.

Fatimah sprang away in alarm until she encountered the back wall of the hotel and could go no farther. She made a soft moan and crouched down with her arms over her head.

Deidre screamed and dashed forward to protect the girl. But there were patches of ice in the rutted asphalt. She slipped and fell down in the middle of the alley, sprawled out at the feet of the attacker. Phillipa and I bounded out of the car, yelling for help, followed by Heather, who first had to extricate herself from behind the wheel.

With a flourish, Fiona drew the rapier out of her walking stick, and (I swear I heard this!) cried *en guarde!* She lunged toward the knife-wielding man, who laughed nastily and knocked the blade out of her hands in a whirlwind strike. With a cry of surprise, she fell against the concrete stairs of the service door.

The attacker, whom we could now see was bearded and turbaned, crouched down over Deidre and held his blade at her throat, glaring at us, a mute warning to keep our distance.

Phillipa and I froze in our tracks, as if we were playing a game of Statues. I felt that my heart had stopped beating, then began again with a fearful thumping. We were so close, I could smell a rancid odor emanating from the man's robes. I concentrated on sending protective vibrations to surround Deidre. I could hear Heather opening the trunk of the Mercedes, rooting around for (I guessed) a weapon.

Fiona, who was behind the crazed attacker, still at the foot of the stairs, seemed to be struggling unsuccessfully to rise. But now she suddenly sprang to her feet. Watching in amazement, we saw her whip her reticule into the air and bash the man on the side of his head. Phillipa said later that it looked as if his eyes popped out of his head in surprise. He dropped the knife and clutched his head with both hands. Goddess only knows what Fiona had in there.

Heather, who had just come up with some kind of iron bar in her hands, looked at the fallen man with amazement. "If thoughts could kill…" she muttered.

"That wasn't magic. That was Fiona!" Phillipa said.

"Same thing." Deidre jumped up and grabbed the curved knife. She lobbed it away from the fallen man in the general direction of the rubbish bin. *The whistles. The fucking whistles!* she screamed at us.

We got it. Three of us blew those bobby whistles for all we were worth.

Phillipa scooped up the rapier from Fiona's walking stick, quickly sheathed the blade, and handed it back to Fiona. "Here, you'd better lean on this," she said, "and do try to look frail and helpless."

As the screech of our whistles pierced the calm, cold night, workers still in the kitchen came running out the service door and were stopped in their tracks by the odd tableau they witnessed in the alley. Someone with presence of mind called the Met on his cell.

Meanwhile, the attacker, still dazed, got to his feet with an odd kind of roar and dived toward Fatimah, who crouched down even lower, shielding herself. But somehow the man became disoriented when he launched himself at the terrified girl, and with his head down like a battering ram, he ran straight into the rubbish bin instead of into Fatimah. His head made an ugly clanking sound against the metal, and he dropped to the ground, apparently unconscious.

"That's good, then," Deidre said, dusting her hands together. "We have witnesses that the assailant dashed out his own brains." She put her arms around Fatimah and drew the girl upright. Checking her over with a concerned look, Deidre adjusted Fatimah's head scarf and tucked in an errant lock of hair. "It's all right now, honey. You'll have no more trouble from him."

Petite Deidre was in danger of keeling over herself with the weight of the fainting girl. Heather strode over and held them both in a firm grip. I glimpsed one of the kitchen workers taking photos with a cell phone.

Almost immediately, a swarm of constables appeared in two cars. There were calls back and forth, and an officer with the rank of commander arrived to take charge. We spent what seemed like an hour or so explaining what had occurred in the back alley and how we happened to be there at the time. The officers were polite but insistent, and they asked the same questions many times, in many ways.

"It's very simple, officer. Night in a strange city, and I was lost," Heather claimed in her most patrician tones. "I had parked here for a few moments to orient myself and check the in-car navigator, when this bearded man appeared suddenly and attacked the young lady from the hotel with some kind of horrid sword. Naturally, we tried to help. My friends blew their bobby whistles, and everyone came running out from the kitchen. Other than that, we don't know who the man is or why he seems to be unwell."

Deidre retrieved the curved knife from the dark corner where she'd shied it. Using a lace-edged hanky to pick it up, she presented it to a WPC. "That terrible man was swinging this at us," she confided in her best little-girl voice. "Lucky he suddenly collapsed, or I just don't know what would have happened."

"It's the first time I've ever driven a vehicle in England, and I found it a tad confusing to drive on the left side of the road," Heather explained further. "I drove around the corner to the right and the next thing I knew, I was in this alley. Golly, it's cold out here." She drew up the collar of her plaid-lined Burberry and shivered ostentatiously.

She'd already put in a call to a London solicitor whose name
had been pressed into her hand by Bart Bangs, her Plymouth
attorney. Bangs had seen her through three divorces and sundry
other legal tangles. When told of our plans to visit Great
Britain, the attorney had wisely alerted a friend in London to
be at the ready.

In deference to her age, Fiona had been allowed to sit in
the car with the door open. She hummed while Phillipa and I
leaned against the fenders, agreeing with every word Heather
said and waiting for whatever would happen next.

"That was neat, wasn't it?" Phillipa murmured to me.
"Abdul the Ripper put out his own lights. Do you think that
was our spell at work?"

"We'll never know," I said. "And I like it that way. Has any
of these officers found out his real name? Or made a connection
with the Ripper?"

"The coppers are not sharing. I trust that they don't quite
understand our interest," Phillipa said.

A rescue wagon arrived to tend to the concussed attacker,
and he was rushed away, accompanied by two police constables,
who were armed only with batons and sprays. I hoped it would
be enough to manage that dangerous madman.

Commander Harris, the officer in charge, took pity on us.
Well, maybe it was pity or maybe it was to escape the reporters
who had begun swarming into the alley, having been alerted to
the possibility of a Big Story by someone on the hotel's staff.
Anyway, we were herded inside and allowed to take seats in the
kitchen staff's rest area. The service door was firmly closed against
the microphones and cameras of the press. Some of the officers
were immediately sent to clear the alley as well. Nevertheless, a
few camera flashes were aimed at our retreating backs.

Just as we were beginning to thaw out, a well-dressed man
in a gray pin-stripe suit walked in through the swinging door
between the dining room and the kitchen and looked around.
Then he headed directly toward Heather, presented his card,
and spoke quietly to the woman police constable who was
guarding us while the rest of the PCs were outside clearing the
alley and Commander Harris was making calls on his cell.

"This is Laurence Watson, my British solicitor. And yours,"
Heather introduced him. "He was kind enough to come out at
this late hour to rescue us from spending the night answering

the same questions over and over without so much as a cup of tea."

The WPC blushed. Tea would have been her job, of course. "The cleaners are in the kitchen now," she explained. "As soon as they're through ..."

Watson (*call me Larry*) smiled reassuringly and shook hands with all of us. "It's a damned good thing I was just up the street at the Embassy Club when you called." His grip was warm, dry, and firm. *Someone to trust*, my inner voice told me. He was also an incredibly handsome man, not tall but well-built and perfectly tailored to show it off. He had finely chiseled features, a typically British long face with something sensitive and Mediterranean about the mouth, thick black hair just streaked with white, and take-no-prisoners gray eyes.

Phillipa flashed one of her dazzling smiles at the solicitor. "I feel we're in good hands at last, Larry" she said. "This has been an exhausting experience." Nevertheless, she seemed suddenly to come to life just when the rest of us were wilting.

Thanks to Watson, we were allowed to return to the Hilton, with warnings to keep ourselves available in case further interviews were required. Deidre voiced our concerns about Fatimah, and the WPC told us that the young lady would be escorted to her home as well.

Although it was midnight, we had tea in Heather's room and conferred with Larry Watson. (*How civilized! How British! What fun!*) Phillipa, who had been going to call Stone in Sussex, where he was staying for the night, still comparing operations with his British counterpart, decided it was just too late to bother and worry him.

Larry was convinced that our assailant would not be freed to repeat his murderous attempts on Fatimah, and for that matter, on us, if he happened to be in a vengeful frame of mind. "You ladies probably don't realize this, but we've had a series of young Muslim girls brutally murdered near some of the best London hotels in the past few months," he said, "so I expect this fellow who attacked Miss Kahtoon tonight will be held without bail and questioned rigorously. It will be quite a feather in the Met's cap if they put an end to these vicious killings."

"Dearie me," Fiona said. "Running into a depraved killer is the last thing we ever imagined might happen to us on our tour of Great Britain's spiritual landmarks."

"You make us sound like a gaggle of elderly pilgrims," Phillipa complained.

"Well, Phil, normally we do lead such quiet, uneventful lives back in the States," Deidre added with a twinkle in her eye.

"Hmmm. Surprising, then, that Bart Bangs would insist I keep an eye on Mrs. Devlin," Larry Watson said, passing his cup to Heather for a refill. "He was quite adamant. Bart's a friend of the family. Known him a long time. Not a chap much given to flights of fancy, I believe."

"Oh, he has his moments." Heather handed around a plate of chocolate digestive biscuits. "I think I may have read something about those murders in one of your tabloids, *The Sun.* The Five-Star Jack the Ripper? You'll keep us apprised, won't you, about what happens to this madman? Do they know his real name?"

Watson consulted his iPhone. "He's just been identified at the hospital as Abdul Hamid, an importer of traditional Moroccan furniture and fabrics."

"*Abdul* Hamid. And we've been calling him Abdul the Ripper. How did we know?" Fiona who had been slumped in the corner of the sofa, came to life with this fresh evidence of our prescience. "Servant of the praiseworthy one. Evidently, he feels himself on a mission from Allah."

"It's a common enough name in the Middle East," I said. "I hope someone at the Met will find out whether the first Muslim victim of his mission was a relation of Hamid's. This killing spree may have been an honor killing run amok. I imagine it would be helpful to have a motive in building a case against Hamid."

Watson put down his cup and looked up at me sharply. "It would be best if you ladies have *nothing more* to do with an attempted crime you witnessed *accidentally*. Fatimah's testimony, along with the depositions you gave after the incident tonight, should be sufficient for the time being. As tourists, you wouldn't want to be kept from your itinerary by having to help the police with their inquiries."

"She's just saying," Deidre said.

"Larry is right," Phillipa decreed firmly. "Not another word, Cass."

"After all, we have *urgent business* at the Crossed Keys Inn," Heather said.

"Yes, yes. We've done all that is necessary here," Fiona said. "And we have other fries to fish. Anyone for a little nightcap, perhaps a tot of Drambuie?"

"Right you are," I agreed briskly. "We'll follow our solicitor's advice to the letter, thank our lucky stars, and get on with our sight-seeing. I believe we've had quite enough excitement for now. As I'm sure our escorts to the UK will agree. Because we *are* going to have to explain this incident to 'the ones who brung us.'"

"Holy Mother! They'll be *so cross* with us." The denouement of our little adventure was just dawning on Deidre.

"Good. That's settled, then." Watson stood and picked up his briefcase. "But I can do something. I happen to have a friend at the Met assigned to this investigation. I could have a quiet word to her about your suspicions, Ms. Shipton."

I didn't need to be a clairvoyant to know that our new solicitor had got an earful of anecdotes about our Plymouth activities from his buddy Bangs. This was confirmed when Watson added, "I assume you ladies will be celebrating the winter solstice at Stonehenge? If there's anything I can do in the way of special passes, please don't hesitate to ask."

Watson said good night and left the apartment, a trace of some enticing masculine scent lingering in his wake. Phillipa sighed and collapsed on the sofa. "Larry almost makes it a pleasure getting in trouble with the law," she said.

"How about the trouble you're going to be in with Stone?" I asked.

CHAPTER NINETEEN

With her 'ead tucked underneath her arm,
She walks the bloody Tower,
With her 'ead tucked underneath her arm
At the midnight hour.
    Traditional British ballad

The jig was up! Our Brown's Hotel encounter was a secret that couldn't be kept.

It began with Stone who was staying over in Sussex where preliminary news of Hamid's arrest had come to the attention of Detective Stern's British hosts and been the excited talk of the Constabulary. The incident report included reference to several "middle-aged" female tourists who had witnessed the suspect attacking a hotel kitchen worker in the alley behind Brown's Hotel and had summoned help with bobby whistles. With an intuitive leap that rivaled any of ours, Stone had divined immediately just who those female tourists probably were and called his wife just as she'd returned to her room after our midnight tea party with Larry Watson.

He read the highlights of the incident report to Phillipa over the phone. "The last I knew, you were going to have afternoon tea at Brown's. But now it appears a bunch of ladies were involved in Hamid's arrest. So, was that you and the Plymouth posse around the back alley where the girl was attacked?"

"Just who are they calling 'middle-aged'," Phillipa complained. "Deidre's practically a child, and I'm still on the good side of fifty."

"That's not the point!" Stone (that gentlest and best-humored of husbands) had shouted over the phone.

"Stone, dear. Here's the thing. Cass got one of those obsessive ideas in her head that she and Heather ought to take a drive through Mayfair, see it lit up at night and whatnot, so the rest of us went along simply to keep her out of trouble. We had absolutely *no idea* that Mr. Most Wanted would show up and try to hack up a sweet little girl before our very eyes. Now do me a favor, dear, and don't make a big deal of this."

"If I believe that story of how you happened to be at the crime scene, will you be trying to sell me London Bridge next?" Stone inquired hotly. "I'm familiar with the usual sub-text of Cass's 'obsessive ideas', you know. Sorry, darling. This already is a big deal. I can't make it back to the Hilton myself tonight, so I'm going to call Conor. He's the closest, and he can keep an eye on the lot of you."

"But we're all totally unscathed, and your Ripper person has been apprehended," Phillipa protested. "What more could you and your friends at the Constabulary wish for? 'Keep calm and carry on,' isn't that the British way?"

"Keep calm? Keep calm?" Stone was shouting again. "I'm a guest of Law Enforcement UK. It's a public relations thing, supposed to be totally unremarkable. If it comes out that you, my wife, witnessed a crime, even participated in the capture of a felon, and the damned British press finds out the connection, it's going to be seriously embarrassing." He took a few deep breaths, deep enough to be audible over the phone, and got his voice under control. "Well, be that as it may, I'll see you tomorrow sometime. For God's sake, stay off the Met's radar meanwhile. Go be a real tourist and stay safe. Love you!" And Stone ended the call, in a tone that was a shade more annoyed than loving, while Phillipa was still arguing the case.

Immediately she called me in my room and repeated their conversation word for word. "Stone's really pissed at me," she wailed. "What a way to start our first vacation abroad!" Like the good friend I am, I assured her that he would probably be even more pissed with whatever Heather dug up at the Crossed Keys Inn.

"Remember Fiona's advice. Try not to worry Stone about the troublesome little details," I suggested.

"Fiona is not my idea of the ideal marriage counselor," she replied crisply.

"For gals like us, your basic crime-solving Wiccans, who're you gonna call? Dr. Phil?"

❧

Meanwhile, Conor was having an after-dinner brandy with his grandpa and some business cronies when he got the call from Stone. Immediately leaving the O'Donnell's new manse (Bridwell Lodge in Essex, a historic manor house lost to its heirs in death duties) in one of the family limousines, he was still muttering Gaelic curses when he confronted Deidre.

As she related the scene to us later, she'd pacified Conor by telling him the whole story, an innocent version she'd concocted on the spot. (Fiona would have been proud.) It was pretty much the same recounting of events that Heather had given to the responding constables.

When Joe came back around two from a Greenpeace presentation on the London Array, the world's largest wind farm, he was surprised to find me still awake. Not only awake, but pretty jazzed up with the night's events and several cups of strong tea in Heather's room. The incident at Brown's hotel had happened so late, it wasn't yet reported in the news, print or television, and wouldn't be until the next morning. But it certainly would be a big noise then, so I related the entire episode with perhaps a few more truthful details about our involvement than Stone and Conor had been privileged to learn. Not that I was more high-minded than my friends, or that Joe's tirades were fiercer. It was just that, as a clairvoyant, I knew the true picture of events would surface eventually, so I might as well get it over with now. Besides, Joe knew me so well, the usual evasions wouldn't fool him for long.

Dick, on the other hand, was the last to learn of our Brown's misadventure. That same evening, he'd flown on American Airlines from Logan to Heathrow to join his wife on vacation, arriving at 5:45 A.M the next morning, British time. But it wasn't until after we'd left for the Tower that a copy of the *Times* was delivered to their room door. Dick had read the headline with a foreigner's disinterest: "Suspect Held in Ripper Murders." But he was instantly shocked out of jet lag daze by the accompanying above-the-fold photo of a young Muslim woman being supported *by his wife* on one side and Deidre Ryan on the other. The caption read "American Tourists Help Foil Attack."

Heather's husband, a big burly guy with a soft heart, a real teddy bear, rarely made a fuss over his wife's friends and their crazy crusades. Just the occasional loving protest when near-brushes with criminals brought danger to the Devlin doorstep. Heather had seemed all right this morning when he'd staggered into the hotel at seven-thirty. She'd kissed him thoroughly, and soon after had taken off with her friends for another day of sight-seeing, leaving Dick to recover from a night of not-quite-sleeping on the plane. Not a word had she said about this so-called foiled attack. Dick spread the *Times* on the rumpled bed and studied it again, still finding it beyond comprehension. Maybe the Times had made a mistake, published the wrong photo. Comforted with this sensible version of events, he'd ordered a full English breakfast from room service, and having demolished that, went back to bed with a cold cloth on his forehead.

In his heart of hearts, he knew it was all true.

∽

It was a good thing we'd left early the next morning to tour the Tower of London. The press had gathered in the lobby hoping to interview the "middle-aged female tourists" involved in the apprehension of the Ripper. Joe, on his way to an early conference, had spotted them milling about with notebooks, microphones, and cameras, and he called my cell with a warning to avoid the lobby. I invited him to catch up with us on the Tower tour, but he said he had this one last Greenpeace meeting before he was on his own.

We five had gathered in the hall near an extravagant vase of flowers on a console table with little gold chairs on either side. I passed along Joe's warning. Immediately, Heather opened her cell and requested that her rented silver Mercedes Benz be brought around to the rear exit behind the hotel.

Still on the phone with me, Joe said, "Do you think you might get away for dinner tonight, sweetheart? Just the two of us." His voice deepened to that intimate, sexy tone I find so irresistible, so of course I immediately agreed to skip out on my friends. "I've already made our reservation," he confessed.

I wondered where. He refused to reveal the restaurant's name. We said good-bye and I closed my phone.

"The Savoy Grill," Fiona said. "I'd bet my best rowan wand on it."

"You could hear our conversation?" I realized now that I had been standing quite close to the gold chair where Fiona was sitting, her walking stick between her knees and a deceptively absent expression on her round face.

"Not ready for my hearing aid quite yet, my dear Cass. Pretend to be surprised when he takes you to the Savoy. Being a sibyl, you've probably had lots of practice," Fiona said. "That's all right then. You two go off and have fun. Phil has her heart set on *Le Poisson* Soho, and the rest of us are silly putty in her hands."

"It's the finest French cuisine in London," Phillipa said firmly. "Not to be missed simply to satisfy a husband's romantic whim."

I ignored her, humming a few bars of that old standard: *I'll take romance …*

"Conor said the food is so artistically arranged he's never been sure whether to eat it or photograph it, but the portions leave him hungry," Deidre said.

"Poor Dick may be a trifle jet-lagged, Heather," Fiona followed her own train of thought. "I wonder if it's really necessary for you to tell him anything at all about the Hamid incident. We'll be dining at the French place tonight, then leaving early tomorrow for the Crossed Keys Inn. Larry Watson seems to think that our involvement in the saga of Hamid is over and done with. The Constabulary has our depositions in hand. Why trouble poor Dick with that whole sordid business?"

"Why indeed?" My slightly sarcastic tone seemed to be lost on Fiona. In my mind's eye, however, I could see the *Times* first page, the paper spread out on a bed somewhere. "Except that Dick will know all about it by the time we get back to the hotel."

༄

There was an extra spring in Fiona's arthritic step while we followed the Beefeater tour guide into the Tower enclosure. Chattering about the reactions of our *significant others* to our latest blunder into crime seemed to have given her some pleasing nostalgic reflections.

"Much as I miss my darling Rob Angus Ritchie, there's something to be said for never having to explain a large charge or a small indiscretion."

"I miss Will, too. Always," Deidre said. "It's as if everything in the past is still there, a room you can almost walk back into, but a story that you can never change, *nor all your tears wash out a word of it*, as the poet says. Meanwhile, life just keeps on moving you along to new places, new loves." She shivered and arranged the scarf that matched her yellow angora tam closer around her neck. The welcome but deceptive sunlight brightened us without heat. It was, as the Brits might say, "bloody cold," but the walls around the Tower green kept out the worst of a cutting wind off the Thames.

"Speaking of loss and love, you ought to read Thomas Wyatt's love poems to Anne Boleyn. *They flee from me that sometime did me seek, With naked foot, stalking in my chamber.*" Phillipa was wound up by the literary history of the place. "Wyatt was accused of adultery with the Queen, and imprisoned here. He may even have witnessed Anne's execution through one of the tower windows. *The bell tower showed me such sight That in my head sticks day and night,*" she quoted glibly. "But Thomas Cromwell got him a free pass. All the other alleged adulterers were beheaded. *These bloody days have broken my heart.* Did you know that Wyatt introduced the sonnet form into English Literature?" Phillipa moved from poem to poem as we toured, while the Beefeater guide continued his less literary patter up ahead of us. We were bringing up the rear of a small herd of tourists.

Thrilled by the legendary ravens that live their pampered lives at the Tower ("enraptured by raptors," as Fiona put it), Heather managed to waylay the Ravenmaster with her questions: why the ravens didn't "fly the coop" (one wing clipped) and what they were fed (raw meat and blood-soaked bird biscuits). Six ravens must be resident in the Tower at all times, but seven are kept (in case one does opt for freedom) because of the superstition that "if the Tower of London ravens are lost or fly away, the Crown will fall and Britain with it."

Meanwhile, Fiona and I were kept busy holding Deidre up as she encountered spiritual vibrations in one room after another. "Kathryn, Kathryn…" she mumbled. "Little Jane.

And Robert, so handsome." Later, she couldn't have told you whose names she uttered, but we remembered. I was surprised. Usually the ghostly vibrations of a popular historic landmark are well washed away by the constant ebb and flow of tourists. Maybe it was different in Britain. Maybe the British reverence for revenants made their ghosts stronger.

"Fifth wife of that degenerate, Henry," Phillipa said. "And poor Lady Jane Grey. Possibly the Earl of Essex. As high-born a bunch of ghosts as anyone would want to meet. What's the collective noun for ghosts, anyway?"

"The usual venery term is a Fright of Ghosts," Fiona said. "But some ghost-hunters prefer a Visitation of Ghosts or a Clanking of Ghosts."

Under the circumstances, there was no danger of our taking the side tour of the dungeons to view the instruments of torture. There was enough angst right out there on the Tower green where Anne Boleyn had been executed by a skilled swordsman brought from France and Margaret Pope, Countess of Salisbury, had been hacked to death by a clumsy English executioner with a dull axe.

We finished our tour with a walk through the Crown Jewels exhibit, which included St. Edward's Crown worn by the present Queen Elizabeth at her coronation. Solid gold with 444 gems, it weighed nearly five pounds. "Can't you feel the magical power of the stones themselves," Deidre murmured. "I must make a deeper study of gems and semi-precious stones when we get home. For our amulets, you know."

"Good Goddess, Dee. You've already weighed us down with enough protective amulets to sink a barge," Phillipa exclaimed.

"Diamonds are a witch's best friend," Fiona declared. "From the Greek *adamas*, invincible." There was something invincible about Fiona herself as she marched along, punching her stick in air to emphasize each point. One of the many rings on her plump fingers was a vintage diamond. "Imbued with magical powers to preserve love, guard homes from lightning, settle lawsuits, and protect the wearer from poisons. Think of all the time Mother Earth took to make each diamond, and other precious gems. I believe the diamonds, sapphires, rubies, and whatnot have lifted our wee girl's miasma of spirits," Fiona murmured, giving Deidre another hug. "Now, let's go get a hot cup of tea and maybe some scones to complete the cure. I believe the New Armouries Café is open."

❦

While we were in the Café, Heather got a call from Larry Watson. She listened for a moment, then took her cell phone out into the courtyard. The conversation took several minutes. When she returned, Phillipa demanded to know what was going on. "If that delicious solicitor wants another meet, perhaps I ought to go with you to take notes or something."

"Down, girl. Only a message, but a worry nonetheless. Larry got an email from Bart Bangs today, sort of an update that Bartie wanted passed on to me," Heather said.

"Oh, what was that?" I asked. Phillipa didn't have the corner on curiosity. At that point, we were walking toward the car, Fiona at the rear, leaning on Deidre.

Heather cast her eyes back toward Deidre and raised her eyebrows warningly. "Nothing we need to discuss at the moment. Privileged communication, you might say. You know how attorneys are."

And that's all we could get out of Heather then. Soon after, she was behind the wheel of her rental, the ghostly silver Mercedes, and the rest of us were occupied with our various prayers and spells to keep ourselves safe in traffic that still seemed wrong-way to us.

"I wish the Vatican hadn't downgraded St. Christopher," Deidre said "I used to take a great deal of comfort from the patron of travelers."

"Now that you're following an older religion, dearie," Fiona counseled, "you may keep whatever saints are dear to you close to your bosom. And let's not forget that Hecate was patroness of safe travel long before Christopher hopped onto the first dashboard."

"Amen, sisters, amen," Phillipa whispered.

So it wasn't until we got back to the hotel lobby that Heather pulled Phillipa and me into the POP bar, while Deidre was shepherding Fiona to her room. With a cursory glance at the wide selection of Pommery Champagnes, she ordered a bottle of classic Brut. "Don't tell Dee," she muttered fiercely, while we watched the bartender pouring the sparkling wine into delicate flutes. "Bartie thought it best for Larry to deliver the bad news himself and offer his moral support."

"What? What?" Phillipa and I chorused.

"Leo Deluca is on the loose again," Heather whispered, although there was no one nearby in the stylish white and gold bar. "Some McLean psychiatrist testified to Deluca's precarious mental condition, and a daft judge allowed the bloody young creep to await trial at home, wearing an ankle bracelet, but allowed him daily visits to Dr. Nutcase at the hospital. His grandmother posted bail. Evidently that old bat has some deep pockets. Right after Deluca's first appointment at McLean, however, he managed to break out of the ankle bracelet and immediately went FTA."

Deluca failed to appear! Houdini could have taken lessons from that slippery little psycho. Such stressful news engenders a thirst. Amid our gasps of horror, we managed to down our restorative champagne and held out our flutes for more.

Heather continued: "Rumor has it that the little bastard was last seen taking off with a long-distance mover headed for LA. No surprises there. So, if he's not hanging around Plymouth, we should have nothing to worry about. Our families are safe from that maniac while he's seeking fame and fortune in the movies, but I've asked Bartie to warn the De Veres and have a quiet word with Bettikins."

"Dee will be hysterical," Phillipa said. "She'll want to go right home."

"But how can he hope to work as an actor when he's wanted as a bombing suspect?" I asked—because basically, I am an innocent.

"Wise up, girlfriend," Phillipa said. "His dear old nana probably has ties to all sorts of Rhode Island establishments. I don't doubt he's already fixed up with a new identity and a changed appearance. You didn't make him as a little old hot dog vendor, did you?"

"Yeah. Stage make-up magic," I remembered.

This being an emergency, I gazed on purpose at the brilliant modern ceiling lights reflected in the mirror opposite me, allowing the usual dancing images to float into my mind's eye. "It will be all right," I said finally. "I see all Dee's little ones gathered around the Christmas tree, safe and happy. We'll only be in England a few more days anyway, and then it's home for Christmas."

"She's never going to forgive us," Phillipa was still protesting. But then she shrugged. "Maybe it's kinder not to worry Dee, though. I imagine it would be a hellacious task to reschedule their flight at this time of year, anyway, not to mention costing the earth."

"We don't want to miss experiencing the solstice at Stonehenge together," Heather said. "And then there's the matter of the Morgan family treasure waiting for us at Crossed Keys Inn."

By the time we'd drained the last drops from our flutes, we'd rationalized away the notion of running home to foil Leo Deluca. It was true that he'd shown a penchant for holding a grudge when we'd encountered him in the past. But we'd got him sent to Juvie, and now he was older, and, apparently, following his very own psychopathic star to Hollywood.

Not that I'd forgotten his recent attempt to demolish a theater and possibly my youngest with it. But if there was any truth to the saying, *Revenge is a dish best served cold,* there would be time enough to bring the murderous munchkin to justice after the holidays.

CHAPTER TWENTY

Sir, when a man is tired of London, he is tired of life;
for there is in London all that life can afford.
   Samuel Johnson

Joe and I had been seated side-by-side at a banquette, where the entire elegant Savoy Grill was in view. We dined on smoked Scottish salmon and Dover sole *meuniere*, with a whole bottle of Soave 'La Rocca', Pieropan, from Veneto, Italy. *This is perfection*, I thought, but there was more to come.

As an after-dinner surprise, Joe had arranged for a car and driver to take us for a ride along the Thames in view of Westminster Bridge, the Houses of Parliament, and Big Ben. Not just any limo, a chauffeured Rolls Royce Phantom, entirely opulent. Among its other elegant appointments, there was a button in back that shut off the chauffeur's view of the back seat.

Such luxurious intimacy is wasted without kisses, but when I caught my breath, there was much to be seen in the cold starry sky. The tipped golden bowl of a moon had risen, rippling a path of light across the water, and when Big Ben struck midnight, the coach did not turn back into a pumpkin after all.

We drove across Westminster Bridge in stately splendor, past 10 Downing Street, so unpretentious, through Trafalgar Square and the Nelson's column by moonlight, then Buckingham Palace and Westminster Abbey, and finally back across the bridge to our hotel. "Is this the London you wanted to show me?" I asked. "Because I'm finding it truly glorious."

"I love London. One of the great cities of the world. Even greater, being here together, though I wish we had more time. Isn't it a pity that we have to shove off tomorrow to some godforsaken inn in Salisbury," he murmured, running a warm, knowledgeable hand across the chilly flesh of my thighs. "But never mind, there will be other times, and this night isn't over yet.

It certainly wasn't. Back in our sumptuous room at the Hilton, Joe turned off the lights and opened the drapes, the starlit setting for our own happy ending to that last night in London. His strong, sea-tanned body was beautiful to me by any light. And he gave me every reason to believe the worship was mutual. We made love with all the time in the world. *Pure magic.*

～

Gathering together for our trip to the Crossed Keys Inn the next morning was like a shock of cold water to my bewitched, bemused state of consciousness. Joe, of course, veteran of many odd-hour watches on ships of the seven seas, was bright and alert, his usual vigorous self.

Heather had hired a white Audi limousine for our motor trip, explaining that it was actually cheaper than traveling as separate couples by train or touring car, and we'd be able to appreciate the scenery in company and at our own pace. The rest of us were simply grateful that a driver came with the limo, so we wouldn't be clutching the arms of our seats while Heather screeched alarmingly through roundabouts. The driver, Ernie Cooper, was a wiry old gentleman with a pronounced cockney accent who'd taken his grandsons to Florida twice in the past five years, and had been thrilled with the low cost of everything in the States.

Every limo in which I've ever been a passenger appears to have been furnished with a younger, hipper crowd in mind, or maybe a rock band. This one sported a pastel leather interior, a full bar, a mirrored ceiling, CD players, and two flat screen TVs. It could accommodate ten passengers, so our party of nine, plus driver, pretty well filled the available space.

Heather had stocked the bar with some famous British beers of every hue from Newcastle Brown Ale to Sam Smith's Pale Ale. Phillipa had procured two well-filled picnic hampers from Marks and Spencer, to keep us from fainting from lack of nourishment, I supposed. As predicted by Conor, those who had dined on French cuisine last night would be ready for hearty British food today.

Deidre whispered to me that each dish at *Le Poisson* listed its calorie content, mostly ranging between 110 and 350. After her appetizer had turned out to be a single Sicilian prawn (butterflied, with bonito flakes and smoked broth), she'd ordered the truffled risotto which admitted to the highest calorie count of any single item on the menu, in hopes of sufficient sustenance. Conor leaned over to show me a cell phone photo of his Slice of North Atlantic Halibut. The minute wedge of fish was surrounded by a zigzag of brown sauce, two dots of caviar, and three crossed asparagus spears, an artful composition on a large white plate.

Ernie found us a pleasant park, austere December trees against a gray sky, where we stopped to enjoy our ample picnic. I'm particularly fond of the Ploughman's Lunch, a hefty cheddar cheese and pickle sandwich. We ate inside the shelter of the limo, then walked around a bit and visited the rest area facilities. The air was chilled and damp, but it didn't actually rain, and who can ask more when travelling in Britain?

After the sandwiches, beer, and almond fruit cake, I just leaned back on Joe's comforting shoulder, dozed a little, inhaling his warm scent, sweet-spicy as bergamot, and day-dreaming about last night. The last thing I heard before I dropped off was Heather explaining to Dick, once again, how she happened to be on the *Times'* first page. Phillipa and Stone were silent, and a little tense. Deidre and Conor leaned their heads together, reviewing images of his Notting Hill assignment for *London Life*; apparently he was over his Gaelic tantrum. Fiona hummed.

A little while later, as we drove into Amesbury, I woke up from my nap with a start, completely aware and alert.

"I dreamed of a skull!" I exclaimed.

Heather laughed merrily, and Phillipa seemed to find the notion equally humorous. Only Deidre frowned a bit. "I've had about enough of British ghosts," she declared crossly. So I said no more about my dream just then and concentrated instead on enjoying the quaint Tudor store fronts and nostalgic old-world Christmas decorations in the villages we passed through. It began to snow, huge soft flakes that stuck to the windows, then slid slowly down, each with its unique cut-out design. We seemed to have entered the landscape of a 19th century Christmas card, leaving behind us all the garish commercial aspects of Christmas at home.

Charles Dickens, we are here!

❧

It was after three when we checked in at our destination. The Crossed Keys Inn looked exactly the way it had been pictured online, a historic Tudor building with a steeply pitched roof, stone-fronted first floor, half-timbering second and third floors, and high chimneys. Swinging in the wind, a rather battered wooden sign depicting the gilded image of crossed keys hung above the heavy double-door entry.

"Wow!" Deidre jumped out of the limo and gazed around rapturously. "How cool is this!" She shone like a single yellow daffodil blooming in the gray and white landscape. It was getting dark already; the shortest days of the year were at hand.

The steadily falling snow gave a breathless timelessness to the scene. We followed Deidre out of the limo, rather lost in wonder; the fragrance of freshly cut fir and pine and the pungent scent of wood smoke surrounded us with the promise of hospitable warmth and Christmas charm. As we moved closer, however, we could see that the original inn, viewed from the side, was considerably larger than it appeared from the front. The inn had been extended more than once through the years. Beyond the building, we could see a garden, winter barren, overlooking a stone church, a picturesque medieval village, and pretty rural scenery.

"Holy Mother!" Deidre exclaimed. "Did you ever see the like, Conor?" Conor, who'd traveled through Britain many times, wisely remained silent, his arm around his delighted sweetheart.

"Let's hope there are decent elevators for Fiona's sake," Phillipa muttered, gazing at the inn's Elizabethan aspect.

"I wouldn't worry. Heather made the arrangements. We've probably taken over the entire inn," I whispered back.

That was not far from the truth. Our party had, indeed, fairly well filled up one of the more recent additions, although Heather had booked a room for herself and Dick in the oldest part of the inn fronting on the street. "If my ancestor has left me a gift, as promised on Samhain, it must be in one of these earliest fireplaces," she said. "Trouble is, they may all be in use."

Having dropped the luggage in our rooms, we gathered for tea in the large paneled keeping room of the old inn, where logs sputtered with welcome warmth in a massive fireplace. Conor was still wandering around with his Nikon. He and Deidre joined us last.

"Do you always keep these fireplaces lit?" Heather asked the innkeepers, Iris and Reggie Harris-Jones, a tall, lean, rather lugubrious couple who bore a passing resemblance to the painting *American Gothic*. They'd made it a point to be on hand with warm greetings for the loaded guest who had booked multiple rooms in mid-winter for an extravagant amount of American dollars.

Heather's bronze hair had grown long again, and she'd pulled it back into a thick braid as she used to wear, although it had proved dangerous in the past, an easy grab. In a soft russet tunic with a loose leather belt over slim pants, she could have passed for Maid Marian. Reggie, who'd been gazing at his attractive guest appreciatively, looked slightly taken aback by Heather's direct questioning of the cheery blazes throughout the inn, but Iris rose to the occasion of dealing with another eccentric American tourist.

"It's winter, Mrs. Devlin. We do have central heating of course, but most guests enjoy the coziness of a jolly fire. If you wish, I can instruct the chamber maid not to light the one in your room."

Dick protested, looking quite disappointed. He may have had visions of enjoying a pleasurable romp with his wife by firelight. I try very hard not to see these things, but Dick's mind was so trusting and unguarded, he was all too easy to read.

"Let Dick have his romantic blaze," I suggested. "I am convinced that fireplaces in use will not stop you from finding your treasure."

"Okay. I trust that's a genuine psychic flash?" Heather looked at me doubtfully.

"Have I ever led you astray?" I hoped there wouldn't be time to answer that one. It didn't help my credibility that Joe was quietly chuckling.

Heather turned to Iris with a sweet smile. "Thank you so much, Mrs. Harris-Jones. We do have to be so careful with my husband's allergies, you know. But apparently, he would prefer the fire to be lit after all. One more question, is Crossed Keys, by any chance, one of Britain's famous haunted inns?"

Reggie took an unlit pipe out of his mouth and leaned forward, eager to answer. "Funny you should mention ghosts, Mrs. Devlin. Some of our other guests are also interested in the supernatural. Manfred and Martha Holstein are staying here. Perhaps you've heard of them? Famous ghost-hunters. Fred's an ordained exorcist of the Universal Life Church, and Martha's a spirit photographer. Authors of *Now You See Me: A Chronicle of Spirit Photography* and *Dorothy in Hell: The Demonology of Oz*. They've been frequent guests of Geraldo Rivera and that televangelist Willie Crookes, talking about their experiences in exorcising haunted houses of the rich and famous and wrestling with demonic possession, especially in children exposed to Satanic literature."

"You don't say, Reggie," Heather replied, dryly. "Yes, I have heard of the Holsteins. Are they here to bust any particular ghost? Or merely grazing through the local dens of devil-worshippers?"

A decided chill was emanating from Heather's aura. I fancied I could see it turning ice blue, casting a frost on our merry party. Dick sensed the change of mood and gave his wife's hand a cautionary squeeze.

"It will be all right," Fiona murmured.

"Holy Mother!" Deidre exclaimed. "Is that the couple of loonies who claim *The Wizard of Oz* is a Satanic figure? And *Alice in Wonderland* is a tale of demonic possession? My kids just love those magical stories!"

"Which only goes to show that *demons are in the eye of the beholder*," Fiona said. "If there's any problem, I will do a baffle."

"What in Hades is a *baffle*?" Phillipa muttered aside to me, settling a gray silk scarf artfully around her black turtleneck.

"I don't know. Fiona keeps coming up with these things," I muttered back.

"Is there any particular ghost story in the history of Crossed Keys that interests the Holsteins?" Heather inquired.

"There is one curious legend ..." Reggie began.

His wife interrupted briskly. "There's no inn in England without its resident ghost, Mrs. Devlin. Personally, I could manage without all those weird doings. Come now, Reggie, we must get on." Iris nodded briskly and hurried out of the keeping room, pulling Reggie along with her. The set of her shoulders said, as clearly as words, *no need to continue humoring these crazy Americans.*

"I'll corner Reggie later, perhaps in the bar," Heather said.

"Yes, good idea. Iris seemed a bit put out. Funny. Most innkeepers seek to capitalize on their ghosts." I said. "Like the boys who ran the Crowninshield in Salem, remember? I wonder if there's a reason why Mrs. Harris-Jones is keeping a low spiritual profile, so to speak. And what in Hades the Holsteins are doing here at this particular time."

"Don't fret, my dears," Fiona said, tapping the crystal pendant under her tartan wool sweater, "I've come prepared to help in the hunt for Heather's treasure. Later. Right now, I'm perishing for one of those scrumptious raspberry tarts on the tea tray. One should never dowse on an empty stomach."

Tea was served by a pleasant young woman named Sheila, who did not demur when Heather asked for a bottle of sherry as well. We basked in the 18th century ambiance of the place, vowing to bring the very civilized custom of afternoon tea back with us when we returned to the States. (Actually, that would never happen. Here everyone's schedule was arranged to accommodate this beatific hour, whereas no such provision was made in our own daytime routines at home.)

"Oh, it's clotted cream, Goddess help me," Phillipa exulted, helping herself from the homey blue bowl on the large round table we had commandeered. "Don't worry about it, Heather. Surely your family ghost will grace you with a few hints in your hunt for the treasure."

"What *is* all this talk about ghost hunting?" Stone asked. "Not more trouble, I trust."

Heather explained about the séance at Burial Hill, and how the Divine Cosmos had arranged for our circle to be here in Britain to help find Heather's bequest and incidentally to celebrate the Winter Solstice at Stonehenge.

Stone shook his head in disbelief and gave his wife an incredulous glance before replying to Heather. "But, Heather, all due respect, my trip was arranged by International Law Enforcement as a publicity thing, not by some spectral pirate of yours."

Phillipa busied herself piling clotted cream and jam on a warm scone and let Heather run with the ball.

"What about Joe's December assignment for Greenpeace?" Heather demanded. "Not to rescue the usual endangered fish being plundered by sleazy fishing companies but to participate in some conference in Britain. You want to ascribe that to *coincidence?* And Conor's family *just chanced* to insist that he and Dee visit Bridwell Lodge during the Christmas season?" She could hardly believe that Stone failed to see the Goddess's fine hand weaving the web of our destiny to be here together right now.

"Synchronicity, perhaps," Joe said. "Who knows how these things happen? We Greeks were raised on the tragedies and understand that we are powerless to avert the will of the Fates in life and love." He smiled at me, not the least disturbed by the notion of being "bewitched." *Sure of himself. Good thing, living with me.*

"You know, Stone," Dick said heartily. "I find it best not to question these amazing happenstances too closely as they may relate to our wives and their arts and crafts. Mysteries of Isis and all that." He leaned back comfortably and beamed at his wife. She smiled back and enclosed them both in a nearly visible rosy aura of love. (I *was* beginning to see auras now, too. Ceres save me!)

"Amen to that," Joe agreed. "Maybe we men ought to form our own association. That way, whenever one of us gets the urge to question a particular twist of fate that throws us in the path of, say, a lunatic killer, another husband talks him out of trying to understand how the ladies got us there."

I aimed a carefully unobtrusive kick at Joe's ankle under the table. As usual, he read my intention and moved out of range. I had to admire his lightning reflexes, among other things.

Stone looked thoughtful, running his long fingers through the fine brown hair that always fell across his eyes. "Well, I admit it struck me as odd that a major murder investigation that had been dragging on at the Met for months would reach a sudden satisfactory conclusion when Phillipa arrived on the scene."

"*Don't blame me*, darling," Phillipa interjected briskly. "It was Cass who saw the whole thing going down at Brown's Hotel."

"Oh, thanks, girlfriend," I said. "Imagine that I did *see* such an event. What were we supposed to do? Inform the coppers that we knew where the next attack would take place? Or just close our mouths and let it happen?"

Joe put his sturdy arm around me, and my defensive stance eased a bit. He said, "Not that I approve of your taking matters into your own hands, but if you had come forward, you might have been accused of being involved Before the Fact. The law doesn't make an allowance for special sensitivities or good intentions."

"Lawyers and doctors are required to report criminal plots," Deidre said. "Why not psychics, as well?"

"The less any of us have to do with the law, especially British law, the better," said Conor, who had been listening with quiet skepticism to this whole discussion. "No offense, Detective Stern. But your wife's involvement is not the question. The question is, do you believe all these psychic shenanigans are *not* just a whole lot of malarkey? The girls just happened to be in the wrong place at the wrong time."

Joe chuckled evilly. I directed another kick that failed to reach its target.

Deidre looked up at the ceiling and shrugged. I could feel her thoughts just as if she'd spoken them aloud. *What Conor doesn't know won't hurt him.*

"What does all that matter now?" Fiona, who had been gazing at the Dickensian prints on the wall and humming, suddenly came back on topic. "The killing has been stopped. The girl was frightened but unharmed. However the murder spree ended is now a moot point."

"Till the next time," Stone said.

"Who knows? Till the cows come home, perhaps," Fiona said. "Speaking of which, why do you suppose the Holsteins are here? I find their Satan rant disturbing. Witches do not believe in Satan. Or coincidence."

"The Holsteins better not be skulking around after the Morgan treasure, whatever it is," Heather said darkly.

"Hey, we're on vacation here, doll. Think happy thoughts." Dick grinned cheerfully. I reflected that Heather, who could rein in a mastiff at full gallop, might actually seem a "doll" to this husky man.

"Tread softly, dear, and carry a walking stick," Fiona advised. She waved hers lightly in the air to illustrate the point, the many silver bangles on her plump arm tinkling quietly.

CHAPTER TWENTY-ONE

God answers sharp and sudden on some prayers,
And thrusts the thing we have prayed for in our face,
A gauntlet with a gift in it.
    Elizabeth Barrett Browning

"Come with me, Cass," Heather whispered to me urgently after breakfast the next morning. "There's something spooky I want to show you."

"What about the others?" My yoga-lithe friend yanked me away from the remaining currant-studded rock cakes on the bountiful buffet. The British really know how to put on a breakfast. Joe and Dick were contentedly loading their plates with the traditional hearty fare. Conor and Deidre were already outdoors; he could not resist photographing the medieval village that provided an idyllic backdrop to the inn. Phillipa and Stone had walked down with them; Stone, the aesthete, was drawn to the ancient stone church.

"Don't want to attract too much attention. Iris, you know." Heather pulled me along a hall that led into the quaint little sitting room in the oldest part of the inn which did not appear to be one of the "public" rooms. I checked behind the open door and there was indeed a small sign: *Private.* The ceiling in here was much lower, the woodwork darker and more burnished with age than in the comfortably chintzy guest parlor and the spacious keeping room where meals were served. Immediately I sensed a chill of secrecy in the room, despite the brisk little blaze in the fireplace. My gaze was drawn to the mantel which was crowded with an assortment of antique Toby jugs, all very charming. But my attention became fixed, with an inexplicable shiver, on one unique item, a skull, which appeared to be made of glass, at the left end of the mantel.

"Is it my imagination, or does that thing have blue eyes?" Heather was still whispering.

An eerie blue light shone through the skull's eyeholes. "There is something," I agreed. "Maybe it's a little light bulb. I think we should bring Fiona in here."

"Look at this," Heather said, tapping her black Sea-dweller Rolex watch. "As soon as I walked in here and touched that skull thing, my watch stopped. My watch *never* stops."

"Maybe it needs a new battery. Hey, let me get Fiona …"

"I had a new battery installed just before we left the States," Heather said. "My phone is fractious, too. Do you have your cell phone in your pocket?"

I did. Mine was a plain jane variety, but Heather's was a new Samsung Galaxy smartphone with multiple features I felt I could never master. Today, however, the smartphone's screen had gone dark. I opened my cell: a cheery blue checkmark lit up, time and date were displayed below.

"Mine's working," I said.

"Touch the skull," Heather suggested, giving me a little shove toward the mantel. "Go ahead."

"You know, Heather, I really don't think we should be in here fooling around with Iris's stuff."

"Just do it."

Gingerly, I went up to the mantel and reached a hesitant finger toward the blue-eyed thing.

Before I made contact, however, an icy voice from the doorway froze us both. "Excuse me, ladies. You probably didn't realize that this is our private family sitting room. I'm sure you'd be much more comfortable in the guests' parlor." Iris stood looking at us with disfavor. Martha Holstein loomed at her elbow. I'd met Martha once at a Plymouth Spiritualist Society meeting. I didn't think she'd remember me, or rather I hoped she wouldn't.

"Cassandra Shipton! I remember you," Martha declared, her bovine cheeks trembling with disapproval. "You and your friends had gone over to the dark side, as I recall."

"Oh, bollocks," Heather said crisply. "Who *is* this person, Cass?"

"Martha Holstein, may I introduce one of those *friends* to whom you refer, Heather Morgan Devlin." I suppose I threw in

Heather's maiden name because the Morgans were practically a royal family of Plymouth. But this would hardly impress Martha; the Holsteins hailed from Allentown, Pennsylvania, where they were much sought after by the would-be-haunted.

"We're very sorry for disturbing your privacy, Mrs. Harris-Jones," Heather intoned regally. "I was so enthralled when I caught sight of your delightful collection of Toby jugs, I'm afraid I couldn't resist having a closer look."

"You ought to put away that Satanic crystal skull," Martha urged Iris in a low voice. "We have to be so careful about evil vibrations and emanations. Crossed Keys could be in grave jeopardy."

"Excuse me, ladies," said Fiona's voice behind the two women in the doorway. She used her walking stick like a shoe horn to wedge herself between the two of them and enter the room, barely glancing at the bone (or skull) of contention, but fully aware of its presence. "I believe the Holsteins are here to exorcise the inn, isn't that right, Mrs. Harris-Jones?"

Our inn-keeper's long face blanched. "That damned thing. As soon as the skull, crystal or glass or whatever it is, showed up on the scene, it made a complete pig's breakfast of all our electronics. I'd have thrown it out in a heartbeat, but Reggie kept insisting that it might have some great value. Mrs. Holstein seems to believe we're the victims of some kind of demonic possession."

"Not something you'd want to advertise," I said. "The wrong sort of guests might be attracted."

"Like you lot of devil-worshippers!" Martha Holstein exclaimed.

"Oh, dearie me," Fiona said quietly. "What a lot of blather and kerfuffle over a few strangelets. If you like, we can raze those babies in a simple little ceremony."

"*Without an ordained exorcist?*" Martha screeched, chins wobbling, hands clutching a Bible to her ample bosom.

"You and your camera and your husband will be welcome, of course, to any official exorcism our circle holds. But first we should hold a wee séance to find out with whom we are trifling," Fiona continued unruffled. "Without its good and true spirit guides, a historic British inn might be as dull and uninteresting as an airport hotel. Now you wouldn't want that, would you, Mrs. Harris-Jones?"

"After all, what's so earth-shattering about a crystal skull," I scoffed. Sometimes the old clairvoyant eye can be blind as a bat.

Meanwhile, Fiona was homing in on the item in question. "Ah, but this is something special," she said, moving closer to the mantel. "Where did this artifact come from, Mrs. Harris-Jones?"

"Straight from hell," Martha Holstein declared.

"The chimney repairman found it when he was re-pointing the fireplace mortar," Iris said. "He said it had been cemented onto a little shelf right above the firebox. Coal black, it was. At that point, I thought it might be valuable, or architecturally important, so I cleaned it up and stuck the thing on the mantel until I had time to investigate. I swear that skull practically buzzed in my hand, but I put that down to imagination. Then my computer began to malfunction in the most annoying way. All the inn's records were at risk. It was Mrs. Holstein who made the connection. But every time I try to move the skull elsewhere, my computer goes down again. Reggie wants to display the skull in a glass case in the guests' parlor, but Mrs. Holstein says we should crush the damned thing and bury its pieces in the churchyard."

"*Oh, no!*" Fiona exclaimed. She looked truly horrified. I suspected it was the librarian in her that deplored the destruction of a possibly historic icon.

"I wonder who put the skull in the fireplace," Heather said. "And why."

"Fiona, you really ought to hold that séance tonight," I urged. "Maybe we can find out what's going on with the skull, perhaps relieve Mrs. Harris-Jones' mind."

"Fred! Where's Fred?" Martha shrieked, fumbling with her cell phone to call for reinforcements. Next thing, she was banging the side of the phone. "What the hell is wrong with this damned cell? Is there no frigging reception in this place? Fred's a real exorcist, and he knows about these things. And if these crazy women are going to have a séance, we must have Fred to exorcise whatever evil spirits possess the skull."

"Mrs. Holstein, you are getting your bloomers in a twist needlessly," Fiona said. She was drawing herself up into a full glamour and would not be deterred, I knew. The plump, affable, older lady slowly faded away and a tall, imperial Fiona emerged. Heather stuck her elbow in my ribs to draw my attention to the transformation, but I was already there. Martha took one look and stumbled a step backwards through the doorway. Iris put her hand flat against her breast, as if feeling for a heartbeat.

"Check this out," Heather whispered.

"I got it," I replied.

"If I can't summon up an answer after dinner tonight, you Holsteins can exorcise the hell out of the inn's electronics tomorrow," Fiona said, and swept her tartan shawl over her shoulder as grandly as if it were an ermine wrap. "And now, ladies, I believe I'll go to my room and meditate. By the way, Mrs. Harris-Jones, I do appreciate being housed on the ground floor. My knees, you know." She flourished her walking stick around the room in such a robust way as to make the two women duck back for fear of being smacked.

Barely hiding our smirks, Heather and I followed Fiona into the keeping room and helped ourselves to another cup of coffee. Phillipa was already standing near the fireplace, shivering from her tour of the stone church.

"Stone is still out there, in a frozen ecstasy over the architecture," she said.

Fiona sighed and sank into a well-padded chair. She was becoming "herself" again as the glamour faded. "I'm going to do some research on crystal skulls," she said. "If Phil's laptop isn't working because of some energy interference that's going on here, I'll give Circe La Femme a call. She's always a deep well of psychic know-how." Fiona had her own esoteric circle of far-flung wise women. Besides La Femme, who was a prominent Salem medium, she sometimes consulted with Anna Amici of the Italian *stregheria*.

"I don't know that there's anything wrong with my laptop," Phillipa said. "I haven't booted it up since we got here.

"I have an idea of the disturbance's source," I said, "but I'm waiting to see what, or who, turns up at the inn tonight."

"What about the others?" Heather wondered. She wasn't so much worried about sweet-natured Dick or imperturbable Joe, I knew, but how would Conor or Stone react to a séance?

"I suspect they'll be bored out of their skulls, so to speak, hanging around the inn while we summon up the good and evil spirits of the place. Why don't we suggest a game after dinner?" Fiona said. She reached into her reticule and brought out two new decks of cards and a box of poker chips.

"I thought Stone didn't play anything except bridge," Heather said.

"And chess," Phillipa said, with a Cheshire-cat smile.

"Never mind the card game gambit," I said. "How are we going to distract Fred and Martha from destroying that skull?"

"And what about poor Dee?" Heather said. "She'll be beside herself if you summon up any real ghosts. Doesn't the poor girl deserve a vacation from ectoplasmic high jinx?"

Fiona said, "My guess is that Dee wouldn't miss this for the world. And I wonder what Conor will make of Martha's spirit photography? He's such a lovely cynic."

"This is shaping up into *one enchanted evening*," Phillipa said.

"*... we will meet a stranger*." I felt sure that something extraordinary would occur. My sixth sense was up and running. "But first, I wonder what's for lunch?" Already I was feeling a bit peckish after the excitement of finding the skull of my dream.

"Mushroom and Watercress Soup or Curried Parsnip, ugh," Phillipa said. "I already checked. One assumes there will be sandwiches of some sort, possibly ham and cheese. The cheddar is really quite decent. Dinner is roast chicken *bonne femme*. That can be a very nice dish, if it's done right. Julia did it *en casserole* with bacon and potatoes."

CHAPTER TWENTY-TWO

Who has not felt how sadly sweet
The dream of home, the dream of home,
Steals o'er the heart, too soon to fleet,
When far o'er sea or land we roam?
Thomas Moore

Deidre and Conor blew in, fresh-cheeked and merry from their walk through the medieval village. After filling two mugs with breakfast tea, Conor regaled us with the array of family photos, dating back to our summer clambake, still stored on his camera. Gripped by a sudden nostalgic mood, the guilt of the vacationer assailed our consciences, inspiring several calls home.

It began with Phillipa who was worried about her new ward Eddie Christie, staying with the Ryan family so soon after being uprooted from living with his aunt, not that Fanny Fearley wasn't glad to be rid of his care. Betti Kinsey answered; *Bettikins*, as she was called by the children and everyone else. The diminutive housekeeper, who was usually as fiesty and unflappable as Mary Poppins, admitted that there had been one "incident" with Eddie's "readings," but nothing she couldn't manage. After all, wasn't she that used to the strange goings-on in Ms. Dee's house, between the red-eyed gargoyles and the poppets that danced off their shelf and now Miss Jenny taking after her mother's wyrding ways.

"Like, what happened with Eddie, exactly?" Phillipa would not be put off with vague digressions.

"Well, Mrs. Stern, nothing too worrisome. I'd got rid of all the newspapers, like you warned me, but some fool left a tabloid advertisement on the doorstep, and Eddie got his hands on it just as I was heading out to fetch the groceries while Mother Ryan was up and about to watch the youngsters. Eddie marched into the kitchen and announced to one and all that the roof of Sachem Superfoods had caved in with the weight of snow on it, and the market was closed for repairs, so I might as well stay home. Being forewarned about Eddie's little quirk, I decided not to point out that it hadn't even snowed yet, that the storm was forecast to begin after midnight. A coastal blizzard. The very reason I needed to get to the store before supplies of milk and bread were wiped off the shelves by a rapacious bunch of storm shoppers. But I did call a friend in the Public Works Department with a warning to watch out for Sachem's roof. Risky, that was, because now he thinks I'm totally bonkers but still needles me for what I like in the numbers this week. Thank God, he paid attention, though, sent a crew to clean off that roof first, and so far, so good. He said a flat roof like that is always trouble."

"So the future can be changed," I remarked with satisfaction when Phillipa told me of her conversation with Bettikins.

"Well, tweaked a little, maybe. The roof may yet stove in, so don't get excited. They had quite a snow storm on the South Shore, but Bettikins is coping," Phillipa said.

"She's worth her weight in doubloons," Deidre agreed. She'd made a call home also, to talk to all the children and Betti. "School's closed but at least we didn't lose power, so Jenny can play videos for the others. Bettikins said that Eddie has been really a great help to her, Phil, apart from that one incident. Not only helping to keep the young ones entertained, he also shoveled the steps and the paths very neatly after the storm, and cleaned off Mother Ryan's car so that she could head out to the casino later. Bettikins said she'd be glad to look after the little sweetheart anytime."

Phillipa beamed, her smile softened by thoughts of the boy. "Everyone falls in love with Eddie."

A mixed blessing, I thought but didn't say.

Then Heather called her new housekeepers, the troubadours Fleur and Roland de Vere, who reported that the Devlin pack had been delighted to cavort about in the deep snow left by the storm, and no, they hadn't been left outdoors too long to get chilled. The dogs had been dried off with towels and spent the rest of the day in the conservatory, wrestling with chew toys and each other. Yes, Fleur had replied to my question, Scruffy and Raffles seemed to be enjoying themselves, as well, especially Raffles, although reprimanded by a few of the females for obsessive sniffing. Scruffy, however, was a little stiff and sore with arthritis, so Fleur had given him a good rubdown with my menthol decoction, a kind of topical herbal aspirin made with wintergreen, just as I had instructed, and he was allowed to nestle by the fireplace with the De Veres, apart from the pack so that he could rest.

"Scruffy seems to have quite an ear for music," Fleur had said. "When I sing, he lays his head right on my knee and closes his eyes." *And enjoys being singled out for special attention,* I thought, feeling much less guilty for abandoning my canine companions to the Devlin menagerie.

Fiona wanted to call the MacDonalds to inquire about Laura Belle, but her relationship with her brother and his wife, the child's grandparents, was rather tenuous and she feared rocking the boat.

"By the time Christmas is over, they'll be quite ready to return little Laura to your care. Remember the last time when Laura's remarks caused some consternation." I assured her. "And if they don't send her back to you by the first of the year, we'll do a little *thing* to make it so."

"Yes, yes," Fiona said thoughtfully. "Well, I have put certain protections around the wee darling."

"I bet you have," I said.

༄

"It was a dark and stormy night," Phillipa said.

As evening came on, so did a howling wind and a drumbeat of freezing rain that threatened to turn to snow before morning.

"Beira has finally caught up with us," Fiona said.

"Beira?" Deidre looked up from her work basket, even more voluminous than Fiona's reticule, and almost as liable to astonish with its contents. Tonight, however, Deidre was domestically knitting argyle socks, one assumed for Conor. This was a work of great precision and many sharp little knitting needles.

"The Scot Queen of Winter rules the days between Samhain and Beltane," Fiona said. "She's the crone aspect of the triple Goddess."

"Personally, I rely on Demeter, the Dark Goddess, as winter comes on. And let's not forget Hecate," Phillipa said. "Has it ever struck you that Wiccans can evoke the perfect goddess for every event in the same way that Catholics zero in on the appropriate saint for every purpose?"

"Don't knock it, Phil. When the going gets tough, I depend on my saints," Deidre said. "Good old St. Anthony when something is lost. St. Francis to restore peace. St. Jude for the worst cases. Where are we going to hold the séance? If we use the parlor, won't we run the risk of being interrupted by one of the other guests? Especially the Holsteins."

"Someone ought to put a bell on that Martha," Phillipa said. "Yes, and the guys are going to be playing cards in the parlor. Bridge, if you believe it."

I had no idea that Joe even knew how to play bridge, or Dick, who seemed more the 5-card poker type. Was I guilty of making assumptions about masculinity? Apparently.

"Conor, too?"

"They need a fourth, and he agreed, albeit reluctantly. His grandmother Eileen is a bridge addict, so he does know the game," Deidre said. "I suppose, if I want to please my *possible* future grandmother-in-law, I'll learn myself."

"Why don't you wait and see how she reacts when you come clean about the kiddoes," Phillipa suggested. "No sense learning bridge to please the old busybody if she's only going to throw you down the castle stairs."

We'd met in the bar for our pre-séance conference, a low-ceiling, smoke stained place with small-paned windows that distorted whatever was on the other side. The room looked as if it would be no surprise to a couple of highwaymen hoisting tankards at one of the time-distressed tables in the darkest corner. The lights were low and threw strange shadows on the paneled walls, but the fireplace was blazing comfortably. Reggie Harris-Jones was bar-tending.

He removed the unlit pipe from this mouth and said, "Whatever you ladies are up to, I think you'll find a quiet corner in the keeping room at this time of night, with the kitchen closed. One of the girls has already banked the fire for the night, I believe."

Fiona took a familiar pamphlet out of her reticule, *Séances Made Simple,* and spread it out on the bar next to her glass of Drambuie. Personally, I thought she knew the instructions by heart, but apparently there were certain deviations in the appendices on which she was refreshing her mind. "I think we'll use wine glasses. They'll testify to unseen presence as reliably as a trance medium. Would you like to join us?" Fiona invited hospitably.

"No, thanks," Reggie said. "Iris would not be best pleased."

"Reggie," Heather said in her most charming voice, "you'd started to tell us about a ghost story or legend connected to Crossed Keys, but you were called away. Maybe you should tell us now, so we'll know what apparitions to expect."

Gazing sadly at the cold pipe in his hand (*how long since Iris had allowed him to light it?*) Reggie held forth with a story he may have told many times. "The Dutch couple who owned the inn before us, the Assendorps, said there was a ghostly presence in the old part of the house that used to thump up and down the little parlor until someone would turn on a light. It looked as if the ghost was trying to find something in the fireplace. There would often be a scattering of soot and chunks of mortar found on the hearth rug in the morning. According to the Assendorps, the old man who owned the place originally had been found dead in that room, and he was reputed to be a smuggler or a pirate or something like that, so they always believed he might be the one haunting the place, looking for hidden loot."

We were all listening now. "And what was his name?" Heather asked.

"Tell you the truth, I forget. Might have been Wright or White. Or Witte."

"First name?" Deidre asked.

"Murray or Morgan, something like that."

We looked at each other without comment.

"Okay, let's get séancing, then," Heather said briskly, reaching up to remove three empty wine glasses from the overhead rack. "Thanks, Reggie. I'll return these later.'

"I don't think you'll see the Holsteins down here tonight. *Shards and splinters, rubble and trouble,* Fred Holstein predicted you ladies would stir up tonight. He warned me to stay clear of your séance for fear of the evil ones." Reggie put the unlit pipe back in his mouth. Conversation over.

"Holy Mother!" Deidre said. "What those two don't know about spirits of the dead could fill a book. And probably will."

Fiona said, "That reminds me, we'll need a chant."

"Working on it," Phillipa said.

CHAPTER TWENTY-THREE

But, soft: behold! lo where it comes again!
I'll cross it, though it blast me. - Stay, illusion!
If thou hast any sound, or use a voice,
Speak to me.
    William Shakespeare

The lights of the keeping room had been dimmed down to two brass sconces on either side of the massive stone fireplace, and the fire banked to glowing embers under ashes.

Deidre put away her sock work and shuddered. "How do I let myself get talked into things like this?" she complained.

"There's a part of you that wants this," I suggested, knowing the ambivalent relationship I have with my own psychic nature. "Make friends with it."

We met for our séance at the same round table where we'd had dinner, and where we would probably continue to gather while we were guests at Crossed Keys. Any table we ever chose immediately seemed to have our names carved on it, and other guests treated it as "Reserved."

Deidre found candles in the tin-lined "porridge drawer" of a weighty old Welsh dresser; we stuck those in holders. Heather had brought her special Goddess candle for the centerpiece. It was white with tiny silver pentagrams imbedded in the wax, silver being sacred to Hecate in particular. Although this was a séance not a Sabbat, just to be certain that we would be working in sacred space (and no evil entities could wander into it), Heather cast our circle with her silver-handled athame. The rest of us lit the four found candles one by one as the quarters were called, representing the four directions;

Heather lit the Goddess candle. The scent of ancient spices swirled around us. The three wine glasses were placed in the middle, between the five flickering flames. Outside in the night, the wind continued to wail its counterpoint, the perfect accompaniment to a séance.

"Let's touch little fingers around the table," Fiona said. One of the glasses slid toward her hand. She pushed it back. "Heather, this is your quest. You call the spirits, and we'll all chime in on Phil's chant."

Heather gazed at the ceiling for a moment, then sang out "Family of Nathaniel Morgan, to me! Morgans, to me! We have come here according to your wishes. What would you have us take away from this inn?"

Silence is never truly silent. Our silence that evening was full of wind, rain, and old-house creaks and groans.

Phillipa began our chant:

> *May the Elders guard our circle,*
> *Evil cannot enter here.*
> *Morgan spirits who have called us,*
> *Let us feel you close and near.*
> *While the veil is thin between us,*
> *Speak your vision, true and clear.*

This we repeated thirteen times, at first in ringing tones, then ever more softly until we barely whispered the last refrain.

The wine glasses slid between the candles. Fiona caught one and Heather another, but the third smashed itself to splinters on the stone floor.

"There's a column of mist by the fireplace," Fiona said. "Does anyone else see it?"

In her high, clear voice, Deidre spoke in a direction to the right of the fireplace. "Why have you called us here? What do you want of us?" Evidently, she was addressing a visible entity that the rest of us saw only as mist.

"Is it the hanged man again?" Phillipa asked, peering into the same direction but obviously seeing nothing. "Agent of sacrifice and change."

"Just for a moment, I saw a man's face, no scar," I said.

Suddenly there was a loud crash somewhere outside. I heard the men in the other room rushing to see out the parlor windows. But we didn't move a muscle.

We sat frozen to our chairs because, at the instant of that noisy distraction, an image had revealed itself, to all of us this time. He appeared in front of the fireplace, a tall gaunt man with the hangman's rope around his neck, open shirt, red scarf around his middle, torn breeches, a manacle around each of his ankles, attached to one another by a chain that would have allowed only short steps. His bronze hair was blowing in a phantom breeze. A shiver as cold as death chilled us to the very bone. He smiled, but it was all rather ghastly. A whiff of acrid smoke wafted through the room. I'd never seen a ghost so plainly, and would be perfectly happy never to repeat the experience.

His eyes, piercing with a light that was not of this world, looked directly at Heather. The color drained from her face, but she stood, facing the apparition and keeping one hand on her chair for support. "This must be Benedict Morgan," she whispered. "Hecate, preserve us."

The voice that floated from the specter's throat and filled the room was harsh and ragged. "The power of the skull. It's for you, woman. The Morgan legacy. Take it and keep it away from others who will seek to destroy you to possess it. Treasures of time will be yours. Guard the secrets of the skull." Immediately the image began to fade.

"*Wait a frigging minute*," Heather cried. "What in Hades am I supposed to *do* with the thing?"

"Try to speak more courteously to a specter," Fiona whispered. "At least, say *thank you*."

"*Thank you*, Great-great-great Uncle Benedict, or whoever you are," Heather said. "Oh, bollocks, he's disappearing fast."

The ghost's last words were barely audible. "Remember… we are Morgans, Morgans, Morg …"

Heather slumped into the chair she'd been using to lean on during the confrontation. "Couldn't he have just tossed us a moneybag of gold Napoleons, or cache of precious jewels ripped off traveling royalty? That skull belongs to the Harris-Joneses now."

"It seems as if the skull has some magic qualities that are unknown to Iris and Reggie," Fiona said. "Best if we don't enlighten them just yet."

Meanwhile, out in the parlor, the men were shouting that some tree had come down in the front yard and half of it was hanging off the roof, propped up on the gutter, threatening the bay window in the parlor.

We heard Reggie rush into the parlor and fling open the front door. "We have to push that broken tree off the house," he cried in alarm.

Iris soon followed him, screaming directions to Reggie as well as to Joe, Conor, and Dick who were recruited to help. Donning anoraks, boots, and gloves thrown their way by Iris, they hurried outdoors to save the window, if that would be possible. Several of the Inn's guests in various states of nightwear, including the Holsteins, came flooding down the stairs. Stone was on his cell phone, trying to raise some official assistance.

Martha, however, was less interested in the calamity in the front yard than in what we five were about in the keeping room. She tottered in sideways on high heel slippers, taking in our table at a glance.

"Brides of Satan in our midst," she screamed, her jowls trembling with agitation. "Don't you realize what you're bringing down upon us? That tree hanging off the house right now is the devil's work, the devil you raised."

"I think you can blame that one on Mother Nature not Satan," Phillipa said, plainly quite irritated with this attack of the mad cow. "Not that we believe in Satan, who was, after all, a Christian invention. Our religion goes back much, much farther, lady."

But Martha, with all her erratic energy at full tilt, had inadvertently crashed through the circle that Heather had cast to protect us. Now it was irretrievably broken. The air began vibrating with unseen beings that had been lurking in the dark corners of the candlelit room. They'd crept through the door our séance opened but hadn't been able to penetrate our circle while it was still intact. We began to see black shapes writhing at the edges of the room.

"Strangelets," Fiona muttered. "I'll have to get rid of them before they take that crazy woman down."

She swung her walking stick in the air, maneuvering it like a wand, and pointed at the apparitions. *"Cease and begone, cease and begone …"* she uttered in her low, imperious magical voice, which in its own way was louder than any shout of warning. *"Children of darkness, get out of our sight, go back to dimensions of bottomless night."*

The creatures squealed like rats, and one of them slid toward Martha, who either saw or felt it, her face going bloodless with horror. She screamed and fainted dead away, toppling with a heavy thud onto the stone floor amid shards of broken glass.

Hearing the commotion, Fred Holstein blustered into the keeping room and fell to his knees at his wife's side. He lifted her head and cried into her ear, "Martha, Martha, what have they done to you? Are you taken?"

"If that doesn't wake her, nothing will," Phillipa muttered, as she wrung a cloth in cold water at the serving sink.

Deidre and I were already crouched beside the woman, she brushing away glass, and I holding Fiona's smelling salts under Martha Holstein's nose. "It's all right, Martha. The room is clean and clear now," I assured her. Phillipa handed me the cold cloth, and I placed it across her forehead. I could hear Fiona behind me, sweeping through the room with her cane-wand, continuing with her *strangelet-begone* chant. I thought that I'd write that chant down in my Book of Shadows as soon as things quieted down. A gal can never tell when she might need to banish some imp from Hades.

Fred had taken out what looked like a pocket-size Bible and a small bottle. Holy water, I assumed, as he sprinkled it liberally over his wife, imploring Satan and all his minions to remove themselves from his wife. The Bible passage he read was "I command you in the name of Jesus Christ to come out of her."

Putting her small hand on his shoulder, Deidre joined in, calling on the Catholic exorcism prayer from memory, "We drive you from us whoever you may be, unclean spirits, infernal invaders, all wicked legions, assemblies, and sects."

A few moments later, Martha sat up, somewhat bewildered and not quite as strident as she had been when she'd entered the room. "Was the Devil after me, Fred?"

"Don't worry, dear. I drove it out of you," Fred said, patting her hand.

Martha hiccupped, and said, "Where's my camera, Fred? Didn't you bring my camera? Do I have to think of everything? We'll write this place up for *Fate*, and maybe there'll even be a TV follow-up."

"Iris will love that, Martha," Phillipa said. But Iris was not party to the Holsteins' plan to feature their inn in an article for

Fate magazine which undoubtedly would be titled something
like "The Crossed Keys Horror in Amesbury"

Meanwhile the front door, not quite latched when the men
rushed outdoors to rescue the bay window, was thumping and
clattering, and the Crossed Key sign banging as if it would
splinter apart at any moment. Possibly not, though. That sign
had obviously weathered many an evil night since its early days
as a refuge for pirates and smugglers. I was betting it would
survive another stormy onslaught.

Heather and I deserted the others to see what was going on
in the parlor. Conor stumbled indoors in a streaming anorak
and brushed the water off his face. "Christ, what a job! Reggie
has an axe, and if he doesn't do himself a mischief or demolish
the bay window with it, I'll be damned surprised. Dick and Joe
are pulling the tree off the house, and Reggie is chopping away
at it. Iris, we need a rope."

Iris hurried away to the back of the house. Conor's vivid
description of the axe had me worried, so I put on my own
parka and rushed outdoors to make certain that Joe wasn't in
danger. Conor soon followed with the coil of rope that Iris had
found, and Iris, suitably bundled up, went with him.

"Reggie, Reggie, you be careful with that thing," Iris
screamed over the wind's shriek. With a rope thrown over the
shattered half of the tree, it could be pulled off the house when
chopped free by the wild blows of Reggie, who was hacking
away manfully while Dick held the rattling window frame in
place. Suddenly, like the finish of a tug-o-war, the branch gave
way, the half attached to the tree swinging up, and the half
attached to the rope springing down, taking Joe with it. He
landed with a thump on the small front lawn.

I ran over to see if he was all right. He was laughing. I gave
him my hand and he jumped up off the ground. "That's the most
action I've seen since we came to Britain," he said, throwing an
arm around me. I translated that as, he missed going to sea on
crazed Greenpeace missions rather than attending high-level
directors' meetings on land.

"Stick with me, honey, and I promise we'll see plenty
of action," I said, hugging him back. Based on history and
prescience, I was sure this was true.

He whispered a suggestion in my ear. "That, too," I said.

CHAPTER TWENTY-FOUR

Ladies, whose bright eyes
Rain influence, and judge the prize.
  John Milton

Afterwards we crowded into the bar where Reggie was celebrating saving the bay window by serving complementary rum toddies. Its diamond panes, he explained, dated back to the 18th century when the inn was built and would have been an irreplaceable loss.

Since we were joined by the Holsteins, we couldn't very well discuss another 18th century artifact that was most pressing to us at present.

"Let's go to the Ladies' loo," Heather whispered to Phillipa and me.

"Oh, no, you don't," Deidre whispered back. "You are *not* leaving me out of whatever you're up to."

With a quick glance our way, Fiona engaged Martha in a friendly discussion about the best sort of camera to use in spirit photography. Could she, for instance, rely on her iPhone to capture that unexpected spectral sighting?

The closest ladies room was rather small for a conference of four, but we managed. "Here's the thing," Heather said. "We've got to get that skull away from Iris and Martha. It's clear that the restless Morgan spirits have called me here with the intention that I should possess the skull, for reasons that I don't fully understand. Yet. And by the way, they wouldn't have become restless and led us here if you lot hadn't insisted on that séance at Burial Hill last Samhain. So you have to help me see it through."

"Of course we will!" Deidre enthused. "That skull was really intended to be your legacy from your great-great-great pirate, Heather, so why don't we simply steal it? That shouldn't be much more difficult than ripping off a towel or two."

"Not on your life!" Phillipa exclaimed. "I've been doing my damndest to keep you all out of the Old Bailey ever since we landed at Heathrow, and I'm not going to allow you to try anything so stupid now that we're clear of London. Besides, it's simple. *Buy the skull.*"

"Possible ..." Heather said thoughtfully.

"But if Iris says no, then what?" I threw on the bucket of cold water that was usually Phillipa's province. "If Iris refuses to sell and then the skull disappears, suspicion will naturally fall on Heather."

"Well, at least Heather has a smart solicitor, gorgeous Laurence Watson," Phillipa sighed. "Worst case scenario, at least we'd meet up with him again."

"Here's what I think," Deidre said. "Before you ever hit up Iris to sell you the thing, we do a little brainwashing with a touch of motivational magic. Fix it so she's afraid to keep the skull on the premises. Goddess knows the Holsteins have already got her pretty skittish."

There was a sharp rap at the door. "Dee darlin', did you fall in there and need my help?"

"Conor's getting restless," Deidre whispered. "Let's take this up again tomorrow. We'll just have to find a way to shake the guys for a while. Honestly, gals like us need a little time on our own to conspire and work the odd spell."

"That's easy," Phillipa said. "Christmas shopping. Best shopping excuse in the world." My friend's nostalgic smile made me wonder just when, where, and with whom she'd stolen off during the Christmas hustle in times past.

So it was agreed. After breakfast the next morning (blessedly clear and bright after last night's storm) we explained that we needed to tour those adorable little antique shops we'd seen when we drove into town. We'd be buying gifts for the children and for the guys, too, so we couldn't have them trailing along.

"But we'll have to come back with packages," Deidre worried as we five set off on foot to explore the Dickensian street. She put a firm little arm into Fiona's to keep her steady on the slippery cobblestones. Wrapped head to toe in what she called the Shopping Macdonald tartan, a bit brighter than the muted Hunting tartan, Fiona stumped along bravely with her stick on one side and Deidre on the other.

"*Shop fast,*" Phillipa instructed. "That darling book store would be a good start. Something Sherlock Holmesian for Stone would be just the ticket."

"A lovely illustrated *Alice in Wonderland* for Laura Belle," Fiona said.

I thought about a really classy edition of *The Ancient Mariner* for Joe. Or *Moby Dick.* Yes!

So we did *shop fast*, and trudged on with our packages to a tiny bright and cheery tea shop at the end of the street, so different from the Crossed Keys Inn with its historical angst. Phillipa waved her hand dismissively at the shy girl waitress. "Oh, just bring us a pot of coffee and a basket of whatever you've got. With plenty of clotted cream."

Over warm scones, we hatched our scheme to detach Iris from the crystal skull.

"We need to inspire Martha to denounce the skull," Fiona said. "I suggest whiff of sulfur, a.k.a. brimstone, my dears."

I did have some sulfur in my Witches First Aid kit, for use in exorcism or for protection, although it could be a bit risky, that bright yellow powder being so powerful and unstable that it was just as liable to brew up negative spirits as to banish them. But the point was, old-time Christians associate sulfur with the fires of hell. So if we burned a bit of sulfur where Martha Holstein would get a whiff and connect it with the skull, she would run away screaming about Satan to Iris.

What we didn't count on was the power of the crystal skull itself to decide into whose hands it would fall. Although we didn't think to ask it for help, the skull had its own agenda.

Before we left the tea room, just to seal our intentions, we held hands around the little table and said a few words, improvised by Phillipa.

All who possess the skull today
Should tremble and beware ...
The legacy can only be
Held by the rightful Morgan heir.

"Oh, but let's do the sulfur thing anyway," Deidre said gleefully.

"Smells like rotten eggs," Phillipa complained. "Sort of a high school prank, don't you think?"

"If you ever have to exorcise a ghost, you'll be glad of a little sulfur," Fiona admonished. "And I believe we have promised to do just that before we leave Crossed Keys."

"I think Iris and Reggie will have had quite enough of our psychic meddling," I said.

"Yes, let's leave them a ghost or two just for a proper historic atmosphere. But personally, I prefer to live in an architecturally designed, ultra-modern ranch house, every board and stone of it blessedly new," Phillipa said. "Not a creak or a groan or a clanking of chains at midnight."

"Well, my house is a fairly new Garrison Colonial," Deidre said, "but some of the poppets I've made keep coming to life at the witching hour and dancing off their shelf."

"That's because you had something witchy in mind when you made them, Dee. What did you expect?" Phillipa said.

"Ladies, ladies," Fiona said. "Cease the squabbling at once! We are Wise Women not the Golden Girls of Plymouth. And we have a mission to fulfill. We must return the crystal skull to its rightful owner, Heather Morgan, of a long line of sea-faring, treasure-hunting Morgans, because only then will we find out what powers it's meant to confer upon us." She wrapped herself grandly in the Shopping MacDonald shawl, picked up her walking stick, and stalked majestically out of the tea room in (I swear it!) a trail of sparkly dust, leaving us to scramble after her with our purchases.

"How does she do that? And what in Hades happened to her arthritic knees?" Phillipa muttered.

❧

Deidre, who was small and quick and had not been caught in the off-limits parlor previously, was commissioned to sneak in there and drop a pinch of sulfur into the fire just as Iris and Martha were heading that way. Shortly after lunch, she got her chance; the two women began some argument out of our hearing and headed past us toward the front rooms that comprised the old inn. Deidre scurried ahead of them.

"I think you exaggerate, Martha," Iris was saying as she brushed past our table.

"My experience with this sort of evil is unequalled in the annals of possession. Why, I remember one place in Ireland— that innkeeper wouldn't listen to me either ..." Martha replied, the rest of her story lost as she bustled on.

We lingered as long as we could, until we were inveigled by Stone into a pilgrimage to the lovely stone church which some of us had not yet toured.

"Worked like a charm!" Deidre chuckled, meeting up with us in the keeping room where we gathered for hot tea after the frigid church. "Details later."

After tea, we whisked Deidre into the parlor. Conor and Joe had gone outside with Reggie to admire their prowess of the night before. Stone sprawled in a cushioned, chintz-covered chair engrossed in a fiendish crossword puzzle from the *London Times*, paying no attention to us. Seated on the windowseat, Dick was intermittingly checking text messages from Dr. Wolf and watching the last rays of the early winter sunset through the bay's charming diamond panes. He made room for Heather to sit beside him, still scrolling and gazing.

Deidre launched into her report. "One whiff of rotten eggs, and Martha jumped like a burro with a burr under its blanket. I ducked out the other door, but I did see the woman rush toward the mantel holding two fingers like a cross in front of her. And say, what do you know? The skull's eyes lit up with that eerie cobalt light, and Martha screamed blue murder."

"What's a 6-letter word for explosive sausage?" Stone asked.

"Banger," Phillipa said. "How did Iris react?"

"She was cool with it at first. She said she'd seen Ol' Blue Eyes before. Went up to the mantel as bold as can please and gave it a little push into place between the Toby jugs. But when she touched it, the skull began to emit this high-pitched whine, the blue light in its eyes went on and off like some kind of demented Morse code. As if that weren't enough, the skull appeared to jump off the shelf and hurl itself at Iris. That did it. Mrs. Harris-Jones screamed and fainted, and Mrs. Holstein cut and ran, didn't even stop to see if Iris was alive or dead. Fortunately, the skull landed on a wing chair by the fireplace."

"Holy Hecate, what did you do then?" Heather asked.

"Rushed into the room, all innocence, and revived Iris as best I could without Fiona's smelling salts," Deidre said. "Luckily, I did have a little lavender spray in my workbag, so I gave Iris a spurt of that. Disgusting smell, sulfur, but it was wearing off a bit and the lavender seemed to help. I sprayed the whole room while I was about it, then I picked up the skull and restored it to the mantel. It flashed a little blue-eye at me in a friendly way. By that time, Martha had returned with Fred, a large silver cross, and a Bible, so I left them to the wrap-up."

"This might be an excellent moment to offer to buy the skull," I suggested to Heather.

"You're buying that crystal thing?" Dick, who had been gazing out of the window abstractedly, suddenly zeroed in on our conference.

"Yes, of course, sweetie," Heather smiled up at her husband as if buying a crystal skull were the most natural thing in the world. "Because I think that's the very Morgan legacy that I was bequeathed by the pirate branch of the family tree. Think of it as sort of a quest. Like searching for the Holy Grail, but not exactly."

"You can say that again," Phillipa said.

"Like searching for the Holy Grail?" Heather grinned. "Different quests for different crests. The Morgan family crest, now, is a rampant lion on a field of vines. Motto, *Spero et Spiro*, Onward and Upward. Morgan is Welsh and has sometimes been spelled Morgaine, how's that for a legendary fillip?"

"*Mor* means the sea, and *gan* or *gaine* is for circle," Fiona added.

"Is that perfect, or what!" Deidre exclaimed.

"The MacDonald family crest," Fiona continued, "or one of them, is a Viking ship with three oars. There's an interesting bit of history there …"

Just then, Joe, Conor, and Reggie stamped indoors, sparing us further excursions into the MacDonald marauding past. Joe went off with Reggie to gather tools needed to secure the Crossed Keys sign that had taken a beating in the storm and was now hanging askew. Conor perched on a bench near the hearth and reviewed the recent photos on his camera. Talk turned to the winter solstice sunrise at Stonehenge on Friday. Sunrise wasn't until eight, but we would be leaving by limousine at six with Ernie Cooper driving. A crowd of over three thousand celebrants was predicted. A day or so later, depending on our various itineraries, we would fly home for Christmas.

"Three thousand solstice crazies beating drums, playing on flutes, ringing bells, singing and dancing, and Goddess knows what else," Phillipa complained. "Did you know there were 'only' fifty or so arrests on drug charges at the winter solstice last year? Hardly a spiritual experience, but here we are ..."

"My dear Phil," Fiona said. "One never knows when and where one's spirit may be touched with wisdom and enlightenment. A solitary walk on the cliffs of Manomet or the fifth inning of a series game at Fenway. Don't sweat the solstice. *The heart has its reasons which reason knows not of.*"

Phillipa gave me a "look" and shrugged helplessly.

Heather said, "Suppose Iris agrees to sell me the crystal skull now that she fears it's possessed by the devil, how in Hades will I get it home?"

"Buy a set of dishes or something and have it shipped. Tuck the skull into a soup tureen in the same package, and just pay the VAT on your china invoice," I suggested.

"That sounds illegal somehow," Phillipa said, glancing at Stone, who was still concentrating on the *London Times* crossword.

"*Harm none, and do as ye will.*" Deidre stated the Wiccan rule crisply. "Okay, let's make it all above board. Buy a few more books at that cute little shop down the street and ship them home. You can declare the value quite honestly by adding whatever Iris soaks you for the skull, with her invoice, and label the goods 'books and artifacts'. Paste on lots of labels from the shop. Fiona might be persuaded to do one of her baffle thingies over the package, you know, to avoid close questioning of the goods."

"Excellent!" Fiona approved.

Although apparently absorbed in his review of photos, Conor looked up and said, "I am shocked—shocked, I tell you—to learn of my fiancée's ability to connive and dissemble."

We exchanged glances. The word "fiancée" had rather jumped out at us all, even Deidre.

☙

Iris Harris-Jones, as it turned out, was just as well pleased to sell her artifact from hell to a potty American tourist for a mere £199. And she supplied an invoice for "crystal artwork."

Carefully wrapping up the skull, Heather packed it with several books she'd bought for Christmas gifts, including a lovely medieval songbook for the De Veres. Patting the skull's head thoughtfully, she whispered, "Bon Voyage, little friend. I still don't know why I have you or what I'm supposed to do with you, but I never look a gift skull in the mouth. Besides, your teeth are bared anyway, and your jaw is even jointed. Rather a neat work of art." The skull's eyeholes blinked blue for one moment and then went dull as Heather enclosed it in tissue paper.

After the package was wrapped, addressed, blessed, and baffled (a Fiona humming spell meant to cause confusion to any over-zealous customs official), Heather called her housekeepers, the De Veres, to caution them to watch out for an important Express mail package from Britain that might arrive before she did. If so, be sure to bring it inside, away from weather and the dog pack, and to keep it safe until she and Dick returned for Christmas. She reminded Roland please to purchase a Christmas tree, and if they were so inclined, trim it with some Victorian decorations they would find on the top shelf of the storage room next to the pantry. She neglected, however, to caution them to keep the package a secret. In fact, Heather even told them that it contained a precious crystal skull with magic properties.

The package, because it included books and was sent by the fastest Express Air Mail from the cute little village post office, would cost almost as much to ship as the price of the skull itself. "Our little blue-eyed friend will probably be there before we are. I'm just dying to play around with its powers, if there are any," Heather said.

I was looking out the window at that moment, admiring how brilliant the winter landscape was now that the storm was over, as if it had washed everything clean. Then a black cloud seemed to come before my eyes, and I saw that package being held by hands that looked faintly familiar.

"Something could go wrong," I said. "A black cloud just came over everything outdoors, and I saw ..."

"Shades of *Dark Victory*," Phillipa said impatiently. "*Neither snow nor rain nor heat nor gloom of night* will stay that package, my dear. We did the pentagram thing, and Fiona baffled it, and sprinkled the package with some stuff from her reticule. Nothing can possibly go wrong."

"Corn pollen," Fiona said. "Many crystal skulls have been carved in South America. Copies of Aztec originals, so it is believed. *Táádidíín* or corn pollen is like a Navajo prayer for protection and continuity of life."

"How will I know if this skull is an Aztec original or a reproduction?" Heather mused.

"*By their works ye shall know them*," Fiona said enigmatically.

CHAPTER TWENTY-FIVE

I speak cold silent words a stone might speak
If it had words or consciousness ...
  Robert Pack

The stones! Even with the crowd that had already assembled at that early hour, the standing stones in the dim pre-dawn lightening of the winter sky were a breath-taking sight that would almost bring us to our knees if we weren't being held up by the mob of celebrants in every kind of bizarre outfit, clapping, stamping, and making variant music.

So having made our pilgrimage on the right day at the right time, with solstice "open access" tickets obtained for us by Larry Watson, we were near the center of the monument, a cluster of white-robed Druids on one side of us, chanting in Gaelic, and a gang of new-agers in rainbow masks banging drums on the other. The air smelled of incense, perfumed but not necessarily clean bodies, nicotine, a whiff of pot somewhere, and a freshening chill wind coming over Salisbury plain from the Northeast.

Conor and Joe had accompanied us. Stone had begged off to go have a farewell pint with his constabulary hosts. Dick had volunteered to tote Heather's many purchases to the village post office. Besides the box of "books and artifacts" already sent expensively by Express Mail, she'd managed to buy additional Christmas gifts in each of the inviting little shops with their Dickensian decorations, far too much to be tucked into her luggage. These packages would be sent by Priority Mail.

Our two stalwarts took their guardianship of our persons very seriously, rewarding any jostling of us with an equal shove back and a menacing look.

"You ladies had better stay close together," Conor advised. "It's a fierce mob of revelers you've got us into." Nevertheless, Deidre's feisty companion was in his element, holding the Nikon above his head to capture amazing elements of the celebration that we would admire later, like the silhouette of two lovers kissing between the stones and a ballet dancer in an exquisite pose just as the rising sun pierced through at its appointed place, brilliantly glimpsed through the gate formed by a lintel. I don't know how he did it in the midst of all those heads and shoulders angling for a better view.

It was a brutally cold pre-dawn morning, but the skies were promisingly clear. "The sun will be aligned with the central Altar stone, the Slaughter stone, and the Heel stone," Fiona informed us, as if we had not all read every scrap of literature on the subject.

"There are a few ruffians here that I'd like to sacrifice on that Slaughter stone," Phillipa grumbled, but she drew a deep breath in unspoken awe as the sun inched up over the horizon. Deidre, on my other side, was jumping up and down with excitement.

It was different for me. As the sun dazzled its way through the stone gate, the raucous cheering, merry-making, drumming, and shrieking seemed to fade away as if someone had tuned down a radio to its lowest volume. I was transfixed in the place where I stood with an elemental joy such as I had rarely felt in my life. It seemed as if all of the past and future had come down to this one moment in which I was completely present, walking the razor's edge, the absolute *now*. I felt Joe's warm, strong body right at my back, with a hand on each side of my waist to guard me from the jostling herd. It seemed to me that we were enclosed together in a connection of spirit that transcended place and time and from which nothing was lacking, perfectly complete eternal love.

I was, in fact, quite transported to another dimension, and if someone hadn't knocked Fiona awry, I might never have come back to earth.

❧

Wedged tightly together, not to lose one another in the crowd, we were all thrown off balance when Fiona stumbled, but agile Heather managed, with Deidre's help, to pull her back up again. One of the two young men who had barreled into our circle was the target of a sharp kick from Conor. The other, taking instant advantage of the situation, jumped for the Nikon. Joe shoved him back with a powerful shoulder, and the hooded kid stumbled away trying to catch his balance.

"Are you all right, Fiona?" Deidre, holding Fiona's other hand, had nearly landed on top of her.

Fiona caught her breath, then used it to cry out *"My reticule, my reticule ... a pox on that little thief who ran off with my reticule! Let go ... let me go after him."* Fiona snatched up her walking stick from the ground and began waving it around in a threatening manner, attempting to draw the rapier within. Joe caught hold of it and held it with the same steely grip that had pulled many a clumsy activist out of the sea.

General panic ensued, with the police pounding into the fray. Before they could ever reach us, however, Deidre and Conor were off like two foxes after the "bloody hooligans", as Conor called them, weaving through the crowd to track down the thugs who had tumbled Fiona and robbed her.

Conor caught up with one of the opportunistic thieves, backed the fellow up against an upright column, and administered a quick hard punch to the midsection that doubled him up. Luckily, the moss green bag was found tucked inside his hooded sweatshirt, because his buddy got away, slipping easily from Deidre's grasp. Conor and Deidre were pleased enough with themselves, however, to have recovered the treasured reticule for Fiona, and they blew off the incident to the police constables who had come to investigate Fiona's screams. *All's well that ends well*, and how do you identify two hooligans in hooded sweatshirts amid hundreds of worshippers and revelers jumping around the circle of standing stones?

Later that morning, as we ate a hearty English breakfast at our regular round table in the Crossed Keys' keeping room, there was considerable teasing of Fiona, who had so often warned us off the dark side of magic, counseling patience and compassion and *karma will get 'em*. Had we not heard her invoking a pox on the young thief and witnessed her making as if to run him through with her lethal walking stick?

Fiona sighed deeply. "There are some things too dear to be lost to the callous thievery of young sociopaths. And there are some transgressions too heinous to go unpunished."

"I am writing those words down in my little notebook right here, *The Wiccan Wisdom of Fiona MacDonald Ritchie*, that I keep in my handbag." Phillipa had taken a small moleskin notebook and a Mont Blanc pen out of her Gucci handbag and was waving it under Fiona's nose. "We'll remind you of this lapse in white magic when one of us finds ourselves tempted to turn some miscreant into a toad."

Fiona signed again. "The art of that hex, turning a man into a frog or a pig or whatever has been more or less lost in antiquity. That's why it's so important to keep notes in one's book of shadows. You think you'll remember the exact spell, but memory can be quite slippery."

"I sense a change of subject coming on," Deidre said. "Speaking of *slippery*."

"I'm just glad as hell we got back here without any unwanted attention from the Stonehenge cops, so we can catch our flights tomorrow without problems," Joe said.

Phillipa said, "It's always something of a neat trick for us ladies to fly out under the radar."

"Not to worry, darling," Stone said. "I have some high-up contacts in the UK law enforcement now. They have your depositions on the Hamid affair in hand. If you keep a low profile for one more day, I think we can get home in good order."

I took little part in the merry brunch conversation. I was still in a state of mild euphoria. Later I asked Joe, "Did you feel …"

"Yes, I did," he said, holding me close. "Now and forever."

⚭

Later, we five held a quiet Yule Sabbat in Fiona's room, where we could be private for a little while. Every room had a fireplace, and a lovely little blaze was burning for our ceremony. Fiona cast the circle with her antique Scottish dagger, which was not quite long enough to be called a "dirk," but was awesome nonetheless. The mantel became our altar, decorated with evergreens (for immortality) and mistletoe (for healing and fertility), the hearth aglow with candles and redolent with frankincense and myrrh. We sang our invocation to Demeter, the Dark Goddess, and exchanged our personal gifts: tiny bottles of blessing oil from my own recipe, amulets with diamond chips from Deidre, and, of course, Heather's candles, different for each of us, imbedded with bright symbols to encourage our yearnings to manifest. Fiona presented us with miniature medicine bags containing Navajo magic of stone, bone, feather, and pollen. Phillipa had made each of us a "tarot box," with different Rider cards laminated on the top. Golden-haired Queen of Cups for Deidre, robust Queen of Wands for Heather, the powerful High Priestess for Fiona, and the Star of hidden knowledge for me.

Every Yule we'd celebrated had inspired its own theme; this year's Yule was pregnant with mysterious and secret possibilities. I thought it must be the influence of the Morgan skull at work.

The next day we flew home to the States, to our families, to Christmas, and to some surprising new incidents connected to Heather's crystal skull and Eddie Christie's disturbing prophecies.

CHAPTER TWENTY-SIX

Within that awful volume lies
The mystery of mysteries!
　　Sir Walter Scott

Since I'd steeled myself against the usual onslaught of grievances and canine hypochondria, I was mighty surprised not to be assaulted with complaints while we were driving Scruffy and Raffles home after our fortnight in England.

Hey, Toots, that girl who sings to us is all right. She knows how to rub sore muscles real good, and she smells of cookies. You can bring her here. We wouldn't mind.

Wouldn't mind. Wouldn't mind. Raffles agreed with his sire.

"You're not complaining about the dog pack? Or the food?"

Those dumb dogs were running around outdoors freezing their asses while I got myself a comfy place by the fire with the girl, the music, and some decent treats. The kid kept himself busy checking out the females, didn't catch on they were all fixed, the poor dumb pup. Scruffy barked the canine equivalent of a quiet chuckle. *The chow is still disgusting, but the girl dropped me a nice oily fish or a neck bone when I wouldn't eat the twigs and bark.*

"She fed you chicken necks!" I was appalled.

Don't get your tail in a twist, Toots. A good fat chicken neck never killed a guy with big strong teeth like mine. I just grind up those babies to a mish-mash.

"I'm going to have a word with that Fleur," I said.

Joe, who had been listening quietly while driving us home, pulled up in our driveway and said, "I wouldn't rock the boat, if I were you, sweetheart. Scruffy is obviously in good health and fine spirits. And we'll need a sitter for New Years Eve. I have plans for us." Then he looked back and met Scruffy's bold gaze with a bolder gaze of his own. "What happens at the Devlins' place, better stay at the Devlins', old guy."

Just WHO does he think he's calling old guy? With his grizzled gray furry face? Ha ha.

Ha ha. Ha ha.

Scruffy's short sharp barks protested the insult, but Joe just smiled, a confident alpha male smile.

࿇

"That damned skull never arrived!"

It was the day after Christmas. I held the cell phone away from my ear while Heather screamed.

"I wouldn't call it 'damned,' if I were you, Heather. 'Thoughts are things.' And, remember, Christmas mail is notoriously slow," I said in the most soothing tone I could muster while contemplating the disaster of my own living room, where a whirlwind of the grand-twins had blown through yesterday. *So much to be done, I've no time for hysterics,* I thought. But catastrophes don't wait for convenient lulls.

"It's not fair!" Heather wailed. "Didn't we do the proper pentagram blessing! Fiona hummed her baffle thingie and sprinkled the frigging package with corn pollen. And I paid that enormous shipping cost for International Express, so that the skull, not to mention my Christmas books, would arrive before the holiday was over. *How could this have happened?*" I could hear the clink of ice cubes as Heather took a breath … and a sip. "Fleur is curled up in the corner of the kitchen, in tears, although I've assured the De Veres that they're not to blame. Still, Roland admitted mentioning that a *valuable* package arriving from England had been entrusted to his care, just showing off, you know, down at that Plymouth club where the artists and poets all hang out, what's it called?"

"Puck's Place." I stared at the Christmas star atop our tree. A pentagram really. It shone silver-bright in the reflection of the antique tin sconces on each side of the fireplace. An instant chill ran down my arms, making me hug myself like a shawl. "Actors from the community theater, too. Heather, I believe your family treasure may have been waylaid by an expert dissembler."

"Oh, no! You don't mean ... but he was seen getting on a bus for Los Angeles!"

"Setting the scene, you might say." I looked past the living room havoc, out the window at the bleak Atlantic shore where gulls screamed as they smashed clams on the rocks below. *Happy as a clam* was a misnomer. The world could be a cold dangerous place. "Deluca has always blamed us for his being sent to Juvie when he was only a youthful psychopath. And he has a revengeful nature. Look how he tried to blow up the Seven Angels theater when he didn't get the part he wanted. His bad luck to run up against me and Fiona, and now he's wanted for the attempted bombing. So I'm guessing he was hanging around Puck's Place, thinking how to get even with the lot of us before he takes off with a new identity, when Roland mentioned the package. Does all this make sense to you?"

"But why me? I wasn't even in Providence when the bomb incident came down," Heather said.

"Sorry, your package must have been just too good to pass up," I said, "but he'll be looking to settle the score with all of us. He knows about the Circle—remember the trial? Your testimony as well as ours?"

"How can he hope to have a career in the theater?" Heather was off on another tangent. "If he's successful and achieves some notice, no matter how he changes his appearance, someone will find him out."

"In this country, yes. Oh, I don't know what he thinks! Damn him."

"Okay. I admit you do make sense, in a *sixth sense* kind of way," Heather sighed.

Deluca in Plymouth! Naturally, this called for a conference. We elected to hold it at Fiona's, where the Turmoil of Christmas Present was not so much in evidence with Laura Belle at her grandparents' house for the holidays. I could only hope Joe would pitch in at home while I was "on assignment." Deidre was glad enough to have an excuse to flee the racket of new toys and videos, leaving Mother Ryan to cope. Conor had already escaped to the peaceful pied-à-terre where he kept his books and photos safe from grubby little fingers.

Phillipa was reluctant, however, to tear herself away from the delight of gifting Eddie with extravagant books, spectacular games, and cashmere sweaters. Still, *duty called.* "A witch's work is never done," she complained, while Fiona bustled about with thistle cups and steaming tea. "I thought we had that nasty piece of work Deluca off our books *twice* before, but he keeps popping up in our lives again like some Chucky-in-the-Box. Is there something different in your cream scones this time, Fiona?"

Our hostess's expression was pure bemused Fiona. "Oh, a pinch of this and a pinch of that," she murmured. Omar sidled from the sofa onto the scarred cherry coffee table where the plate of fragrant miniature scones was on offer. Fiona gave him the brush off, but dropped a crumb of scone onto his window cushion where he could snap it up.

"I believe it's the *eye of newt* that gives her scones that *je ne sais pas*," I said.

"Never mind swapping recipes, ladies" Deidre said. "Let's get out that old grimoire and find something to put Deluca out of our lives once and for all."

"*Hoist with his own petard*, as Fiona is so fond of saying," Phillipa suggested.

"You really should have asked Dee and me to go with you to Providence," Heather said. "You needed a full circle to get that wily blackguard off the streets for good and all."

Meanwhile, Fiona got the decrepit, moldy Books of Shadows out of its special silk wrappers and laid it on the coffee table. Omar hissed, slitted his copper eyes, and jumped off the window cushion. He retired in lordly splendor to one of the mismatched bookcases where he posed on the top shelf like a statue of Bast.

"I fear that our antique grimoire spooks Omar," Fiona sighed. "But my new familiar, Blod, can be trusted to carry forth the spell where it needs to go."

"Blod?" Deidre looked up from carefully turning the book's pages.

"It's Blodeuwedd her owl," Phillipa said. "Perches in the tree out there, invisible by day."

I looked out the big window at the rowan tree, gray-limbed in the December mists, and thought I spied pale eyes in a white face peering back at me. A few scarlet berries still clung in clusters of fine branches, like drops of blood. I wondered on what small timorous creatures Blod dined in winter. Closing my eyes would not shut out the cruelty of the natural world and men's hearts.

"Earth to Cass, Earth to Cass … come home now, we're working here," Phillipa said. "Dee has found something brilliant. Read it out to us, Dee. Cass is just beginning to focus."

Deidre read: "To Stop the One Who is Evil. Prepare a life candle that will burn as many days as you wish, and seal in it the essence of the man. Gather ye five stones cast up on the shore—birth stone, heart stone, journey stone, fate stone, doom stone—and place them in a circle with the life candle at the center. Light the candle and set watchers to keep it burning to the end. When the candle is finished, the one who must be stopped will be finished of his evil. Throw the stones back into the ocean where they will never be seen again."

"Oh, lovely," I said. "That one's too black for me. Do you seriously want to be visited by the blow-back karma of this?"

"Think, Cass!" Deidre stood up and absolutely waved her fist. "Remember what Leo did to his own innocent family members, and what he tried to do to our children. And now, the nice old theater where your daughter might have been a victim when a bomb blasted out the place."

Fiona took Omar into her lap and stroked his head as if to read his thoughts. Or maybe that was exactly what she was doing, because she said, "Omar is very fond of Laura Belle, and he's not a forgiving soul."

"Omar is not required to be a forgiving soul," I said crossly. "But we are bound to the white side of magic. Turn that page, Dee!"

"What do you suppose I could use as 'essence of the man'?" Heather's tone was thoughtful.

"I think I can find the right stones on Cass's beach," Deidre said. "In fact, I can see them in my mind's eye."

"Now you sound like Cass," Phillipa said. "But I vote with Cass, *no, no, a thousand times no*. What else have you got, Dee?"

And so we went on squabbling, what to do about Deluca. I was sorry that I'd started all this by voicing my suspicions that he was hanging around us still and had probably stolen Heather's skull right off her doorstep. But I *was* suspicious, and he *did* have the treasure in his murderous little hands. *I knew it in my bones.* But in the end, we agreed to table the magic until another day.

The skull, meanwhile, was not resting easy in Deluca's grasp.

But the days got away from us. Heather was still fussing and fuming, of course, her beautiful Christmas books and her Morgan treasure gone astray. Deidre got busy with her children still on school vacation and her shop, Deidre's Faeryland, buzzing with after-Christmas sales. Phillipa was using the hiatus to take Eddie on fun trips, to the Science Museum in Boston, Faneuil Hall, and the Freedom Trail. Fiona was entertaining (and consulting) her Salem buddy, Circe La Femme for a few days. And I had New Year orders to fill. Prosperity Pillows, Lady Luck Oils, Bless-This-House Besoms (made traditionally with ash wood staves and fine birch twigs), and Sizzling Senior Love Potions were big sellers.

Circe contacted her spirit guide, the Princess PauWau, on Heather's behalf. The Indian maiden assured Fiona that no black spell would be needed. "My Aztec brother is very powerful and will bring himself home," Circe had channeled in Princess PauWau's voice.

When Fiona called with Circe's spiritual message, Heather remained surprisingly calm. She said only, "The ghosts of Morgans Past are no slouches either, Fiona. The Morgan treasure will find its way back to me, and that little psycho will die," Fiona reported Heather's exact words to me later that day.

"That doesn't sound good to me, Fiona. I'd bet my best cinnamon besom that she's created that deadly candle we vetoed. It will be up in that turret meditation room, burning its black vibes to bring down Deluca."

"I wonder what she's using to represent his essence," Fiona said mildly.

"Hecate only knows," I said.

Joe had booked our New Year's Eve months ahead at the Omni Parker House, and it was an evening to remember, although I have to confess I didn't exactly notice the clock striking midnight as we left the merry-makers and retired early for a private celebration. I do remember, however, that the Boston sky was ablaze with fireworks, which seemed at the time theatrically appropriate.

Those bedazzled memories were all I would have for a few weeks, because right after New Year's Day Joe was back to saving the planet from environmental despoilers. Greenpeace was mounting another campaign against the pirate fishing operations off the coast of Africa, just the kind of assignment that put a sparkle in Joe's eye and the fear of Posieden into my heart.

With a cheerful grin and his old gray duffle bag over his shoulder, Joe left on January 2 to join the *Gaia* in Portugal; the Greenpeace vessel was setting course for the southern coast of Africa where one notorious trawler with massive nets was scooping up entire eco-systems, over-killing fish and even damaging the coral. Activists would try to board the monster ship with banners, and of course would be prevented from doing so by beefy Dutch sailors while a great video for future fund-raising was shot from the *Gaia*.

"Promise you'll stay on the ship and let the young idiots get thrown off the monster ship," I had pleaded.

He answered with good-bye kisses that addled my powers of persuasion. "My entire job will be just to keep the *Gaia* running for a quick getaway. Trust me," he'd said.

As if …

CHAPTER TWENTY-SEVEN

Fear is sharp-sighted, and can see things under-ground,
and much more in the skies.
Miguel de Cervantes-Saavedra

Christmas vacation was over, and Deidre breathed a sigh of relief.

All her children were in school now, Bobby, Willie Jr., and Annie at Massasoit Elementary, and Jenny at Cedar Hill Middle School, where she was two years behind Eddie Christie, Phillipa's new ward. Annie was in pre-kindergarten for only a half day, but Deidre employed Betti Kinsey to watch out for all of the youngsters at whatever time they came home. Deidre could now throw her considerable energies into minding the shop, as well as creating water sprites and faery dolls for her spring line. Her voluminous workbag went with her everywhere, chock full of new models for the coming season.

Laura Belle, Fiona's grandniece and the joy of her solitary life, was back again in her arms. Once the little girl's mother had returned to her job as an attorney for The Hague Abduction Convention in the Netherlands, a civil law mechanism for parents seeking the return of their children from other countries, Laura Belle's grandparents were glad enough to return her to Fiona's care. There was something disconcerting to the MacDonalds about their granddaughter. So Laura Belle was now in pre-kindergarten with Annie, who was quite the chatterer; nevertheless, the two had become fast friends.

On a quiet Monday morning right after the New Year's festivities, Deidre invited me over to Faeryland to see her newest renovation of a Victorian dollhouse that was the centerpiece of her shop. She knew how I loved every doll furnishing that graced the elegant mansion, from tiny chamber pots under the beds to coin-size cast iron frying pans in the kitchen. And then there were miniature books in the library! *What fun!* I'd brought with me a two-inch bonsai rosemary tree and some thimble-pots of French thyme for Deidre to plant by the dollhouse's garden gate. I found her merrily engaged in lacing cobwebs in its attic and arranging a ghost to pop out of the matchbox-size armoire.

"Oh!" I breathed, clapping my hands together like any five-year-old.

"You may play with it, if you are very, very gentle," she said in a motherly tone, as if I weren't a head taller than she. Deidre kept the glass doors to the library of the dollhouse locked away from sticky little fingers, but she opened it for me with a tiny gold key.

"Goodie." Reverently, I smoothed my finger over the library books on the shelves. One book was lying open on the diminutive library table. "Oh, where did you get this adorable atlas?"

"There are rare book dealers who know where to find miniatures, many of them from some collector's estate. Listen, Cass, I have a problem."

"What a surprise, Dee!" I said. "And here I thought you invited me over for a play-date." I turned the pages as delicately as I was able, revealing maps from England to Scotland to Ireland, each image perfectly drawn. Studying the detail with a magnifying glass, I was entranced, although aware that Deidre's real agenda was about to be revealed.

"Ha! You're nearly impossible to surprise, Cass, as you well know. So now, tell me what I should do about Conor's grandmother Eileen? I mean, if one of us doesn't find the nerve to tell her about my family, my relationship with Conor is never going anywhere, you know what I mean?" Sitting on a high stool behind the counter, Deidre was sewing gossamer wings on a bevy of silver faeries who bore an uncanny resemblance to those we'd glimpsed once in Jenkins Park while picnicking with the children.

These serious intentions were such good news! I could hardly wait to tell the others. But I forced myself to focus on the problem. "You have rightly supposed that I am the wisest woman in the Circle then?"

"Oh, bollocks, Cass! Fiona's ten times wiser, as you well know, but you're the witch who can see into the future, if you put your psyche into it. You can tell me how the revelation will be received."

I closed my eyes and sighed dramatically. "Oh, dear. That doesn't look good at all."

"What? What?" Deidre leaned over the counter anxiously.

"I see a large bosomy woman chasing you down the stairs, wielding a shillelagh."

"Oh, you are so full of malarkey. This is important, you know."

"So, am I to take it that you want to make an honest man of that world-traveled leprechaun?" I dodged the ball of silver mesh that was hurled my way. "My advice is just to tell the woman. Show her that cute Christmas photo that Conor took, with the kids, the doggies, and all."

"It's not your *advice* I want, Cass. I want your clairvoyant prediction. How will the old dame react?"

Deidre hotted the tea pot from her electric kettle, then added three scoops of Irish Breakfast Tea, and cut slices from a raisin-studded soda bread. Conor's influence was in evidence. Deidre's taste had once run to supermarket tea bags and arrowroot cookies. I pondered the chameleon nature of women in love, as evidenced by my own odyssey into Greek cooking.

"I'm not a mind-reader, you know," I protested.

"Yeah, yeah. I know you, Cass. All you need is to focus on a shiny object," Deidre said. In an obviously pre-planned maneuver, she quickly pulled a saucer-size gold pentagram out of her workbag and held it aloft so that it shone brightly in the overhead light and reflected the gleam directly into my eyes.

"This is so unfair, I refuse to be coerced," I complained, turning to shield my eyes, but little Deidre only giggled and danced around so that the star continued to shine on my face.

There was no help for it. I felt myself beginning to drift away. At first, I heard a woman scolding and laughing at the same time, but I couldn't make out any of her words. Then I floated into a cellar room where a shadowy person was hunched over a workbench, attaching wires to some receptacle the size and shape of a lunchbox. After that, I didn't remember anything.

Feeling quite nauseated, I came out of my trance to the sound of Deidre sniffling back tears, saying the Hail Mary prayer, and splashing my face with cold water. *"Mother of God, pray for us sinners* ... what in Hades did you see, Cass? It couldn't have been as bad as all that, could it?"

"Thanks a lot, Dee. Just what I needed was another ominous warning," I said weakly.

"Eileen O'Donnell? Oh, don't tell me." Deidre poured boiling water into the tea pot.

"Are you kidding? After you cornered me with that gold thing? But Eileen O'Donnell is not the problem," I said weakly. "Not the real problem anyway. After the first shock, she'll adjust. That scene did not end in tears, because I distinctly heard her laughing. But after that scene faded, I saw another. I saw a man in a cellar, I think, putting together a bomb. For when, for where? That's what we've got to find out."

"Do you think it was Deluca?" Deidre asked urgently.

"I don't know. I just don't know for sure. Damn this psychic trap! I only catch a glimpse of the future, never the whole story."

Any further discussion had to be tabled right then. Two young women came into the shop. One had hair the color of goldenrod, the other copper, but they both wore the identical hair styles of everyone else their age, long and straight, gleaming with good conditioning. They were looking for some cute little girl pocketbooks that they'd seen in the Faeryland ads. The pocketbooks opened to reveal a family of elves or pixies, one of Deidre's adorable creations. A tiny mirror, comb, and hankie completed the ensemble. Irresistible. I would absolutely have to buy one for my granddaughter Joanie, and something comparable for Jackie as well.

"What do you have like that for boys?" I asked.

The shoppers had made their selections. Wrapping two of the pocketbooks separately in tissue for her customers, Deidre gestured to the other side of the tree on which the bags were displayed. Jack and the Beanstalk kits held the story book, packets of magic beans, a bag of gold coins (chocolate), and an unfolding beanstalk made of nylon rope. The women continued to browse the after-Christmas sales, exclaiming their way through a heap of stuffed magical creatures, faery pillows, and mythical lunch boxes.

"Excuse me, Ms. Ryan," one of the young women said, "but I've heard that, you know, you're like an expert on herbs and spells. Is that true?"

Deidre chuckled and held out her hand to indicate me. "You must have heard about my friend Cass Shipton. That's her right there, lurking behind the dollhouse. She's the expert on herbal spells."

There was nothing for it but to step out and hand the two young women my business cards. *Cassandra Shipton, Earthlore Herbal Preparations and Cruelty-Free Cosmetics*. I wondered what they were after in the way of magic spells, but I pretty much guessed that they had love potions on their minds. For their husbands? Their tennis instructor? The fitness guru? Perhaps they were single mothers just looking for a guy. In the moment of giving out the cards, touching their hands, and looking in their eyes, I knew more than I want to know, as was frequently the case. Even worse, I could see the nimbus of light around each young woman's head and shoulders. There was a red flair around the blonde's jaw. Bummer. I had never wanted to extend my clairvoyance to auras, but it was happening despite my best effort to shrug off this new psychic wrinkle.

"You may want to check out my online shop," I said. "I have some after-holiday sales as well. And it's totally private. Also, be sure to keep that dentist appointment."

They looked at each other. The young blonde grinned. "Thanks. I'll look you up this afternoon. But how did you know about the dentist?"

Her copper-haired friend interrupted, "Now, this stuff you sell, it's all perfectly legal?"

Deidre replied for me, "It's just herbs, my dear. Herbs are still perfectly legal. And Ms. Shipton's products have such fun names, like Conjure Your Dream Lover Pillow, Sensational Sex Bath Salts, and Passion Potion XOX. That's perfectly legal, too."

"Don't help me, girlfriend," I muttered, then added to the eager young things, "There are also Wise Woman Teas and Blessed Home Candles." I didn't think they were worried about finances, though. The gifts they'd just bought and those they were contemplating were fairly pricey.

"I'll take this one," the copper-haired gal said. "My daughter Harper is really into horses."

"That's Arion, the immortal horse of Adrastus," Deidre said.

The blonde decided on the mermaid.

"In Greek mythology, she's an undine, a sea faery."

"You're beginning to sound like Fiona, the walking encyclopedia of myths," I said.

"Well …" Deidre dimpled. "It is what it is." Her customers were leaving with overflowing totes emblazoned with Deidre's Faeryland. "Good luck with the passion potions," she called after them and chuckled wickedly.

"Desperate housewives of Plymouth," she said.

"Love potions work pretty well, you know," I defended. "Maybe because they focus intention, which is such a powerful force."

"That's why none of *us* ever needed a love potion," Deidre said.

"Phil used one of my blends once. On Stone, as a matter of fact, when they were dating. She liked that it had oregano in it."

"Seems to have worked rather well," Deidre said. "Too bad she didn't take a slug of it herself."

I ignored that and went back to playing with the dollhouse. The library held an exquisite copy of Alice in Wonderland.

"Aren't these miniature books fearfully expensive?" I wondered.

"Yes," Deidre said. "It's one of the ways I stash away funds, unbeknown. This kind of collectible item increases in value more reliably than blue-ribbon stocks."

"Does Conor know about this little collection? And is it insured?"

"No he doesn't, and yes it is," Deidre said. "The insurance company requires me to have a state-of-the-art security system. So behave yourself, Cass, you're on Candid Camera." She pointed up to the corners of the ceiling; the surveillance wasn't too obvious, or I was too dumb ever to have noticed. "A woman needs her own private nest egg, so my mother taught me, and her mother before her. It might be an Irish thing, I don't know. This particular policy is a separate deal, a rider on the dollhouse and its contents, everything fairly valued."

"Hey, Dee, you're a totally independent woman, the sole owner of this thriving doll business." I peered into the darling dining room, the table set with miniature Canton Export china, gleaming under the light of a crystal light fixture. "And Conor has his own lucrative profession. I think you can relax now."

"You never can tell about the future. It's simply a question of being able to spend extraordinary funds without answering to anyone. In case I ever get married again."

"*Extraordinary*, like what, Dee? Gambling losses? Blackmail?"

But Deidre's pretty mouth was set in a stubborn line. She wasn't about to shake off the family paranoia.

～

I drove humming like Fiona, thinking good thoughts about Deidre's future, but my pleasant mood faded rapidly when I found Phillipa in my driveway looking like the bearer of grim tidings.

"I just took a chance. Best to discuss this in person. Thank the Goddess you're home," she said.

"Now what?"

"Good to see you, too, Cass. Let's go inside," she said.

Gotta pee! Gotta pee! Scruffy and Raffles met me at the kitchen door, dancing around urgently. I let them onto the porch, and they dashed through the pet door.

"Stone had an upsetting message from his British counterpart," Phillipa said, divesting herself of the black parka and cashmere scarf. "What's for lunch?"

"Not too upset to eat, then? How about tuna? Italian tuna, fried peppers and mushrooms, artisan bread. Coffee?"

"Wine! There's been a rumor came down from MI5 that Abdul Hamid has reached across the pond to an American confederate, possibly a young cousin or a nephew."

"That sounds ominous." I poured chardonnay from the bottle that was open in the refrigerator into two pressed glass tumblers, my everyday wine glasses, which had the advantage of being as large as Old Fashioned glasses.

"One of our own citizens, actually," she continued. "A disaffected engineering student with an Afghanistan family background, Robert Azizi. Recruited by a mullah who's on the terrorist watch list. Robert's new name is Mohammad Abdul Aziz Al-Waladi. The British guy, Gordon Burns, wasn't supposed to get involved, but I guess he liked Stone and thought he ought to get a heads-up" Phillipa downed half the wine in her glass.

"And this affects us, how?"

"Do you know what a fatwa is?" she asked.

"Some kind of Islamic judgment. Salman Rushdie comes to mind. Subject of a fatwa issued by the Ayatollah Khomeini after writing a book perceived to be an irreverent depiction of the prophet Mohammad. Lived in hiding for years."

"Well, the good news is that we're not important enough to merit an official fatwa from Ayatollah Anybody, but Abdul Hazrad may have laid the responsibility of a personal fatwa on his young American relative," Phillipa said.

"A fatwa on who?"

"Whom do you think? On the tourists who were responsible for thwarting Abdul's spree of so-called honor killings. The gals who got his ass thrown into jail, or g-a-o-l as dear Larry would say it. You do remember that front page photo of Heather and Dee comforting little Fatimah Khatoon, who is now the prime living witness and being held in protective custody?"

"*Jail* and *g-a-o-l* are pronounced exactly the same, Phil. How do you know all that? Gordon Burns wouldn't have mentioned the photo. Did you happen to put in a call to 'dear Larry' and now you're just dying to talk about him?"

Phillipa looked out the window. "Your doggies are heading for their pet door."

I opened the back door. The big fellows hurtled in and went straight for their water bowl, slobbering on the kitchen floor as usual. "Don't change the subject, Phil. Did you have a chat with Laurence Watson?"

"As a matter of fact, yes. He's Heather's British solicitor, after all, and I thought he should know what Burns had told Stone. He's getting in touch with Bartie Bangs, but he's relying on me to warn Heather and Dee. It's his opinion that, since we five are so notoriously connected in Plymouth, the warning ought to extend to all of us. *Another nice mess you've gotten us into, Stanley.*"

"*Me?* Why am I always being blamed." I busied myself heating up the peppers and mushrooms, while Phillipa drained most of the oil off the delicious *tonno* into a cup.

Save some fish oil for us, Toots. Fish oil makes our bones strong and our coats shiny.

Shiny! Shiny!

"Because you're the one who has the visions that lead us into trouble every time. What do you want me to do with this oil?"

"Just save it in that little cup. Scruffy and Raffles like it drizzled on their dinner. So now we have some young terrorist wanting to exact revenge as well as that nasty piece of work Deluca who's lurking around with the same idea. I wonder which villain it was that I *saw* making a bomb?"

"A bomb?" Phillipa looked at me sharply with her expressive dark eyes. "Who knows? It was *your* vision. Right now we've got to worry about warning Heather and Dee, and Fiona, too, of course, about the fatwa. And it's time for some serious protective magic. I hope that purloined skull doesn't give Deluca any special powers that were promised to Heather." Phillipa cut the tuna and pepper sandwiches with a savage flourish.

I got a pot of coffee ready and put the bottle of chardonnay on the table. Phillipa slid the sandwiches onto plates, and we sat down at the kitchen table and dug into our lunch.

Surprisingly, I found I was quite hungry.

"Danger always gives me an appetite," Phillipa said. "Stone is fit to be tied, naturally. I think he wants me to get myself to a nunnery and stay there until the situation is resolved. Larry sounded quite concerned, as well. We had a nice chat."

"Oh for Ceres' sake, Phil," I said. "A nunnery is the last place I'd ever expect to find *you*."

"I think that's what worries Stone," she said. "The best thing would be to call a meeting so we can break the ill news to the others and plan a strategy at the same time. Have you seen a weather report this morning? There's some talk of a coastal storm over the weekend. Might be rain, but probably snow, depending on the air temperature."

"Talk about the Gathering Storm. I wish Joe were here instead of on the sunny coast of Africa. In times of danger and snow accumulation, a man comes in so very handy," I said.

"Oh, you don't fool me, Cass Shipton. You're still besotted with that brawny Greek adventurer," Phillipa said.

I smiled and turned away, getting up to flip on the coffee. The five of us had never been eager to discuss the details of our love lives. On the other hand, we regularly read each other's minds, which was quite disconcerting enough.

Suddenly I felt a chill travel from my neck right to the bottom of my spine, like a shaft of ice. What in Hades was that? Something was pushing at my psyche, but I shook off the feeling. Just another psychic false alarm. Still I sat down in a hurry, my legs weak and trembling.

"Hey, Cass, what's wrong with you?"

"Oh, just another figment of my fevered brain," I said.

"Do you think maybe we had too much wine?" Phillipa opened the back door to toss the bottle we'd emptied into the recycle bin on the porch.

"Speaking of besotted," I said, pouring coffee into our cups and setting out a plate of brownies, thankful I'd made them from scratch. Phillipa, of course, turned up her nose at those handy mixes. "I do think Dee has made up her mind to marry Conor. I don't know what *he's* made up his mind to do, but it won't matter. At least she loves him as a man and not as another of her children, which was the case with Will."

Phillipa clapped her hands together in uncharacteristic enthusiasm. "Oh, joy! A handfasting!"

"I rather think it will be a traditional Catholic ceremony," I said.

"Well, a handfasting *later* then."

CHAPTER TWENTY-EIGHT

Heaven from all creatures hides the book of Fate
All but the page prescrib'd, their present state.
    Alexander Pope

That well-worn axiom "be careful what you wish for, you may get it" came to mind when Joe called right about suppertime, ten in the evening where he was. He sounded strangely muffled.

"I'm all right," were his first words. Whenever someone you love begins a phone conversation with those three ominous words, it bodes ill.

"What happened? Where are you?" I shouted across the Atlantic, noting that the connection was not great, Joe sounded so faint.

"In Abuja. Nigeria. At the National Hospital."

I must have screamed or something like that, because he hastened to comfort me with soothing words, especially the word *home.* "Listen, sweetheart. I'm really all right, and they're sending me *home.* I'm coming *home.* I'll be *home* by Thursday."

It must have worked; my wits were returning to me. "What exactly do you mean when you say you're 'all right'?" I asked suspiciously.

"It's just a back thing. I've got good drugs for the pain, and I've been assured that I'll heal up in a week or two. Or maybe three. But the thing is, I'm using a wheelchair temporarily because every once in a while my leg goes numb and just gives out on me. There's some fear that I could break my hip or crack my head if I keel over. But I can use crutches for short distances, like getting from the car to the house."

"Oh, Joe, how awful for you! What happened?" Imagining my robust, active husband confined to a wheel chair and high on one of the currently prescribed super-strong pain-killers, whose effects he would hate, I managed not to cry, barely. "Oh never mind, honey. Naturally, I'm curious, but you can tell me everything later. The important thing is that you're all right, and you'll get better. So don't worry. Everything will be fine once you get home. We'll be fine. Shall I make an orthopedic appointment for you?"

"Greenpeace has already taken care of that. Boston Medical on Monday."

Greenpeace hadn't taken the coastal storm into account, but appointments can always be rescheduled. I might need some help, though, and a plan was already forming in my mind. "Let me know when your flight to Boston is due, and I'll meet you at the arrivals gate. I assume the airlines will have someone watching out for you?"

"Yes, wheelchairs get VIP treatment. Listen, Cass, I've got to go now. My nurse has to do some stuff, and he's standing over me glowering. I'll call when I know more details."

"Okay. I love you, and I'll see you soon."

"I love you, and I'll see you soon," he echoed.

After we'd hung up, I realized that I was still burning to know how he got hurt. What dumb macho thing had he done, who had he tried to rescue, why hadn't he stayed out of harm's way as he promised? Well, that story would wait until Joe got home, and would probably be a glossed-over version of the truth anyway.

Could things be worse? Well, yes, but not by much. When troubles descend, you need to avoid brooding over the big picture, just keep going, and *do the next thing*. My "next thing" was to call Tip, who was part of the plan that had taken shape in my mind right after Joe told me about the wheelchair. Tip, Thunder Pony Thomas, the boy I had once fantasized about adopting, was now a student at the University of Maine majoring in anthropology with a minor in American Indian music. We shared a deep bond formed through many past adventures. When I called to ask if he were free to give us a hand with Joe in the wheelchair, the oncoming storm, and a couple of threatening psychopaths looming on our horizon, Tip actually laughed, with that characteristic Indian humor that came with a straight face and a chuckle held back until it became a cough. "Sure, Aunt Cass. *Same old, same old?* I'll be able to get away okay, not to worry. 'Family emergency on the reservation' should work all right. I can leave first thing in the morning, settle in before the storm hits Plymouth. Now tell me about these two psychos? Are they partners?"

I confessed that they were actually two separate threats and related most of what had gone on to precipitate each crisis.

I told him about the Hamid fatwa first, and the possible recruitment of Robert Azizi to carry it out, since I knew, when I got to Deluca, rational discussion would descend into angry shouting. Tip knew Deluca, and how dangerous he could be. They'd both gone to school in Plymouth, the same years but different schools, and they'd had an early run-in at a track meet which had involved Deluca trying to disable the rival team. Later, Tip had helped Joe to rescue our little ones from Deluca's evil intentions.

"*Kihci-Niwskumon ehtahs yut npeci!* Why the hell didn't they keep that SOB in jail?" Tip spat the words. I'd rarely heard him resort to the native Passamaquoddy language. An appeal to the Great Spirit?

"As you know, Tip, the rules for juvenile detention are fairly lenient. But now Leo's wanted for a bombing threat in Providence. When he gets prosecuted this time as an adult, the law won't go so easy on him."

"I'll be there by noon tomorrow," Tip said in a quieter tone. He'd be traveling on his bike, a well-loved but rather banged-up Harley. "Ah …"

I knew what was coming.

"Ah … have you heard anything from Jordan lately?"

"Not much, Tip. Christmas card, different address, but still in Salem."

"Maybe I'll give her a call, you know, after we get things sorted out."

"It would be nice to get in touch again. I love that girl. She reminds me of Freddie, same irrepressible spirit."

"Yeah. Well, see you tomorrow then," Tip said, his tone now charged with emotion.

After the call ended, I thought how easy it was to anticipate the resurfacing of Tip's passionate crush on Jordan Rivers. What was it Joe had said? "It's called first love, and it's supposed to end in heartbreak. She is older, and bolder; he is young and vulnerable. It's a learning experience."

So if I were psychic enough to read Tip's thoughts, how come I hadn't felt a thing when the love of my life got himself a crippling injury? I thought back, had there been any kind of twinge, a dream even? Holy Hecate, *yes!* That onslaught of chill while Phillipa was here at lunchtime, that I'd pushed away, rather agreeing that we might have had too much wine at lunch. What's Rule Number One for clairvoyants? *Never ignore any flash of insight*, however brief or unwelcome.

I guess I just wanted to be normal, not always buffeted by sights, sounds, and feelings hidden from others. For every time my visioning had saved someone, there were a dozen times when it had made my life a quagmire of conflicting emotions. It seemed as if everyone else had a thicker skin than I, an armor against too much knowing.

Obviously, I was in immediate danger of feeling quite sorry for myself.

The dogs had come in from their last run of the starless evening, having exercised their own special kind of foresight, scenting everything surrounding the house and finding no danger, breathing in the promise of snow, then tearing inside to shake off January's burning cold from their fur.

Hey, Toots! You look as glum as a pup who's run into a skunk. Anything a loyal companion can do? How about a cuddle and couple of treats?

Treats! Treats!

Dogs always know how to lighten up human angst. The three of us curled up on the sofa and watched a favorite old film *Bell, Book, and Candle*, peacefully for the most part, except for their need to growl at Pyewacket every time the cat appeared on screen. I enjoyed a cup of hot tea with honey and a dollop of Myers's Rum, and they munched their evening Milkbones. Later I watched the local weather report. The storm was stalled in Pennsylvania leaving great drifts of snow in its wake. No telling how long it would take to reach us, but the forecaster's best guess was Thursday morning with an expected accumulation of 8 to 10 inches. If Joe arrived tomorrow or early the next day, at least I'd have him settled before the roads became impassable. And Tip would be here to help, *dear Tip.*

It would be all right. Tomorrow, first thing, while Tip was still on the road, I'd call the others for a meeting of minds and a little defensive spell-work. Then, I'd sprinkle sea salt at the borders of my property, whisk away evil vibes indoors with my cinnamon besom, anoint the window and door sills with protection oil (lavender, hyssop, mugwort), and smudge the whole place with sage. Yes! My heart chakra was filled with strength and resolve.

But when I finally pulled back the white chenille bedspread and got under the quilts alone (Scruffy and Raffles not being allowed on the "big bed") the specters of fear and uncertainty returned and sat in the corners of the room like a row of Deidre's red-eyed gargoyles.

 ⌒⌒

Deidre arrived mumbling about neglecting her shop, and what was all this about, another of Cass's phantom threats? Phillipa, who knew what was brewing, smiled a Mona Lisa smile as she busied herself unpacking the applecake she'd made. Heather had brought Honeycomb, her golden retriever, for a "play date" with Scruffy and Raffles (her pup from that unsanctioned union at an earlier date). And Fiona was as unperturbed as always, a little aura of sparkles around her coronet of braids. (Yikes! I was seeing *her* aura, too.)

I shooed the three dogs out into the backyard, where Honeycomb, no doubt, would sneer at Scruffy and tumble Raffles, all in good fun, hers.

"Is this about Deluca?" Heather asked, unwrapping herself from an endless designer scarf of green and rust. "Any news of the missing skull?"

"No. But Deluca is not the entire story." I poured coffee and let Phillipa tell the tale of Abdul Hamid, his young relative, and the possible fatwa.

"So, along with the threat of Deluca's shenanigans, we now have to cope with some revengeful terrorist descending on us and our families?" Deidre asked crossly.

"I fear we are faced with *the evil of two lessers*," Fiona said. "The pursuit of justice is fraught with potholes. But I wouldn't worry about the Aztec skull, Heather. Circe says it will work its own way home."

"So let's just worry about who's building the bomb I saw in my vision, and where it's going to be detonated," I said.

"Well, you're the seer." Phillipa passed around slices of applecake. "You tell us."

"We'll need to create a sphere of light around us right now," Heather said. She reached into a hand-woven tote at her side. "I've brought some purple patchouli candles that will shield us from evil while we summon a protective aura and consider our next move."

Honeycomb had commenced to bark so sharply that I feared it would be a total distraction, so I let the three rascals back into the house. Scruffy and Honeycomb made a dash for the living room, where I knew she would soon contrive to take over the window seat that was Scruffy's accustomed post.

Heather set up the three fat candles on my kitchen table, a long slab of weathered oak of the kind often labeled "distressed." They were filled with minute silver swords and pentagrams. Soon the room was filled with the strong perfume of patchouli, earthy and musty-sweet.

Raffles, who'd positioned himself hopefully under the table on which I was cutting wedges of cheddar cheese to go with the cake, got up with a unhappy snort and went to join Scruffy and Honeycomb in the living room.

Dumb kid! Didn't I tell you? When those dames start lighting their candles, the wise canine will pull in his tail and vamoose.

Vamoose! Vamoose!

Move over, big boy. You're in my stretching spot.

That Honeycomb was quite a prima donna. "Play nice," I said to the snarling maneuvers in the living room. Tip would be here soon, and my two dogs would be ecstatic.

With a tinkle of silver bangles, Fiona waved her be-ringed hands around us, summoning the blue-white cloud of security and healing to keep us safe. We did the new (or was it old, after all?) Bane and Baffle spell designed by Fiona, which involved a lot of humming and drumming on the table, and then we did the Wall spell we had used so effectively in the back alley of Brown's Hotel in London, when Hamid had run his own head into a dumpster. Meanwhile, Phillipa improvised her way into a new chant, so we sang that out thirteen times, from soft to loud, reversing our usual order on this occasion. Why? It just *felt* right to end with force and resolve.

> *By this circle's hearts and hands,*
> *By this circle's true commands,*
> *All we love are safely held,*
> *All we hope for shall be well,*
> *And he who troubles us shall learn*
> *That evil is its own return.*

໖໐

When Joe called from LaGuardia the next afternoon, he was just one short flight away from Logan. How glad I was that I had Tip to go with me! The promised storm had begun lazily with a few flakes out of a silver sky, just enough to keep the windshield wipers on low, but there was no telling how quickly it would accelerate.

A young airline attendant wheeled Joe into the Arrivals concourse, while he tried his best, with a jaunty wave and wide smile, to look like a guy who didn't need a pretty girl's help or even a wheelchair. He pointed confidently to the crutches attached to the chair, but I could see that little line of pain beside his mouth. I leaned over to kiss him and we hugged, awkwardly. The kiss was reassuring, though, sure and strong.

"Tip! Great to see you," he said a moment later. "I'm guessing Cass thought she'll need some help hauling me around. You're still in college, aren't you?"

"Exams are over. Aced those, so I'm just taking a week off," Tip said airily, leaving it to me to spill the other problems, or not. "I'll go get the luggage, Aunt Cass. Am I looking for the usual sea-stained gray duffle?" This from Tip who'd arrived yesterday with only a well worn backpack, a flute case, and a pair of snowshoes hitched to his bike.

"Of course," I said. I handed him my keys. "If you would, you could also pick up the RAV and meet us at that door right over there. We'll be waiting by the curb."

Tip jogged off on his assignment, leaving me to decide on how much of the current craziness I would spring on Joe right away. Wheeling him over to a bank of chairs, I sat beside him, holding his hand. We gazed at each other, drinking in the simple happiness of being together again, so deep that I almost felt I were the one who had just come home. Aware that I was getting teary again, I brushed my eyes and said, "It's such a great relief that you're here, safe, in one piece. How's the back?"

He shrugged, studying my face with that direct blue-eyed gaze. "What's going on at home?" he asked. "*Something*, that's for sure. Those worry lines aren't all for me." He touched the space between my brows gently.

"I guess I should never play poker," I said. "Let's wait until we're on our way to Plymouth, because you're going to have a lot of questions. We'll sit in the back together and let Tip be chauffeur. He's a better snow driver than I am, anyway."

"Yeah, I heard that forecast on the plane. Major storm expected tonight. Guess I got back just in time, while the airports are still open. But the storm's not important, is it?"

"No, honey. That might be the least of it. Come on, let's go to the door and watch for Tip."

Tip pulled up to the curb about ten minutes later and hopped out to help with the wheelchair. Joe was already maneuvering himself toward the car on crutches. Mindful of the collapsing leg problem, I held him securely by the back of his belt all the way.

Tip drove through the increasing snowfall without comment, while I told Joe about the missing skull, and the possibility that Deluca had stolen it and was still hanging around with evil intentions. Joe murmured something unintelligible and held my hand more tightly. "And what else?" he asked shrewdly. This man could read me far too easily! So then I launched into Gordon Burns' warning to Stone about Hamid's young relative here in the States.

When at last I had finished, I sighed and looked out the window. "All this and a blizzard, too," I said. "Some homecoming."

CHAPTER TWENTY-NINE

The snow had begun in the gloaming,
And busily all the night
Had been heaping field and highway
With a silence deep and white.
    James Russell Lowell

Despite the rising wind and swirling, stinging snow, when we'd guided Joe (determinedly on crutches) into the house, and settled down around the fireplace after dinner, the aura of peace and familiarity was so comforting, it was impossible to believe that we were in danger of anything more than a blizzard.

And a blizzard was what we got! At 11:00 PM, just when we were about to turn in, the electricity failed, but anyone who lives in Plymouth is ready for any and all such emergencies. Many folks had gone upscale with home generators (sissies!), but the rest of us equipped ourselves with plenty of heavy duty flashlights, lanterns and candles, a battery-operated radio set to WBZ, and a stack of dry firewood.

The fire was already keeping the living room warm with a nice bed of red coals that needed only a log or two to blaze up again. Our bedroom on the ground floor would benefit by a little of that heat, but Tip would be upstairs in the frigid second floor.

"Scruff and Raff will keep me warm, won't you, guys?" And sure enough, the two dogs padded upstairs with Tip and settled down to their task. If the electricity had not been restored by morning, he and I could build a second fire in the kitchen fireplace, and the whole downstairs would be reasonably livable. There was plenty of dry wood stored on the porch, in case.

Joe's sigh of relief, when he lay down at last, spoke of the pain he must have been enduring, sitting up in the wheelchair all evening.

"Would you be more comfortable if I slept on the couch?" I asked.

"Are you crazy? Slide over here and let me put my arms around you," Joe growled softly, so I did that. Although wearing my thickest flannel nightie and a pair of socks as well, Joe's body, as always, radiated more heat than a space heater. I shrugged off the shawl I'd layered over the nightie.

"Do you think we could …?" he murmured, running his hand up under my flannel layers.

"Maybe," I said, shifting closer to give that warm hand more opportunity. He was wearing the monk's robe with a hood that I'd given him for Christmas. The front of it was open against me, and his intentions were apparent. "But I'm afraid I might do some damage to you when I'm not thinking."

"Don't worry. I love you most when you're not thinking. Best medicine in the world for aching bones," he lied.

I was very careful. He only yelped in pain a little once. The rest was sweet, slow, satisfying, and who knows? Possibly medicinal.

༄

We were woken abruptly by the sound of a crash somewhere near the front door. "Snow sliding off the roof," I murmured. The electric bedside clock was no help, its digital face blank. Joe looked at his watch, which obligingly lit up when he pressed something. 3:14 AM.

"I'll just go look out the window," I sat up and put my feet on the floor, which was unbelievably icy even through my socks.

"No, you don't." His hand closed like a steel handcuff around my arm. "That wasn't any snow slide." He pushed himself up and reached for his crutches. Propping them under his arms, he struggled into the living room and grabbed the old cast iron poker.

Right about then, Scruffy rushed down the stairs, surprisingly without a warning bark. A bemused Raffles followed his sire's footsteps warily.

Fully dressed in worn jeans and AIM sweat shirt, probably sleeping in his clothes, Tip sidled down against the wall, his moccasins soundless on the braided-rug stair treads. Joe was in the living room, already standing on his crutches with me beside him. I wondered why Joe and Tip seemed to be sensing more danger than I did. Clairvoyance could be so unreliable!

Scruffy was snuffling with great intent at the front door in the living room. Someone must be out there! Tip began putting on the snow shoes he'd left at the bottom of the stairs.

We were all extremely quiet, listening. *A scraping on the front step.* There would be no point in trying to fling open the seldom-used, squeaky, heavy front door. A door like that doesn't have any fling left in it. But Tip already had his hand on the old wrought iron latch. If he thought he'd be able to open *that* door quietly, he was sadly mistaken. Although Joe had lubricated the hinges and lock the last time he was home, it was still a big old irascible monster. The latch flew open with a jolt and a bang, and Tip pulled it open, not without some effort. Scruffy tried to push past me, but I held both dogs firmly by their collars.

Nothing there!

Tip surveyed the tracks around the front door. "He came in from the main road, but these tracks are heading to Jenkins Park. I'm going to follow," he said. "I'll take Scruff, Aunt Cass. The snow's deep but he'll manage."

I let go of Scruffy's collar but not that of his disgruntled, whimpering offspring. The two of them, the young man and the old dog, raced to follow the footprints. A man had come down the long drive, through the pines that screened Route 3A, to the garage where Joe had his workshop, to our front door, and then into the woods beyond.

How helpless Joe must feel, propped on crutches, clutching a poker he couldn't possibly swing without toppling over, avidly watching the running pair while the winter storm nearly blew us over in our own living room.

Peering intently into the darkness, my hold slackened, and when Raffles suddenly got it into his head to bolt, I lost him. He galloped out of the door barking wildly, but he didn't follow his sire. Instead, he seemed to be obsessed with the big old rhododendron beside the front door. I leaned out to grab him and see what he was so interested in, hoping it wasn't a skunk wintering somewhere under the house.

It wasn't. It was a backpack under the still-green leaves. "Oh, sweet mother Ceres, save us," I said. "Joe, there's a backpack out there—you don't suppose ..."

Joe pushed himself forward with difficulty, craned his neck around the door. "Get Raffles in," he said. *"Jesu Christos*, I'd move the thing, but ..."

"Not on your life, or Tip's either. It might go off the moment you touch it." I floundered onto the front step in my socks, which seemed inclined to freeze me to the spot. I could just reach far enough to haul Raffles toward me inelegantly by the tail until I could grab his collar again.

"Don't let him go!" I handed the nervous dog to Joe, hoping he didn't end up being pulled off his crutches. My cell phone? Now, where did I leave that? I yanked myself off the icy step, leaving one sock stuck there, and ran for the kitchen, where the phone was just where I'd left it on the counter. Usually I would have taken it into the bedroom with me at night, but when Joe was home, I was more careless about that. I punched in 911. "Holy Hecate, they'll never believe this."

It must have been a busy night at the emergency switchboard. The gal who answered, once she understood that there was no health emergency or imminent threat, was not all that excited about a backpack abandoned beside my front door. What made me think it might be a bomb? (How much time did she have, I wondered). She would send a patrol car to investigate as soon as one became available. "Shut the front door, retreat to the interior of the house, and stay on the line," she sighed.

Tip and Scruffy came back, Tip lightly on his snow shoes, Scruffy up to his belly in snow but prancing importantly. *No need to get your tail in a twist, Toots. We scared them away all right.*

"Gone," Tip said succinctly. "In the general direction of the Sterns' place, so you probably ought to call Mz. Phil."

I pointed wordlessly to the rhody where Raffles had discovered the backpack. "I called 911. I don't think they're as worried about that thing as I am," I said. "They'll send a patrol car when they can." I glanced at Joe, noting that he was still holding the poker.

Tip pulled my sock off the front step and handed it to me. By then, between Tip stamping off his snowshoes and Scruffy shaking his rump, we had our own indoor drift of snow on the inside doormat, not to mention the white stuff blowing through from the outdoors as we stood there. "You'd better shut the door for now," I said to Tip. "That's about all the dispatcher could recommend. Like the old 'duck and cover' defense for an atomic attack."

"Duck and cover?" Tip struggled with the heavy door, got it shut, and threw the latch with a mighty thud.

"The Cold War, kid, when everyone was building bomb bunkers and stocking up on canned goods," Joe said to Tip in an avuncular tone.

"I'll ring back in a few minutes," I said to the 911 dispatcher and ended the connection while she was still arguing. Ignoring Tip, I called Phillipa to warn her of an intruder heading her way. The phone rang four times and went to voice mail. I handed the phone to Tip and said, "Keep trying."

Without consulting either man, I dragged a straight chair to the mantel and took down my grandma's .22 rifle. Now where in Hades were those bullets? Every time I hide something in a safe place, I forget where the safe place is.

"What in hell do you think you're going to do with that rifle, Cass," Joe demanded.

"Load it," I said. "As soon as I remember where I hid the bullets."

"You'd better let me have that, Aunt Cass. I've been hunting with my father and the old chiefs since I was ten," Tip said. "You, on the other hand, hardly know which end of that Winchester is up—no offense. Nice rifle, by the way, pre '64."

"I feel better with a weapon in my own hands," I said.

"That's trouble right there," Joe said. "What else did the dispatcher tell you?"

"To move into the interior of the house," I said. Good idea, *the farther away from the front room as possible.* As we herded ourselves into the kitchen, I looked at my cell. No answer yet. I tried Phillipa's number again.

Meanwhile Tip got a fire going in the kitchen fireplace. It would take a while for the little blaze to take the icy chill off the room.

"This is one of those times I wish I had a gas cooker like Phil," I said, looking at the useless tea kettle on the stove.

Thinking of Phillipa, I took the phone back from Tip and tried her number again. It occurred to me then that we should all be checking on one another. Witches' phone tree. We were all on each other's speed dial.

This time she answered. "Missed your call. Power's out. We were getting wood for the fireplace. Eddie and I are holding the fort, with Boadicea," she said by way of hello. "How's everything there?"

"Uh oh," she said when I'd finished my worried report. "How very weird. Do you suppose our friend Leo is out and about? Tip says he took off into the park? I'll keep an eye out, though I doubt he's headed here. But then, who knows how sadistic psychopaths think? There's a gun in the lock box upstairs, as you know, but I can never remember the combination, and Stone won't write it down. So I'd better phone him this instant. He's out rescuing someone, of course, but he'll send some help for you right away. And me. Do you really think you need to call out the bomb squad? In this weather?"

"What's the weather got to do with it?" I screamed in her ear.

"All right, all right. Sit tight. You're in the kitchen? Good. Stay out of the front room."

The front room was where Joe was clumping about right now, in search of his bottle of Jack Daniels in the parson's cabinet.

"You be careful and listen to Boadicea," I said. "She'll know if Deluca is lurking outside. Remember that he saw you in that Starbucks when we got his laptop away from him. And he knows who you are."

"Stone will see we're well guarded," Phillipa said. Her voice had a slight nervous undertone. "And what about Fiona? After all, she's the one who shot at Deluca."

"At least she's armed," I said. "As I intend to be as soon as I find the rifle bullets for my .22. You'll check on the others, especially Fiona?"

"Of course. Call me back the instant the squad arrives. And give that rifle to Tip, you idiot."

As soon as I stopped trying so hard to jog my memory, my unconscious mind tossed up the answer. I remembered where I'd stored the damned bullets, in an empty glass jar labeled

Periwinkles on the top shelf of my spice cabinet. (Made sense; periwinkles are used to banish evil influences.) I got on a chair again to fetch them down, handing the jar and the rifle to Tip. He loaded it quickly, laid it on the empty chair beside him, and pushed it in under the table.

We were all drinking whiskey in the kitchen when the bomb squad, summoned from Middleboro, arrived with lights blazing to push their way to our front door with a small plow attached to their van. (Good! Tip and I wouldn't have to shovel a path to the front door, in case we still had a front door.) Two bomb squad officers surveyed the backpack and lowered it into the bomb pot with an extremely long remote grabber. The guy in charge, who went by the name Ranger, had a Sam Elliot mustache and laconic manner, minus the Elliot twinkle in his eye. The other guy, Pete, was as round as the bomb pot and clearly miserable with a Rudolph-red nose.

"Someone's idea of a prank," Ranger muttered. Nevertheless, they would maneuver the pot into the field reserved by the fire department for that purpose and attempt to set off the bomb safely. We breathed sighs of relief as the suspicious thing was hauled off our premises.

It was 5:00 AM and still dark when the officers returned. "What do you make of this?"

Ranger asked, holding up some kind of costume that he'd found in the backpack when he'd finally deemed it safe to open. "And this?" It was a stage dagger with a note pinned to it.

I read the words aloud: "'Double, double toil and trouble, Fire burn, and cauldron bubble, Trouble that you've heaped on me, Soon I will return to thee.'"

"Wasting police time and resources," Ranger snapped. "Does this prank make sense to you, M'am? Know the perpetrator, do you?"

"Yes, I know who left this backpack here to frighten us," I said. "Guess he's in a mood to play games. I just feel lucky this wasn't a real bomb like the one he made to revenge himself on Seven Angels." Realizing that the officers were still looking puzzled and angry, I filled them in on Deluca's background and the charges in the current warrant for his arrest. Now they looked interested but even more perplexed. I counted on Stone to make sense of the situation later.

"What the hell does Deluca think he's doing, tramping about in the snow to deliver stupid threats?" Joe, who had hauled himself up on crutches to examine the note, sat down heavily in one of the kitchen chairs. "Makes me wonder what he's planning for an encore."

CHAPTER THIRTY

By the pricking of my thumbs,
Something wicked this way comes.
    William Shakespeare

At 7:17 AM, the power was restored with a brilliant flash of all the lights that had been on when the electricity failed.

Good thing! I was beginning to feel seriously caffeine deprived after a night's sleep that had more or less ended at 3:14 AM, although I did doze a bit after the disgruntled bomb squad left. Surprisingly, they did not regard the backpack as criminal evidence, despite my hysterical reaction to its presence under my rhododendron bush. No bomb, no crime.

Although there's no substitute for a good night's sleep, it's always been my belief that a big protein breakfast comes close. Between frying up sausages, eggs, and polenta ("cornmeal mush" to Tip) and toasting English muffins, I studied the contents of the backpack, which I had laid out on my desk in the old borning room off the kitchen.

The stage dagger with the threatening note. Plastic boots with fold-over tops. A gray wig; might have been the one in which Deluca had disguised himself while playing a hot dog vender in Providence. I'd draped the bulkiest item over the desk chair: a tartan cloak with a big fake silver broach in the shape of a rampant dragon brandishing a sword. I didn't need Fiona to identify the light blue and red plaid as Clan Macbeth, the Thane of Cawdor being a menace to all who stood between him and his desires, not unlike Deluca.

"You're very quiet this morning," Joe said, leaning on his crutches and pouring more coffee for the three of us.

"I'm just thinking. About that stuff in my office. What it means, if any meaning is intended." I reached for another English muffin, fortification for the snow shoveling to follow.

"The guy is a lunatic, Aunt Cass." Tip poured maple syrup on his slab of crusty polenta. "Don't expect any useful evidence out of that pile of crap."

"He's a clever lunatic, though," Joe said. "He didn't choose to taunt you with a Macbeth costume for nothing."

"Yeah, but Macbeth got his in the end," Tip said. He wiped up the last drop of syrup with the last bite of muffin and brought his plate to the sink. "I'm going to get started on the driveway. Always got to be ready for a quick getaway."

"I'll be out to help in a few minutes," I said as cheerfully as possible for a gal who hated snow shoveling.

"No need, Aunt Cass. Honestly, you should stay in the house and do the visioning thing on Deluca till you figure out what he's up to. Why don't you get out that medicine pillow?"

An attractive offer except for the pillow part. He was referring to my least favorite psychic aid, a prototype so powerful that I never again combined those particular herbs in one pillow. The Psychic Visions Pillow which I sold online was a pale, safe imitation. Meanwhile, I had the damn original *somewhere.* (I routinely managed to lose it.)

Once again I pummeled my memory for an answer, but none was forthcoming.

Tip picked up the rifle still on the kitchen chair and stood it in the boot closet under the stairs. He took out an old pair of Joe's boots and pulled them on; they were heavier than the ones Tip had brought with him for snowshoeing. "Remember that it's loaded," he said, and headed out the kitchen door, closely followed by Scruffy and Raffles, exclaiming joyously.

Let's go, let's go! The kid and I will keep away pesky squirrels and wicked crows while you play in the white stuff.

White stuff! White stuff!

"Did you look in the freezer?" Joe asked.

I looked at him sharply. "What makes you say that?"

"It's the most unlikely place I can think of to hide a pillow." He stumped around on his crutches, turning his back ostensibly to make another pot of coffee, but really to hide an insufferable grin. "And you've hidden it there before."

Just to prove him wrong, I went right down cellar to the long coffin-like freezer where we keep enough frozen foods for an army of hungry refugees, in case such a horde should pass through Plymouth. And there it was! Right between the giant bag of mango chunks and a stack of foil-wrapped lamb chops. *Merde!* (as my youngest daughter would say.) I grabbed the pillow. It was covered with a blue fabric, printed with herb sprigs, both the color and those particular herbs (mugwort, mimosa, rosemary) being elements of clairvoyance. How tempted I was to toss it out the cellar door into the snow! But no. There is honor among psychics. I carried it into our bedroom for a consultation, steeling myself for Joe's robust laugh.

But he wasn't in a laughing mood. He was listening to my cell phone, which I had left on the kitchen table. "Phil," he said succinctly, and passed it to me.

"What's going on?"

Phillipa spoke briskly. "The officer Stone sent over to Fiona's to guard the premises can't get into the house. Guess why!" Without waiting for my reply, she continued. "Fiona is crouched down by her window, aiming her Glock at him. I never should have warned her about Deluca. She thinks the uniform is just another one of Deluca's clever disguises."

"Not answering her cell?" I asked, with no real hope that Fiona would pick up in the middle of a perceived crisis. But right at that moment, I happened to glance out my bird feeder window, where a snowy owl was perched, glaring at me. "Wait. Oh, good! I think Blod's here. That's rather significant, don't you think? Like the bird's on our wave length. What if I tell the owl to bring Fiona a message? Might work."

Phillipa groaned. "Stone has promised that the officer he sent to guard Fiona, Doug Murphy, will attempt to reason with her before he's forced to report the standoff and someone at headquarters sends for a SWAT team. He realizes that she's just scared. I'm going right over there right now. I've almost got my car free of snow, and by the way, what do you think I found hanging on my radio antenna? A Paw Sox cap, like the one Deluca was wearing at Starbucks. Boadicea is going nuts over the boot prints."

"Another warning! What can he be thinking, tramping about in the snow like that?"

"What, indeed? Wants to strike a little terror in our hearts, I guess. But, I can only handle one crisis at a time. I'm off to Fiona's now. I'll drop Eddie off at Dee's. Maybe I can save the situation before Fiona gets arrested for attempted murder of a policeman. Or shot. Doubt they'll shoot, though, with Laura Belle in the house. But you go ahead and try the owl thing. After all, it worked for Harry Potter. Oh, wait—that was fiction, wasn't it?" She ended the call abruptly.

I tiptoed over to the window. Blod (or whoever) was scattering sunflower seeds he'd found under a layer of snow in a contemptuous manner. "Sorry, no fresh mousies this morning," I whispered. "Listen, Blod, this is very important. You have to fly right back home and warn the Lady Fiona that the gentleman outside her house is there to help not hurt her. Got that? Help not hurt. *Go right now. Shoo! Shoo!*" I tapped on the window, subliminally conscious that Joe was watching me in a worried way. "Listen, honey—either you believe in magic or you don't," I explained to him. "I do. This is called *Acting in Accordance.*" I shook the damned pillow at him. "Now I'm going into the bedroom and meditate before I'm tempted to turn you into a toad."

I thought he would never stop chuckling, but I left the kitchen with all the dignity I could muster. Fiona has told us that the toad spell is lost in antiquity anyway.

I curled up under our quilt, and leaned my cheek on the pillow. The house was still chilly, and the pillow was even colder. I let my mind wander thoughtlessly for who knows how long? Long enough. Suddenly I sat up with a jolt of knowing. *Trouble, trouble, boil and bubble.* Simple enough; Deluca was invoking the Scottish play to hint that Fiona would be one of his prime targets. The dashing imitation 17th century Italian boots (Seven-league boots!) symbolized his own swift getaway. The cap and the gray beard were reminders of his encounters with us in Providence.

"He's going after Fiona and Phil and me," I said when I emerged from the bedroom. "I just don't know in which order."

Joe made a move toward the boot closet, hampered by his crutches, and suddenly his leg simply collapsed under him. Going down as directly and suddenly as I have seen trees fall in Jenkins Park, he hit his head on the corner of the stairs. I screamed, but evidently not loud enough to be heard above the chorus of barking outdoors. In an instant, I was crouched beside Joe, calling his name.

"I'm all right," he groaned, clutching his brow. "I only hit my head. Wicked headache."

"Oh, honey, there might be internal bleeding. Or you might be concussed. I have to call 911 for a rescue wagon."

"Don't, Cass!" he said in as commanding a tone as a man on the floor clutching his head can manage. "They'll take me to Jordan Hospital. And I don't want to leave you alone. It's dangerous, as you already know."

"I'll be going with you, honey. Tip will hold the fort and take care of the pups. He's has the .22, and he's a strong, clever boy."

The dispatcher sounded weary, either from being on duty all night or dealing with another Shipton emergency—or both. But the Rescue response was timely, and there was already a path to the front door cleared by the bomb squad.

Once it was established at Jordan that Joe wasn't bleeding into his brain, Dr. Blitz still wanted to keep him overnight. "He'll need to be watched for symptoms of concussion, okay? But you don't have to stay Ms. Shipton, okay? Come back for him in the morning, okay?"

"Okay," I said. "As soon as he seems to be sleeping peacefully."

Joe did fall asleep, finally, so I decided to go home. While I was warming up the Rav in the parking lot, I saw that I'd missed several calls from Phillipa and hadn't read her text messages either. No point now. I called her back instead.

"I tried to get you!" she complained. "Where in Hades were you?"

I told her about Joe's accident and our trip to the hospital. "I'd left my cell in my coat pocket in the waiting room," I explained. "How's the situation with Fiona."

"Murphy used a bullhorn to talk her down from full panic. He threw his identification onto the front step. Fiona claimed that Laura Belle spoke up from behind the sofa where she was supposed to be barricaded and said, "It's all right to open the door for the nice policeman, Aunt Fifi.""

"So then, she put down the Glock and opened the door?" I asked hopefully.

"Not immediately. Not that she didn't believe her grand-niece, who only tells the truth, as we know. But she was still hesitant. Deluca can be very believable, and you recall that he once made off with the youngsters, like a veritable Pied Piper, and tried to drown them in Eel River? But apparently, just then, there was something going on in the backyard that got Fiona's attention. And Omar was causing a ruckus at the door to the backyard, trying to claw his way through."

"Yes—and then?"

"Fiona opened the door and surrendered her Glock. Office Murphy is still there, outside, on guard."

"Anything else?"

"All right, all right. Fiona is saying that Blod turned up, perched on the window ledge, and pecked at the glass with a message. That's what was driving Omar bonkers. The damned owl has never come that close to the house before."

"And the message was?"

"You'll have to ask Fiona. Meanwhile, at least she isn't waving a gun around. She brought out some coffee and scones to the squad car, and even used her magical voice, but no way was Doug giving back her weapon."

"Good man. As long as he stays there and watches out for them."

"What about you? You're alone in the house with Joe in the hospital."

"I have Tip, Grandma's rifle, and these two protein-packed guard dogs. I should be fine. You take care yourself."

Of course, I couldn't resist calling Fiona. "How come you gave the Glock to Officer Murphy?" I asked.

"A little bird told me to," she said. "Officer Murphy's a sweet boy, really. Still out there, poor dear. Won't give me back my Glock, though."

"Good."

"All I have left is a little .38 special, but that's in my lock box. Can't be too careful with children. I've always kept my Glock in the lock box as well. It's really strange and magical the way I got the .38. Remind me to tell you the whole story sometime. Of course, it's a revolver so there's the problem of recoil. Fortunately, I have a strong hand."

I hesitated to stop the flow of Fiona's ramble until I was satisfied that she was not in immediate danger of some firearms violation. Phillipa would follow up on this tidbit later.

∽

Everything being clear and quiet on this cold, sunny Sunday morning, Tip called the beautiful Jordan Rivers, whom he'd met at the Morse site in Salem, where she'd been a photographer and cataloger. They were both majoring in anthropology, though at different universities, he in Maine and she in Massachusetts, but Tip's crush on Jordan had little to do with shared interests. A couple of years older than he, she was electric and alluring, with West Indian features and a brilliant, graceful style all her own. We (Joe and I) thought there had been a brief physical relationship that Tip wanted to pursue and Jordan did not. Whatever, she must have been glad to hear from Tip and welcoming, because soon after he admitted to the call, he wondered if I'd be okay if he met Jordan for dinner that night. The roads to Salem were relatively clean, he avowed. In the bright sunshine of day, there seemed to be no immediate dangers. Unless of course, I needed him to help with Joe.

The impassive expression he tried to keep on his face during this self-sacrificing offer would not have fooled any mature woman, especially not a clairvoyant. "Of course, if you feel there's a threat from that SOB Deluca, I'll stay right here."

"Deluca may have wanted only to scare us into fits before he disappears off the police radar. I have the .22 and the dogs, and the patrol cars will be checking on all of us," I said. "Dr. Blitz wants to keep Joe another night, especially because of the sudden collapse of his leg business. A few more tests to be on the safe side. So you go ahead and have a good time. Give Jordan my love. Joe won't be discharged until ten tomorrow morning. So if it's too late to come home, feel free to stay overnight." I did the expressionless thing, too, when Tip shot me a suspicious glance. Could I possibly be matchmaking? *Who, me?*

Tip left early in a gladsome roar of the Harley. I filled a few orders, then after lunch I took the dogs (who'd begged for a ride) and went to Deidre's house. I had a few cautions to impart.

"Keep in mind it was you and Heather in that *Times'* photo where you were credited with helping to capture that nasty terrorist, Hamid," I warned her over some very nice French Press coffee in her jonquil-yellow kitchen. I'd left Scruffy and Raffles in the car to avoid their harassing the poodles. "If Abdul Hamid's nephew is out for revenge, he may come calling on you. Stone's aware, and there are officers keeping an eye on your place, but you need to be doubly alert, Dee."

"Really, will we never be done with that London incident? It was just another of your chancy visions that got us to Brown's Hotel that night. The wrong place at the wrong time *again*. Well, not the wrong time for that little Fatimah Khatoon, I guess. Anyway, I've told Conor about this latest worry, and I got quite the lecture in return." Deidre's busy fingers kept themselves occupied with sewing faery shoes onto faery feet. "I think the underlying theme of his harangue was the dangers of running with the wrong crowd, namely you witches. Not that he doesn't like you all, he does. But it's not escaped his notice that mayhem and murder seem to follow us wherever we go, and he'd just as soon that his *carabhaidh* wouldn't wind up in so many dire straits and police reports."

"And Grandma O'Donnell has been clued in to the real extent of your family? How did that go? Are you officially engaged, then?"

"*No*, he hasn't asked me, 'officially.' It went pretty much as you saw it. At first she paled and fell into her chair in a swoon. Then she turned purple and clutched for her smelling salts and a tot of whiskey. But after a few minutes, she seemed to recover and began to laugh. She never did say why. All she said was, 'You're such a little thing, too. To think I was worried about your hips.'" Deidre grinned. "Evidently she's looking ahead to my bearing a passel of future O'Donnells."

"Good Goddess! And are you? Looking forward to another child with Conor, I mean?"

Deidre sighed and patted her flat little stomach. "As the *stregheria* and Doris Day would say, *Que sera, sera*. But I rather think Conor has no notion of settling down as a family man any time soon. He so enjoys assignments in far-flung places. Lucky for me that I have such excellent nannies and can play at being a free soul from time to time."

I asked no more questions, although plenty of them occurred to me.

"Okay. I'm glad the old girl came around. Meanwhile, you keep everything locked up tight. By now, the police patrols that Stone alerted must be spread pretty thin. Do you have anything in the house to defend yourself with? I suppose not, with the children."

Deidre smiled and glanced up at an open shelf where several grotesque figures with glittering eyes lodged between *The Joy of*

Cooking and *The Microwave Gourmet* were glaring at me. "Well, there are my gargoyles, of course. I've promised a couple of those to Heather for protection. They're medieval, you know, employed by the Catholic clergy to scare evil spirits away from the church. And Heather's going through her own medieval phase, what with the De Veres and all. But I guess you mean something more traditional. Will's old firemen buddies are on call if I think I need something or someone. Better not mention the possibility of my borrowing a weapon to Phil, though. You know how she gets."

We said good-bye, and I headed off to Fiona's, where I walked the dogs up and down the street for a few minutes, then stashed them back in the car because of Omar.

"Hold the fort, guys. If you're very, very good, we'll stop by Dunkin' on the way home."

We canines get used to being abandoned and forgotten. It's a dog's life. I'll have a raised cinnamon cruller.

Cruller! Cruller!

"Everything's been as peaceful as Tut's tomb before Carnarvon found it," Fiona said. "I wonder if we haven't been getting ourselves all worked up for nothing. I finally got rid of Phil and her pleas of caution, and I told that young officer that he might as well go along, too. Just ask someone to drive by occasionally, and if he sees a light in the front window, he'll know I'm all right. I've got that one on a clapper, so if anyone breaks in here, I can clap it off in a jiffy. Officer Murphy kept my little Glock, though. Cheeky of him. I'm a Senior Citizen, you know, and I'm entitled to my rights." She handed me a thistle-painted mug of steaming lapsang souchong.

"Last time I checked, that meant a discount at the movies not the right to threaten a cop with a weapon," I said.

"Oh, don't be a nit-picker. *Fore-armed is fore-warned.*"

Fiona seemed in good spirits, and I didn't doubt that the need to protect Laura Belle would call forth some hidden resources we none of us knew.

My last stop was at Heather's where my dogs were always welcome, although Scruffy was too snobby to enjoy the camaraderie, except for his unrequited interest in Honeycomb, who gave him the usual surly lip.

"The reason you have to be super-careful," I said, "is because you and Dee were in that photo in the *Times*. If Hamid has incited his nephew to some maniacal fury, you may be his first stop."

Heather poured us each a glass of sparkling Prosecco. I'd had about enough caffeine for one day anyway. I sipped the restorative beverage with relief.

"Do you really think anyone could get in this house without my canine brigade going into a frenzied alarm mode?" she asked. "Say, since Joe's not being discharged until tomorrow morning, why don't you and the pups stay for dinner? Fleur is making a traditional medieval eel pie, and some other interesting dish, I forget what."

"No, thanks," I said promptly. "I promised the dogs I'd stop at Dunkin's on the way home. You must never break a promise to a dog, as you know. They have better memories than elephants, and they make sure you never forget, either."

"Tell me you're not allowing those lovely healthy animals to be poisoned with fried doughnuts!" Heather exclaimed.

"Of course not, Heather! The girl at the drive-up window at Dunkin's keeps some special high-fiber, tooth-cleaning biscuits just for canine customers."

She raised one eloquent bronze eyebrow but let that one go.

"Actually, if push comes to shove," she said, "Roland has a crossbow, and he knows how to use it."

So, with one thing and another, I drove toward home feeling quite confident in our readiness to meet whatever danger came our way, not discounting the force of magical intention as chief among our weapons.

I didn't forget to make the pit stop I'd promised my furry friends, where I also bought myself a chocolate doughnut, an adult treat known to have no redeeming value, smirking to think it might have been a slice of eel pie.

CHAPTER THIRTY-ONE

Must helpless man, in ignorance sedate,
Roll darkling down the torrents of his fate?
  Samuel Johnson

It was blissfully warm and snug at home. There's nothing like a loss of power to remind us of our daily blessings. The oil heater was running its heart out in the cellar; I could almost hear a calculator clicking every time it roared to life.

I brought in split logs from the porch, stashed them in the kitchen wood-box, and built up the fire in both the kitchen and the living room. An aura of hominess and coziness filled the downstairs; but the house seemed empty without Joe. I was so glad that he was home from Africa, battered though he was, and would be released from the hospital tomorrow. Still, I was fairly adapted to the "feast and famine" of his frequent absences. There were even advantages to *down time* in a marriage. A chance to reflect on the person you are by yourself. But not too long away from each other, of course; the best times were those we spent together, no matter if we were grubbing out the herb gardens in spring or traveling to thrilling places.

Tip called just as I'd got the fireplaces blazing cheerily; he asked if everything was quiet in Plymouth, no signs of psychos lurking about, no problems at the house needing a man's expertise to sort out.

I knew where this was going. "It's okay Tip. Why don't you stay over tonight, and come back early tomorrow morning to help me get Joe home? Give my love to Jordan."

"You won't get too lonesome there on your own?"

"I always have my friends close by, the medicine women."
I used the name that Tip had given us. "And Joe is only a cell
phone call away. In fact, I'm going to call him now."

And I did that. Somehow you always ask people in the
hospital what they had for dinner and what they were watching
on TV and/or reading. Joe had been served his dinner ages ago,
"some chicken slop," and he was watching the BBC program
about the Acropolis Museum in Athens.

"You sound a little sad. Do you want me to come over for
a visit?" I asked.

"No, that's okay, sweetheart. Just a twinge of nostalgia for
the mother country. You'll be springing me out of here first
thing tomorrow, right?"

"Dr. Blitz gave his blessing?"

"If I don't pass out overnight," Joe said. "See you in the
morning. Miss you, love you."

"Me, too," I said.

"But that's why a gal needs her canine companions," I
said to my furry audience of two. "For sensible conversation
and cuddles." I settled onto the living room couch, enjoying
the cushions' scent of anise, purslane, and rose petals and
sipping a glass of iced dry vermouth with a twist of lemon,
an aperitif I'd learned to enjoy during quiet moments of our
Italian adventure. The peaceful interlude lasted for several
sweet minutes, then ...

Hey, Toots ... what's for dinner?

Dinner? Dinner?

Actually, I was getting hungry myself. "I'm thinking
about those braised chicken breasts in the freezer," I said. "And
some nicely spiced rice. But first, why don't you guys take a
run outdoors before dinner?" I emptied my glass and stood
up, stretching, and ambled into the kitchen, where I noticed a
message on my cell phone, which I'd left on the table as usual. I
let the dogs out the back door so they could whisk through the
pet flap on the porch, while I read the message.

It was from Phil: "Eddie read another headline. Yesterday!
Afraid to tell me. *Break-in and Shooting in Plymouth.* Tell Tip,
keep that rifle ready. I'm calling everyone."

Oh, swell. Tip was off romancing in Salem. I guessed I'd
better not tell Phil that, or she'd be sending in the Marines. I
refilled my vermouth glass, found and unwrapped the chicken

breasts, and put them into the microwave, pressing Rapid Defrost.

What were the odds of that headline referring to me? After all, I'd been warning everyone else to beware of dangerous enemies showing up on our doorsteps. But Eddie's headline could just as well refer to some family get-together of the Finches gone awry. That big frowsy Wanda Finch had threatened me with her rifle more than once. All the Finches were red-haired hot heads. They ought to have their own reality show; Plymouth's answer to Duck Dynasty.

All the while I was rationalizing away my fears, I was checking the window locks very carefully. Now I let in Scruffy and Raffles. "Everything cool out there, guys?" I bolted and chained the door.

Scruffy swaggered in and occupied himself with a long, sloppy drink of water. He looked up finally, dripping onto the floor as usual.

Chased away some dumb squirrel.

Dumb squirrel! Squirrel!

Raffles took his sire's place at the water bowl.

Almost too quiet, I thought. Tip would have said, "Must be Indians out there."

I fed the dogs, then carried my own dinner on a tray into the living room and watched *Sixty Minutes*. When it was over, I scrolled through the Guide looking for some good old movie. Scruffy, who had taken his usual post on the window seat, stood up and bristled.

I peered over his back into the darkness. Scruffy and Raffles began to bark in earnest now, whether sensing my frisson of alarm or something else, I didn't know. A chill ran from my neck right down to my root chakra. Maybe some bold raccoon banging the trash receptacles, I thought, but that wasn't the feeling I was getting.

Too late! There was a thump on the porch. I wheeled around toward the kitchen, thinking I would just get that loaded rifle from under the stairs, in case.

There was another crash, a fearful one, as someone kicked in the kitchen door. The dogs snarled and moved toward the hooded figure standing there, grinning, a pistol in his hand. My knowledge of guns is minimal, but I thought it might be a semi-automatic.

"Call off these damned dogs or I'll have to shoot them." Leo Deluca's hood fell back revealing his boyish features and tumble of black curls as he backed away toward the door, where a broken chain dangled from the lock. A hateful smile sat oddly on his baby face.

I grabbed Scruffy's collar and hauled him back toward the living room and our bedroom beyond, with him struggling and coughing all the way. Raffles turned toward us, startled and uncertain what to do without his sire's lead. I whistled and he followed as I dragged and pushed Scruffy into the bedroom, growling. It took all my strength to close the two dogs in and slam the door.

"It's all right, Scruffy. You two be quiet now."

Scruffy didn't believe that for a minute. He continued to bark vociferously and scratch at the bedroom door. Raffles followed suit. As I was in the living room, I naturally glanced at the front door. No way to open that quietly to escape, and I wouldn't have left the dogs to their fate in any case. Besides, I was in Deluca's direct line of sight through the kitchen-to-living-room door. I returned to the kitchen and faced him.

"What do you want here?" I demanded. "The police are watching this place, you know. They'll be driving by any minute now."

Deluca laughed—a false stage laugh. *"The lady doth protest too much, methinks.* As if I would believe you, Ms. Shipton. You know what I've come for, don't you? Payback is a bitch, isn't it? Sit right down there, hands on the table. I'd be very sorry to kill you right now unless you insist."

I eased myself into a kitchen chair, the sink at my back, never taking my eyes off my nemesis. Deluca shrugged out of the backpack he was wearing and took out an oblong package, about the size of a shoebox, which he placed on a counter near the stove, across the room and out of my reach. This was followed by a roll of duct tape.

The chill in my body had nearly frozen me solid, but I managed to hold out the index and little fingers of my left hand in the stregheria sign to ward off evil intentions. The hardest thing to do when truly in danger is to surround oneself with the blue-white aura of protection, but Goddess knows I tried.

Keeping the pistol trained on me, Deluca came so close I could smell the ugliness of his intentions in his sweat and breath.

"Put your hands behind the chair," he ordered. I obeyed reluctantly, my thoughts and intentions sizzling against this indignity. He stuck the gun under his sweatshirt, somewhere at the back of his jeans, taped my hands together, then my feet. Looking at me with nasty satisfaction, he smiled and considered my mouth. "Later," he said. "After we've talked."

At least I would be able to speak, for now. If only I had Fiona's magical voice. Even Phillipa could manage it sometimes. Or maybe I would find a way to call for help. I glanced at my cell phone on the table. *Impossible now*, I thought.

But Deluca had caught my look. I could see it on his face; he began to plot a new angle to his master plan.

"Hmmm. Let's have a look at this speed dial," he said, taking my cell phone in hand "Which of these old gals was with you in Providence? The crazy one with the gun—I remember. That's Fiona Ritchie. And the dark-haired one who looks like the Wicked Stepmother in Snow White. Married to that detective. Yes. Phillipa Stern. Well, hell. Might as well get the whole coven together. *Double, double, toil and trouble, fire burn and cauldron bubble.* They sure as shit got together to testify at my trial. And all that humming. What was that about?"

"Your guilty imagination has run away with you. You're the only one responsible for your conviction, and even then you got off easy, tried as a juvenile. This time, with the Seven Angels incident, you're going down for a much longer time."

He studied the cell phone thoughtfully. "A text message, I think. I wouldn't trust you with an open phone line. You might try to warn your friends. After all, this is shaping up to be quite a party, and I wouldn't want any of you to miss the entertainment. Let's have a look at the style of your other texts. 'Blessed be'... 'Merry meet' ... very nice. That should give an air of authenticity. *Fair is foul, and foul is fair.*" He sat down at the table opposite me and began to compose a text. "Simple, plausible, and urgent. What fun to get all those accursed accusers here, and then we'll see whose tune is humming now."

Deluca gazed intently at the small screen and continued to key in messages rapidly with both thumbs. "*If it were done when 'tis done, then 'twere well it were done quickly*" he muttered.

In spite of my desperate situation, I could almost smile. It was the thought of us five in one room, an over-powering spiritual presence that made most men rather jumpy without being aware of why they were suddenly a bundle of nerves. On the other hand, rising anxiety is not something one wants to encourage in a psychopath.

But surely something would ring false in whatever he was writing. Otherwise, I worried, the others would indeed rush over into harm's way, and if they were hurt or killed, it would be all my fault. Still, with the thought of their solidarity, at least I felt an element of hope. I only wished that Fiona still had that Glock in her reticule. I said, "My friends aren't all that easy to fool. They'll know something's wrong. I'd be surprised if Phil or Dee isn't alerting the cops this very minute, and they'll soon be surrounding the house."

"Text messages are delightfully anonymous," he said. "I doubt they'll get wise."

Deluca had his own cell phone. I could see it in his shirt pocket. Not a regular cell phone, I thought. That's the remote control detonator. And that package, the bomb I'd seen in my vision. Would my friends fall for the phony texts? What could I do? Not much, duct-taped hand and foot. I studied the ceiling, as if the bunches of dried herbs hanging from the beams would give me some kind of inspiration.

"Here's what's coming down," Deluca said. "First, we'll have our little reunion. Then when I leave you and your friends to consider your sins, you're going to have as long as it takes me to get back to my car to think about how many times you witches have ruined my life. And then … BOOM. *These our actors, as I foretold you, were all spirits and are melted into air, into thin air.* Good-bye Cass Shipton and her weird sisters, her mutts, and her lovely seaside cottage. My parents used to have a lovely seaside cottage, too, until they had to relocate because of you and your circle from hell."

I thought the longer I kept this madman talking, the better chance there was that one of the others would text me back and get suspicious when I didn't answer, or even that the patrol would swing by and check on the car, whatever car Deluca had parked out there.

Scruffy and Raffles had begun to quiet down in the bedroom, just the occasional growl and lonesome yelp. Well, they were safe in there for now. Whatever happened, I wouldn't try to open that door and take a chance that one or both of them would get shot.

Deluca sat down at the table across from me. The terrifying package looming behind him on the counter, he fiddled with his own cell phone, frowning in complete concentration. I hoped to the Goddess that he knew what he was doing and wouldn't set off that bomb by accident. Not that I wouldn't like Deluca to be *hoist by his own petard*. But somewhere else, not here.

"If you leave now, you may be able to get away before the SWAT team shows up," I said.

"The wicked stepmother should be here first," Deluca said. And he was right, Phillipa lived the closest. Only ten minutes later (perhaps the longest ten minutes of my life, watching this lunatic fiddle with his cell phone attached to what surely was a bomb and mumble lines from Shakespeare to himself) I heard Phil's footsteps on the porch stairs. Familiar footsteps; the dogs barely woofed.

"Hey, Cass … I hope this is important. I had a very delicate lemon curd in the works. What in Hades happened to your doors?" Phillipa stepped into the room wearing a black leather jacket and a pilot's silk scarfk. "Uh oh, I see. The Bad Seed has turned up again." She unwrapped the scarf as coolly as if the appearance of a felon in our midst were an everyday occurrence. (Come to think of it, that might be true.)

"Sit down right there," Deluca ordered. He pulled the pistol out of his belt and waved it to indicate a chair halfway down the long table from me.

"He texted everyone," I said.

"Shut up, bitch, or I'll tape your trap," he snarled.

"Well, I hope the others are quicker on the uptake than I was," Phillipa said, eyeing Deluca's truly frightening expression and moving reluctantly to the chair he had indicated. "Mine said, 'Come to my house as quick as you can. I have something incredible to show you. Merry meet and blessed be!'"

"And that sounded like me?"

"Well, no actually. I thought maybe you'd been hitting Joe's Jack Daniels. Or Heather's treasured skull had surfaced and was addling your brain."

"Shut up! Shut up! This isn't any fucking tea party." Deluca stepped behind Phillipa and pulled her arms back cruelly.

"Hey, what do you think you're doing?" she demanded.

He put the pistol on the sink so that he could quickly and efficiently tape her hands together. "That skull! *Alas, poor Yorick.* What the hell was that all about? The fucking thing practically destroyed all the electronics in my workroom," Deluca said. "But, since it looked like a museum piece, possibly valuable, I threw it into the trunk of my car. Then the damned car battery started to act up, so I dumped the skull."

"Ouch, you little savage! That hurts," Phillipa said. "Where?"

Deluca pulled the tape even tighter, then began to tape up Phillipa's ankles. "Hold still or your friend here will suffer."

"Tempting ... but I'm fond of her," Phillipa said. "My question is, where did you dump the skull?"

"What do you care? You'll never see it. I threw it into the woods, and good riddance."

"Do you mean Jenkins Park?"

"I hear another car," I said. "Sounds like the blue bomber."

Having trussed up Phillipa, Deluca stood and faced the door with a wicked grin, the pistol aimed steadily at whomever came in next.

"Hello! Hello!" Fiona's musical voice sailed ahead of her. She stepped into the kitchen wearing several layers of the MacDonald tartan and took in our sorry state with one sharp glance of her gray eyes. "Dearie me, young man ... what's going on here?" Without breaking eye contact with Deluca, she began to reach into her reticule. Deluca leaped forward and knocked the reticule out of her grasp with his left hand in an artful move that was reminiscent of stage sword play. It slid halfway across the kitchen floor and stopped against a table leg.

"Shit," muttered Phillipa.

"Sit yourself down at the other end of the table, Madame Ritchie." It was a long table, and he was positioning us at a distance from one another. You're just in time for the party," Deluca said with almost playful menace, twirling the roll of duct tape in one hand.

"Now, Lee, you don't want to use that tape on an old lady like me," Fiona said softly in her magical voice. A shadow seemed to fall across her face and her hair darkened. "Why, I'm old enough to be your grandmother, and my skin is as delicate as paper. Tape will tear my poor arms. How is your grandmother? Bianca, isn't it? I bet she's praying right this very minute, as I am, that you won't ruin your young life just when the future is all before you, like a theater as the lights go up and the curtain rises." As I watched, Fiona seemed almost to take on the appearance of Bianca Deluca, complete with that little stoop in her back, but with more of a kindly expression than I'd ever seen on that miserable old bat's face.

For a moment, Deluca looked bemused, almost in a trance, but then he shook his head sharply and gave Fiona a push into the chair he had designated to her, with her back to the fireplace. "I know what you're up to, Madame Ritchie," he said agreeably, "and it won't work on me or any other true actor."

Fiona sat down, and Deluca turned his attention back to the door. Had he forgotten to tape Fiona's hands after all? She sat demurely with her hands behind her, just as if he *had* taped them. Meanwhile, a racket outside took his attention—and ours.

There were two voices, arguing. "It's Dee and Heather" I mouthed silently to Phillipa and Fiona. As we all watched the kitchen door intently, Deidre skipped in like little red riding hood—actually wearing a small red wool cap and carrying her work basket; a gargoyle peeking out from the top; Heather strode in afterward, holding a gargoyle in each hand, like two puppets.

"Dee seems to think these babies will scare away evil. What's that you gals have wrapped around your ankles? Good Goddess, is that duct tape! Oh, look what the cat dragged in!" Heather exclaimed, spotting Deluca, who was leaning nonchalantly on the counter beside his suspicious package. "I think we're looking at the ideal test of Dee's gruesome dollies." The large sleeves of her russet cashmere coat fell back as she shook the gargoyles in Deluca's direction.

"We think we were followed! There's a black Buick that's been sticking to us like paint," Deidre exclaimed. Then she, too, came to her wits and took in the picture before her. "Oh it's that little Gobshite again. Holy Mother of God, what do you have there?"

"Followed by whom," Fiona asked, slowly returning to her own self but retaining her musical magical tone of voice.

"Don't know!" Heather said. "Right behind us, though. Dee thinks it's a police officer or maybe one of her firemen buddies, but I'm not entirely sure."

Deluca aimed his pistol at one of the gargoyles and fired a shot! The fuzz flew off the top of its head but the little red eyes only glittered more menacingly. A window to the porch exploded. Heather screamed, and Deidre threw herself between the table and the sink. The dogs in the bedroom set up an unholy chorus of howls.

The noise was deafening, and the lingering smell of gunpowder disgustingly acrid. My kitchen had suddenly become a battleground.

"Is your hand all right?" I asked

"Holy Hecate, that scared me." Heather wiggled her fingers experimentally. "Okay, I guess. Listen, you son of a bitch …"

"Shut up, the whole gaggle of you!" Deluca screamed. "You two get your asses into those chairs over there," Obviously, he feared he was losing control of the situation, just as I had imagined he would once our circle was complete.

"Listen, Lee," Deidre said, venturing to stand again, but still behind me, Phil, and the table. The seriousness of her tone was somewhat at odds with the pointed red cap sliding over one ear. "You'd better leave here while you can. You're a fugitive and there are cops right outside. I'm not sure why they followed us here, but they're going to be very glad to see you."

As if to prove the point, there were heavy footsteps on the porch stairs, and the door to the porch crashed open. A man's figure appeared in the broken kitchen doorway. The shotgun in his hands was hung from a sling around his neck. He pointed it toward us, where we were frozen in disbelief behind the table, as he released the safety.

CHAPTER THIRTY-TWO

Who would not rather founder in the fight
Than not have known the glory of the fray?
    Richard Hovey

Although Deluca's eyes were bugged out in shock, he pointed his pistol at this new intruder with unwavering aim. The stocky, dark young man wore a turban with an MIT jacket and jeans. He seemed unfazed, stiff and curiously unresponsive to his precarious situation.

"I think what we have here is a Mexican stand-off," Phillipa said, sotto voce. "Is this golem who I think he is?"

"Allahu Akbar, Allahu Akbar," shouted the stranger, flourishing his shotgun at us women, seemingly unconscious of Deluca. I could see the hilt of some kind of short sword sticking out from under his jacket. This did not look good. I hadn't thought I could be any more frightened than I'd been confronting Deluca, but I was wrong about that. I was helpless now, tied up in a web of tape, and this madman had a sword. My heart was beating like a trapped butterfly.

Difficult as it was to take a breath, I managed to say, "Ladies, I believe this gentleman is Robert Azizi, whose uncle Abdul Hamid we ran into while we were in London."

"Allahu Akbar," Azizi repeated in a dazed way, as if he were drugged or hypnotized. Perhaps that's what it took, religion at the hypnotic level to convince a decent student intent upon becoming an engineer to abandon all that in favor of killing women to restore the honor of his family.

Fiona began to whisper, drawing the attention of all. She had drawn her tartan shawl over her head and was intoning something that sounded like Arabic. *"Qūlū ma'ī Qūlū ma'ī, Allāhu Allāhu, Allāhu Akbar! Allāhu fawqa l-mu'tadi."*

"Get out of here, you towel-head," Deluca screamed. "Or else you're dead."

"In confusion, there is opportunity," Deidre muttered. She crouched down again, eased behind Phillipa, and began to work away at the duct tape.

A moment later, Heather moved in back of me and tugged at the edge of the tape holding my hands together. "Damn, I think I've broken a fingernail," she complained.

Deluca's hysterical tone seemed to bring the first sign of conscious life to Azizi's eyes. He looked at Deluca with surprise, at the pistol in the young man's hand, then around the room at Fiona, seated sedately by the fireplace and the rest of us, bunched up behind the long oak table, where Heather and Deidre were surreptitiously trying to free Phillipa and me. Azizi lifted the shotgun a little, as if trying to guess its weight, then ...

The second explosion inside my kitchen, louder than the first, rocked us all and assaulted our ears with a deafening pain. The air, still smoking with the caustic smell of gunpowder, got a refresher. Deluca was knocked back toward the birdfeeder window. Looking completely shocked, he grabbed his stomach and slid down the cabinet to the floor. Glass had shattered above him, most of the shards blasted outwards into the yard. His pistol slid across the floor and was stopped at the refrigerator. Blood began to ooze between his fingers. The dogs went into another frenzy of barking and howling.

Heather abandoned the half-unwrapped duct tape, leaving it to dangle around my fingers, and flung herself over the pistol.

Azizi looked down at her as if she were some strange species of lizard slithering at his feet. He swung the shotgun around and pointed it directly at Heather's head while she was still trying to free the pistol underneath her.

Fiona sprang up from her chair and tossed the tartan shawl over Azizi's head, throwing off his aim. The shotgun went off with another shattering blast, this one taking out the lighting fixture. It fell with a mighty crash right in the middle of the kitchen table. Only a light over the sink now illuminated the kitchen. I nearly toppled over in my chair. Fiona grabbed her reticule, still where it had fallen against the table leg, and lifted something out.

At last Deidre's nimble fingers had succeeded in freeing Phillipa, while I was still working at my bonds, which were partially loosened. Under the circumstances, they both crouched down behind the table. Despite the carnage in the kitchen, Phillipa crawled over on her knees to help me get free.

Azizi roared in rage and pulled the obscuring shawl away from his eyes. Just in time for Fiona to hit him with a blast from the pepper spray she'd been carrying in her reticule. He screamed and scrubbed at his eyes, dropping the shotgun at Deidre's feet.

She picked it up and checked the chamber. "I wonder which thingie is the safety," she said. "Oh, here. I think I've got it."

Phillipa finished unwrapping the duct tape around my hands, leaving me to deal with the ankles, stood up, and took a cell phone out of her jacket pocket. ""I believe it's time to call 911. We'll need an ambulance, too. No, two ambulances. Oh, yes ... and the bomb squad. I take it that thing on the counter is Deluca's? Where's the remote?"

"Ceres save us! It's in his shirt pocket. What if Azizi had hit that pocket?" I wailed, as I began to work on my ankles. "Fat chance of getting the bomb squad out here after that false alarm we had."

Phillipa was already talking earnestly to the dispatcher. I thought it was a good thing she was married to a Plymouth detective. A call like that needed all the credibility it could get. As it was, the woman was keeping her on the phone, describing our ordeal.

Azizi was still wailing, even louder than I was.

"I'm putting the remote in my reticule for safekeeping. Don't worry, I've disabled it," Fiona said, kneeling down beside Deluca. "Leo is alive but unconscious. Cass, get Azizi's jacket and shirt off him. Don't pull them over his head, cut them off with scissors, and flush his eyes with cool water. Wash his face, too, with some non-soap face cleaner."

After moving Deluca's limp hand out of the way, Fiona began to put pressure on the wound in his abdomen, crooning to him in a voice I recognized as a replica of his grandmother's.

"What was it that you recited to this Muslim character, Fiona," Deidre asked, keeping the shotgun trained on Azizi. "I didn't know you spoke Arabic."

"*Say it with me, say it with me: God, God, God is the Greatest, God is above any attacker!*" Fiona recited, then returned to her comforting monolog, only interrupting it long enough to ask, "Do you have some kind of a large gauze pad, Cass?"

I stopped bathing Azizi's face and said. "There's plenty of first aid stuff in the downstairs lav. Heather, would you have a look? Dee, keep that gun on Azizi in case he recovers."

"Not to worry," Deidre said, her gaze and her aim never wavering away from the MIT student writhing on the floor while I bathed his face. Heather stuck the pistol in her belt and went off to rummage around in the lav.

"Be careful with that thing," I called after her.

"I feel like Annie Oakley," she yelled back. "And it's a good feeling." A moment later she was back with a fistful of gauze pads for Fiona, who pressed them to Deluca's wound.

He opened his eyes, groaning in pain. "*Our revels ... our revels now are ended,*" he mumbled. Anything else was lost in the shrieks of sirens, the screeching of vehicles in the driveway, and the thunder of police and EMTs rushing in to take over. Ahead of them all, Phillipa's husband, white-faced and grim, whose arms enclosed Phillipa in a fierce grip, demanding to know what was going on here.

Phillipa explained succinctly. "Deluca. Gunshot to the abdomen. Just became conscious again. Azizi. Pepper spray. And there's a bomb over there beside the stove. So ... how was your day?"

Heather gently uncurled the shotgun from Deidre's tight grip, grabbed one of the officers, and dropped both weapons into his hands. I recognized him as Heather's cousin Cliff Morgan, who almost grinned at her but then thought better of it and resumed the severe expression of an officer of the law. Stone directed others to remove everyone from the house as quickly as possible.

I grabbed my lumber jacket and the leashes off the hook by the broken kitchen door and dashed into the bedroom to free the dogs, who'd finally stopped barking, outmatched by the cacophony in the driveway when it had reached fever pitch. "Come on, you guys. We've got to get out of here."

It's about time, Toots. What's with all the fireworks? The kid is really spooked.

Spooked! Spooked!

As were we all.

I don't think I've ever seen EMTs move faster. The sight of the bomb squad van may have given them extra motivation for speedy evaluations. The two ambulances swerved around the other vehicles and out of our yard, sirens wailing, taking out a bank of rosemary bushes on their way. We ladies were herded into two patrol cars. Officer Bronk, in charge of our evacuation, wanted to leave the dogs behind. Numb as I was, I struggled with him to keep hold of their leashes while Heather screamed in one ear and Officer Morgan had a quiet word in the other until Bronk gave up. The fire trucks remained at the house, along with the bomb squad, whose chief had given me an incredulous look in passing.

We were then driven a safe distance up the main road, where the dogs insisted on getting out of the car.

Gotta pee!

Gotta pee!

I jumped out and walked Scruffy and Raffles a short way into Jenkins Park, still keeping them on leash. As we moved through the woods parallel to Route 3A, Scruffy began to pull and strain against his collar in the distracted, excited way of a dog who has scented something disturbing.

"What in Hades are you after, Scruffy? This is no time for a squirrel chase, so I am *not* letting you run, Mister."

Fiona handed over the remote detonator to the bomb squad technicians, who peered at it and at her incredulously. She smiled modestly. They used long-handled hook-and-line equipment to maneuver the bomb out to the containment pot and drove away to detonate it safely. Only then were we allowed to return to what remained of my house. Detective Stern had taken it on his own authority to forego the crime scene tape that would have sealed off the premises, and he expedited the forensic team gathering evidence. The photographer took pictures of every shred and shard, nothing I'd ever want for my photo album. Stone maintained it was not the evidence but our testimonies that would nail the case shut on Deluca, if he lived that long, and then he shunted everyone out and returned to Middleboro to make his report. Deluca and Azizi were both rushed to Jordan Hospital, treated for their injuries, and held under guard. Deluca was in ICU for the time being; it was expected that Azizi would be moved to Plymouth County Correctional the following day.

As soon as everyone left, Heather began with great industry to sweep up the glass. "We have to get this stuff off the floors before the kitchen will be safe for your dogs," she explained. Shut up in the bedroom again, Scruffy and Raffles were indeed complaining about neglect and ill-treatment.

Deidre and Phillipa got the light fixture off the table and stashed it on the porch.

"I guess I'd better call Dick," Heather said reluctantly, after her final sally with a wet mop. "Maybe he can do something about that kitchen door, just for tonight."

While Deidre wiped down the counters with handfuls of wet paper towels, Fiona built up the kitchen fire. With the smashed bird feeder window and the window to the porch blocked with ill-fitting cardboard and a back door that wouldn't quite close, we needed the extra warmth.

I dreaded bringing Joe home tomorrow to this mess, the biggest challenge yet to his do-it-yourself prowess. Well, Tip would be here to help. "I guess I should just be grateful that the whole house didn't blow up with us in it," I said.

"Ah, Pollyanna, the Glad Girl," Phillipa said, Somehow she'd managed to brew a large pot of coffee and scramble a bunch of eggs with sausages and a tower of toast on the side. By then it was past two, and we were all exhausted and famished.

The floor having finally passed Heather's inspection, the dogs were allowed out of the bedroom but were intimidated enough by the general shambles to hop onto their L.L. Bean faux sheepskin beds and curl up out of the way.

Eggs! Are those eggs? Good for a canine's shiny coat. Gives us lots of energy for guarding the den. Hey, Toots!

Toots! Toots!

"In a minute, you mutts."

"If Azizi had not arrived when he did, or if he'd come at a different time ..." Deidre said, eyeing Phillipa's platters with the hunger of the newly reprieved from death. "I feel we were blessed with a divine intervention, don't you? Surely the Holy Mother …"

"*Man proposes, the Goddess disposes.* I am often confounded by the inexplicable twists of fate. Let's do a circle of gratitude before Dick gets here," Fiona suggested.

I looked around at the broken windows, the hole in the ceiling, the dent in the table, and the door hanging oddly on its hinges. "Sure, Fiona, why not?"

"Well, okay, but don't let the eggs get cold," Phillipa said.

Heather lit a fat green candle she'd given me at Christmas. Its strong fragrance of frankincense and myrrh helped a little to dispel the reek of gun powder and the sickening iron smell of blood that had invaded my home. We held hands around the newly distressed table, and Fiona spoke for our hearts.

> *All good comes from the Goddess,*
> *And to her we give our praise,*
> *Thankful that Her power saves us*
> *And protects us all our days,*
> *Grateful for her many blessings*
> *As we follow in Her ways.*

❦

When Tip wove in on his Harley at eight the next morning, he was aghast and embarrassed at not having returned in time to help us face our attackers.

Having just staggered out of bed after too few hours sleep, I was clutching a mug of coffee and looking around my own kitchen with the despair and disbelief of a war refugee after the battle.

Pulling myself together, barely, I reassured him, "It was for the best, Tip." I was imagining how Tip would have reacted to Deluca's menace. "I fear you'd have got yourself killed trying to take down Deluca. As it was, Azizi did that for us. I would say we were lucky, but I truly believe we were blessed."

I told him how the confrontation had gone down, with Fiona the heroine who'd disarmed Azizi with pepper spray.

"Chief Medicine Woman of the Plymouth clan," Tip said. "That pepper spray is nasty stuff. I've heard tales." He surveyed the shambles of my kitchen with dismay and determination. "What time is Joe getting discharged?"

"We have to leave for the hospital in a couple of hours. Not much we can do," I said. "Our first task will be to keep Joe from trying to repair the destruction. Dick fixed the door, sort of, but I really have to call a locksmith."

"Joe can direct operations, and I'll follow his instructions. The worst thing for him will be the idea that he wasn't here to protect you."

"For which I'll be eternally grateful. We're safe and well, that's all I care about." I also cared about my beloved kitchen, but this was no time to wring my hands. We'd get that back in shape eventually.

"How's Jordan?" I finally thought to ask.

"She's all right." Tip turned his head away, inspecting the patched-up back door. I could read a world of disappointment in the set of his shoulders. "Going to Seattle in June. Got a summer gig at the Burke Museum, artifacts from Columbia River and Puget Sound. Might transfer to University of Washington in the fall."

"You'll miss her."

"I'll be okay." Tip turned back with a lopsided grin that wouldn't have fooled anyone, certainly not me. "Who knows what this year will bring? And besides, I'm going to be pretty busy myself. I'm thinking I might switch my major to law, you know. Music, too, of course. Double major."

"That's the spirit." I thought I might do a little ritual to bless Tip's hopes and plans at Imbolc. How good it would be if he found a captivating new love to banish any lingering fantasies about Jordan. Not that I wanted to meddle!

༖

While I was waiting for Joe's discharge to be processed, Dr. Blitz, who'd seen us through many another emergency, quietly clued me in with the privileged information that Deluca was recovering surprisingly well from his stomach wound, and the doctors were projecting a date at which he might be transferred to Plymouth County Correctional Facility. Jordan Hospital would not be sorry to see him go; high level prisoners interfered with the daily routine, which was hectic enough already.

About my husband, Dr. Blitz said, "I know Mr. Ulysses is impatient, okay? But do your best to keep him on those crutches for a while longer, okay? He's still liable to a sudden collapse of that right leg. Avoid stairs, okay?"

"Okay," I said.

Joe's orthopedic specialist at Boston Medical had recommended a follow-up evaluation in three weeks. He would discuss the issue of crutches or no crutches at that time.

Looking into Dr. Blitz's kindly but abstracted gaze, I thought he understood the situation in its reality. Joe's patience was wearing thin and thinner. Soon enough he'd throw away those crutches with some Greek oath and that would be the end of it.

"Or if he won't listen to reason, walk the stairs with him, in back when he's going up, in front when he's going down, okay?"

"Okay," I said.

∽

On the way home, I tried as gently as possible to explain to Joe what had transpired while he was tucked up at the hospital. He listened quietly, too quietly. The tightening of his jaw and the narrowing of his eyes spoke of his helpless anger louder than words.

At least he didn't blame me ... too much. "It's your karma, I know, but you have to take more care in the future. I don't think I could bear it if I lost you to one of these quixotic crusades of yours," he said in a low, reasonable, loving voice, which made me feel much more guilty than any heated words could ever have done.

All hell broke loose, however, when Joe clumped in on his crutches and took his first look at the condition of the kitchen—the cabinets he'd remodeled, the light he'd hung, the broad plank floor he'd refinished. "*Jesu Christos!*" he roared. "I'd like to kill those two bastards with my own hands."

I sent a little paean of thanksgiving to the Goddess of a Thousand Names that Joe would never have the chance to face Azizi or Deluca again.

"Phillipa says Leo has lost a lot of blood. He's in a world of pain right now. They've sent for his family." I didn't add that Deluca was no longer listed as critical, according to Dr. Blitz, and might soon be transferred to the County. "As for Azizi, he's looking at a long, long sentence for attempted murder, multiplied by five. Probably forever," I said placatingly.

"Lucky for him," Joe said in a tone I barely recognized as my good-natured husband's.

CHAPTER THIRTY-THREE

Attempt the end, and never stand in doubt:
Nothing's so hard but search will find it out.
    Robert Herrick

"That little devil Deluca is like a cat with nine lives!" Heather exclaimed.

It was barely past lunch, and I'd fled to Heather's for a little peace and quiet while Tip held the fort. I'd left Joe swearing at his infirmities while Tip did his best to restore the kitchen, which was impossible of course. Joe was already talking about a complete remodeling. Is anything as depressing as the thought of having one's kitchen enter a long period of upset and confusion? I'm not in favor of the death penalty but I might make an exception for the guys that shot up the heart of my home.

Heather had viewed this latest news from the hospital as a good excuse for an afternoon tea party in the Conservatory and had called all the others to join us. Deidre was tied-up with year-end inventory at her store, but she agreed to skip out for an hour. She and Phillipa were bemoaning the fact that we'd all have to testify in court against Deluca … again!

"As Wiccans, we are healers and therefore bound to rejoice at his recovery," Fiona said thoughtfully.

"Oh, bollocks," Deidre said, stabbing her little needle into the Green Man doll whose breechclout she was stitching on his sylvan body.

"On the other hand," Fiona continued, "that little assassin once tried to drown my darling Laura Belle, and your kids, too,

Dee, so I don't feel the necessity of going overboard on the well wishing."

"Amen, sister, amen," Deidre said.

"It's Federal prison for Leo this time," Phillipa said. "Unless his attorney manages a plea of insanity."

"What attorney? Not that mellifluous Owen Llewellyn, the honey-voiced Welshman who saved Leo's ass before!" I poured some of Heather's excellent Amontillado sherry into my empty tea cup.

"Deluca's a bombing suspect who tried to blow up a public theater. That's terrorism and that's Federal. He may recover from being shot in the stomach, but he's going to be out of our lives for a long, long time," Heather assured me.

Meanwhile, Fleur de Vere had wafted in with a tray of medieval sweetmeats, which she called *pokerounce and coffins*. Phillipa inspected them with suspicious interest. They turned out to be honey-drenched nut treats and custard tarts, both quite delicious.

"Excuse me, Miss Heather, but were you talking about Leo Deluca whose picture was on the front page of the *Patriot Ledger?*" Fleur asked.

"For heaven's sake, Fleur. Just call me Heather. None of that feudal nonsense, please. Why do you ask?"

"When Roland and I were working King Richard's Faire last summer, we met up with an actor at the Shakespeare Out-of-Doors performances. He was going by the name Richard Burbage, but that Leo Deluca in the paper looks exactly like him. Roland always thought that Richard was on the run from someone or something. The article said Deluca had been shot during a home invasion at Ms. Shipton's house, so I just wondered if it could be the same person."

With all of us suddenly looking at her avidly, Fleur's pale skin flushed with embarrassment. "We did *Midsummer Night's Dream*. Richard was brilliant as Puck. I played one of Tatania's handmaidens, Peasebottom, and Roland was Robin Starveling, the tailor."

"Did everything go well with the production?" Fiona took Fleur's tray and put it down on a rattan side table. Bangles softly tinkling, she put a comforting arm around Fleur.

"Well, yes. For the most part. Until the end, when there was some trouble with the manager about our wages. He'd promised a decent bonus for the acting, but then he claimed that those who were already employees of the Faire were not entitled to further compensation. That included Roland and me, of course. Richard said he wasn't an employee of the Faire and demanded what he'd been promised, but the manager made some excuse about knowing Richard was using a false name, so he'd better just settle for room and board."

"In other words, the manager stiffed you," Heather said. "Then what?"

Fleur's eyes filled with tears. "It was terribly disappointing! Most of us were trying to save up for winter when the Faire would be closed. Richard left in a huff before the last performance. Good thing, because a bunch of the actors got sick and threw up all over the stage."

"*Quelle surprise!*" Phillipa said.

"Thank you, dear," Fiona said. "It must be distressing to remember those troublesome events."

"Will Richard go to prison now, do you think?" Fleur asked.

"You're damn right he will," Deidre said.

Fleur picked up some empty dishes and fled back to the kitchen.

"Good to know Leo never lost his herbal skills," Phillipa said.

"King Richard's Faire must have been where Leo hid after he skipped out on parole. What bothers me most is Deluca's continual ability to get away Scot-free," Fiona said. "I think when we are called as witnesses, there ought to be a serious humming spell as well."

"Yes, yes, but what bothers *me* the most is the thought of that creep just throwing away my Morgan treasure," Heather said vehemently. "That we went all the way to England to rescue!"

"Extraordinary adventure, though," Phillipa said.

"Granted, but …"

"The winter solstice at Stonehenge was an unforgettable, transcendent experience, well worth the trip," Fiona added. "If that crystal skull is as powerful as I believe it to be, it will find its way home to you eventually. Keep the faith."

☙

Feeling guilty for my absence, I picked up an apple strudel at Bunn's Bakery on my way home. As I came up the porch stairs, I was greeted by the sight of Joe's crutches propped on one of the wicker chairs, even sooner than I had predicted. I just hoped my many healing rituals would keep him from collapsing, as Dr. Blitz feared might happen.

Joe had sanded the kitchen table and was preparing to rub it down with a Miniwax stain that would disguise the damage. The broken cabinet door had been removed, and the interior shelves put in order and dusted. Tip was changing the broken glass in the bird feeder window. I was lavish in praising my two handymen while brewing a fresh pot of coffee and laying the strudel out on the counter beside the cups.

How I would miss Tip when he returned to the University tomorrow, leaving me the dubious role of handyman's helper!

Scruffy bumped against me hopefully. *How about a walk in the woods, Toots? I'm losing my superb muscle tone, sitting around here while the furry-faced guy fusses. I need a good run!*

Good run! Good run! Raffles nosed the leashes hanging by the battered kitchen door with a hopeful canine grin.

"Okay, I'll take you guys out into Jenkins Park, but no wild running after everything that moves today." I put on my parka again, took down the leashes and clipped them firmly to my companions' collars, resigning myself to Scruffy's grumblings.

We strode off into the park together. It was cold but not unbearably, the dense trees protecting us from the frigid ocean winds. It was hard to believe that Imbolc was only a week away, the first stirrings of spring celebrated in the Wiccan calendar.

Raffles walked with a mannerly gait, reveling in many deep sniffs of the fetid leaves and invisible droppings of small animals. At least, it was too cold and dry still to worry about deer ticks and other canine hazards just yet.

Scruffy, on the other hand, was prancing and pulling in a most annoying way, turning our enjoyable ramble into a tug-of-war. "What in the world has got into you?" I asked crossly. "Can't you even behave as well as Raffles?"

Never mind the insults, Toots! There's something crazy out there. Can't you hear it? Gotta find out what's going on. Keep the kid here, and let me run. Gotta go! Gotta go!

Scruffy was behaving in an erratic, impulsive way, as if he were sensing something really unusual. Could he be sensing coyotes or even a wolf? I wondered if black bears ever roamed around Plymouth woods, maybe a refugee from Myles Standish State Forest? Whatever was putting the hair up on his back, I didn't want him—or any of us—having to tangle with it.

"Not on your life! We'd better turn around and head home now."

It took a bit of hauling to drag Scruffy back to the house. He was pulling and digging in his claws in a crazed fashion. At least Raffles pranced along at a perfect heel. I wondered if senior dogs ever slid into dementia.

Take that thought out of the law!

CHAPTER THIRTY-FOUR

All that is gold does not glitter,
Not all who wander are lost;
The old that is strong does not wither,
Deep roots are not reached by the frost.
  J. R. R. Tolkien

When I think about it now, I believe it was the near hysteria induced by being the target of terrifying vengeance from both Deluca and Azizi, two fanatics worlds apart in their central delusions but equally venomous, that made me so extremely careful not to let my canine companions run free in the Park for the rest of January. A hard month anyway, alternating between coastal snow storms (major hits to the South Shore and Cape Cod) and single digit freezes that penetrated right to the bone. Not a good time for man nor beast.

But then came the first of February, a Major Sabbat, Imbolc, when Brigit (Brighid, Bridget, or Bride) waves her white wand to breathe life into the mouth of dead winter. Patroness of poets, seers, prophets, gold-workers and smiths, Brigit is the most revered goddess of the British Isles. (Christians, unable to lure the common people away from the veneration of Brigit, wisely made her a saint.) All wells are sacred to her.

Among the Pagana—Druids, Wiccans, and country folk who lived by the seasons—Imbolc embodies the return of life, the lactation of the ewes, the flow of milk, the foaling of lambs, the promise of spring. The days are becoming longer, the sun stronger, willow branches are thickening yellow, and fields will soon be prepared for the sowing of seeds. Imbolc is a celebration of fertility, too, as most Wiccan holy days are. (A couple of weeks later, Valentine's Day, will blossom out with every symbol of sexual love.)

There would be additional blessings for us to celebrate at this Imbolc. Our enemies were in the hands of Federal prosecutors. Everyone in our circle, including members of our extended families, human and animal, was safe from harm. My kitchen was temporarily in working order (awaiting the major remodeling of Joe's dreams). My online herbal business and Deidre's doll shop were suffering a bit of a lull, but we were confident that the first burst of forsythia and lilac would bring forth the usual spring demand for love potions, flea banes, and faery princesses. So we kept busy stockpiling our wares.

It was a fine season to curl up with a good book, however, and Fiona was fairly swamped at the Black Hill branch library where she reigned alone except for the *de rigueur* volunteer matron. Phillipa was happily steaming up her state-of-the-art kitchen with stews and soups for her next cookbook, *Lobster, Quahogs, Venison, Corn: More Native Foods of New England,* which was enough for Heather to pin on her Stop Cruelty to Crustaceans button, citing a recent study claiming that lobsters feel pain when being cooked. Fortunately, Heather was too busy at Animal Lovers, finding homes for stray, freezing mutts, to face her own dilemmas—that fish and shellfish were a big part of her quasi-vegetarian fare at home. She claimed that Dick has some humane way of tapping lobsters on the head and rendering them unconscious before boiling them.

It was still too cold to celebrate Imbolc at the lovely stone circle that Heather had built at her place, and Phillipa was eager to try out new recipes on the usual guinea pigs, so it was decided that we would gather on the eve of February first at her home. Fiona would be our high priestess, so that Phillipa would be free to organize the feast.

A good choice! In Phillipa's formal living room, a blazing fire in the copper-hooded fireplace that dominated one wall was the perfect antidote for the winter doldrums, while under floor-to-ceiling windows on the other side of the room, green and flowering plants flourished, a sign of things to come. An impossibly white gardenia had opened its fragrant petals for the occasion. Zelda, Phillipa's sleek black cat, posed glamorously on a cream silk pillow, and Boadicea, the old boxer, lay awkwardly supine on a Turkish rug by the hearth in utter contentment.

Fiona called the quarters and drew our circle with the 18th century Scottish dirk she used as her athame. We lit Heather's white, yellow, and lavender candles, imbedded with miniature symbols of spring. Melted snow in a blue pitcher, and salt in a copper bowl were set on our altar, the hearth. (It was necessary to give Boadicea a shove to one side. She stalked off grumbling and hopped up on the apricot sofa.)

Fiona had suggested that we bring our besoms to this ritual. Imbolc, along with the New Year, was a time to clean out the old and make room for the new. Brooms were such a stereotypical symbol that we giggled like girls, admiring the different designs. Mine was a traditional bunch of the plant broom, *Cytisus scoparius*, saturated with essential oil of cinnamon, as the Shipton women's herbal journals had instructed (to draw love and money, enhance libido, and protect from evil). Deidre's broom was store-bought, painted yellow, with a cascade of floral ribbons. As tall and willowy as she was, Heather's broom had been made from a sanded, polished young sapling, and ornamented with a moonstone, its brush her favorite shade of rust. Fiona brought a blackened, dangerous-looking implement, forged iron and ancient Scotch broom, only enlivened by the tartan ribbon tied around the handle. Phillipa, who deplored the image of witches-on-brooms, impatiently grabbed one of three hearth brooms hanging by the fire; handmade wooded handles and long straw skirts.

"*A broom of one's own* is so important to women, as Virginia Wolfe has written so eloquently," Fiona sang out cheerfully.

Phillipa and I exchanged the usual raised eyebrows. Who would say *nay?*

Phillipa chanted a rhyme and we repeated it thirteen times as we danced around in a circle briskly brushing away all negativity, and incidentally spooking Zelda and Boadicea, who sensibly fled to the kitchen where they would be safe from accidental pokes.

> *Out, out, all fusses, fumes, and frets,*
> *Begone, all sorrows and dark regrets,*
> *All rot and evil, all danger and blight,*
> *We banish from hearth and home tonight.*

There was, after all, plenty of negativity to sweep away, in view of our recent encounters. We even raised our brooms and drew pentagrams in midair (from the bottom left point for banishing) with zesty punches. After that robust ritual, it took a while to come down to earth, restore meditative breathing, and resume our Imbolc with dignity to form a healing and wishing circle. I included a heartfelt blessing for Tip to find a true love, if not a forever love, to sweeten his university studies.

"I wonder where the broom-riding myth got its start," Deidre said when we'd opened the circle.

"An uncomfortable thought." Phillipa passed around aperitifs of chilled extra dry Vermouth with a twist of lemon to restore our strength. "Worse than thong underwear."

"It originated in the idea that women steeped in herbalism had learned to rub themselves with ergot on a wand in order to enjoy orgasmic hallucinations," Fiona said.

"Some horny clergyman probably made up that one. Early porn." Heather held out her glass for a refill. "Where were they supposed to get ergot, anyway?"

"Moldy rye bread," I said. "There doesn't seem to be any end to the weird powers attributed to witches. The better to burn those attractive, evil hussies. After a thorough inspection of their naked bodies, of course."

"You'd better sweep that thought out the door, too," Deidre complained.

So we did. It was time for Phil's amazing feast in Imbolc's milky theme. Lobster-Tomato Bisque, Shrimp Macaroni and Cheese, and Baby Spinach Salad with Caramelized Walnuts. Dessert was coconut cake in the shape of a baby lamb. About a million calories, I decided, but worth it.

◦◦

The ceremony of Imbolc seemed to have settled my nerves and brought back my old confidence in the goodness of life and the protection of the Goddess. The week after Imbolc, I finally let the dogs off the hook—the leash, that is—in Jenkins Park. Immediately, Scruffy took off through the woods without a backward glance. Raffles and I looked at each other in amazement. "You stay right here with me," I warned him sternly. "Just in case it's skunks or a porcupine that has your sire in a tizzy."

But we couldn't stay there. When Scruffy set up a howl that the Hound of the Baskervilles would have envied, we had to follow through the prickly winter underbrush. Whatever trouble he'd got himself into, it was up to me to rescue him, and I couldn't very well leave Raffles tied to some tree. I chose a stout branch from the plentiful deadwood of late winter to carry. An excellent club, in case.

It was a long, damp slog, but we finally found Scruffy not far from the main road, Route 3A, about half-way to Phillipa's place. He was standing over a fallen tree with his head thrown backwards like the silhouette of a wolf—albeit, a shaggy one.

I moved forward with extreme caution. Whatever he had cornered under that tree, at least it couldn't be very big. But if a raccoon, those babies could be extremely nasty when cornered. I brandished my improvised club and crept forward cautiously. Raffles stayed right at my heel.

About time you got here, Toots! There's something weird under there. It's beeping.

"I can't hear anything," I said.

My superior Briard ears detect sounds far above what you humans can hear. Scruffy swiveled his ears in different directions. The offspring of an unsanctioned union between a purebred mother and an enterprising terrier (species unknown), Scruffy's ears had escaped the cropping that had once been popular for registered Briards, although now outlawed throughout Europe, but he managed to perk them up when the need arose.

"Yeah? So what have you got there, some weird tracking device?" I peered into the hollow below the toppled tree. Scruffy was right. I'd have to take the beeping on faith, but I could see that the glass thing half covered with mud was blinking a steady stream of blue and may have been beeping, too, for all I knew.

I leaned over for a closer look. My heart skipped a beat in excitement. Could it be true?

Scruffy had found the missing Morgan skull!

❧

"Don't touch it!" Heather screamed in my ear. I moved the cell phone a few inches away. I was still standing in the cold, damp woodland with two unsettled dogs looking at me with reproach. "I need to consult Fiona before we move the treasure. She impressed upon me that proper rituals, smudging and so on, must be observed before I bring the skull home. Because its powers may have been jammed or damned or something from rattling around in that creep's possession."

"*Remain calm, Heather.* I'm going to take the dogs home now. When you and your purification team show up, I'll guide you to the place where we found your treasure, when I trust you will have a proper thank you for Scruffy and me."

"Wait, wait! Surely you're not going to leave the skull unguarded?"

"It's hidden under a fallen tree. No one has discovered it in all these days since Deluca tossed it out of his car. I think it will be safe for another hour or so, don't you?" I ended the call before I had to listen to more. Because right now I needed to clip leashes onto these fellows and take them home to be toweled down and warmed up. Me, too. Maybe Joe would have made a fresh pot of coffee.

I found Joe measuring my cabinets, not a good sign. I never wished for him to be summoned to a new assignment, usually, but if that happened soon, I wouldn't have to face the messy disruption of my kitchen just yet. As long as the room was reasonably cleaned up, I wouldn't miss that one cabinet door very much. In fact, it looked rather nice to see my ceramic casseroles all neatly lined up, like something out of Martha Stewart's magazine. Perhaps I should consider glass doors on the next lot.

"Scruffy, I think you've earned a special reward. That was a very important discovery you made in the Park today." There were sautéed chicken livers in the refrigerator. I put one in each dog dish, and the dogs appeared to inhale them, so fast did they disappear. Then they licked remnants of fragrant oil as if trying to remove the lettering on the bottom of each dish: *Good Dog*.

Meanwhile, I made the fresh pot of coffee myself. Then I changed from my damp muddy clothes into a clean, dry sweater and slacks, ready for the onslaught of Heather's crew. While I waited, I told Joe what Scruffy had discovered. "Heather wants some kind of a ceremony out there in the Park before we dig out that skull and return it to her."

Scruffy and Raffles seemed rather cowed by their morning's adventure. They curled up on their kitchen beds in thoughtful nose-on-paws positions, eyes and ears taking in everything we said.

"A strange business all around," Joe said, helping himself to a steaming mug. "You suspect the skull has some extraordinary mystical powers, don't you?"

"If it's truly crystal. And especially if it's of Aztec origin. Let's assume that the skull was valuable, and Heather's pirate ancestor knew that when he hid it for her at the Crossed Keys Inn. He would have had to actually look into the future and foresee her existence in time. Possibly with the aid of the skull."

"If you're right," Joe said, "possession of the skull will be a dangerous business. There are people who would stop at nothing to get their hands on such a thing—nutty necromancers, crazed collectors of Aztec artifacts, avaricious museum directors. You'd better warn Heather not to tell anyone, and I mean *anyone*, what she's got. Remember that's how she lost the skull the first time? Roland de Vere shot off his mouth at the Plymouth Art Club."

"You're right, honey. I'll have a word with her, but you know Heather. Discretion is not in her nature. Still, as a Moonchild, she's a keeper. What she sees as hers she'll hang onto at all costs," I said. Already I could hear cars arriving in our driveway. The dogs barely stirred. Good. I would leave them at home with Joe while we unearthed Scruffy's find.

Hastily, I threw on my old green lumber jacket that hung by the kitchen door and ducked out of the house to meet the others. Phillipa, who had walked over, was just emerging from the Park. "When I passed that old log, I saw the damned thing in there blinking away," she whispered to me. "No good is going to come of this."

"Never can tell," I whispered back, then motioned for Heather, Fiona, and Deidre to follow as we retraced Phillipa's footsteps to the fallen tree.

Phillipa was right. The skull was still blinking blue in an even more agitated fashion. And now it was beeping as well, at a range our human ears could detect.

"Oh, look, listen!" Heather cried. "I believe it's greeting us."

"*Hello, suckers*," Phillipa muttered.

Fiona got right to work scattering salt in a circle and softly intoning blessings, some of them in Gaelic. Deidre lit sage sticks and began smudging everything in sight, the fallen tree, the skull, and us. Heather had brought a picnic basket with a cover and also a staff made in the same style as her broom but taller, a polished natural sapling, only this one was set with a turquoise stone. Brandishing the staff in midair, she drew an upright pentagram of protection over the skull's hiding spot, beginning with the top point of invocation.

Phillipa said, "Oh, all right." She thought a moment, with her poet's abstract gaze, then gave us an impromptu rhyme.

> *Ancient power, pirate's prize,*
> *Let no stranger steal thee,*
> *Share your powers, strong and wise,*
> *As our hands reveal thee,*
> *But hide yourself from envious eyes,*
> *Let our arts conceal thee.*

We continued to repeat the rhyme while Heather gingerly knelt down and loosened the skull from its lair. It stopped blinking and beeping for several worrisome minutes, then resumed when she enclosed the skull in its blue silk carry-all and laid it in a velvet lined basket.

"Come up to the house and have some tea and gingerbread," I invited. Heather was the only one who didn't accept, anxious to take her treasure home to show Dick.

Before she left, I knocked on the Mercedes window until she opened it, then leaned in. "Two watch points," I said. "One, your computer is going to be fried if you get *Poor Yorick* too close. Stick it up in the turret room. Two, Joe advises that you tell no one about it until we have a chance to see what it can do and how much someone might want to avail themselves of its powers. And that means the De Veres as well."

"Roland never intended any harm," Heather said. "But, yes, I take your points. Both of them. I did have the turret room in mind. And you can stop calling our crystal friend 'Yorick'. We'll need a nice dignified Aztec name. I'll put Fiona on it."

⟨⟩

The next afternoon, which was Sunday, we got together at Heather's to psyche out the skull. It was a little awkward getting Fiona up the ladder to the turret room, valiantly hanging on to her reticule, but we managed.

Heather had set the skull in a small niche that once held an astrolabe; the niche was now lined with silk drapery. "Blue seemed appropriate," Heather said, as the skull slowly blinked blue lights through its eyeholes. She showed us a red cord threaded through the silk, like a blooded vein. At a slight upward flick of her fingers, the cord closed the silk over the skull. Another wave of her hand slid a wooden panel down over the niche, so that it appeared to be part of the wainscoting. "I had this covered niche made for the astrolabe. It's been in the Morgan family since the days of the China Trade, and my dad seemed to think it kept our family on a safe course through the generations. Who knows? The astrolabe is behind locked glass in my office now."

"We could name the skull *Toci*," Fiona suggested. "That's one of the Aztec matronly goddesses of fertility, death, and rebirth. The one that's easiest to invoke. Some of those divinities, Huitzilopochtli or Chalchihtlicue for instance, only an Aztec priest could be expected to pronounce." Nevertheless, the many-syllable names fell trippingly off Fiona's tongue.

The skull continued to blink sedately, obviously not agitated by the proposal.

"Gosh, it never occurred to me that this might be a woman's skull," Deidre said.

"Why not?" Phillipa said testily. "Psychic power is not the exclusive property of males. As witness, this circle."

"That's a debate we don't need to have any more," I said mildly. "Since men have cornered religion, women get to play with enchantments, sacred and profane."

"Women priests!" Deidre said. "To see that, I might go back to the Church."

"Without giving up the Goddess, I trust?" Phillipa asked.

Ignoring our digression, Heather said, "I suppose I could take it to some kind of forensic lab." She opened a cabinet in the wainscoting and took out a bottle of Strega, which she poured all around in the tiny Venetian glasses she'd had sent back from our Italian trip. (Kidnapping and other mayhem had not deterred her from shopping for Murano.)

"No need," Fiona said, reaching forward to touch the skull with a much be-ringed finger. "See here, how Toci's brow ridges are not as pronounced, while the upper margins of the eye orbits are sharper?"

"Sharper than *what?*" Phillipa demanded.

Fiona reached into her reticule, took out a computer print-out, and unfolded it. The illustration depicted two skulls, one male and the other female.

"Chin more pointed, with a larger, obtuse vertical forehead angle of the jaw," she read. "I know we don't have a male skull at hand to compare, but I think you can see that the artist who carved Heather's skull meant to portray a woman."

"Sold," Heather said. "Toci it is."

"I guess we ought to meditate," I suggested reluctantly. "Perhaps whatever powers Toci holds will make themselves known to us in a meditative state." To tell the truth, I was not normally big on meditation. Falling into trances at odd moments had made me wary of deliberately invoking transcendental states.

"Good idea," Phillipa naturally agreed. "Maybe Cass will go off into la-la land with Toci."

I sighed. Heather and Fiona nodded. Deidre put down the leprechaun doll on whom she was sewing curled green shoes. We closed our eyes and breathed in, out, in, out, in the prescribed fashion, silently reciting our individual mantras. Mine was *I Am, I Am, I Am.*

By the time I got to the sixth or seventh *I Am*, I felt myself jolted away from the turret room, from the Morgan home, from Plymouth itself, gliding through the pale gray winds of time. I came down in an earthen room, with golden light streaming through slits in the wall like narrow windows. A man in roughly woven tan clothing was seated at a table, carving a block of crystal. He spoke in a strange tongue, and yet I could understand him; he was reciting spells of power and sorcery. I thought I understood some of the Aztec words. The vision faded, and I zoomed back to the present, feeling disgustingly nauseated. "That Strega!" I complained.

"Holy Mother, she's back!" Deidre exclaimed. She seemed to be patting my hand anxiously. I heard Fiona's bangles somewhere close and breathed in the acrid smelling salts she was brandishing under my nose. I waved the noxious stuff away.

"Cass, tell us, what did you see?" Heather demanded.

"The man who made this skull invested it with powers. He spoke in his own Aztec language, but I understood some of the words meant "life after life" and "oracle." The problem is that I don't know how much I imagined and how much was true clairaudience. Toci may be able to voice predictions, presumable through one of us, as the oracle at Delphi was the voice of Apollo. Also she may strengthen the gifts we already have. And give us insights into our former lives."

"That's because all time is one in the psychic sense," Fiona said. "Past and future are ever present for those who can experience the timeless. That's what you do, Cass."

"Yeah, maybe," I said. The thought was rather overwhelming. "But only in glimpses."

"I'd like to know who I was in a former life, wouldn't you?" Deidre dimpled mischievously. "I suppose Cleopatra has already been taken, though."

"Yes, by Cleopatra," Phillipa said. "And every other idiot who claims to have been her."

"Speaking of Delphi," Fiona said thoughtfully. "We should travel there someday. Personally, I've felt the Pythia calling me, haven't you?"

"Could we please stay on topic," Heather said crossly. "Right now, we have our hands full of this Aztec treasure."

"Next Esbat, let's give the 'life after life' thingie a try," Deidre suggested.

"What about the oracle power, how do you suppose that will manifest?" Heather wondered.

I said, "Watch out, Heather. You may be its instrument."

"How will I know my own thoughts from Toci's?"

"You'll know," I said. "Probably by some accompanying physical symptoms."

"Or perhaps through you, Cass. The virgins at Delphi would swoon after prophesying.," Fiona said.

"They were breathing in some drug vapors from crevices below the temple," Phillipa said. "In other words, they were stoned."

"Life after life," Fiona mused. She hummed a few bars of *Where or When.* "*I wonder if we five have lived before,*" she improvised to the melody.

"Okay, let's do it," Heather said. "Next Esbat, the March moon, Worm Moon, the stirring of earth, the hint of spring."

It might have been my imagination, but Toci seemed to beep an affirmation.

CHAPTER THIRTY-FIVE

Dust thou are, to dust thou returnest,
Was not spoken of the soul.
  Henry Wadsworth Longfellow

So it was that, at the next Esbat, the March Worm Moon, we gathered in Heather's turret meditation room to discover, if we could, the "life after life" powers of Toci. The grinning crystal skull rested in a teak-wood stand within its customized niche on the blue silk that could instantly become a carryall simply by pulling the red cord threaded through its hem.

It was just at sunset. Although we faced east not west, the drift of clouds was tinged with coral and violet and the lifting, gliding gulls over the Atlantic reflected the last gleams of the sun. Moonrise was early, 6:54 PM. Resting on the various floor cushions that were the only seating, we watched the moon appear like a huge bronze medallion out of the ocean, turning from deep gold to silvery white as it moved higher in the sky. Heather lit pure white candles that she'd placed on the windowsill circling the room above the wainscoting; they were scented with cheerful, uplifting bergamot.

We hesitated. Not even Heather wanted to be first. So it was Fiona who bravely laid her be-ringed hand on the pulsing skull, its blue eyes glowing with power. The inner fire of her antique diamond ring seemed to leap to meet the crystal's energy. She stood perfectly still, head bowed as if listening to the slightest whisper in the air. I could see a rosy aura leaping around her entire form; something intense was happening that went beyond the usual (but incredible) glamour that Fiona could project around herself.

After a time that might have been only minutes, she turned toward us, solemn but smiling. "All blessings flow from the Goddess! This explains so much," she said.

"What? What? *What?*" we demanded.

"Impossible to say how far into the past I traveled, but it was well before the Europeans came. When I touched the skull, I slipped into a trance—that must be what happens to you, Cass. What an overwhelming, surreal experience! I can hardly wait to tell Circe who is such an old hand at astral travel and the like. Anyway, when my vision cleared, I found myself gazing down at my feet shod in hemp sandals. As I gradually looked up. I saw my body clothed in a back-and-front fringed apron, a turkey feather robe, a handsome necklace of stone and bone. Only this wasn't my body as it is now. I was younger, shorter, browner, standing in the sacred circle in the Canyon de Chelly. I was aware, I *knew* that the center of the circle was the earth's birth canal from which all life emerged. I recognized myself as a medicine woman of the Anasazi." Fiona plumped down heavily, looking dazed but energized. "Now I understand why ... oh, everything that draws me back to the cultures of the Southwest."

"Holy Mother! I want to try that, too." Deidre jumped up from the cushion on which she'd been perched, embroidering silver faeries on a pillow with the words *Only Believe* in silver script. She rested her small right hand, where she now wore the gold wedding band from her marriage to Will, on the skull. The glow in its eyes faded and dulled. Deidre stamped her size-three shoe and exclaimed *"In ainm Dé,"* one of several Gaelic oaths she'd picked up from Conor. Gradually the blue light came up again, just like a gas ring turned to High. The skull beeped softly.

"Oh!" Deidre cried out, and then stood immobile, a mask of wonder, like a child listening to a faery story.

We waited. Phillipa checked her watch and held up three fingers when a subdued Deidre returned to this time and place.

"First, I saw my round-toed shoes and my hands. which were spotted and lined, older than I am. I was repairing the lace around the neck of an undergarment. My mistress, Kathryn, was standing by the window, just a barred stone slit, crying. I *remembered* where we were and why. My mistress, just a high-spirited girl really, who'd been crowned queen only two years past, was going to be *executed* the next day, for adultery, high treason against the King, that fat smelly old Henry. She was only 21. Of course, of course—don't you recall how crazy I was when we toured the Tower of London? But in my vision, *back then*, all I wondered was, for whom would I sew now? Even though I was a most skilled seamstress in the court, no lady would want to be cursed with bad fortune by employing me." Tears ran down Deidre's face.

Fiona got out her smelling salts and waved them under her nose. Phillipa put her arms around Deidre. "Hey, Dee! No wonder you always have that busy needle in your hand! Now you just let go of that grim scene you envisioned. You don't want to get as addle-headed as Cass, do you?"

"Yeah? Well, just you go next, Phil. Put your hand on that damned skull, and let's see how easily you shake off that past life thing, if that's what it was." Deidre grinned wickedly, having effectively cornered her comforter.

"A past life, maybe, or a psychic connection with the past life of a kindred soul, no one knows for sure," Fiona decreed. She was making notes in a little tartan-covered notebook she'd taken from her reticule.

So what else could Phillipa do? She strode up to the skull, stone-faced as it pulsed blue and bluer at her approach, placed her cook's hand (short, unpolished nails) on its head, and closed her eyes. Several minutes passed before she opened them again. Meanwhile, Deidre had, almost unconsciously, continued embroidering with her usual industry, and Fiona kept scribbling. I had absolutely no desire to play this game, but I would. *Esprit de corps* and all that. I glanced over at Heather, and was gratified to note that she was visibly pale.

Phillipa rejoined us in the present with a start, her dark eyes unreadable as she collapsed on the floor pillow where she'd been seated earlier. "Sweet Isis, what a shock! No one ever told me there could be a sex change in these flights of fancy. Give me a shot of liqueur, please, whatever you've got up here."

"It's Strega, of course, Phil," Heather said, opening a cabinet in the wainscoting and taking out a bottle of the yellow gold. She proceeded to pour it into the Venetian glasses; we passed them around. Phillipa drained hers and held out the glass for more.

"Why do we see our shoes first? Mine were covered in the blood of infidels. My silk tunic was drenched, and my armor dripping. I have never seen so much blood, a regular shambles. I was a Muslim warrior. In Morocco, I believe. It was like Custer's last stand. Our sultan, who was gravely wounded, insisted on being strapped onto his saddle so that he could lead the charge. An entire Portuguese army came up against us, and we killed them all, many thousands. Allah be praised."

"You're still in the fugue, Phil. I think you mean, Goddess be praised," Fiona said. "The last crusade. Young King Sebastian's remains were sent back with an honor guard to Philip of Spain, who returned the favor with an emerald the size of the boy's heart, plus his weight in rubies. They don't fight wars like that anymore." She sighed regretfully.

"Yeah, no style at all. Just slobs with smart bombs," Deidre said, plunging a fine little needle into her cushion for emphasis. "Do you, like, just memorize *everything*, Fiona?"

"The colorful stories seem to stick in my brain," Fiona admitted.

"Oh, Hecate preserve me, I'll go next," Heather said, jumping up from her yoga crossed-legs perfect posture and striding toward the skull, which welcomed her with a toothy grin and eerie glowing eyes. *Some treasure*, I thought.

Heather laid her long slim fingers against the top of the skull, started, then appeared to enter into an instant trance. We were respectfully quiet, Phillipa keeping an eye on her watch. Just as she held up three fingers, Heather snapped back to the present time, with a look of pure amazement.

"It was the dogs. The dogs who saved me, poor loyal hounds," was the first thing she said.

"Where? When? What happened?" we clamored.

"It was shoes first, just like the rest of you," Heather said, looking out the window at the darkening water as she told of her vision. "Mine were leather, scuffed and muddy. My dress was long, but I'd hiked it up in my belt, the better to work I think. My hair was bound up in a net of some kind. In my hand, I held a small scythe, and there was a heap of cabbages at my feet. I felt a terrible responsibility, like a great weight on my shoulders, and gradually I realized that there were family members and other people who must be protected. I heard horses from a long way off, and I knew they had come to compel me to marry a man I despised. Someone who stank of cruelty and sweet decay. A forced bedding would be as good as a wedding, and then he would have the legal right to my manor. I ran into the wheat fields, vowing to cut my wrists with the scythe if I couldn't escape. But it was my hounds who saved me, jumping and howling and attacking. I had a pack of them to keep wolves off the sheep. As I crouched between the stalks, I could hear the dogs snarling and tearing, until one by one they were silenced. Whatever happened then, no one followed me. I was safe, I thought, for that day. I would ride to my uncle and call on my cousins to move in here and help defend my land."

Heather turned and poured herself a slug of Strega, offering the bottle around, but we all shook our heads, as we absorbed the stories we had been living through. "Medieval, I guess," she said thoughtfully. "Those blessed, rowdy dogs."

We all turned our heads to look at Fiona.

"Don't look at me," she said. "Yes, probably Medieval. Women didn't get to own much, or not for long. I can't say what year, though."

My turn, no help for it. I pulled myself up, not a graceful springing to my feet like lithe Heather, who'd probably had several lives of working out in the fields under her belt.

The skull winked a blue wink when I put my hand on its cranium. Instantly I felt as if the rug of time had been pulled out from under me and I was gliding like one of those gulls on ageless winds, lifted and then gently put down in a new place.

Before I even opened my eyes, I smelled fire.

"I looked down at the new world under my feet." I related my story. "Cobblestones. Soft leather boots, rather shabby. Voluminous skirts over ample hips. A basket on my arm. From the smell of it, herbs. I was still a young woman, long heavy hair coiled up under a scarf. I bent over, not wanting to attract attention. There was a patient waiting for me, but fire burst out of the cathedral and we all began running for the bridge. Then the wind changed direction, went south and brought the fire with it, engulfing the houses and shops on the bridge. But I was surrounded by a struggling crowd still impelled toward the burning bridge by the mob behind us. I tried and tried to push myself in the other direction. Finally I broke free at the edge of the bank and fell down into the river. There were boats, people trying to escape the fire. I hoisted myself up onto the wale of one, but a man in a fur hat and a velvet doublet struck at my hands with an oar. My skirts were sodden, dragging me down.

Burning wood was falling off the bridge. A piece of it struck that man in the face, and he fell into the river. So I pulled myself into that boat with the help of a woman who was already there. 'Good,' she said. 'Good riddance to that cheapskate master.' She grabbed one oar and gestured for me to take the other."

"The year was 1212," Fiona said. "One of the great fires of London, although not the greatest. Started in Southwark Cathedral. London Bridge was a ruin for years afterward."

Phillipa gazed out the window at the Atlantic and shrugged. "Ask a librarian …"

We were quiet for a long time after, gazing at the candles, the moon, the stars. A few purple wispy clouds drifted over the sky, sometimes obscuring the moon, sometimes revealing its brilliance like the drawing back of a stage curtain. After a while, Heather went downstairs and asked Fleur to bring us a pot of Assam tea and some mugs.

Heather pulled the cord that enclosed Toci in its silk shroud and flipped the panel shut. When Fleur appeared a short while later, poking her head above the trap door and sliding the tea tray across the floor to Heather, there was no skull to be seen.

The tea was as strong as coffee and went a long way toward clearing my head of the fog of astral travel. "I wonder what else we took into ourselves when we entered that time warp," I said.

"Something, that's for sure," Deidre said. "I feel prickly all over, like an excitement brushing across my skin, the way you feel with a low-grade fever."

"Or when you come face to face with Michelangelo's David in Florence," Phillipa agreed. "Not exactly sexual, but something in that neighborhood."

"A runner's high," Heather said. "I feel that way sometimes when I've run past the aches and pains."

None of us could dispute that. She was the only runner in our circle; in fact, the only athlete, with more muscle than all the rest of us combined.

Fiona said, "Brrrrr. The ghosts of the Anasazi walked right through me. What we're feeling must be the power of Toci. Possibly it will wane after a bit, but we might try calling upon it in case we're ever in a tight spot again."

"Without turning over a card of my tarot deck," Phillipa said wryly, "I can predict that's a good likelihood."

"Well, I'd just as soon that future tight spot isn't in an airplane with Fiona ever again," Deidre said with her usual impish grin.

"Or terrorists wrecking my kitchen," I said.

"Or a crazy man blowing up my housekeeper," Heather said.

"We mustn't let yesterday take up too much of today," Fiona said.

"I don't see why ..." Deidre began. "Shouldn't past lives be like a lesson in something?"

"Not at all," Fiona said. "Unless the lesson is the eternal survival of spirit."

"Also, put your trust in dogs, not men," Heather added. "Of course, Dick is different. But my first three husbands ..."

Phillipa picked up the theme. "It's not all that much fun being a man, if it means having to defend your country and kill people. War is a miserable business, in any era." She looked down at her black sweater. "Maybe I'm still in mourning."

"Don't run with the crowd, but then I never have, in this life anyway," I said. "I almost went up in flames with London Bridge. Disaster happens so unbelievably fast. I'd just come from the kitchen of the cathedral courtyard. Probably bringing mint, sage, and rosemary to the chief cook, and suddenly, *whoosh!*"

"I wonder if those 13th century priests were celibate," Phillipa said. "Fiona?"

"The Catholic Church was working on it," she said. "Not a popular plan, but celibacy prevailed finally."

"I believe Ireland was one of the last hold-outs," Deidre said.

∽

"How did it go with the skull?" Joe asked.

By the time I got home from the Worm Moon Esbat, he was in bed, worn out no doubt from designing replacement cabinets in his workroom.

"The skull took us on time trips that may or may not have been previous lives," I said, slipping into the luxurious green velvet robe I'd bought from Victoria's Secret online.

"Did you meet me there?" Joe stretched out his hand to take mine. I sat down beside him.

"No. But I saw London Bridge go up in flames. I was an Herb Wyfe, I guess you could call it."

"But we *did* meet in our past lives. I'm sure of it," Joe said. "I wonder what would happen if you and I consulted that crazy skull together."

"I'm game," I said, leaning over for the kiss that was always waiting for me.

CHAPTER THIRTY-SIX

Vision is the art
of seeing things invisible.
   Jonathan Swift

A call from one of my children is always an event; to have each of them call in the same morning is downright incredible. Actually, it's my daughter-in-law Freddie who calls me most often, with news of my grand-cutenesses. After that, Becky keeps in touch fairly often, but her absorbing career in family law at Katz & Kinder and the travails of her love life don't leave much time and energy for checking up on old Mom, unless of course the ladies and I have been in the headlines again. But that home invasion of my seaside cottage by two raving psychos, a source of worry and embarrassment *then*, was old news *now*. Still, I rather credited Toci with ratcheting up our family rapport.

Whatever the crystal skull had imparted to us seemed to have had an energizing effect on our lives and our psychic skills. It would take time and experience to discover how the Toci phenomenon would play out.

Cathy, who hardly ever calls, called first, her voice at full dramatic pitch, "Muth-er! How are you, *chérie*? Irene said I must call you at once to see if you are all right, since I dreamed last night that you had climbed onto the roof, which is an old joke."

"Yes, I know the joke. That was kind of Irene. I am in good health, honey. But I want to hear all about you two! Have you completed your work in the film? The bar scene where you get torn to ribbons by zombies? I'll bet you were both agonizingly wonderful."

"Oh, that old *merde!* Tis done, tis done, and we barely survived that *imbécile* film editor and his inexcusable cuts. René has a marvelous scream, though."

"And the Seven Angels Repertory Theater? *Les Liaisons Dangereuses?*

"*Oui, Mama.* Irené says I am incredible as *une amie de Cecile.* The play goes up in two weeks. Do try to make the opening night! You and Joe, of course. And then when *A Midsummer Night's Dream* goes up in June, René will be a Puck *ravissant.*"

"How lovely! But will you be able to continue staying with friends through June?"

"Irene knows this young professor at Brown who's going to England for the summer, leaving behind three cats and a *charmant* apartment. She's offered our services as free house-sitters and cat-keepers. He leaves on May 1st."

"Perfect! You're planning an extended stay then? Is the theater going to take you on, I hope?"

"Here's René," Cathy said in a tone of infinite weariness. Our conversation had already gone on longer than most.

"Idylla Schimmer has made some vague promises," Irene said. "Life in Los Angeles, scrabbling for parts and all, was *très fatiguant* for Cathy. She's so delicate, you know. So, if Seven Angels pans out, we may look for our own place in Providence. Push comes to shove, I could find some work at one of the restaurants to fill in between gigs."

"Oh, my dear, I am so delighted! Tell Cathy how thrilled we all will be to have you living nearer."

Before I even had a chance to rush the good news to Joe, who was out in his workroom contemplating the fitting of glass doors to my new kitchen cabinets, Becky called. (Things really do happen in threes, so that practically guaranteed a call from Adam very soon, Goddess be praised!)

"Are you all right, Mom? I had this dream about you last night."

"Tell me I wasn't on the roof," I said

She laughed, a deep, rich, sweet laugh that told me more than she would want me to know in advance of her announcement. But Cathy wasn't the only actress in the family. I can do a very convincing *what a surprise!* "Close," she said. "You were on a brilliant white terrace overlooking an azure blue sea. Maybe that was a roof, after all."

"I'm just fine, Becky. Keeping my feet on *terra firma*. And how are you, honey?"

"Well, there is news, Mom. Guess what!"

"I can't imagine," I lied.

"Johnny and I have decided to get married. I know you like him, so I guess that will be all right with you."

"All right! I'm absolutely thrilled! I had no idea you were getting serious." Only a slight twinge of conscience there. "Have you set a date?"

"Well, the thing is, Johnny doesn't want the whole three-day Italian *festa,* you know, so we may do something ultra private and quiet."

"Okay, but I insist on being invited. I have to give you a proper blessing."

"Do I have to invite Dad, too?"

"Let's worry about the logistics later, honey. Right now, let's just be gloriously happy."

"Works for me!" Becky laughed again, that woman-in-love-and-loving-it laugh that so gave her away.

We talked a little longer, mostly about how brilliant and caring Johnny was and what a difference he had made in her life and how much they had in common, et cetera. Which was fine. There was just that one little dark place in Johnny that I couldn't manage to read. But I thought I would give that reading another try before he became my son-in-law. Not to change anything, just to be prepared.

I sat at my desk in the old borning room with my hands practically on both phones, land line and cell. Adam called a few minutes later.

"Your line was busy all morning," he complained.

"Sometimes I get calls," I said.

"Well, here's the thing, Ma. I'm worried about Freddie. You know those people who never forget her special talents."

He meant the CIA for whom Freddie had been successful in the past at remote viewing and fiddling with sensitive machinery. "Yes, I remember," I said cautiously.

"They're after her again, and I don't like it much. I wonder if you could talk to her?"

"I don't know that she'd welcome an interfering mother-in-law," I said.

"Better you than me." Adam sighed. He, too, had sometimes been used to carry the odd message. As vice-president at Iconomics, Inc., a computer security firm, his work often took him to London, Tokyo, Singapore and other cities where Iconomics had offices.

"I'll sound her out," I promised. "Maybe she's not that keen."

"Thanks, Ma. Oh, and by the way, speaking of 'viewing,' she says not to be surprised if you take another trip. She's *seen* you, you know the way she does with the remote viewing thing, on some kind of a white patio that overlooked the Mediterranean."

"Ah, the roof again. 'Your mother is on the roof.'"

"Is that a joke?" Adam remembered.

"A man who lived with his aunt and a cat went on a trip and asked his friend to call if there were any emergencies at home. Shortly afterward, the friend did call to tell him that his cat had climbed up on the roof, fallen off, and died. The man scolded the friend for tactlessness and explained that he should have said, the cat climbed up on the roof, then waited a day to tell him about the fall, and then, in another call, to say that the cat was dead. A few days later, the friend calls the man again. He says, 'Your aunt Rose climbed up on the roof today.'"

"Sick humor," Adam laughed.

"Trouble is that Cathy and Becky saw something similar. Makes a person nervous."

"I'm not a clairvoyant, or whatever you call it, like you, Ma, but I'm betting the girls are catching the vibes that you're going to take another trip. Mark my words!"

Rather a turn of the tables, I thought. A scene passed before my eyes almost too fast to decipher. Blazing sun, dazzling white roof, blue sea. I pushed it away and said good-bye to my son, promising to find out what Freddie was up to, if anything.

❦

With Joe's request in mind, I visited the Morgan mansion that afternoon. We settled in the conservatory, which doubled as her family room, although the "family" consisted of twelve or so dogs she always has in residence. The floor was littered with chew toys and plastic bones.

Sensing that Heather might be reluctant to share her treasure's extraordinary ability to energize one's spirit and evoke past lives, I started out on the defensive. "Remember who went along as muscle when you bulled your way into that demented Willie Hogben's compound with the excuse of rescuing his three wild dogs?" I reminded her. "Now Joe just wants this little favor. He wants the two of us to go up into your turret room and see what Toci has to say about his and my past life. If we were together, you know."

"Very romantic," Heather said dryly. "You remember that I was warned against outsiders wanting to avail themselves of my crystal skull's power."

"*Outsiders!*" I cried, setting down my tankard of medieval grog with a bang. It slopped over onto a tapestry covering the conservatory table. I only hoped it was expensive and irreplaceable.

"Hey, Cass the Clumsy. That's antique needlepoint from a French monastery. Roland located it on eBay, thoughtful boy. And I didn't mean outsiders in that sense. I merely meant, outside our circle of five."

I watched Heather mopping up the grog with a "dog towel" kept by the conservatory door for inclement weather. "And didn't the two of us help you to take possession of that damned Morgan legacy?" I said when she had finished.

"All right, all right. I take your point. But no one else except Circle members. And their significant others." Heather revised her rules.

She was safe there, I thought. I couldn't imagine Stone or Conor being seized by the notion of a previous life with his beloved. Only Joe with his Mediterranean soul would believe that he'd recognized me at first sight. In fact, I'd confessed to a similar intuition—which helped to explain that crazy night we met. I drifted off into memory for a heartbeat or two, then shook myself back into the present.

"All right, then. Thanks, girlfriend. We're counting on the declining Worm Moon to guide us, so we'll be over when it rises tonight." I scooted out of there before Heather could change her mind. As I drove away, looking back at the

handsome old mansion with its Widows Walk turret, I had
a nano-second image of flame, which I brushed away with a
shrug. You'd think I'd get comfortable with my life of sudden
flights of fancy but they still made me jumpy.

"It's fine, honey," I told Joe. "Heather doesn't mind a bit. I
said we'd be over then when the moon rises."

"8:59 PM." Joe always kept track of time and tide. But a
fleeting expression crossing his face told me that something
else besides our little adventure was afoot.

"You've got another assignment," I guessed easily. "So you
must have said that your health is back to normal? And you
have Dr. Blitz's approval?"

"I suppose I should be used to your reading my mind, but it's
still disconcerting." He had the grace to look shamefaced. "Dr. Blitz
signed off on me. 'You're doing okay, okay?' he said. And I feel
quite well, really. My back is perfectly fine, and we're only sailing
the Gaia into some major ports on the Eastern seacoast to give tours
of the ship and lobby for a coal-free future. Piece of baklava."

"Sure, sure," I said. I checked my third eye for glimpses of
danger and disaster. "When are you leaving?"

"Tomorrow. I'm joining the ship in Wilmington, North
Carolina." Joe pulled me into his arms in a maneuver designed
to prevent further argument. As usual, it worked pretty well. I
rested my chin on his shoulder, letting myself and my dratted
third eye go quiet with the sensual feel of him, the strength and
sweetness of his body.

"It's a good thing, then, that we've planned to consult Toci
tonight."

☙

"This is truly spooky," I said.

Joe and I sat together on cushions, facing Toci, whose
eyeholes blinked blue very slowly, as if trying to teach us some
Aztec Morse code.

"She's psyching me out," Joe said.

After a while, the blinking picked up to a cheerier pace. "I
think she's accepted you," I hoped. "Let's put our hands on the
crystal before she changes her mind."

The room was redolent of past incense, the many aromatic candles that had been burned in this room by Heather to accompany all her moods and wishes. We'd opened one of the high windows a few inches. The chilly March breeze sent a not unpleasurable shiver across my neck. In the windows to the right of Toci's niche, the Worm Moon, now a half-sphere like a tipped gold bowl, rose above the Atlantic. Joe's hand tightened on mine. The moment had come.

"Toci of the Aztecs, we ask you to grant us a glimpse of our joined past, as you hold all time in your infinite sight," I said quietly in the stillness of the isolated room.

We laid our hands, still joined, on the crystal skull. Almost immediately I lost the sight and feel of Joe sitting beside me as I slid into the blue-gray currents of time that are fearful and wondrous at the same time. At the back of my mind was always the worry that my return ticket might get lost in the mysteries of astral travel.

Having lost touch with Joe entirely, I felt myself floating toward earth alone. As before, I was looking down at the place where I had landed. My feet were shod in rope sandals. My gaze moved up my body. I wore a loose garment of light-colored wool, cinched and bloused by a thin woven belt and held up by two silver clasps on my shoulders. My hands were bare of rings. I put one hand up to feel my hair, which seemed to be long and knotted up off my neck. The one escaping strand was golden-brown.

Looking around me cautiously, I saw that I was on a terrace overlooking the sea. The smell of brine and fish floated up from below where there were several roughly constructed wooden wharfs. Wooden ships with single square sails, most of them rolled up, filled the bustling port. One or two sails were unfurled, straining in the wind as those ships moved closer to shore. A small army of men, dressed in little more than loin cloths, were unloading crates and jars from the docked ships. I knew they were slaves. Other men, a dozen or so sailors, were coming ashore from one of the ships. Straining to see the one man I was watching for, I felt a surge of joy as his familiar form strode toward me. Although he was still just a distant figure, I recognized him, a jaunty walk and trimmed black beard I would have known anywhere. He was wearing a flat brimmed hat, which he swept off his head and waved in my direction.

I wanted to run down the stone stairs toward the waving man. But right then my ears were filled with a wild singing sound and I was drawn upward and backward into insistent eddies of time, like being reluctantly pulled out of a dream, a dream where I wanted to stay. Abruptly, I opened my eyes. I was back in the turret room. My hand had slipped off the skull, and I sank back on the floor pillow. Beside me, Joe was just opening his eyes.

"Corinth, I think," were his first words. "We were both in Corinth. BCE, from the construction of the ships in the harbor. You were on the terrace waiting for me. *Jesu*, you were like a beautiful vision. I had been at sea for many months. The building behind you was a temple. I hope to hell you weren't some priestess sworn to lifelong vows of chastity. You didn't look all that virginal, though. Rather wild and wise, actually."

"And you? What was your station? You looked quite brown of skin, your beard black as onyx. You waved and smiled at me."

"Station? Are you kidding? I was master of that ship and all the souls and cargo aboard her, of course."

Joe put his arms around me, and we both became aware of how chilled we felt, far more deeply than could be accounted for by the March breeze coming through the barely opened window. The cold hand of time was shuddering across our skins, almost like a warning: *do not get lost out here.*

"*Enough,*" Joe said. "I don't think we need to know more, do you?"

"It might be dangerous," I said, burying my face against his neck, a place of shelter and comfort. Then I thought of that bottle of Strega in the wainscoting cabinet. Just the thing to warm our hearts.

Soon we were sipping the strong yellow liqueur in fragile Venetian glasses. I felt Joe looking at me with that particular familiar smile. "I have an idea, O priestess," he said, nudging me down, the weight of his body pinning me to the pillows.

"So I notice," I said. "But not now, not here. Let's go home, honey."

But Joe wasn't listening, sliding his hands under my sweater.

"Wait, Joe," I said. "Don't you smell smoke?"

"No one will come up here now," he reasoned unreasonably.

"I'm not making this up," I said. The drift of air coming in the window had changed from the smell of damp woods and the sea beyond to something that alarmed me. As soon as I identified it as smoke, dogs downstairs in the house began barking.

"That *is* smoke!" Joe finally got it. He jumped up and pulled me with him. In a moment, he had the trap door open, and we were clambering down the ladder, Joe first, taking care that I was supported as I descended.

We rushed downstairs, following our noses to the kitchen, where we found a scene of utter domestic chaos. Something in the oven was billowing clouds of sooty smoke. The Mexican tiles above were blackened, and the air was foul. Dick was jockeying a huge pan cover over whatever was burning. In the hall, Heather was shooing the small dogs who slept in the house into the dog yard beyond the conservatory. Fleur was weeping, and Roland was huddled with her in a corner of the kitchen.

Taking in the situation with one swift glance, Joe grabbed fistfuls of pot holders and took hold of the roasting pan with Dick's cover still on it. "Where should I take this?"

"Out to the stone wall," Dick said. "I'll see if I can wave this damned smoke out of the house before everything reeks of it."

I ran to help Heather. Picking up the De Vere's little Italian greyhound, Fra Angelico, who seemed to be immobilized with fear, I followed Heather into the dog yard. "Didn't you call the fire department?"

"We were going to, but then Dick thought he could smother the mess in the oven and spare us the thundering herd and the water damage."

"How did it get so far along? Don't you have smoke alarms?"

"Not any more—we pulled out all the batteries. Those alarms drive the dogs crazy when they chirp in the middle of the night, you know." Heather closed the conservatory door with a sigh. The frantic barking outdoors was now somewhat muffled.

By common assent, we sank down on the cane sofa and let the men deal with the aftermath. I thought I would give Heather the smoke alarm lecture when she was feeling stronger. "How did it get started? Surely no one was cooking at this hour?"

Heather sighed again. "Apparently, Fleur had decided to roast some birds for tomorrow's lunch, basting them with some medieval sweet sauce that caught fire at that high temperature. Probably meant to be used over an open hearth where it would be constantly watched."

"Well, you caught the blaze in time it appears. Joe's off to North Carolina on assignment in the morning. I'll come over after he leaves and help you wash those tiles."

Fleur was still sobbing softly in the corner, partly muffled by Roland's chest. He averted his gaze when I tried to send him an encouraging smile.

"Roland will take care of the clean-up, I'm sure," Heather said. "The kids feel very bad about this."

∽

That proved to be true. The De Veres felt so bad that they disappeared with their little "Angel" sometime before dawn. By the time I showed up, Heather was scrubbing and cursing all by herself, Dick being tied up in surgery that morning.

"They left a damned note," Heather said. "Apparently they'd been offered a gig at the Scarborough Renaissance Festival that's opening in Texas on April 5. *Now what am I going to do for help around here?*" she wailed.

I hardly dared to imagine an answer to that one. The problem of Heather's housekeepers was fast becoming our personal urban legend.

Taking a sponge from the bucket of hot soapy water, I set to work scrubbing the Mexican tiles. "Maybe Phil will have some ideas," I suggested.

Heather brightened. "*Yes!* I'll ask her to read the tarot for me. You know how things just come to her when she's concentrating on those cards." Never one to waste time thinking when action was on offer, Heather dried her hands and rang up Phillipa on her cell. I heard her describing the fire, the sooty carnage, and the disappearance of yet another perfect couple from her domain. Presently she ended the call.

"What did she say?" I asked.

"What kind of a friend laughs fit to kill through one's whole description of a serious domestic crisis?" Heather sputtered. "When she finally stopped cackling, all she said was 'Have tarot, will travel.' What's so funny? That's what I'd like to know."

"Probably she just got a bit giddy with relief at the thought of the danger you averted," I said with as straight a face as I could muster.

∽

"Thank the Goddess, we have seen the last of eel pie and boiled *sallat*!' Phillipa said, laying down the Queen of Wands with its lions and sunflowers to signify Heather. She continued to construct the Celtic cross with what turned out to be a preponderance of Wands and Cups.

"Not to worry, my friend," she reassured Heather, tapping the final card, the Ten of Cups. "This is a card of perfect family happiness."

"But what about all these restless Wands?" Heather asked doubtfully. "And the card that crosses me, the Five of Wands with those guys trying to bash each other over the head?"

"Yes, knaves with staves," Phillipa admitted. "There may be a bit of restless activity before you reach that rainbow of domestic bliss. You must simply trust in the Divine Cosmos to respond to your true intentions, the unspoken desires of your heart." She sighed and pushed the cards together before Heather could quibble further.

"Phil, you're looking just a tad downcast," I said. "How are things at home?"

"Two things at home are of note," Phillipa said. "Emma Christie is being released from court-ordered rehab, and what that means to Eddie I'm not sure. Whether she will be able to provide a good home for her son is still a question. Second thing, Eddie hasn't read a single future headline since the 'break-in and shooting in Plymouth.' Which was us."

"Aren't these two good things? Heather asked. "Mother and son reunited. No more bizarre incidents to disturb his family."

"I'll miss him," Phillipa said simply. A single tear rolled down her cheek—reluctantly. Phillipa never cried. She brushed it away impatiently.

I understood how deeply she felt the probability of that loss, having parted with Tip in much the same way. So I rattled on, the way you do to allow a friend to pull herself together. She turned away and surreptitiously dried her eyes. I reminded Phillipa of how close Tip and I had become in later years. "Youngsters remember the love, after all. And they come back. As for the headlines, it may be that Eddie's outgrown his quirky talent for prophecy. That happens sometimes with psychically gifted children when they reach puberty."

"If you can manage to let the kid go with good grace, Phil," Heather said, "I guess I can stop kvetching and learn to do a little cooking."

Phillipa and I glanced at each other. "You do make a lovely salad," Phillipa admitted. "That romaine with pecans and blue cheese is quite tasty."

I put my arms around both of them, group hug. "Noble, that's what you are, both of you. There is nothing we can't get through together with the Goddess's help and a little booze."

"Yes! We ought to drink to that!" Heather exclaimed, brightening instantly. "Why don't I make a pitcher of margaritas? I have a Milagro Romance that's quite nice." Not waiting for our reply, she hastened into the newly cleaned kitchen, pausing only to put a Jimmy Buffet CD into the Bose player.

"I like her style," Phillipa said. We smiled at each other. *"Let go and let Goddess."*

༄

My impromptu invitation to lunch didn't fool Freddie for a moment.

"Okay, witch-in-law, what's on your mind?" she demanded as soon as we were settled into our booth at The Walrus and the Carpenter with plates of local oysters and a bottle of Pinot Grigio. Hers were raw, mine were Rockefellers, as I decline to eat anything that's still living, except maybe yogurt.

"I'm a little worried about your continued association with that Free Fall Club, you know the one to which I refer?" The tables in this little oyster bar were close together. Better not to mention the CIA by name, even in the lowest not-to-be-overheard whisper.

"*Adam is worried*, you mean." Freddie's hair was raven black again, a pixie look that suited her gamine face. (The natural shade was chestnut brown and curly, not seen since the twins' first birthday.) Palest lip gloss. Slouchy sweater dress and thigh high boots. The boots were nice for the continual spring rains, but those inches of bare flesh between boots and skirt must get mighty chilly. At least she hadn't reintroduced the nose ring, and there were no dragon tattoos.

"He loves you very much. The Free Fall gang just uses you, and then tosses you into thin air without a decent chute," I said, maneuvering a forkful of garlicky spinach and oyster toward my mouth.

"I know where to draw the line, you know," Freddie said. "I won't try my so-called 'powers' on any living thing that might be harmed. I've resolved to be like, you know, Superman. Work only for truth, justice, and the American way. Especially after that guy who threatened my babies just collapsed at our feet clutching his chest. You recall that incident?"

"Vividly. I don't think you should blame yourself. The man had a weak heart anyway," I lied. "The FF Club is not going to tell you whether the end results are true and just."

"Yeah, well that's why I turned down this latest gig. I just thought it would be fun to have lunch together and admire the way you eased into the lecture." Freddie filled my glass and her own.

"Adam will be relieved," I said.

Freddie sighed. "It's a good thing your son is so incredibly hot and I love him to pieces. Otherwise, a girl could get a little restless just being a wife, mom, and electronic genius."

"I don't usually suggest this, but if push comes to shove and your feet are going to sleep, take a little trip to the Mohegan Sun. Just be careful. Roulette might be best, so you can't be accused of card counting."

Freddie's smile was pure Cheshire cat. "I might just do that. And afterwards, I'll take the kids to Disney World. Or better yet, The Wizarding World of Harry Potter."

CHAPTER THIRTY-SEVEN

A *wild dedication to yourselves*
To unpathed waters, undreamed shores.
    William Shakespeare

On my way home, I stopped at Fiona's to dispel the Margarita mist with a cup of her strong lapsong souchong and to gossip a bit. Laura Belle was next door playing with the new kitten, so I could spill the whole De Vere story without alarming the fragile little girl.

"I've known from the first night we met that Fleur de Vere will cause the occasional fire wherever she goes," Fiona remarked after I'd filled her in on the night's events. "Wasn't she there at that Thanksgiving conflagration? It's not malicious, it's just her karma."

"Just delivering rolls. She left right away. Don't think you should have told Heather?"

"Maybe *cause* is the wrong word," Fiona, as usual, went off on her own tangent. "It's more as if little fires will spring up in her neighborhood."

"Firestarter!" I exclaimed.

"I wouldn't put it exactly that way. I would say, if she wants to avoid the heat, she ought to stay out of the kitchen. Shortbread?"

I reached into the tartan tin. Omar eyed me with disfavor, spit out some Persian profanity, and leapt onto the windowsill.

"What's going on with him?" I wondered.

"Blod's back. Don't you see her there in the rowan tree? Circe and I are experimenting with sending messages back and forth by owl."

"How's that working so far?"

"Well, there is the problem of interpretation."

"One hoot for yes, and two hoots for no?"

"Now you sound like Phil. Nothing is that simple, Cassandra," Fiona said reprovingly. "All I will say for now is, our spiritual communication is progressing. *A bird in the bush is worth two in the hand,* I always say."

Making a mental note to pass that one on, I said, "Speaking of Phil ..." and related the news of Eddie and his mother.

"Inevitable, I'm afraid. But as you told her, Eddie will come back. We'll include Eddie in our Ostara ritual, of course. It's best to leave such things open-ended, though. Just a request for his well-being, whatever is best for the boy. And then there's Heather's housekeeping problems. I confess I'm rather at a loss on how to phrase our call this time."

"Maybe we've been *too* open-ended on that one," I suggested.

"Once we've let go of the matter and released our intentions to Ostara, the resolution will be out of our hands, literally. But I do pray that whomever She sends to the Devlins will be unencumbered by odd quirks of fate and run-ins with the law."

"That doesn't seem to be too much to ask," I said. "Good fortune for Eddie and good housekeeping for Heather."

∽

Ostara, goddess of Dawn, goddess of spring—soon after the Worm Moon, we celebrated the return of Ostara at the universal vernal equinox, a day and night of perfect balance. Wiccan Sabbats are not held on a date imposed by religious history or secular agenda; they follow Earth's yearly journey around the Sun. There's something powerful and authentic about a ceremony that has been going on ever since pre-historic farmers first looked up at the sky and began to record the passing of days and the movement of stars.

We held our Sabbat at the Morgan stone circle, where we danced off the chilly March evening with abandon and raised a heartwarming cone of power to carry our intentions into the Divine Cosmos.

In April, we celebrated Easter, too, of course. Deidre wouldn't have missed the chance to decorate Easter eggs and organize charming baskets filled with flowers, frogs, faeries, and fancy candies for the youngsters. Phillipa baked cardamom-scented braided breads with whole eggs nesting in them. Heather added a Rabbit Retreat to her animal sanctuary for the rescue of pet store bunnies abandoned by careless children. I began to uncover mulched perennial herbs, each one a joyous revelation. And Fiona scandalized her neighbors by bathing her rotund naked body under the April Moon, which she called variously the Sprouting Grass Moon or the Fish Moon. "Rejuvenates the skin," she recommended the practice to all of us, "better than those pricey so-called ageless skin creams. And has an estrogenic effect on dryness elsewhere." She winked meaningfully.

"Won't do, Fiona," Phillipa said. "Stone would have to arrest me for indecent exposure. But I would like a few lessons in that glamour of yours. Seems to me it's even more rejuvenating than streaking in the moonlight."

We had teased Fiona into teaching us about the glamour on other occasions, but none of us felt we'd truly grasped that most desirable talent. Fiona sighed, smiled enigmatically, and seemed to be considering how to explain the inexplicable. We were gathered on my architecturally incorrect porch, no longer glassed-in but screened for spring, with a briny breeze coming up the slope from the seashore. It was three in the afternoon, and we were enjoying the first iced tea of the season, spiced with mint from my garden. Heather had offered to show me how to make a proper mint julep, but we'd opted for clear heads while attempting to understand the glamour. That is, if we were able to make sense of Fiona's hums and hints.

"Might be easier to teach you how to fall in love," Fiona said. "Or catch a falling star in a wish bowl." She reclined on the wicker settee and gazed into the middle distance.

"What in Hades is a wish bowl?" Deidre muttered.

"Quiet," Phillipa whispered, "or you'll throw her off the track."

Fiona chewed a mint leaf thoughtfully. *"The glamour* combines the kind of charismatic energy the best actors employ and the sort of mass hypnotism some gifted preachers practice and the just plain pheromones a woman exudes when she finds a man attractive, those invisible chemical signals that might bring some stranger straight across the room singing *One Enchanted Evening.*" She paused and took a long swig of iced tea.

"That's all very colorful, but I'm still clueless," Phillipa said.

"I guess it's like Louis Armstrong said about jazz," Heather said. *"If you have to ask, you'll never know."*

"No, it can be learned, because I learned it," Fiona said. "First I located a quality of blending or invisibility—within myself, you know—so that I could sneak in and out of government offices and wreak some havoc. That was in my Berkeley days." She sighed nostalgically. "And I find, the older I get, the easier it is to slip by unnoticed, just a harmless old lady."

Phillipa snickered.

"Yes, but what about that thing where you suddenly look so regal, even taller?" petite Deidre asked enviously.

Fiona laughed, her deep infectious laugh that always compelled us to laugh as well. "For that, you need to summon your goddess self. It's a kind of spiritual confidence that attracts attention."

"But *how* do you do that?" Deidre demanded.

Fiona remained unperturbed. "So tell me, when you look in the mirror first thing in the morning, what do you say to yourself?"

"Cass, what a mess your hair is," I said, smoothing back my wild mop. I badly needed another appointment at Sophia's Serene Salon.

"Your eyes are all puffy again, Dee," Deidre said. *"Maybe it's time to jump on the wagon."*

Heather grinned. "Never! But I do worry about my neck. I check for flab."

"I bemoan this frown line between my brows." Phillipa rubbed the offending line with her finger.

"Well, then—lesson one," Fiona said. "Here's what I want you to say to yourself instead. And it must be the first thing you say. *You are beautiful. You are blessed. You are guided. You are loved.* And believe it as you say it. That's the important part, your belief in yourself. Because *you are* all those things. Every woman is a goddess. Not necessarily Venus—unless it's the Venus von Willendorf—but a goddess nonetheless."

We were silent for a few minutes, absorbing that idea, memorizing the words.

"All right then. What's lesson two?" Deidre demanded.

"Lesson two is the way you get to play in Carnegie Hall. *Practice, practice, practice*." Fiona said. "And while you're practicing lesson one, I have an idea to propose. Another spiritual journey."

That silenced us all. Finally, Phillipa asked, "Where to, O Divine One?"

"I'm thinking … *Hellas*, the Hellenic Republic. We'd pay homage to the Oracle at Delphi, to the Pythia. Visit Athens and the Temple of Athena Nike. Restore our connection with those ancient goddesses and wise women."

"*The Isles of Greece, the Isles of Greece*," Phillipa recited dreamily. "*Where burning Sappho loved and sung …*"

Greece! I had to admit to myself, that was a truly electrifying prospect. My imagination sprang immediately to Joe and I making an excursion to Corinth as well. "Next year perhaps," I said. "Why not?"

We were silent then, with the silence of friends so attuned to each other that words are sometimes superfluous. But then the reflective mood was shattered like a mirror into a thousand pieces. The quiet porch was suddenly filled with the screams of sea gulls discovering a school of bluefish just off the shore.

What was awaiting us next in the abundant feast of life?

∽

On Saturday we all received a mysterious text from Deidre: "Come over for brunch tomorrow. Mother Ryan is taking the kids to College Pond very early, so *blessed peace*. I have something glorious to show you. You'll never guess!"

Phillipa called me a few minutes later. "She's engaged, isn't she?"

"Don't you think we should allow the girl to reveal her own news?"

Phillipa cackled like the Wicked Witch of the West. "*As if*."

༄

A half hour later, it was Heather. "Should I bring a magnum of champagne? Or is that too obvious?"

"You think?"

"I'll just leave the cooler in the car until Dee tells us she's finally got engaged. Do you think she'll want us to be matrons of honor? Is it possible to get Phil to lighten up on her black weeds?"

"I'm more worried about talking Fiona out of her tartans." I said.

"I just hope Dee doesn't insist on our all wearing the same color. I mean, mine is clearly an autumn palette, you're spring in all its shades of green, and Phil is starkly winter."

"Oh, just think! Jenny and Annie will be flower girls, *so cute!*" I was beginning to feel quite enthusiastic at the prospect of another Circle wedding.

"If she goes for pink, I'm really going to put my foot down."

༄

Phillipa called again. "What's Dee going to do about Will?"

"How do you mean? Will's buried at St. Timothy's cemetery."

"Sure. But she still keeps his hats all lined up on her closet shelf. Their wedding photo is tucked away in the drawer of her bedside table. And Mother Ryan's room is like a shrine. In fact, it *is* a shrine, complete with candles."

"Let's just trust Dee to find her own way through the thicket of memories. And besides, she hasn't really told us the glad tidings yet," I reminded her.

༄

Fiona was next. "I suppose the O'Donnells will insist on a church wedding, soon I hope, so we can hold the handfasting while the weather is still fine. Do you think Conor would go along with a Midsummer's Eve ceremony? Dee would make such an adorable Titania!"

"Will Conor be comfortable with our presence at a church wedding?" I wondered.

"Of course. Traditionally, it's very bad karma to leave a witch off the guest list."

∽

Heather's second call: "Perhaps it would be good if Fiona didn't hum during the ceremony. And none of your *strega* hand signals to avert evil, either!"

"I think you can trust us to behave ourselves in a mannerly fashion."

∽

Phillipa's third call: "You know, I could do a gorgeous wedding cake. But I suppose Eileen O'Donnell will have her own ideas about that."

"I think we'd best leave Grandmama to run the show," I said. "Did you know that Dee has never met the parents? They've been working at a medical center in Ghana. So probably they're really good people."

"Or crazy. Or both. How interesting, though. I wonder what they'll make of Dee and her four little ones."

And so it went, back and forth, until finally we gathered in Deidre's dining room at ten on Sunday. Time for the denouement.

∽

Presenting her offering of fragrant cinnamon rolls, Phillipa looked around the table with reluctant approval. It was laden with quiches, scones, Irish soda bread, fruit, and preserves, and everything looked amazing. A woman in love can accomplish miracles.

"You've outdone yourself, Dee. Where's Conor?" Phillipa asked.

"Hiding in his little apartment. He says he sometimes finds the five of us all together in one room a tad unsettling," Deidre said.

"So ... what's this glorious *something* you've brought us here to admire?" Heather asked ingenuously.

"Yes, no more keeping us in suspense!" Phillipa demanded.

Fiona beamed and reached into her reticule. I just hoped she wouldn't bring out the corn pollen until after Deidre's announcement.

"It's official! I'm engaged to be married!" Deidre declared happily. She held out the secret she'd been hiding in her apron pocket, and no wonder; it was that impressive. Gone was the jade parrot ring. Deidre petite hand was weighed down by a magnificent oval diamond in a lovely old-fashioned setting.

"Dee! I'm astonished! We all thought you'd never get around to making an honest husband of that charming Irishman!" Phillipa caroled.

"Well, he's been hinting around all year, dropping the word fiancée, you know, but this time he actually got down on bended knee, with this lovely ring in a blue-velvet box," Deidre said. "He even looked a little nervous, as if he wasn't quite sure I'd say yes. Can you imagine?"

"Darling, I just happen to have a bottle of champagne in the car—and I think it's still cold," Heather said. "I'll just pop out and get it. We must have a toast!"

"Oh, Dee, how happy you'll be together!" I exclaimed. "Conor's so lucky to have the love of an amazing and talented woman like you. And he's rather brave, too. Because look what he gets in the bargain."

"A ready-made family, a passel of witchy friends, and the occasional ghost sighting," Phillipa said.

"You could knock me over with a crow's feather!" Fiona declared, sprinkling the bride-to-be with corn pollen.

"Oh, don't overdo the shock and awe, guys," Deidre said with a sudden impish grin.

"I don't know what you mean," Phillipa said.

Deidre gave us all a long speculative look. "And there's another thing. We'll be five married ladies now. So maybe it's time we reformed. Conor did make me promise that there would be no more dangerous shenanigans, you know. I mean, there he was all formal and serious. Vowing a lifetime of love and his hope for a marriage uncluttered by criminal types."

"Of course!" "Absolutely." "Not to worry, Dee." we chorused.

There were a few moments of silence that lasted until Fiona chuckled softly, her irresistible chuckle. That did it. The rest of us laughed until we cried. Even Deidre collapsed in giggles.

"Well, we can *try* to stay off the wild side," Deidre said.

Heather retrieved the champagne from her car cooler and opened it handily. She'd brought five flutes as well. When we each had one in hand, Fiona proposed the toast.

"Here's to Dee and Conor—may they live happily ever after, blessed by all the good faeries of Dee's imagination and all the gods and goddesses of Conor's Celtic heritage. Especially Brigit, goddess of hearth and home, whose feast day was Imbolc, just past."

"And here's to the Circle, friends forever," I added after Heather had promptly refilled our glasses. "May Brigit, mistress of healing, prophecy, divination, and the magical arts, bless us all."

When we five lifted our glasses, the air between us seemed almost to sparkle with energy. Whatever happened, there was no way our future could be uneventful. There would always be new challenges and adventures, but we would live up to them. With the magic of friendship, anything is possible.

'

Johnny Marino's Ziti Casserole

Goddess bless a man who knows his way around a kitchen! Becky's fiancé produced this dish (in greater quantities, of course) for Cass's After-Thanksgiving Family Dinner.

½ pound ziti, cooked according to package directions
1 tablespoon olive oil
(About) 3 cups Chunky Tomato Sauce (recipe follows, or use store-bought chunky sauce)
3 tablespoons grated parmesan cheese, divided
1 pound ricotta cheese
About 12 small, sweet, whole leaves of basil (or shred 6 larger ones)
4 ounces mozzarella cheese, sliced, slices quartered

Cook the ziti, drain, and mix with the olive oil.

In a 2 ½ quart gratin or baking dish, layer 1 cup of the sauce,1 tablespoon of Parmesan and half the ziti. Add a second layer of 1 cup sauce, 1 tablespoon Parmesan. Next, drop the ricotta by tablespoons over all, spread gently with a table knife. Arrange the basil leaves on top. Layer on the remaining ziti, the remaining cup of sauce, the remaining tablespoon of Parmesan, and arrange the mozzarella quarter-slices on top.

Cover loosely with foil (tented above cheese) into which you've cut three slits.

Bake in a preheated 350 degrees F. for 30 minutes. (If you refrigerate this dish before baking, allow 10 to 15 additional minutes.) Remove foil and bake another 10 minutes. Let rest 15 minutes before serving.

4 servings.

Chunky Tomato Sauce with Peppers and Mushrooms

3 tablespoons olive oil
8 ounces washed, sliced white mushrooms
2 Italian frying peppers (or Cubanelles) seeded and cut into chunks
½ cup chopped onion
2 cloves garlic, minced
1 (28-ounce) box Pomi chopped tomatoes (or other canned chopped tomatoes) with juice
3/4 teaspoon salt
Freshly ground black pepper, to taste
2 peperoncini (Pastene piquant peppers—optional)
2 tablespoons fresh chopped flat-leaf parsley
1 tablespoon fresh chopped basil leaves

Heat the oil in a large non-stick pan. Stir-fry mushrooms, peppers, and onions until softened, fragrant, and slightly browned, 5 minutes. Add the garlic and continue to stir-fry for 1 minute. Add the tomatoes, salt, pepper, and peperoncini. Simmer with cover ajar for 30-40 minutes, stirring occasionally, until thickened to a sauce consistency. Stir in fresh herbs.

Fleur de Vere's Medieval Braised Chicken with Saffron Cream Sauce

"I wonder if the De Veres will serve eel pie." Fiona smiled at me impishly … "Eels! Oh, good Goddess," I exclaimed before the front door opened and Dick Devlin welcomed us into the Victorian red parlor.

2 or more split chicken breast halves with skin and bone, about 3 pounds
Salt and pepper
Olive oil as needed
Generous sprigs of fresh sage, rosemary, and thyme; remove leaves from stems and mince
¼ teaspoon saffron threads
1½ cups hot chicken broth
2/3 cup heavy cream (must be heavy cream, not light or half-and-half)

Preheat the oven to 375 degrees F. Salt and pepper the breasts all over. Pour a little olive oil into a heavy baking dish or pan that's about 3 inches deep. Place the breasts in the pan and drizzle some oil over all. Bake on the middle shelf for 30 minutes.

Mix the minced herbs with about 2 teaspoons of oil and spread the paste over both sides of the chicken. Continue cooking for another 20 minutes or until the thickest part of the breast registers 170 when tested with a meat thermometer. Remove the breasts to a platter and keep them warm. Drain the fat from the pan, keeping the crusty brown bits.

Crush the saffron threads between your fingers. Add the saffron to the hot broth and stir to dissolve. Pour into baking pan, scraping loose the brown bits, and simmer until reduced by a third, about 5 minutes. Whisk in the cream, and simmer, stirring often, until slightly thickened, about 5 minutes.

To serve, slice the breasts and drizzle half the sauce over the slices. Pass the rest in a sauce boat. Garnish with sprigs of fresh rosemary, if desired.

4 servings.

Phillipa's Shrimp Macaroni and Cheese

Phil's amazing feast in Imbolc's milky theme: Lobster-Tomato Bisque, Shrimp Macaroni and Cheese, and Baby Spinach Salad with Caramelized Walnuts. Dessert was coconut cake in the shape of a baby lamb. About a million calories, Cass decided, but worth it.

2 cups milk, divided
3 tablespoons butter
3 tablespoons flour
½ teaspoon ground mustard
¼ teaspoon salt (the cheese adds plenty more)
¼ teaspoon white pepper (black is okay, too)
dashes of cayenne pepper, to taste
2 cups shredded sharp cheese
½ pound casserole elbows, medium shells, or any macaroni shape you prefer, cooked according to package directions
About 2 tablespoons seasoned crumbs
12 to 16 cooked, cleaned, shelled large shrimp, about ½ pound, with tails on

Put 1 1/2 cups of milk and the butter in a large heavy saucepan, and heat slowly until the butter melts. Pour remaining 1/2 cup cold milk into a jar, add the flour, mustard, salt, and pepper. Close tightly and shake until the mixture is smooth. Pour the milk-flour mixture into the heating milk, turn up the heat to medium high, and stir or whisk constantly until the mixture bubbles and thickens. *Sticks easily*, so keep stirring right to the bottom of the pan. Lower heat, and simmer for 3 minutes, stirring often.

Remove from heat and stir in the cheese. It will melt from the heat of the sauce. Stir or whisk a few times until smooth.

Preheat oven to 350 degrees F.

Cook ziti or any noodles according to package directions. Drain and spoon into a 2 ½ quart gratin or baking dish. Stir in cheese sauce. Top with crumbs. Stand shrimp in the macaroni, tails up.

Bake the casserole for 25 to 30 minutes or until bubbling.
4 servings.

Heather's Romaine, Pecan, and Blue Cheese Salad

Heather said, "I guess I can stop kvetching and learn to do a little cooking." Phillipa and I glanced at each other. "You do make a lovely salad," Phillipa admitted. "That romaine with pecans and blue cheese is quite tasty."

6 to 8 cups torn romaine leaves
1 cup pecan halves
1 cup shredded carrots
1 Vidalia onion, peeled and ringed (use large rings only)
1 cup Blue Cheese Dressing (recipe follows) or store-bought dressing

Combine romaine, and pecans in a large bowl. Toss. Pile shredded carrots in center, arrange onion rings around the sides of the bowl. Drizzle dressing on top.
4 or more servings.

Blue Cheese Dressing

½ cup mayonnaise
½ cup sour cream
¼ teaspoon black pepper
1 cup crumbled blue cheese, divided
¼ to ½ cup plain yogurt

Combine mayonnaise, sour cream, pepper, and ½ cup blue cheese. Blend or process until smooth. Thin with yogurt to the desired consistency. Stir in remaining ½ cup cheese.

Made in the USA
San Bernardino, CA
08 March 2015